SHADOW PACK

MARC DANIEL

Text copyright © 2013 Marc Daniel

To Louise, Victor and Valentine.

Acknowledgements

Writing this book was a long and not entirely pain-free process, and a number of outstanding individuals need to be acknowledged for the help they provided along the way.

My first thanks are due to Darwin and Katherine who were brave enough to soldier through the initial draft of the novel. Without your helpful suggestions and comments the story would have looked a lot different, and not in a good way.

I am equally grateful to Amy and Susan for their insightful perspectives on the characters. Your remarks helped me see my cast through a different lens and contributed to their development into more personable individuals.

I will be forever indebted to Michelle for the time she spent painstakingly hunting down typos and the like throughout the manuscript. Without your eagle eyes many errors would have gone unnoticed all the way to publication.

Sarah, at Cornerstones Literary Consultancy, provided the professional editing touch the manuscript required and for which my readers will no doubt be grateful.

A very special thank you is owed to Jasmin. As if reading the whole manuscript three times prior to publication was not good enough, she graciously put up with countless hours of silence in the house only interrupted by the sound of my typing. Thank you for your support throughout the whole process, Jasmin. Michael would have never become who he is today without you.

Cover Design: Ivan Zanchetta (bookcoversart.com)

Michael Biörn Series

Novels
Shadow Pack
Unholy Trinity

Short Stories
Michael Biörn -A short autobiography

Download your free copy at:

http://bit.ly/MichaelBiornBackStory

Chapter 1

The first ring of the phone brought him wide awake. Michael Biörn lifted his three hundred pounds of muscle, sinew and bone from the comfortable armchair in which he had been dozing off by the fireplace and dragged his 6'4" frame to the kitchen. The cabin wasn't big enough to require more than one phone and since the jack was already in the kitchen at the time the cabin had been assigned to him, he hadn't bothered moving it to a different room. He had never been a fan of electrical work and the kitchen was as good of a place as any for a phone.

The stars shining in the clear September night sky of Yellowstone National Park didn't provide much light in the room, but he didn't need much light to find the phone.

Michael lived in the middle of the park, in an isolated cabin near Canyon Village. Most park employees lived by the North entrance, but Michael sought more isolation. Seclusion was in his nature, the nature of his beast. He would have loved to just get rid of this damn phone, but the park services needed a way to get in touch with him other than knocking on his door. Since radios tended to be unreliable in mountainous regions, Michael had finally agreed to have a phone at home. He had stood his ground, however, when a few years later his boss had tried to hand him a cell phone. Today, he was one of probably three American adults who did not have one.

As he grabbed the receiver, Michael lifted his hazel eyes towards the small cuckoo clock hanging above the cabin front door. Nine o'clock, not a good sign. Nobody ever called him this late with good news.

"Hello?"

"Good evening, Michael," answered the voice of Bill Thomason, his boss. As expected, the man sounded troubled. After the usual apologies for calling late and bothering his employee at home, Bill finally came to the point of his call. "We have a couple of hikers missing. A boy and a girl."

"How long?" Michael enquired while his fingers attempted to tame the unruly waves of his brown hair.

"Two days. They came to backpack for Labor Day weekend, but they were supposed to head home on Monday. The mother of the girl called us. She was worried something had happened to them."

"How old?"

"Early twenties, college kids."

"Has the mom called the highway patrol? Maybe they crashed on their way home."

"She called everyone under the sun. We were the last ones she thought of contacting."

"Maybe they took a detour and are having a good time in Vegas… college kids will do that!" argued Michael, knowing all along that he would still need to get his butt out of the house and go looking for those kids.

"It's possible, but she's convinced otherwise. At any rate, we need to check it out," replied Thomason.

"Fine," conceded Michael. "Where are we going?"

"Pebble Creek campground. Meet me there in an hour."

Chapter 2

The Alpha was getting worried. Jack, the wolf he had sent for the assignment, had not reported back to him for debriefing, and that couldn't be a good omen. He flipped once more through the 153 channels available to choose from, but only to confirm there truly was nothing worth watching this late in the night.

Like all Alphas, he was a man of action, something that came with the territory. You didn't become Alpha by being quiet or accommodating, but by fighting your way to the top of the pack. Lately, however, he had been forced to rely on others to do the heavy lifting, and this passivity was making him increasingly restless.

Maybe he could take care of the next project himself... that would relax him a little.

His phone finally chimed, indicating the arrival of a text message. He looked at the screen and felt relieved. It was from Jack:

Job done, but ran into problems.
Need to talk ASAP regarding damage control.

The Alpha thought for a second before replying:

Meet me at the arboretum in 2 hours. Be presentable!

The arboretum was within Memorial Park, and he knew from experience that this part of Houston would be practically deserted this late in the night.

Chapter 3

Michael Biörn saw Bill Thomason's truck parked in the Pebble Creek trailhead parking lot and rolled to a stop next to it. With the exception of a beat-up Ford Fiesta parked on the other side of Bill's truck, the lot was empty.

The two men came out of their trucks at the same time, each holding a backpack. Bill was in his mid-fifties and had only ten years on Michael, but his gray hair and slumped posture made him look older. His short cropped beard was barely longer than the other man's day-old stubble, but Michael's hair tended to grow significantly faster than average.

"Is that their car?" enquired Michael, his breath visible in the already cool September air.

"Yep! That's the license plate listed on their backcountry permit. They were supposed to go up Pebble Creek Trail and spend the first night at campsite 3P3. Then they were to head down Slough Creek, spend the second night at 2S1 and continue down Slough Creek Trail back to civilization the next day."

"That's over twenty miles," remarked Michael. "You're planning on searching all that tonight?"

"I have a group heading up from the Slough Creek trailhead with satellite radios; they'll let us know if they find them before we do."

In addition to the standard issued weapon, a Sig P239, 9 mm, each ranger carried an aerosol can of bear spray holstered on his belt. Bill was also carrying a rifle on his back, which could come in handy in case their worst fear came to be realized.

There were two types of park rangers. The friendly ones, found in visitor centers, were paid to answer tourists' questions and take them on backcountry hikes. The law-enforcement ones, on the other hand, made sure the aforementioned tourists behaved themselves while in the park, and only had to be friendly towards them if they felt like it. Both Michael and Bill belonged to the second category.

For the type of rescue mission Bill and Michael were about to under-take, a backcountry ranger would usually have been part of the group. Backcountry rangers typically knew the backwoods of Yellowstone bet-ter than their law-enforcing counterparts, but Michael was an exception to that rule. He had spent more time alone in the backcountry of Yel-lowstone than anyone else alive, and everyone working in the park knew it.

Hiking the backcountry of Yellowstone National Park meant being about as remote from civilization as one could possibly be while still within the lower forty-eight states. Cell phones didn't work for the most part, and, depending on where your hike took you, you could be as far as a day's march away from the closest road.

All backcountry campsites in Yellowstone were isolated and far enough away from the trail that they were essentially invisible to hikers not knowing their locations. Michael knew exactly where he was going, though, and Bill followed in his footsteps.

It took them a little over three hours to reach the vicinity of the primitive campsite where the young couple was supposed to have spent the first night, but Michael had known long before reaching the site that something had gone terribly wrong. He had picked up the smell of blood when they were still half a mile away. Blood and something else, a scent he had recognized only too well: grizzly bear. Of course, he hadn't men-tioned the smell to Bill; it would have raised questions Michael didn't want to answer. Both men were advancing with headlamps on their fore-heads, although only one of them truly needed it. Michael could see about as well at night as he did in the daylight, but he had to maintain appearances.

They took the side path that parted from the main trail and led to the campsite. Michael stopped as soon as the path opened onto the forest clearing where the site was located and gestured for Bill to be quiet and turn off his headlamp.

It was the night of the new moon, and only the stars illuminated the macabre scene. A couple hundred feet in front of them were the remnants of a two-person tent, which had been flattened and shredded to pieces. The barely recognizable shape of a dismembered human body was lying a few feet from the tent.

Bill would have probably walked straight to the body if Michael hadn't held him back by the sleeve, while pointing at the dark shape crouched on the ground under the trees lining the clearing.

"You think that's the bear?" asked Bill in the lowest voice he could manage.

But Michael didn't have to guess; he knew. The smell was coming straight from the dark shape.

"I do," he replied simply.

With extreme caution, Bill deposited his backpack on the ground and, using the rifle's night scope, took aim at the dark shape. He quickly confirmed what Michael already knew.

"It's a grizz. I'd say around four hundred pounds… looks like it's sleeping."

Even though he resented it more than anyone could ever imagine, Michael knew what had to be done. A bear that had killed a human could not be allowed to live. But he sure wasn't going to be the one shooting it!

Suddenly, the wind turned and the grizzly picked up their scent. It awakened and rose. Bill fired twice in rapid succession, placing two bullets in the animal's heart.

As they reached the hiker's mutilated body, Michael picked up a scent he had not noticed at first. The odor had been masked by the stench emanating from the days-old corpse, but it was undeniably there. A more subtle fragrance… fear. Relying on his nose for the general direction, he started searching the thick evergreen canopy that spread all around the campground and quickly identified the origin of the odor. Perched in a nearby tree, about fifteen feet from the ground, was a white human shape. A female from what his nose could tell.

Chapter 4

Detective David Starks and Lieutenant Steve Harrington were digging into their breakfast burritos at the local Taco Cabana when the call came in through the radio. After swearing profusely at the bad timing, the two cops asked for a couple of doggy bags and were on their way.

When they arrived at the address given by the dispatcher, a coroner's van was parked in the driveway and a couple of officers in uniform were making sure none of the curious neighbors ventured inside the house. In addition to the two or three Houston PD cruisers parked in front of the house, numerous Harris County Sheriff Department vehicles blocked all access to the street.

"Why is the Sheriff Department involved in this?" Harrington asked the officer guarding the front door.

"The victim was Chief Deputy Mark Sullivan, from the Harris County Sheriff Department."

Harrington's eyes met David Starks' and he knew his old partner was thinking the same thing he was—another cop!

Harrington looked tired at this moment, although it was difficult to tell for certain whether fatigue or concern was more responsible for the lines on his closely shaven face. Naturally, the somewhat slumped shoulders and slightly protuberant stomach weren't the artifacts of a man in his prime, but the lieutenant was nearing fifty, and was past his prime. Standing beside Starks didn't help his case either. Starks, in his early thirties and weighing a hair over 200 pounds on a 6'2" frame, looked more like a model than a cop. Although his golden complexion, deep blue eyes and semi-short blond hair played their part, his charisma alone sufficed to explain his popularity among women.

"Let's go have a look," he said as he walked through the door and passed a score of police officers, sheriff deputies and coroner's staff all busy doing something.

The scene in the living room, however, was not what they had expected. Over the past year, several high-ranking police officers had been murdered, most of them execution-style, but this one looked different.

For one thing, the amount of blood soaking the living room carpet was astonishing. How could so much blood have come from a single body? The riddle was partially answered when the detectives realized that some of the blood belonged to the dead Rottweilers whose bodies had been shredded and the pieces scattered across the room.

"Are these Sullivan's dogs?" Starks asked one of the deputies.

"Yes. Chief always liked attack dogs."

"It looks like these found their match," noted Harrington more to himself than for anyone's benefit.

Sullivan's body was not in much better shape than his dogs', but at least he was mostly in one piece. A large chunk of his throat had been torn away, which would make the medical examiner's job easy when the time came to determine the cause of death. The air conditioning inside the house had done a good job preserving the bodies; the air was slightly tainted but still breathable.

"What happened?" asked Starks. "Did his dogs kill him before turning on each other?"

"It's doubtful," answered the deputy. "If you look at the carpet, there's a set of tracks that can't belong to either dog. They're way too big."

Harrington and Starks walked over to the bloody paw prints indicated by the deputy and had to agree with the man's assessment.

"What in heaven's name could have left a track this size?" asked Starks bewilderedly. "A lion?!"

"I don't have the faintest clue," replied his friend and colleague. "But I know someone who might."

Chapter 5

Michael had been in bed less than an hour when the phone rang. "You've got to be kidding me!" he muttered to himself.

The rescue mission had taken most of the night. The young woman had been half dead from starvation and dehydration when Michael had found her hidden in a tree. Given the circumstances, she had been very lucky. With the exception of bruises and scratches received from branches while climbing up the tree, she was mostly unscathed. Unlike black bears, adult grizzlies couldn't climb trees, and this fact had saved her life.

All they had learned from her before she had passed out in Michael's arms was that the bear had attacked them in the middle of the night four days earlier. She had been hiding in the tree ever since. Without food or water, it was a miracle she had survived. Her boyfriend hadn't been so lucky. The bear had fed on his corpse every day since the attack, and there really wasn't much left of the kid to bury.

The chopper dispatched to retrieve the young man's body had brought a medical team to take care of the girlfriend. Once the medics had put her on IV fluids, her condition had improved fairly quickly. Within a couple of hours she had awoken and started giving more details about their nightmarish experience.

Soggy from rain, they had made it to their campsite late on Saturday night. After setting up the tent, neither had had much appetite and they had decided to just go to bed. She knew the basic rules to follow when camping in bear country, and she had asked her boyfriend to pull their food up a high branch out of reach of bears. "Bears don't like rain either, they won't bother us," had been his reply. The grizzly had proven him very wrong.

"You'd better have a really good reason for waking me up, Bill," Michael growled as he answered the phone.

"Good morning, Michael. It's good to hear your voice too. Had I known you'd turned into a lazy-ass son of a bitch who doesn't get up before noon, I'd have waited for the afternoon to call you," replied Steve Harrington on the other end of the line.

"Steve?! Is that you?"

"Who else would dare talk to you this way, old fart?"

"I guess it *is* you. Well, sorry for the greeting, but I had a busy night and just got to bed."

"Nothing serious, I hope?" enquired Steve.

"Depends if you consider a twenty-year-old kid ending up in a grizzly's stomach serious or not, I guess. Not to mention his half-starved, traumatized-for-life girlfriend," replied Michael, using his most subtly sarcastic tone. "But enough about me. To what do I owe the pleasure of your call?"

"I'm working a homicide down here in Texas, and I could use your help."

"We're talking about a coyote homicide and you think the local game warden isn't qualified to apprehend the poachers?"

"No, we're talking about a cop and his two Rottweilers torn to pieces by something that leaves tracks the size of a frying pan," answered Steve in a stoic voice.

"I see…"

There was a pause in the discussion while Michael assessed the possible implications of his friend's revelation. After a few seconds he resumed:

"And you think whatever left those tracks is not… *natural?*"

"Well, if I knew I wouldn't be calling you. You're the expert in *unnatural* things!"

"I prefer the term praeternatural, but I get your point. What do you want me to do?"

"I'd like you to come down here and give your expert opinion. I talked to my Captain about this and you'll be reimbursed for your plane tickets and lodging expenses. You'll still have to pay for your food though. We don't have the FBI's budget."

"What kind of cheap-ass outfit do you work for?" Michael didn't wait for an answer; he had already made up his mind to go to Houston. If those paw prints were truly as big as described, Steve would definitely need his help.

"OK. I need to make a few arrangements here, and I'll be on my way. I'll let you know my flight number, and you can pick me up at the airport."

Chapter 6

The Alpha sat quietly as Jack told him what had taken place at the chief deputy's house. He asked a few questions which Jack nervously answered before being dismissed. Once alone, the Alpha stared blankly across the empty room, assimilating what he had been told. What had gone wrong, if anything? What action had to be taken, if any? He was the Alpha, the undisputed leader of the pack, the general. He could not let this pass without careful review and an assessment of the potential fallout. If damage control was required he would need a plan for it.

The unnaturally large paw prints on the carpet had been noticed. An expert was being brought in who would surely identify the prints as well as the mayhem. Those two factors would indisputably lay the blame on a wolf: a very large wolf.

For the police to announce the presence of a 250-pound wolf in downtown Houston without an explanation or a logical plan for its capture, would no doubt cause embarrassment for them and a field day for the press. They were going to play this one close.

Wolves, for all practical purpose, had been eradicated from Texas in the first part of the twentieth century. In addition, wolves in excess of two hundred pounds could not be found anywhere in the world. The largest wolf on record had been shot dead in northwestern Bulgaria in 2007 and had weighed a hair under one hundred and eighty pounds. Moreover, instances of wolf attacks on humans were scarce, far apart, and none had ever occurred inside someone's home in the presence of two attack dogs.

Jack's misstep, if there was one, was not only placing the entire operation in jeopardy, it threatened the survival of the whole pack. On the other hand, Jack could hardly be blamed for having committed an error. Most wolves placed in his position would have reacted in the exact same way. Staying in control of one's wolf in the heat of battle was a difficult thing to do under normal circumstances. Staying in control of one's wolf in the heat of battle when the opponents were attack dogs was nearly impossible... especially for an omega! And Jack *was* an omega.

If only he had cleaned up the mess instead of leaving it behind for the cops to find and stick their noses where they didn't belong. An involuntary morphing was not something a werewolf could reverse of his own will, however, and the Alpha knew it all too well. Time was the only remedy, and it could sometimes take days for a werewolf to morph back into its human form.

Under the circumstances Jack had done the right thing by leaving the house as soon as possible while he could still benefit from the cover of darkness. A 250-pound wolf roaming Houston residential areas in broad daylight was the sort of advertisement the pack did not need.

After pondering all the factors, the Alpha convinced himself that Jack couldn't have done anything differently and consequently was not responsible for the mess he had created. Therefore the omega would be allowed to live. A good thing! An Alpha always despised having to kill his own wolves.

Chapter 7

Steve Harrington's black Honda Accord was racing through the streets of Houston. The vehicle still had the new car smell Michel Biörn loathed so much.

"Did you just pick it up at a dealership on your way to the airport?" asked Michael, irritated.

"No, actually I've had it for six months. Maybe your nose is a tad too sensitive," replied Steve scornfully.

Michael did not respond to his friend's provocation; he just wasn't in the mood for their typical verbal jousts. Spending most of the day in airports and planes designed for people half his size had not left him in a cheerful disposition.

"As a matter of fact, this is the first new car I've ever bought. I got it to celebrate my promotion."

"Promotion?" asked Michael, suddenly interested.

"Yes, Sir! I'll have you know that you're riding with a Lieutenant, so it's time to show some respect," replied Steve in the snootiest tone he could manage.

"My mistake, Lieutenant. I just hadn't realized one got promoted for sleeping on the job down here in Texas. Took you long enough though. You were Detective for what... forty, fifty years?"

In reality, Steve was in his mid-forties, just like Michael. The difference between the two was that Michael had been in his forties for over a thousand years.

Chapter 8

Danko Jovanovich, aka The Serb, was finishing a plate of Peking duck in one of the fanciest Chinese restaurants in the city. The size of his gut was a clear indicator the man had never skipped a meal in his life. A pair of chopsticks lay discarded a few inches from his plate; eating with twigs was best left to savages. The Serb considered himself civilized and therefore ate with a fork, a tool he deftly used to engulf pieces of duck large enough to choke a hippo into the gaping pit of his mouth.

Danko was a smalltime bookie working for the Russian mob; after dabbling in all type of illegal activities, he had found his vocation in the world of illegal street fighting.

Underground street fighting had always existed, but its popularity had been relatively limited in the US until the arrival of the MMA tidal wave. MMA, or Mixed Martial Arts, was a combination of various fighting styles mixing up punches, kicks, wrestling, choking, and pretty much anything one could imagine. The style had initially been created to identify the best fighters, regardless of their fighting style. For this reason, the belligerents were to fight under a very loose set of rules that had initially allowed everything save for biting and eye gouging. However, as MMA grew in popularity and started attracting more and more spectators, the barbarity had to be cleaned out of the sport. Nowadays, MMA was following a complex set of rules intended to protect the fighters and as such had become just another fighting sport. The irony of the situation was lost on the overwhelming majority of fans, but the few who realized MMA fights had lost their sole purpose in life started actively seeking the thrills of the good old days. Illegal street fighting was the answer to their prayers.

In payment for his service, The Serb was entitled to pocket ten percent of the bets' profits, which lately amounted to a cozy sum. Danko was greedy, though, and ten percent no longer satisfied him. As a bookie, he was in the best possible position to be creative with the accounting. Of late, however, he had been exceedingly creative. Thus far, there was no indication his employers had noticed anything amiss, and he intended to keep it that way. The Russians weren't the forgiving type.

Danko placed forty bucks on the table, got up and exited the restaurant. The establishment, like most in Houston, was located in a strip mall. The closest parking spot he had found had been a hundred yards away, and he now had to walk the distance with a belly full of duck meat. He loathed exercising in general and walking in particular.

He was halfway to his car and already sweaty from the muggy evening heat when he realized he was being followed. He turned around quickly, in the same motion grabbing the gun holstered on his belt, but a hand trapped his wrist in a vice-like grip before he had a chance to draw the weapon. The hand belonged to a burly six-foot man with emaciated features. Next to him was another man, a bit shorter, but his eyes scared the living hell out of Danko. A predatory aura emanated from both men and The Serb picked up on it immediately.

"Good evening, The Serb. How was the duck?" asked the second man.

"G-goood…" replied Danko after a few seconds. Beads of sweat were now dripping from his forehead. "Who are you? And what do you want from me?"

"Relax! We're basically colleagues! We too work for Dimitri Ivanov," replied the first man with an all-but-friendly smile as he pulled Danko's gun out of the holster. "And you won't need this where we're going."

The shorter one grabbed Danko under the arm, and they started walking in the direction opposite to Danko's car.

Danko did not know these men, but they couldn't have screamed hitmen any more if the word assassin had been tattooed on their foreheads. The Serb knew beyond any doubt that getting in a car with them equaled a death sentence.

With the exception of an elderly couple, the parking lot was empty and nobody would come to his aid if he called for it. This was not a time for procrastination; this was a time for action. In a motion surprisingly quick for a man his size, Danko rotated his upper body and punched the goon holding his arm in the throat. The hitman's trachea emitted a sinister cracking noise. As the man reflexively brought his hands to his throat, Danko immediately reached for the small caliber he always carried in an ankle holster, but the other man was faster. Before Danko could reach the gun, he was lifted off his feet and slammed headfirst onto the ground. Then everything went dark.

Chapter 9

Black-lettered yellow plastic tape reading "CRIME SCENE DO NOT CROSS" barred access to the driveway. Steve Harrington and Michael Biörn ducked under it and walked to the front door of Chief Deputy Sullivan's house. The lieutenant pulled out a key from his pocket and unlocked the door.

The bitter-sweet smell of blood assaulted Michael's nostrils as soon as he stepped through the door. It only took him a few more seconds to detect another, more subtle odor still lingering in the air... wolf.

Aside from being free of cops and missing a dead body, the house looked the same as it had when Steve had first seen it a day earlier. The Rottweilers' bodies had not yet been removed and the smell of flesh in the early stages of decomposition tainted the air. The taupe living-room carpet was soaked with the victim's blood, which had also splattered all over the cream-colored walls.

"So, what do you think?" asked Steve, while Michael was still trying to get a feeling for what had happened.

"I think the room's a mess," Michael mumbled, still assimilating the surrounding mayhem.

"Way to state the obvious, thank you very much. Anything more insightful?"

"Well, for one thing, this house stinks of wolf."

"Wolf..." repeated Steve thoughtfully. "Now that's interesting. Is it a wolf that left these paw prints?" He pointed at the biggest set of tracks on the carpet.

"Yes, no doubt about it," answered Michael pensively, his thoughts racing through the implications of this discovery.

"So, nothing special about them? They just belong to a common wolf?" asked Steve hopefully.

"They do belong to a wolf, but they are definitely too big for a common wolf. The smell in the air is wrong too. The beast that left these tracks would weigh anywhere between two hundred fifty and three hundred pounds." He turned to face Steve. "A werewolf."

The detective's face turned green at the announcement. "You're kidding, right?" he asked halfheartedly.

"Unfortunately, I am very serious."

"But I thought you were the only one left out there? The only one of your kind?"

"As far as I know, I am the only one of my kind still alive. But I am not a werewolf, Steve. You of all people know that." Steve's face reflected his state of mind better than any discourse would have, and Michael felt sympathy for his friend. The lieutenant was neither prepared nor equipped to deal with these sorts of things.

"But you never said anything about werewolves! When you told me that there were others out there with special talents and that the less I knew the safer I'd be, I just took your word for it. But now a werewolf has killed a cop in his home, in the middle of the city. It's time you tell me the whole story."

Steve's iPhone rang before Michael had a chance to respond. The lieutenant checked the caller ID and answered, "Dave, what's up?"

"I'm at the restaurant. I've been waiting for you guys fifteen minutes already. That's what's up," replied David Starks on the other end of the line.

"Shit! I hadn't realized it was so late. We're leaving Sullivan's house right now. We'll be there in ten minutes."

Chapter 10

The drive from Sullivan's home to the restaurant where Detective Starks awaited them only took a few minutes. Not nearly enough time for Michael to answer even a tenth of his friend's questions.

"Here we are," announced Steve as he parked the car just in front of the restaurant.

"I'm not planning on discussing the existence of praeternatural beings roaming the planet in front of your friend," warned Michael. "So you'll have to be patient a couple more hours before you get your answers."

"All right. But don't think you're off the hook," replied Steve. "As soon as we're back in the car, we'll resume our little conversation."

They walked to the hostess and asked for David Starks' table. The detective was sitting at a booth near the bar, and he got up to greet them.

"David Starks," he said in a cheerful tone as he extended a hand towards Michael. "And you must be Michael Biörn, wildlife specialist and Steve's army buddy."

Michael caught a glimmer in the detective's eyes that made him feel uneasy. The man's odor was strange as well. Difficult to identify for certain—which in itself was odd enough—but Michael perceived what seemed to be a very faint mixture of adrenaline, perspiration and excitement, with maybe an even more elusive touch of fear.

"How do you do?" said Michael as he shook the other man's hand, his face an expressionless mask.

The three men took their seats and spent the next five minutes absorbed by the menu. When the waitress came to enquire about their selection, Michael ordered the biggest steak in the house, a 24-ounce T-bone, while Steve and David ordered steaks of a more manageable size.

David was the first to break the silence following the waitress's departure. "So, what did you think of the crime scene, Michael?"

"It's a bloody mess, that's what I think," he answered cautiously.

"Michael thinks the big paw prints belong to a wolf," interjected Steve, shooting a glance at Michael.

But Michael wasn't paying any attention to him. Using his peripheral vision while seemingly staring at the wall, he was busy observing David.

"Wolf... that's interesting. Not too many wolves in Texas," replied the detective. "I wonder where they found it."

"Who's they?" enquired Michael.

"We suspect the mob might be behind this, but we're not too sure on that one," offered Steve.

"A man and his two dogs are shredded to pieces by what appears to be a wolf, and the police suspect the mob?" asked Michael incredulously. "Could someone please explain to me how you reached that conclusion?"

"We have been working a case for a couple—"

The arrival of the food stopped Steve in mid-sentence. The steak, though rare, was overcooked for Michael's taste, but it was usually the case. In the intimacy of his cabin, the ranger never bothered cooking his meat. In public, however, eating raw steak was frowned upon, and Michael could not afford to attract too much attention.

"You like your steak bloody," observed David.

"I'd eat it alive if I could," replied Michael in a tone he hoped was humorous.

The answer generated a twinkle in the detective's eyes that was not lost on Michael.

"As I was saying," resumed Steve. "We've been working on a case for the past couple years, which we believe is linked to organized crime. Over the past twenty-six months, five cops have been murdered execution-style across the city. Most of them near or at their domicile."

"What do you mean exactly by execution-style?" questioned Michael.

"One bullet in the head and two in the heart," replied David.

"That's rather different than siccing a wild beast on your victim, isn't it?"

"It is. And that's why we're not positive about Sullivan. But he was the Harris County Sheriff Department's Chief Deputy, and that fits our profile."

The three men fell silent for a few minutes. Michael was making a mental summary of the situation, trying to find an explanation for the presence of a werewolf in what was suspected to be a mob-sentenced assassination.

Michael had inhaled his steak within five minutes of it being served, and his companions took advantage of the break in the discussion to finish their own.

"What were the pieces of evidence collected on the crime scene at Sullivan's?" Michael finally asked. "I noticed the yellow tags disseminated in his living room."

"A couple of guns were found on the crime scene. The other evidence collected was mostly pictures of foot and paw prints," replied Steve.

"From what I saw, there was only one set of foot prints," commented Michael.

"That's right, Michael," replied Steve. "And they belonged to the victim."

"Under the circumstances, two guns would seem to be at least one too many then, wouldn't they?"

"You noticed that too," concluded Steve as he was getting up. He then grabbed his iPhone that was lying on the table and headed for the restroom.

A moment of uncomfortable silence ensued, which was quickly broken by David. "So I hear you and Steve go way back?"

"I guess it's been about twenty years. I was his sergeant in the army."

"Rangers, right?"

"That's right."

"Must have been tough, especially in Somalia…"

"Yes, it was. We almost didn't make it once or twice."

"I know… Steve told me the two of you had fought at Mogadishu…"

The battle of Mogadishu, better known as Black Hawk Down, had been a tough one for sure, but nothing in comparison to the one during which Steve had learned Michael's secret. Their team had been sent on a recon mission behind enemy lines, but they had been ambushed by the enemy. Their entire team had been wiped out that day and Steve and Michael had been the sole survivors. In the heat of battle, outnumbered five to one, Michael hadn't had a choice. The only chance he'd had to save at least some of his men, and possibly himself, had been to morph. In front of bewildered assailants, he had turned from man to beast and killed them all. He had received a few bullets in the process, but nothing he couldn't recover from. Steve had witnessed his transformation and, after a long explanation between the two men, had promised Michael his secret would be safe with him.

Steve came back from the bathroom and handed his phone to David. "I grabbed the wrong one. This is yours. I went to call Marjory and found a text message from a lady named Katia who wanted to see me tonight…"

"I'm sure it's a mistake. I don't know anyone by that name," replied David unconvincingly.

"I'm sure… He doesn't look it, but David is quite the ladies' man," commented Steve, approvingly shaking his head.

David, apparently embarrassed by his partner's comment, found nothing to reply.

"Well, it's getting late anyway. I'll drive Michael back to his hotel and we can reconvene in the morning," said Steve before adding, "Who knows… if you're lucky, maybe Katia's still waiting for you."

"She'd better be," answered David jokingly.

Chapter 11

Danko Jovanovich woke up with a splitting headache. He was lying down on his back on some hard surface. It didn't feel cold, though, so he assumed it was hardwood. His eyes were still closed, but as he was slowly coming out of his beating-induced nap, he could hear voices in the background. He must have moved involuntarily because he heard someone saying, "He's waking up." The statement was quickly followed by the sound of feet shuffling on the hardwood floor.

"Good morning, sleepy head," said a man in a tone that sounded a little too honeyed to be honest. "We were starting to think you'd never wake up."

Danko cautiously opened his eyes. Blinded by the warm electric lighting in the room, he took a few seconds to fully assess his surroundings. From where he was lying, he could already distinguish half a dozen persons standing around the room, four men and two women, but there might have been others he couldn't see. It wasn't looking good.

He quickly identified two of the men as his assailants, but he'd never seen the others before.

It was still pretty dark outside and it looked more like the middle of the night than the morning in spite of what the man had said.

"I am glad you could join us, Danko," said the man who had first spoken to him.

"It didn't look like I had a choice."

The room was large, about twice as big as you would expect a living room to be. The floor was definitely hardwood: good quality, too, from what he could tell. Oil paintings hung on the walls, but Danko was not in a mood to pay attention to them.

"One always has a choice, Danko. For instance, you had the choice to be honest with Dimitri's money, but you chose not to be," replied the man in a lecturing tone. "That was not a very smart thing to do, by the way. No one ever told you that stealing from the mob was about as good an idea as petting a wild tiger?"

Danko didn't bother replying. He knew denial was useless and preferred focusing his attention on a way to get out of this alive. His interlocutor was clearly the boss. The others' body language left no doubt about this point. Their attitude towards him was deferential, almost as if they were afraid of the man. He wasn't particularly tall or bulky—though definitely in good shape—but there was something imposing about him, something that made you listen when he talked. Although he probably was in his late forties, he appeared to be in his prime. His thick black hair showed no sign of thinning, and only the faintest of wrinkles were visible at the corners of his eyes. His aquiline nose was supported by a strong jaw line, and his eyes seemed to see through your body all the way down to your soul.

"Who are you?" Danko asked finally.

"Who am I? Don't you know that curiosity kills the cat?" replied the man, smiling. "Oh well, I guess it won't hurt to tell you… I am Peter Clemens."

Danko had never heard the name before, but the fact that he obtained it so easily could only mean two things. One: it wasn't the man's real name; or two: Danko wasn't going to live long enough to do anything with it.

"Max, help our guest to his feet," said Clemens.

A six-foot-tall man grabbed Danko by the arm and jerked him up in the air. Danko was not a lightweight, but the man lifted him off the floor as easily as he would have a feather.

"You haven't asked yet where you are, but I'll tell you anyway. You are in the heart of Sam Houston Forest," said Clemens. "Ivanov wants you dead, but he isn't here so we don't really have to listen to him, do we?"

Danko wasn't sure where this was going, but if Clemens offered him a way out, he'd take it without discussion.

"I'm listening," he replied, swallowing hard.

"My friends here could use some exercise, so why not kill two birds with one stone?" said Clemens. "If you can make it out of the forest without my men catching you, you are free to go…"

"And if I don't?" interrupted Danko.

"Then you'll wish you had died here and now."

Chapter 12

Michael Biörn spun around in his bed for the twentieth time. Exhausted, he had turned in for the night an hour earlier, but his racing mind simply refused to go to sleep.

The ride back from the restaurant had turned into a reenactment of the Spanish inquisition, starring Steve Harrington as the inquisitor and Michael in the role of the suspected heretic.

After an hour and a half of questioning, Steve was still going strong when Michael had finally refused to answer any more questions until he got some sleep.

The questioning had not been strictly unilateral, however. Michael had also tried to learn a few things from his friend, but Steve was not very knowledgeable in the domain of the paranormal. He had never heard of any praeternatural creature aside from Michael, and Michael had been forced to explain the difference between werewolves, shape-shifters (who, for the most part, also happened to morph into wolves), vampires, and himself.

At first, Steve had thought Michael was pulling his chain when he had started talking about vampires. Funny how people were... they could see their friend turning into a wild beast with their own eyes, but still acted all skeptical when you started mentioning blood suckers... Strange! Especially considering how Hollywood had spent the better part of the past twenty years showing werewolves and vampires as mortal enemies.

In all fairness, Hollywood, for once, wasn't too far off. Werewolves and vampires didn't play well together. No one played well with vampires, though, so the werewolves couldn't really be blamed for it.

Where Hollywood had gotten it mostly wrong, however, was in presenting the blood suckers and werewolves as mortal hereditary enemies. Vampires had plenty of enemies, but only one historical nemesis: the shifters. Shifter was short for shape-shifter, also known as skin-walker.

Although the shifters morphed into wolves, they differed from werewolves in many ways. For one thing, the change was always voluntary and instantaneous, and, unlike werewolves who could weigh as much as fifty percent more in their wolf form, shifters retained the same body weight when shifting. That still made for really big wolves, but not nearly as big or scary as the werewolves.

Another significant difference was that shifters were always of Native American descent and were born with their shape-shifting abilities. Werewolves, on the other hand, could be of any lineage and, with a few exceptions, were born human and subsequently turned into wolves.

What had kept Michael from sleeping had not been his friend's questions, however, but his answers. Although Michael had felt an instinctual dislike for David Starks, whom he had met for the first time at dinner,

Steve had vouched for his old partner.

"*I trust him as much as I trust you,*" had been his exact words. "*We were partners for over eight years and I never saw a hint of dishonesty in his behavior. Marge and the kids love him!*"

Michael had not pressed the issue. After all, Steve was a cop and should have noticed something if there had been anything suspicious going on with his partner. Michael had strong instincts, but he was also the most asocial being one would ever meet, and this tended to influence his judgment. He didn't always need a good reason to dislike people. He'd once suspected his own boss, Bill Thomason, of being a witch because he'd found a couple of dead ravens in the man's trashcan. But witches and sorcerers were rarely careless enough to leave evidence of their craft for others to find...

Since Steve was utterly clueless about magic, Michael had only brushed on the topic of witchcraft, simply mentioning witches and their more powerful colleagues, the sorcerers. It was already plenty of information for the poor lieutenant to digest in one evening.

Henceforth, Steve would be an *Initiated*, a human aware of the existence of praeternatural creatures... but praeternatural creatures only. Michael hadn't mentioned a word about the supernatural beings. Warlocks, wizards, elves and mages weren't to be trifled with.

Chapter 13

The moonlight had cloaked the forest in an eerie glow, which did nothing to soothe Danko's already strained nerves.

He had been released from the house twenty minutes earlier and been told he would benefit from a fifteen-minute head start. He had started running as hard as he could, but he had rapidly been forced to slow down and adopt a pace more suited to his physique.

After following the narrow dirt road leading away from the house for about two hundred yards, he had made a ninety-degree turn and dived straight into the woods. The maneuver had been intended to throw off his pursuers and buy him a little time. After that, he had run straight ahead, on several occasions barely escaping decapitation by low-hanging branches.

A howling sound rose from the entrails of the woods, startling him. The call was quickly answered by a second howling, and a third, and a fourth. Danko had not spent much time in the forest, but he was pretty sure the presence of coyotes in a place like this was to be expected. The fact the howling sounds seemed to be getting closer was a bit more unnerving though.

Danko mentally cursed the years of sedentary lifestyle and

overindulging, which had turned him into the out-of-shape blob he was today.

Out of breath, he kept running, although at a pace that most people would have considered walking. Suddenly a slightly unearthed root caught his left foot and sent him flying in mid-air.

He landed on his chest, the shock driving the air out of his lungs. He was still struggling for oxygen when he noticed the small forest trail beneath his feet. He gave himself an additional thirty seconds to recover from his fall before he started running down the trail in the hope of covering more ground, now that trees kept mostly out of his way. At least the howling sounds had stopped. It had to be good news.

Chapter 14

Katia's car was parked in front of Detective David Starks' house when he got home. David was paranoid and obtaining the key to his house was a privilege few had earned in the past. Katia Olveda was not one of them—at least, not yet.

She got out of her car and met him at the front door. She was a gorgeous brunette of about 5'5", with curves of the type men brag about to their friends.

"Hello, lover," she said in a southern drawl she somehow managed to make sexy.

"Good evening, gorgeous," replied David.

"Late night. Is everything all right?" she asked, as she approached to kiss his neck.

"I think so," he answered, still thinking about Michael Biörn. "I had a work dinner. You know how it is."

Katia knew exactly how it was. Dating David implied a lot of concessions… but he was worth it. At least she hoped so.

David Starks was lying in bed, wide awake. Katia had left his house an hour earlier, looking a bit more disheveled than when she had first gotten there. Sex with Katia was always fun. She was just kinky enough to constantly keep it interesting. Katia, however, was not on David's mind at the moment; Michael Biörn was.

Biörn was the type of man who emanated palpable raw power. Most would have attributed this feeling to the man's imposing physique, but David knew better. He had felt the beast trapped within the man, and it had frightened him.

A faint cracking sound from the stairwell attracted his attention. It was probably nothing else than the house shifting, but the detective had learned to be cautious. His life often depended on it.

He grabbed the Smith & Wesson he kept on his nightstand and headed for the bedroom door on tiptoes.

Chapter 15

Danko knew he was being watched; he could feel it in his soul. The small hair that had risen on the back of his neck a few seconds earlier had just reinforced his certitude. Somewhere behind him, eyes were boring a hole in the back of his head.

Utterly out of breath, he stopped running. This was the end of the journey, and there would be no happy ending. Slowly, he turned around to face his executioners.

Whatever he had expected to see, this wasn't it. He could have sworn he'd find Clemens' goons standing behind him, but instead there were five monstrous wolves of the type only seen in B sci-fi movies. So much for his coyote theory...

Describing the beasts as gigantic would not have done them justice. Danko was pretty sure he'd seen horses smaller than these.

The largest creature was standing in front of its fellow beasts, a mere ten feet from Danko. Its fur looked a solid black under the moonlight, unlike the other beasts that appeared mostly gray.

One of the gray wolves took a few steps towards Danko, but a loud growl of the black one made him fall back in line, whimpering. At least it was clear who was in charge.

There was something unnatural about the beasts, aside from their size, that Danko could not pinpoint. Maybe, had he been less terrified, he would have noticed the monsters' eyes. These weren't wolves' eyes; they were human.

As if answering a silent call, the pack started moving towards Danko in perfect synchronization. A second later, they had him surrounded.

The back of the black wolf was as high as Danko's belly button, which placed it around four feet. Its head was only a few inches below Danko's, who could now clearly appreciate the size of the beast's jaws.

The wolf scent filled his nostrils. This was too much for his sphincters, which released their contents in his pants.

The black wolf's upper lip pulled apart to reveal three-inch fangs, but the beast wasn't growling... he was smiling! A hideous, sardonic smile, which froze Danko's blood.

In a flash, the wolf lashed forward, sinking its teeth in the man's belly. This was the signal the others had been waiting for. The feeding frenzy began.

Chapter 16

Steve was over an hour late. This was totally out of character, and Michael was growing increasingly worried. He picked up the receiver and dialed Steve's cell phone for the third time. Still no answer. He replaced the receiver on the phone and right away picked it up again. This time he called information in hope of obtaining Steve's landline number, but Steve wasn't listed. Cops rarely were, for obvious reasons.

Fifteen minutes later, Michael was in a cab on his way to midtown. He didn't know Steve's address, but he had been at his friend's house once before. Having a photographic memory, he remembered exactly how to get there. It had been over ten years though, and he hoped Steve hadn't moved in the meantime.

The cab stopped in front of Steve's place, a modest two-story wooden house built in the seventies, whose front porch harbored a swing in serious need of a paint job.

Michael paid the fare and extracted himself from the cab's backseat as fast as he could manage.

He smelled the blood from the sidewalk. He ran towards the house and turned the front door knob. It was locked. Not bothering to ring the bell, he shouldered his way through the door. The frame gave in with a loud crack, and he rushed inside the house.

The first floor was deserted, but he noticed bloody tracks on the stairs. He leaped upstairs in two strides and followed the bloody prints straight into the master bedroom.

Steve and his wife, Marge, were in their bed—at least, what was left of them. Their bodies looked like they had been run over by a tractor pulling a chisel plow. Blood splattered the walls and soaked the sheets, pillows and mattress. The carpet had been relatively spared from the crimson shower, which indicated they had been killed in their bed without a chance to get up.

Recalling the couple had two daughters, Michael ran to the girls' bedrooms, but they were both empty and the beds were made. He remembered that both girls attended college, and he felt slightly relieved.

He walked back into the main bedroom to look for a phone, but changed his mind when he found Steve and Marge's cell phones lying in puddles of blood on their respective nightstands.

He walked back downstairs, found a phone hanging on a kitchen wall and dialed 911.

Chapter 17

William and Brad Ferguson had woken up early that day and driven straight to Sam Houston Forest to hunt rabbits, the only thing one could legally hunt this time of the year. Given the choice, most boys in their late teens would have preferred being in bed to roaming the woods this early in the morning on a Saturday, but the identical twins belonged to a different class. They had arrived in the heart of the forest before sunrise, and it was still dark when they set out on their quest.

The brothers moved slowly, stealthily through the thickets, their lanky bodies skillfully avoiding the branches and thick brush whose rustling could have betrayed their presence. They knew the place well and had no problem orienting themselves in the morning twilight. This early in the day, the forest was teeming with wildlife. Squirrels, armadillos and deer were a dime a dozen. They had even seen a couple raccoons, but so far, no rabbit.

They had been creeping through the woods for about thirty minutes when William suddenly cried out, "Shiiiit! What the fuck!"

The first light of dawn had lifted the uncanny, surreal atmosphere of the woods brought upon by the moonlight, but Danko's mutilated body did not require special lighting to unnerve anyone.

Brad, who had been following William at a short distance, came running, alarmed by his brother's scream. Brad liked to think of himself as a tough guy, but the view of the bloodied mess that had been Jovanovich was too much for his stomach. Before he had a chance to turn around, he regurgitated his breakfast on Danko's remains.

William's stomach was a bit stronger, and he managed to fight back the urge to be sympathetic to his brother. He pulled out his cell phone from his pocket and dialed 911.

"911, what is your emergency?" answered a composed female voice.

"We found a body in Sam Hou—" started William. His words died in the receiver but were quickly replaced by a gruesome gargling sound as blood started spurting out of his torn throat. The wolf could have decapitated him easily, but he chose to let him bleed to death instead.

The beast then turned its attention to the brother who, quickly recovering from his stupor, was aiming at him. The bullet caught the animal in midair but didn't slow him down. Before Brad could pull the trigger a second time, the wolf was on him, ripping him apart with claws and fangs.

The werewolf had never liked hunters, but he had to admit, they tasted really good. He looked around and sniffed the air to make sure no one had witnessed his little snack. He then retreated to his hiding spot behind a couple of thick bushes and waited for the cleaning crew. They had better hurry if they didn't want to spend the day picking up pieces.

Chapter 18

The forensic team was passing the entire bedroom through their fine-tooth comb, looking for fingerprints, hair, and other potential clues in the oddest places. They had, of course, noticed the bloody animal tracks on the carpet and immediately drew a parallel with those found at Chief Deputy Sullivan's domicile.

In the meantime, Michael was the subject of intense questioning by homicide detectives Lewis and Salazar. Cops were always very suspicious of people who found bodies. Finding a fresh body avoided the whole nuisance of needing an alibi and made murderers' lives much easier.

"Why did you bust open the door instead of calling the police?" asked Salazar.

"For the third time, I just reacted on instinct. I knew Steve well, and when I saw his car in the driveway, I knew something was wrong," replied Michael, who couldn't tell the officer he had smelled blood from the middle of the street.

"And you and Harrington knew each other how?" asked Lewis, a semi-attractive thirty-something woman with auburn hair held back in a short ponytail.

"We were in the army together before he joined the police. He called me a couple days ago asking me to come to Houston. He wanted my opinion on some tracks found at a crime scene."

"Ah yeah, that's right... you're the tracks expert," said Salazar sounding utterly unconvinced. "So, Mr. Expert, what's your professional opinion. Is this the same killer that killed Sullivan?"

"No," replied Michael simply.

"No?" Salazar sounded genuinely surprised this time. "And why do you think that?"

"Because the paw prints are different. They still belong to a wolf, but a different one."

Michael would have preferred keeping this piece of information to himself, but the forensic team would reach the same conclusion sooner or later, and then he would have even more questions to answer.

"So we have two homicidal wolves, working as a team, who target cops at their domicile. That's your story?" asked Lewis visibly irritated.

The two of them were clearly trying a bad cop-worse cop variation of the famous good cop-bad cop routine. Michael just wasn't sure which one was playing the part of the worst cop. Of course, the intimidation technique would have probably worked better if he had been guilty of something, or if he hadn't been a good foot taller and 150 pounds heavier than his interrogators. At 5'7", Salazar wasn't much taller than his partner and appeared in significantly worse shape. While Lewis looked to be in good shape despite her two pregnancies, Salazar's belly gave the impression he was expecting a child of his own.

"I don't need to come up with a story, lady," replied Michael finally. "I'm not a homicide investigator. It's *your* job to come up with something that makes sense. I am not even saying the wolves had anything to do with the killings. I'm simply telling you the wolf tracks at Sullivan's and those found here belong to two different animals."

Lewis and Salazar clearly weren't used to being spoken to that way by a suspect. It took them a second to recover from the shock.

"Listen to me, sir. We are investigating a murder here, and if you do not cooperate, we'll have you arrested for—" started Lewis.

Michael, who was not in a mood to be threatened, interrupted her in mid-sentence. "No! *You* listen to me! The people slaughtered in there were my friends. They had two daughters. Someone should call them and let them know. Someone should also call Detective Starks and tell him his old partner was murdered."

Chapter 19

The Alpha ached all over. He had had very little sleep lately—particularly the night before—but he wasn't complaining. He was working towards his great scheme, and the physical pain was a minor nuisance that would soon go away. It always did.

The killing had been worth staying up late. The fear he had glimpsed in his victims' eyes was reward enough. The Alpha thought he might even have seen a flicker of recognition in those eyes at the very end. He wondered... but that didn't really matter anyway.

Things were starting to look better. With a little help from providence, he had found a way to use Jack's mess to the pack's advantage. The art of improvisation had always been one of the Alpha's strong suits. He was maybe not the strongest wolf out there, but he was one of the brightest, and none of his wolves dared to question his leadership.

Chapter 20

Michael parked his rented Chevy Malibu in the parking lot of Memorial Hermann Hospital. The only two cars available when he had visited the rental agency had been the Malibu and a Toyota Matrix. Since the Matrix did not come with a can opener, he had opted for the Chevy. The Malibu cost $10 a day more than the Matrix, but this was of little consequence to Michael, who had been able to put aside a nice emergency stash over the past thousand years. A good thing, too, for with Steve dead, he probably wouldn't be reimbursed for any of his travel expenses. This was the very least of his concerns however. Steve and Marge had been murdered, and that was the only thing he could think about. Of course, the fact that their killer, in all likelihood, was a were-wolf only added fuel to the scorching fire that roared inside him. Michael hadn't been concerned with the wolves in many years, more years than most people would see in the course of their lives, but that didn't mean he had forgotten. He would never forget.

The hospital smell had hit him as soon as he had parked the car, but as he entered the building the odor became almost unbearable. With a sense of smell seven times better than a bloodhound's, Michael was over-whelmed by the amount of olfactory information available to his nose. While a mere human would have simply noticed the characteristic anti-septic odor associated with medical establishments, he detected the un-dertone fragrances the industrial strength disinfectant attempted to cover. Hospitals smelled of blood, urine, sweat, feces, fear, anxiety, and pain.

Michael asked the receptionist for David Starks, and she directed him to the fifth floor. Once on the fifth floor, he walked straight to the nurses' station. A nurse, busy transferring information from a clipboard to a computer, answered his query without lifting her eyes from her work. "Last door on your left, the one with the officer standing guard."

Michael walked to the uniformed cop, introduced himself, and asked to see Starks. After the cop replied that no one outside medical staff was allowed in the room, Michael had just started explaining his connection with Lieutenant Harrington when the door was opened by a stunning brunette. Steve's comment about Starks being a ladies' man came back to his mind as the woman extended a hand towards him.

Chapter 21

Dressed in a blue Armani suit and matching tie, Dimitri Ivanov looked nothing like the Hollywood stereotype of a Russian mob-ster. And unlike your stereotypical Italian mobster, the headquarters of his villain empire weren't located in the dimly lit back room of some family-owned restaurant. Dimitri Ivanov was a businessman who offi-cially ran a successful import-export enterprise from the fourteenth floor of a modern-looking building in downtown Houston. His cropped curly black hair, close shave, flat stomach and erect posture successfully pro-jected the middle-aged professional image he was cultivating for the world to see.

Ivanov's staff was better armed than the local S.W.A.T. team, but this was Texas after all, and an honest citizen was entitled to the right to bear heavy artillery to protect his interests.

A knock on the door interrupted the mob boss in the middle of his discussion with Igor Petrovich.

"A package for you, Boss," shouted a voice on the other side of the door.

"Let him in," Ivanov told the giant who watched the door.

The giant was Stanislas Erzgova, Ivanov's personal bodyguard. Stan had been in the Russian Special Forces for a few years before deciding that, if one was going to be in harm's way, organized crime was a more lucrative venue than the military. As far as muscle men were concerned, Stan was one of the brighter ones.

The door opened on a shaggy-looking man in his mid-twenties. He was holding a thick envelope that he dropped on the boss's desk.

"It's been checked, Boss. It's clean."

"Thank you, Vadim, you can leave us now… and go get a haircut!"

Vadim departed with the look of a schoolboy who had to take home a bad report card.

The envelope was unmarked. Dimitri opened it using the penknife he kept at all times on his person and pulled out a small book: Danko's accounting records. A card was accompanying the book:

With Compliments,
P. C.

The inscription had been left by a laser printer, and Ivanov was sure no fingerprints would have been found on the note if someone had cared to look. Peter Clemens was a prudent man.

"It looks like our friend Danko was reunited with his maker," said Ivanov.

"Sleazeball," commented Igor Petrovich, who was sitting across Ivanov's desk.

Petrovich had quickly risen through the ranks of the organization to become Ivanov's official second in command. As cunning as he was ruthless, Petrovich was a man people feared for good reason. He wore his dirty blond hair cut above the collar in an attempt to cover the scar which started below his left eye and went all the way down to his jaw— a souvenir left by the razor of a well-intentioned Mexican competitor who had exhaled his last breath on Petrovich's shoulder with the Russian's knife buried deep in his guts.

"I have to give it to him, Petro. Clemens gets shit done."

"I could have done it myself just as well, Boss, or sent one of the guys… and it wouldn't have cost you a dime," replied Petrovich.

"I know, Petro, I know. But I can't afford to risk losing you for a scumbag like the Serb. You're too valuable to me. Using Clemens makes good sense from a business point of view. I've explained it to you before."

"I know, Boss, but I still don't get it. He charges 50K a pop. You don't think we could get it done for much cheaper?"

"Probably, but I like his style," replied Ivanov, smiling.

Clemens' style was not the reason Ivanov used his services, but Petrovich didn't need to know that. Knowledge was power, and Petro was powerful enough already. Igor didn't need to know Ivanov employed Clemens' services because he couldn't afford not to. He didn't need to know that Clemens and his friends were the single largest threat to Ivanov's organization… and he sure as hell didn't need to know that Clemens was the reason Ivanov never went anywhere without silver bullets in his gun.

Chapter 22

"Mr. Biörn, I presume?" The woman's skin displayed a pleasant natural tan common along the Mexican border. Her silky hair was black as ink and flowed in waves over her shoulders down to her mid-back.

Katia Olveda was used to seeing men lose their composure when they first met her, but her looks did not seem to particularly affect Michael. He shook her extended hand and simply replied, "How do you do?"

He didn't bother asking her how she knew who he was. His sheer size was a dead giveaway. He had been described on several occasions as "The Hulk without the green".

Katia observed Michael a brief instant before turning her attention to the uniformed cop watching the door. "It's all right, officer. Detective Starks will be happy to see Mr. Biörn."

The officer nodded and with a ceremonious "Yes, Ma'am" stepped away from the door. Katia was leaving and did not follow Michael back into the room.

David Starks was sitting in bed wearing a hospital gown that clearly showed the multiple bandages covering his arms and torso. He also had a very large piece of gauze taped over his left shoulder, which went all the way to the base of his neck. His face had not been spared by the ordeal either. Long claw marks were visible on his right cheek and forehead, and one of his eyes had turned an ugly yellowish color.

Overall, he looked beaten and tired, but nonetheless Michael saw his probing eyes studying him intently.

"Michael. How kind of you to come visit. Please have a seat," said David in a voice made drowsy by the painkillers.

Michael picked a chair that had been used by Katia Olveda a few minutes earlier and, after drawing it a few feet away from the bed, sat on it.

"How did you know I was here?" asked David.

"After Steve and Marge were murdered, I tried to get in touch with you. I went to the police station, but your Captain refused to tell me where you were. It took me four days to finally convince him to tell me what had happened to you. I only found out this morning that you'd been attacked the same night Steve had been murdered."

"I heard you were the one who found them?" said David, almost apologizing for asking.

"Yes. And it wasn't a pretty scene," replied Michael. "Could you tell me what exactly happened to you?"

"I could, but why do you want to know?" asked David, who already knew the answer.

"I want to find the bastard who killed Steve."

"This is not a Park Ranger's job, Michael," replied David without irony.

He was staring into Michael's eyes in a way Michael did not like at all—a way that made him feel nervous, agitated, dangerous. Once again, Michael had an uneasy feeling in the presence of David Starks. He could have sworn the detective was trying to hide something from him, except that now, he didn't really seem to be trying anymore.

"But you're not quite a simple Park Ranger, Michael, are you?"

Michael did not say a word; he just stared the detective down until David eventually dropped his gaze.

"I am not your enemy, Michael, no matter what you think. We want the same thing out of this, but we need to be honest with each other."

"I'm listening," replied Michael cautiously, letting his tense muscles relax a little.

"Let's start by answering your question." David readjusted the pillow behind his back, bringing a rictus of pain to his bruised-up face. "It was about 4.15 a.m. I was lying in bed awake when I heard some noise downstairs. I grabbed my gun and went to check it out. As soon as I got to the bottom of the stairs, I could smell it, like a dog smell but stronger. I walked to the living room and there it was. I didn't get a chance to pull the trigger. It pounced at me and sent me flat on my back—"

"What was *it* exactly?" interrupted Michael.

"It looked like a wolf on steroids!"

Michael seemed to be pondering David's answer while the latter resumed his story. "I had let go of the gun in my fall but it had dropped close enough that I could reach it. That's what I did, and it saved my life, for at the same time Wolfy was going for my throat—" David paused for an instant, visibly agitated.

"Are you all right?" asked Michael.

"I'm fine. Would you mind pouring me some of that water?" David pointed at a bottle on the bedside table.

Michael obliged and David took a couple of sips before continuing. "My reaching for my gun made the beast miss its target and instead of my throat, he shattered my collarbone."

Michael's eyes were instinctively drawn by the bandage around David's shoulder.

"You can't put a cast on a collarbone." David had followed his gaze.

"How did you get out of this alive?" asked Michael with just a hint of suspicion in his voice, which David did not seem to notice.

"I got lucky. He had his teeth sunk into my shoulder, but I now had my gun in hand. I emptied the magazine in the animal's side. That got its attention."

"What happened next?"

"It was visibly hurt, but not hurt enough. It got off me and ran, shattered the nearest window, and then it was gone."

"How did you get to the hospital?"

"The gunshots woke up the entire neighborhood. The neighbors called 911 and they found me on the floor, unconscious."

Michael considered David's tale for a minute. It sounded plausible enough, but didn't make much sense. He had the definite impression David was holding something back.

"So that's the whole story?"

"It's the whole story, and the way you're staring at me as if I just made it up is starting to get on my nerves, Michael."

"I'm just not of a very trustful nature, and you have to admit, the whole thing sounds fishy," replied Michael without apologizing.

The two men were silent for a few minutes, lost in their respective thoughts.

"Michael."

"Yes?"

"I know what attacked me, and I know it wasn't a simple wolf," said David very seriously.

Michael was suddenly very attentive. "What was it then?"

"You know what it was as well as I do, and probably a lot better… It was a werewolf."

Michael looked at him skeptically and then, in a voice dripping with sarcasm, said, "I assume your gun was loaded with silver bullets then…"

"Drop the act, Michael!" answered David. "You know very well that silver has no particular effect on praeternatural beings."

This time Michael took him seriously. The fact that he even knew the word praeternatural was a sign David Starks was to be taken seriously. Most people would have called a werewolf supernatural, but they would have been wrong.

"What do you know of praeternatural beings?" asked Michael.

"Enough to be able to recognize one chewing on me," replied David without humor. "Enough to tell that you know them too. From the minute I saw you, I knew you weren't human."

Michael neither denied nor confirmed the claim. He just did what he had always done best. He listened.

"Look, Michael, I don't ask you to trust me with the truth. Just listen to what I have to say." David reached for his glass of water. "I never knew my real dad, he left my mom when she was pregnant with me, but she married a man who raised me as his own. This man was a werewolf. I was raised by a werewolf. Do you really think you can fool me? The way you walk, the way you look at people, the way your attention gets caught by sounds and odors nobody else can detect. I can feel the animal inside you as clearly as if I saw it, Michael."

Michael looked at David. Not a challenging gaze, just a tired look, the look of someone weary of having to hide his true nature day in and day out.

"I am not a werewolf, David," said Michael finally.

"Maybe not," replied David, "but you're not human either."

Chapter 23

Detective Edward Salazar did not particularly shine in the intellect department, but he was dedicated to his job and relatively good at it. He could find the apparently irrelevant piece of evidence that would eventually break a case. He just typically wasn't the one doing the breaking.

His partner, Detective Samantha Lewis, on the other hand, was as sharp as the stiletto shoes she wore off duty. She was also good at getting confessions. The cute demeanor she could fake had tricked scum into confiding in her more than once.

Today, however, her wits and cuteness were of no help. Lewis and Salazar had been reviewing the evidence for over an hour, and they were getting nowhere fast.

After Lieutenant Harrington's murder and the attempt on Detective Starks' life, Lewis and Salazar had been assigned to the investigation, which also included Sullivan's assassination. The *modus operandi* common to the three cases was original enough to guarantee a connection between them. Now they just had to find it.

The mob angle was still being favored but didn't seem to lead anywhere. Over the past two years, half a dozen high-ranking police officers had been murdered at home. The majority of victims had belonged to the Houston PD, but the Harris County Sheriff Department and the state police had also suffered casualties. The last two victims, Harrington and Starks, had been the officers in charge of the investigation. Up to that point, the mob hypothesis made sense. Organized crime going after cops, although unusual, was not without precedent. The recent shift of *modus operandi*, however, was harder to rationalize.

One could perfectly picture a hitman shooting a cop at point blank range in his living room. On the other hand, imagining a mobster taking the time to train wolves simply to kill cops in the most gruesome manner was just a bit farfetched.

"Maybe the mob's trying to send a message," said Salazar, still staring at the evidence board where pictures of the various crime scenes were pinned. "That would be their style… trying to scare us out of their business."

"Unlikely," replied Lewis. "For one thing, Sullivan, as far as we know, had never worked on a case involving the mob, so why would they kill him? In addition, mobsters kill cops when they have no choice, not just for fun. It's bad for their business. It raises too much attention and motivates us to go after them."

Salazar didn't reply. As usual, Lewis' arguments made sense. The phone rang and he picked up the receiver.

"Salazar. Yes… Are you sure? Different ones, for sure? OK, thanks for letting me know."

He took a small notebook out of his coat pocket and scribbled down a few lines before turning to Lewis who was staring at him with a questioning look.

"It was the lab. Biörn was right. The wolf tracks found at Sullivan's and Steve's belong to two different wolves. It was confirmed by the analysis of the hair found at both crime scenes."

"After all, he *is* the wolf expert…" she replied pensively. "What about the blood found at Starks'?"

"The lab didn't get to it yet. They think they'll have the answer within a couple days," responded Salazar as he placed the notebook back in his pocket.

"If it belongs to a third animal, I swear I resign and sell my services as wolf hunter," interjected Lewis. "That's got to pay better than a cop's salary anyway!"

Chapter 24

Lying on the bed in his hotel room, Michael was reflecting on the discussion he'd had with David Starks in the afternoon. He was feeling less suspicious towards the detective now that he knew about his past. If David had been raised around werewolves, he was an initiate: a human without special abilities, but who was aware of the existence of praeternatural and supernatural beings. Michael knew from his past as a berserker that it was possible and even likely an initiate would be able to sense the animal nature hidden inside his human body.

A thousand years had passed, but Michael remembered vividly the initiates who had fought at his side in the streets of London in the year 995 during the raiding of England. The berserkers' corps of Olav Tryggvasson's army had been composed of a few praeternatural beings, but the majority of the warriors had been purely human… initiates. Over the centuries, many theories had been put forward by scholars of all eras and nationalities to explain the enigma that were the berserkers of

Norway, to explain the lethally destructive fury of these men who waged battle with such bestial ferocity that they were feared well beyond the borders of modern-day Scandinavia. Some historians had postulated the berserkers used drugs to induce their uncontrollable trance, while others believed they had simply donned beasts' pelts and worked themselves up into a destructive trance prior to battles. None had gotten it right. The truth was that the initiate members of the berserkers' corps were simply able to feed upon the raw animal power of their praeternatural brothers in arms. This borrowed energy gave their troops a sense of cohesive rage in battle where the initiates wreaked havoc almost as much as their beastly brothers. In the end, the initiates spent so much time in close quarters with their praeternatural counterparts that any one of them would have been able to recognize the praeternatural nature of a stranger on first encounter.

David's experience as an initiate didn't seem to extend past were-wolves, however. He looked at Michael with a mixture of curiosity and speculation, apparently unable to place his true praeternatural nature.

There were many questions Michael had wanted to ask the detective: questions that required answers. He had refrained, however. He simply wasn't ready to trust the detective just yet... which left him in a conundrum. He still needed to understand how werewolves were connected to the case, but he hoped someone other than David could provide answers on the subject.

He sat up on the bed, picked up the phone on the nightstand and dialed a number he hadn't used in ages. The phone rang three times before a female voice answered. "Hello?"

"Heuu... Hello?" Michael hadn't been expecting a woman to answer the phone. "I'm looking for Ezekiel."

"Sorry, you have the wrong number."

Michael was pretty sure he had dialed the correct one. His memory was as good as they got. After a second of reflection, he asked, "Were you recently assigned a new number by chance?"

"No. I've had this number almost five years."

"Well, sorry for the bother," said Michael, hanging up.

He was distraught; now he had no way to contact Ezekiel. It had been over ten years since he had last spoken to his friend, and for all he knew Ez could be long dead. Unlikely though... wizards weren't particularly easy to kill.

The phone rang, interrupting his train of thoughts. He picked up the receiver.

"Michael Biörn! What do you want from me, stranger?" boomed a familiar voice.

"Ez? Is that you? How did you know I was looking for you? I thought the lady who answered the phone didn't know you?" asked Michael, surprised.

"Oh, but she didn't," replied the wizard mischievously.

"So how *did* you know?"

"Michael Biörn, I am a wizard of the second circle. Do you really think I need someone to forward my calls in order to know you're looking for me?" Ezekiel sounded falsely hurt. "The spell allowing this miracle, which seems to amaze you so much, is about as difficult to master as blowing on a rope to make a knot disappear…"

"Sorry, Ez, I guess I had forgotten I was talking to the greatest wizard in history," replied Michael in his most humble voice.

"Flattery will lead you nowhere, my friend!"

"It was worth a try… I'm in Houston. Do you think we could meet somewhere for dinner or a drink? I have a couple questions I'd like to ask you."

"Are you buying?" asked the wizard who, in truth, had even fewer money concerns than his eon-old friend.

"It goes without saying."

"Then I will try and see if I can free my schedule for you."

Chapter 25

Peter Clemens parked his Dodge Viper next to the only vehicle on the lot, a black Mercedes limousine with windows so dark one could not see through them from the outside. The parking lot belonged to a church, and since there was no service scheduled for the evening it was deserted.

Clemens got out of his car and nodded to the large man who was opening the Mercedes' back door for him.

"Good evening, my friend," said Ivanov in the slight Russian accent he always had when he spoke English.

"Good evening, Dimitri," answered Clemens, settling down next to the mobster on the limo's back seat.

"I hope the traffic wasn't too bad. Not easy to get around town this time of the day."

"No, it isn't. But surely you didn't ask me to drive all the way here to talk about traffic?" Clemens' cordial voice contrasted with the nature of his question.

"You are right, we are business men. Time is money. Let's cut the bullshit," replied the mob boss. "I wanted to see you because I hear things from my informants… things I don't like. Maybe you already know what I am talking about?"

"Maybe I do, but just to be safe, why don't you tell me?" answered Clemens in a neutral tone.

"There are rumors on the street that three cops were murdered in less than a week. Have you heard about this?"

Clemens seemed to contemplate the question for an instant before saying, "Why don't you ask your driver to go check the pressure in the tires?"

Ivanov looked at him for a second.

"Very well. Sergei, go keep Stan company."

"Yes, sir," replied the driver, exiting the car and closing the door behind him.

"And now, can you tell me what you know about this?" asked Ivanov in a slightly irritated voice.

"I probably know as much as you do, no less, no more."

"Have you heard that the cops believed some wolf was the killer?" enquired Ivanov.

"That's the rumor, yes."

"So, what can you tell me?"

"I can't help you, Dimitri. I know nothing about these murders, and if I did, I still wouldn't have to tell you anything." Clemens spoke in an amicable voice that wasn't enough to veil the threat in his answer. "But out of courtesy and respect for you, I would probably let you know anyway."

Ivanov looked Clemens in the eyes for just a few seconds before lifting his gaze back to the man's forehead. He didn't like looking into Clemens' eyes. There was something scary about them. They were the eyes of a predator.

"Do you have any idea who is behind this?"

"I don't. Maybe the Italians… Who knows?" Clemens didn't sound convinced.

"That could be their style, but they haven't been seen in Houston since the Mexicans kicked them out three years ago," replied Ivanov pensively.

"Maybe they're back, now that the Mexicans are out…"

"If they are back, nobody told me. As far as I know, we are the only ones in the city, and I intend to keep it that way."

Chapter 26

Michael understood why Ez had picked this particular restaurant as soon as he walked into it. The subdued lighting provided by lit candlesticks on the tables and the walls gave the establishment a peaceful atmosphere and enhanced the anachronistic feeling given off by the rest of the decor. The battleaxes, flails, flanged maces, mauls and shields hanging on the walls, the coarse wooden benches and dining tables, the metal wine pitchers—all was designed to project the diners back to medieval times.

But the interior decoration—reminiscent of an epoch both men had known—had not been Ezekiel's sole motivation; small and mostly empty, the place was above all discreet.

Seated at a table in one of the back corners, Ezekiel was sipping from a metal pint. A few patrons had costumed themselves in Middle-Age fashion to enhance their dining experience, and for a change Ezekiel, wrapped in a long gray cloak, did not look completely out of place. His pointy wizard hat still looked a bit over the top though.

Michael had to drag the wooden bench a good three feet away from the table before he could fit his hulk of a body on the seat facing his friend. That meant his back was to the door, a position he did not particularly like, but he could count on Ez to warn him of incoming trouble.

"Long time, no see, my friend, as they say these days…" opened Ezekiel with a smile.

"It's all a matter of perspective. What are ten years for you and me?" replied Michael without humor.

"Are you going to get all melodramatic on me? Because if that's the case, I have better things to attend to. Like finishing my hair-growth slowing potion, for instance."

"No melodrama. But let me know when you're done with that potion of yours. It could come in handy," replied Michael a bit more cheerfully.

"That's better. Now what's the matter? What are you doing in Houston? I don't suspect you came on a simple courtesy visit, did you?"

"I wish I did, Ez, I wish I did…" Michael trailed away as the waiter approached the table with menus. He and Ezekiel made their choice quickly, from a selection designed exclusively for large carnivores, and got back to business as soon as the waiter was no longer within earshot.

"You probably didn't know my friend Steve Harrington. We were in the Rangers together about twenty years ago."

"I can't say I knew him. But I do know he and his wife were murdered in their home a few nights ago by something that looked like a wolf." Ez lowered his voice.

"News travels fast around here. Although I believe the cops are trying to keep it quiet. I haven't seen anything about it in the papers or on TV so far."

"Neither have I," replied the wizard, "but when three cops are attacked at home by wild beasts in the middle of the country's fourth largest city, it does tend to raise some eyebrows in our small community."

"Are you looking into it?"

"No. It's not really our business to go investigate cops' murders, especially if magic was not involved, and from what we can tell, it wasn't."

Michael nodded slowly in agreement. He already knew this much.

"I already visited two of the crime scenes. As a matter of fact, I'm the one who discovered the bodies of Steve and his wife," he said in a somber tone. "One thing is for sure. Werewolves were involved. At least two different ones. Their tracks and stench were all over the place. And from what I hear, they left DNA evidence behind them as well."

"Now that wasn't a very smart thing to do, was it? It's not like them to attract attention. Especially since they really don't need to morph into their wolf form to kill someone..."

"I know. This whole business is fishy. It just doesn't make sense. If the general public learns about the existence of werewolves, particularly in this context, it will be war. And the wolves have nothing to gain from that, beside extinction," agreed Michael.

It didn't matter that a wolf could easily kill a dozen armed men and walk away unscathed; there were at most a couple thousand wolves in the country, and they were not bullet proof... at least not entirely.

The waiter brought a cauldron and set it in the center of the table. The thick stew had a smoky aroma and contained pieces of meat the size of a fist. Using a ladle, the waiter poured generous portions into large wooden bowls, which he placed in front of his guests. He then poured lavish amounts of a thick red wine into tin goblets before departing with a hearty, "Feast well, my lords."

Large wooden spoons being the only utensils available to do the feasting, the two friends used their hands to fish the chunks of meat out of their bowls. This didn't bother either one of them, however. In the course of their existence, they had both spent more time eating with their hands than with silverware.

"So, what did you want to ask me?" resumed the wizard.

Michael finished up a chunk of pork the size of a quail in one swallow before answering, "You've been living around these parts a long time—"

"Only a couple hundred years," interrupted Ezekiel facetiously.

"Anyway, long enough to know the neighborhood. What can you tell me about the praeternatural community?"

The wizard wiped his hands and mouth on an oversized napkin made of linen and sat back on his seat. "Starting with the obvious, we do have a few werewolves."

"How many?"

"I don't really keep a close tally, but I'd say at least thirty or forty. The Houston pack is one of the largest in the country."

"Who's the Alpha?"

"A man called Peter Clemens. He has a big house in the middle of Sam Houston Forest. The rumor is that it is also used as the pack's headquarters."

Michael made a mental note of the name before asking, "What does this Clemens do?"

"You mean aside from leading a pack of werewolves?"

"Yes. I mean for a living!" Michael ignored his friend's sarcasm.

"I believe he runs a small investment company."

"And on which side of the fence does this pack stand?"

"Now that's hard to tell for sure," answered the wizard. "They are not obviously on one side or the other. I hear from some sources that they could be working part-time with the local mob, but it would need to be confirmed. They don't exactly qualify as cub scouts... but for the most part they don't cause enough trouble for us to concern ourselves with them either."

Michael thought about his friend's statement for a minute before asking, "Any lone wolves in town?"

"Not that I know of," replied the wizard contemplatively. "That wouldn't go well with Clemens. He's way too territorial to allow it."

"Anything else? Vampires maybe?"

"No vampire whatsoever; the Houston pack is too big for them to hang around town. There are hearsays of a couple shifters, but they are in hiding. The wolves would see them as competition and hunt them down if they found out. But I don't have to tell *you* that..."

Michael was indeed all too well aware of this. The territorial and aggressive nature of the wolves towards other predators was the reason he was the only one of his kind left alive. It was also why he was hiding out in the middle of Yellowstone. He truly loved the park, but the hiding was getting to him.

"Any magicians?" he asked finally.

"Your garden variety of witches and sorcerers. We had trouble with a sorcerer whose head was getting too big for his hat a few years back. But we took care of the problem, and they've all been playing nice ever since," answered Ezekiel, boasting slightly.

"What about your folks?"

"You mean wizards or supernaturals in general?"

"Both."

"Well, aside from yours truly, there are three other wizards in town. All good people, although one of them is a bit arrogant, if you know what I mean..."

Michael almost asked Ez if he were talking of himself, but thought better of it.

"There are also two or three elves."

"Elves? That's unusual! Aren't they a bit far from a real wood in a city this large?"

"Yes, they are. And a little too far from their kindred too, if you ask me. It's not good for an elf to be on his own... these folks need company!"

"Are they causing any trouble?"

"No. At least not around here. They keep to themselves, antisocial folks. If you ask me, I don't think they are here of their own will," answered the wizard in a conspiratorial tone.

"What do you mean?"

"I think they're exiles."

Ezekiel's theories weren't always as sound as his more factual state-
ments, so Michael didn't pry further into the issue.

"Any Warlock?" he asked.

"A Warlock? On my turf?" exclaimed the wizard, outraged. His outburst turned a few heads in their direction. Taking notice, he resumed in
a muffled but still appalled voice, "What kind of a wizard do you think I
am? Do you really believe I would put up with that kind of nonsense?"

Michael didn't think so, but seeing his friend work himself up had
made it worth asking.

Chapter 27

After J.F.K.'s, this was by far the largest funeral Michael had ever attended, and he had been to plenty. There were over a hundred cops
present, including Frank Dacosta, Chief of Police, and the Executive Assistant Chief of Police Thomas Maxwell. All were wearing ceremonial
uniforms. In comparison to the imposing police representation, the family members and friends were few and looked almost out of place.

It had been raining all morning, and even though the rain had finally
stopped and the sun was making a tentative appearance, the air was still
heavy with the smell of damp soil. Unfortunately for Michael, the earthy
smell was not strong enough to cover the odor of embalming chemicals
emanating from his friends' oversized casket—Steve and Marge were being buried in the same coffin.

Michael was standing by David Starks, in the first row, just a few feet
away from the coffin. David, dressed in a black suit, looked better than
the last time Michael had seen him. Even the scars on his face looked a
lot better than they had a few days earlier in the hospital.

Immediately across from the two men were the deceased's daughters
surrounded by a dozen relatives. The youngest daughter, Lucy, was a
redhead who would have been considered pretty under other circumstances. Currently, she held a white handkerchief under her nose, and
her face was puffed up by the crying she had been doing all day. Clad in
a knee-length black dress, she was holding her sister's hand tightly in her
own and did not look like she would ever let go of it. The oldest daughter, Olivia, was wearing large sunglasses that covered half of her face.
Her brown hair had been pulled back in a bun and her slender neck disappeared in the collar of a dark gray skirt suit. Unlike her sister, her behavior did not show any emotion, but her apparent composure was betrayed by the tears pearling from time to time down her cheeks.

The Reverend finished his oration and asked the family if they would
like to say a few words. When they all declined, he called the Chief of
Police to the pulpit.

Frank Dacosta gave a ten-minute speech praising Steve Harrington's exemplary service record and vowing to do everything in his power to catch the perpetrators of this atrocious crime. The discourse was well rehearsed and meant to be heartfelt, but it only sounded stale and generic.

♋

Michael walked towards Lucy and Olivia Harrington to present his condolences. Lucy, supported by an uncle and still drowning in her tears, barely acknowledged his presence, but Olivia surveyed him from behind her opaque sunglasses.

"Who are you?" she asked in a low voice that sounded as if she was fighting back a sob. "You look vaguely familiar."

"I am Michael Biörn. I was a friend of your father. We used to be in the army together."

"You're the one who saved his life, aren't you?"

Michael simply nodded.

"Didn't you use to come by the house when I was a kid?" she asked, her voice sounding slightly more assured.

"I did visit once or twice. But that was a long time ago, I'm surprised you remember."

"Oh, I remember." Her lip curled into the shadow of a smile; Michael's physique wasn't easily forgotten. "You haven't changed much."

Before Michael had time to add anything, David Starks arrived to present his condolences to Olivia.

Michael took a couple steps back to give the two of them some privacy. That's when he caught an odor that sent his internal alarm system haywire.

The scent was coming from the left, somewhere behind him. He slowly pivoted to find the origin of the danger and met the gaze of a man who was staring at him. The man was well built, though small in comparison to Michael, and wore the Sheriff Department's uniform. He was surrounded by a couple of fellow deputies conversing in low voices. The deputy continued staring at Michael a few seconds before turning his head towards his companions. At least he knew better than to try and stare down a larger predator. This observation did not comfort Michael very much, however. A wolf had seen him, and soon the whole pack would know he was in town.

Chapter 28

"You've got to be kidding me!" exploded Detective Samantha Lewis, bent over a sheet of paper on her desk.

"What is it?" asked Salazar.

"That's the genetic analysis report for the blood samples found at

Starks'," answered Lewis, still reading.

"And? What does it say?" asked her partner, sounding impatient.

"It says, in short, that two different blood types were found on the scene. The first one belongs to David, but the second one is not human. It belongs to a wolf—"

"We already knew that!" interrupted Salazar.

"I *know* we already knew that," answered Lewis, not hiding her irritation at her partner. "What's new is that the wolf blood was left by yet a third animal. It doesn't match the DNA from the hair samples found at Harrington's or Sullivan's place."

"You've got to be kidding…"

Chapter 29

Michael Biörn was sitting in a comfortable, if not luxurious armchair in David Starks' living room. The floor tiles had been wiped clean of the mess made by David's struggle with the werewolf, and the room now mostly smelled of pine-scented cleaner. The wolf scent was still present, but very faint; it had been over a week since the attack. This scent was different from the one Michael had picked up at Harrington's though, quite different; it was not a match for the one he had smelled at Sullivan's either. A third wolf…

David entered the room with a mug of steaming coffee in one hand and a mug of tea in the other. He placed the tea in front of Michael. "Do you take milk or sugar?"

"Do you have honey?" enquired Michael. "If not, sugar will do."

"I believe I do," replied the detective, disappearing into the kitchen. He came back a moment later holding a small plastic bear filled with honey, and a coffee spoon. He handed both to Michael who added five generous spoonfuls of honey to his tea.

"You sure like your honey," commented David with a smile, settling down on a leather sofa facing his guest.

"I do," answered Michael simply.

"So, tell me why you're here. You were rather cryptic on the phone."

Michael took a sip of his tea before answering, "I came to you with a proposal."

"I'm all ears…"

"I believe we could help each other out. A sort of mutually beneficial association," said Michael, observing his host.

"What exactly do you have in mind?"

"We are both looking for the same thing: the bastards who killed Steve… and who tried to kill you. You know the city, you know the case, and you know a few things about werewolves." Michael paused to drink another sip from his mug.

"All right, I see why I would be of interest to you. Now tell me what you bring to the table," answered David in a businesslike tone.

"You may think you know werewolves because your step father was one… and that may be so. But that knowledge won't save you the next time they try to rip your head off your body. You got lucky once; it won't happen again." Michael gave David an instant to digest the statement before continuing. "What I bring to the table is my expertise of the werewolves and my protection."

"Your protection? You're a tough cookie, Michael, I'll give you that. But we are talking about werewolves here. I don't see how a mere human could protect me against them." David spoke in a falsely candid voice. "Unless, of course, you are admitting to be more than a mere human…"

"I am not admitting anything like that, but believe me when I say that a werewolf will think twice before attacking me."

"Good enough!" replied David, a satisfied smile on his face. "Does that mean I can count on you to tuck me in bed every night?"

"That's not what I had in mind, but I can sleep on your couch if it makes you feel any safer," said Michael uneasily.

"Thanks for the offer, especially since you seem serious about it. But I'm afraid having a three-hundred-pound fulltime babysitter would negatively impact my lifestyle. Plus the captain has posted uniforms outside my house already."

"That's probably a good thing, as long as they are carrying heavy artillery."

"They are. Colt Anaconda loaded with 44 Magnums, if you want to know. Specially authorized for the occasion."

"That should at least slow them down," replied Michael thoughtfully.

"But that doesn't solve our problem…"

"Which is?"

"Which is that you are not a cop, Michael, at least not a real one… no offense."

"None taken."

"I couldn't bring you in on this case even if I wanted to. And on top of everything else, I am no longer in charge of the investigation. After what happened last week, I have become too personally implicated in the case to be allowed to stay on it."

"Who's in charge of the investigation then?" asked Michael.

"Some colleagues of mine, Detectives Lewis and Salazar."

"I bumped into them at Harrington's after I discovered the bodies. They didn't strike me as particularly bright," commented Michael.

"Don't underestimate Lewis. She's a sharp one. Salazar not as much, but he's no dummy either, and he carries his weight."

"Listen, even if they were the best cops on the planet, you and I know they are no match for what they are up against. Werewolves might, in a pinch, let cops arrest them in order to protect the pack or the secret of their existence. But if Lewis and Salazar come anywhere close to the truth, they will be eliminated without a doubt," said Michael calmly.

"Fine! You made your point. Where do we start?" conceded David.

"We start with the obvious suspects. What do you know of the were-wolf community in the region?"

"Not a whole lot," answered the detective, caressing his three-day beard meditatively. "After my stepfather disappeared, I did my best to stay away from them."

"When did that happen?"

"Sixteen years this past month," answered David after a second of reflection.

"What happened, exactly?"

"Nobody knows. He left for work one morning and was never seen again."

Michael wondered if David's stepfather's disappearance had influenced him in his career choice. He asked, "Do you know a man by the name of Peter Clemens?"

"Doesn't ring a bell. Why? Should I know him?"

"It would help. Let me enlighten you."

Chapter 30

"Tom?"

Executive Assistant Chief of Police Thomas Maxwell recognized the Alpha's voice immediately. He had been expecting this call.

"Yes," he answered.

"I need you to keep me informed of any development in the investigation. We can't afford to be caught off guard. Is this understood?" asked the Alpha in a tone accustomed to giving orders.

"Yes sir, absolutely. I will personally keep an eye on the cops in charge of the case."

"Good. And if they get even remotely close to finding out about us, you pull the plug on the investigation."

"I understand. But sir, if I may ask, what is our next move going to be?"

Chapter 31

In a coffee shop across the street from the police station, Michael sat slowly sipping on a cup of tea. He was waiting for David Starks to come pick him up.

David had called him in his hotel room shortly after Michael had returned from getting lunch.

"I found our ticket in," the detective had said excitedly as soon as Michael had picked up the receiver. "Our ticket to Clemens' house."

Now that David knew about Clemens, he hadn't wasted any time and had already come up with a way to pay the Alpha an official visit. Michael had to admit that sheer luck had played a major part in their good fortune.

After getting out of the hospital, David had been assigned to a missing person's case: two brothers who had gone hunting in Sam Houston Forest and had never returned. A 911 call had been placed from one of their cell phones, however, and traced back to the center of the forest. After studying a map of Sam Houston, David had noticed the call had been placed less than two miles from Peter Clemens' cabin, giving him a perfect excuse to pay the Alpha a visit.

The coffee shop door opened and David walked in. He located Michael immediately and motioned for him to come. Leaving his cup half full on the table, Michael walked over to the detective.

"Let's not hang out here too long," said David in a voice just low enough to prevent eavesdropping. "If other cops see me with you, they'll ask questions I'd rather not have to answer."

Michael nodded his understanding.

"Let me walk to my car and you can join me in thirty seconds. OK?"

"Works for me," answered Michael.

The car was parked in a space reserved for police vehicles a few hundred feet down the street. David wasn't halfway to his car when he heard a woman's scream. He turned around and saw a man running on the sidewalk holding by the strap something that looked too small to be a purse. A woman was running after him but quickly losing ground.

"Stop him! He stole my camera," she screamed.

As the man was passing the coffee shop at full stride, Michael simply stepped in front of him, effectively stopping him in his tracks. The man, who couldn't be a pound over one eighty, bounced off Michael and landed on his back, the wind knocked out of him. Michael, who had not even flinched in the collision, was holding the camera by its strap.

David and the woman reached Michael at the same time.

"Thank you, sir," said the woman, gaping at Michael who was used to seeing that reaction from people meeting him for the first time.

"How stupid do you have to be to snatch a camera in front of a police station?" asked David, bewildered, as a couple cops in uniform were already showing up to collect the half-knocked-out thief.

"Are you an officer?" the woman said to Michael who didn't get a chance to answer before she turned her attention to David, saying in a flash of recognition, "Detective Starks! What a coincidence, I was actually looking for you."

David sounded a little uneasy and less than truthful when he replied, "Sheila Wang! What a good surprise."

In response to Michael's unspoken question he explained, "Sheila is a reporter for the Houston Post. Anything you tell her can, and most definitely will, be held against you."

"Now, Detective, you know that's not fair. All I want is to ask you a few questions about your assault," replied Sheila in a voice as sweet as honey, her eyelashes playing their part as well.

Sheila Wang looked definitely more like a Wang than a Sheila. About 5'3", petite, with straight dark hair worn in a bob and slightly slanted eyes, Sheila could not hide her Chinese heritage. Most people would have considered her attractive, but she was not attractive enough to coerce David into an interview.

"How did you hear about that?" he asked, not hoping for an answer.

"You know I can't reveal my sources, Detective," she told him with a smile Michael found quite attractive.

"And you know I won't tell you a thing," David replied, copying her smile before turning to Michael and saying, "Let's go, we've wasted enough time."

As the two men were walking towards David's car, Sheila called to Michael, "Sir. What's your name?"

He turned around to look at her and after a second of hesitation answered, "Michael Biörn."

Chapter 32

Victor Grey, known in some circles as the Chemist, stood in front of a complex-looking distillation set-up made of Vigreux columns, glass alembics, and countless glass coils. At one end of the set-up, an electric heating mantle was supporting a large flask containing a dark yellow liquid. The boiling liquid was sending vapors through the columns and alembics, which cooled the gases down before resending them back into the boiling flask. A small fraction of these vapors, however, was traveling all the way through the glass labyrinth and making it to the end as a colorless liquid dripping one drop at a time into a much smaller flask.

With his short stature, his untamed reddish hair, and his oversized belly, Victor more closely resembled a barbarian of old than a nerdy scientist, but he knew his way around a lab.

The distillation step was the most meticulous part of the process, which was why the Chemist was paying close attention to the details. If the heating were too harsh, the coveted molecules would decompose and the whole batch would be lost, but if it were too gentle, the brew would not be refined and would therefore be unusable.

The flowers contained the sought-after ingredient in a very diluted form, drowned in a sea of other molecules of no interest to his customer. The right alkaloid needed to be isolated from the complex mixture in order to warrant the potency of the final product.

This was a very interesting project from a scientific standpoint—interesting and dangerous. These were calculated risks, however. If one were careful, this particular substance was actually less hazardous to make than heroin, and the Chemist had had plenty of experience making heroin.

Victor did not know his customer's identity. The small bright purple flowers were delivered to him on a regular basis by a feral-looking black man wearing a thousand-dollar suit, who also picked up the final product when completed. This guy was not the man Victor talked to on the phone though, he was just an underling. The phone guy was the real boss, Victor was sure of that.

What Victor did not know was what his customer did with the product. He couldn't sell it or even use it as such... the pure form would have killed anyone. So, someone, somewhere, had to be converting it into something useful.

The Chemist knew better than to ask questions though; his customer paid him handsomely for his discretion. Still... he wondered.

Chapter 33

The dirt road leading to Peter Clemens' cabin in the heart of Sam Houston Forest was narrow, and particularly winding. On several occasions, Michael had expected David to hit one of the trees edging the path; but the detective had negotiated his turns with dexterity, and they had finally made it to the cabin.

Upon seeing the house, Michael decided that calling it a cabin had to be the misnomer of the century, or maybe his definition of the word was simply a bit dated.

The garage was separated from the house, but only at the ground level. The second story of the house connected with the second level of the garage, and the bridge between the two buildings offered protection from the weather to anyone walking from the garage to the house or vice versa. All in all, the two-story house had a footprint exceeding 3,500 square feet, which seemed rather large for a couple with no children.

The fact Clemens and his wife had no children was not surprising to Michael, however. Werewolves often suffered from fertility issues, especially when trying to conceive a pure-bred. They were generally more successful in their unions with humans, but the resulting offspring only had one chance out of four to be a werewolf.

Werewolves born of the copulation between a wolf and a human were called half-bred. Half-bred wolves were weaker and less dominant than their full-bred brothers, but since werewolves had such a hard time reproducing between themselves, most of the born werewolves were half-bred.

David rang the doorbell and a tall burly man opened the door. Peter Clemens' gaze immediately went to Michael, totally ignoring David as if he had not even noticed the detective.

"Peter Clemens?" asked David, holding out his badge. "I am Detective Starks from the Houston Police Department, and this is Michael Biörn."

Michael was hoping Clemens wouldn't notice David hadn't introduced him as a detective.

Peter Clemens slowly shifted his eyes to David, finally acknowledging his presence.

"Yes, what can I do for you, Detectives?" asked Clemens, who had been quick to regain his composure—but not quick enough. David had definitely seen panic in the man's eyes. Panic and hatred… this was going to be fun.

"We have a few questions we'd like to ask you. Would you mind if we came in?" asked David.

The Houston pack Alpha seemed to hesitate an instant before making up his mind. "No, of course, please come in." Clemens knew his hesitation had been a mistake and he hated himself for it. One could never show weakness in front of an enemy, and Michael was definitely an enemy.

They followed him to the living room where a man and a woman were sitting. As Michael entered the room, both of them abruptly got up, visibly agitated.

"These gentlemen are with the Houston PD," said Clemens to the man and the woman. "Please do sit down, Detectives."

David and Michael sat down on one of the empty couches while the others, obeying the Alpha's veiled order, settled back into their seats.

"This is my wife, Isabella, and my friend Karl," explained Clemens.

The man was as tall as Michael, and although his muscles were visible under his business suit, the ranger still had a good fifty pounds on him. Not a hair was visible on his closely shaven scalp, but a well-trimmed brown beard swallowed half of his face.

The woman was in equally good shape and was clearly a force to be reckoned with.

Karl and Isabella were not nearly as good as Clemens at hiding their emotions, and to the detective's trained eyes, their nervousness perspired through every gesture they made.

Karl's gaze was focused on Michael with the intensity of a laser beam, while Isabella's eyes kept flying from Michael to her husband like drunken butterflies. Although Peter Clemens was apparently looking at David, Michael knew the Alpha was in reality watching him from the corner of his eye. Michael always made wolves nervous, especially when there were only three of them around, and these three were definitely wolves.

"Mr. Clemens," said David. "We are investigating the disappearance of two brothers who were last seen on September 11th. Their names were William and Brad Ferguson."

"I am afraid I don't know these names," replied Clemens in a controlled voice that was meant to be amiable.

Michael shifted position, and Isabella jumped in her seat. For a fleeting instant, David thought he saw fangs between her slightly parted lips.

"Bella, could you bring these gentlemen some coffee?" said Peter to his wife.

David and Michael quickly declined the offer, but she still left for the kitchen.

"Your wife seems nervous," remarked David.

"It's understandable, I believe. She's not used to seeing the police in our home," replied Clemens, smiling.

"Quite," said Michael.

This time Clemens could not disguise the daggers in his eyes when his gaze met Michael's. The other wolf, sitting on the edge of his armchair, looked ready to jump at Michael's throat at any moment. David was thoroughly enjoying the show.

"I have a couple of pictures to show you." David took out photographs of the missing brothers from a file he was holding. "Could you please tell me if you recognize them?"

"Never seen either one," answered the Alpha, after staring at the pictures for a short instant. "But why are you asking me?"

"A 911 call was placed from one of their cell phones the day they disappeared. The phone's GPS tracker was active and we were able to trace the call's location. It was placed less than two miles from your house."

Isabella Clemens still hadn't returned from the kitchen when David and Michael took their leave a few minutes later.

Chapter 34

The instant the door had closed on the departing 'detectives', Isabella jumped out of the kitchen. "What the hell was that?" she exclaimed. "What was that *thing* doing in our house? Is he a cop?"

Isabella was not exceedingly beautiful, at least not according to commonly accepted canons of beauty, but she was attractive in her own way. Athletic and lithe, her body could be considered deadly in more ways than one. She had fine features—although her nose was a bit long and her eyes sat a little too deep in their sockets—emphasized by thick blond hair that fell in waves over her shoulders. A stranger would not have noticed any of these features at the moment, however—only the extreme nervousness that brought her beast to the edge of her skin. It wouldn't have taken much more stress for her to morph involuntarily.

In contrast with his wife's extreme agitation, Peter was showing no emotion. He simply went back to his armchair and sat down in silence.

"Do you want me to follow them?" asked Karl.

Peter, still lost in his thoughts, replied by a negative nod.

"Snap out of it, Peter," said his wife. "What are we go—"

"Be quiet!" he interrupted. He had not raised his voice, but his tone was unmistakable. It was an order, a command from the Alpha to a sub-altern wolf.

He remained meditative for another few minutes before saying in a reproachful voice, "You could not have followed them without being noticed Karl." He added more neutrally, "You are my Beta, I need to be able to count on you to make the right choices."

He was not really upset with Karl. The presence of that man in the house had clouded his second's judgment, and Peter could hardly blame him.

"But what *was* that thing?" asked Karl timorously.

"That wasn't a wolf, was it?" said Isabella.

"Did it smell like a wolf, darling?" asked Peter rhetorically. "It was obviously not a wolf."

"Whatever that thing was, it was a predator for sure and definitely not human," said Karl. "It is on our territory, Peter… it needs to be removed."

"I could not possibly agree more," answered Peter. "How do you propose we do that?"

"The same way we always do," interjected Isabella, looking more feral than ever. "With teeth and claws!"

Isabella was a dominant wolf, ferocious and vicious. As Peter's mate, she benefited from a status almost equivalent to his in the pack. The Alpha female took orders from her mate only.

"I appreciate your enthusiasm, darling, but I would like to find out more about this man before sending my beloved wife after him. I have the feeling this particular prey could be more than even you can handle."

Neither Isabella nor Karl objected to Peter's remark. They too had sensed the quiet strength emanating from Michael Biörn. A type of raw power unfamiliar to them, but undoubtedly present.

Chapter 35

As if celebrating the arrival of fall after months of drought, the rain had just started pouring again. When it rained like that, the roads could be flooded in less than an hour… that was Houston for you!

Waiting in her car for her partner to return from his doughnut run,

Detective Samantha Lewis was watching the raindrops explode as they landed on the windshield. Salazar was going to get soaked simply for giving into the doughnut-eating cop stereotype... moron! Tired of waiting, Lewis started reading the report she had grabbed on their way out of the office.

Salazar opened the passenger door an instant later and sat on Lewis' leather seat, drenching it in the process. Thankfully for him, Lewis was too absorbed by her reading to notice.

"I brought some for you," said Salazar, opening the box of doughnuts he had brought back with him.

She ignored him, still reading.

"Hey! I'm talking to you."

"What?!" she finally answered looking at him. "Can't you see I'm busy?"

"I said I brought you some doughnuts." He held out the open box.

"I'm on a diet," she replied, getting back to her reading.

"Again?"

"Shut up, asshole! You'd do well to do the same! It'd be cheaper than buying new sets of pants every six months," she scolded.

But her outburst did not affect Salazar who just shrugged before sinking his teeth into a raspberry jelly-filled doughnut.

"And watch out for my seat! You're getting sugar all over it."

"What are you reading?" he asked, unperturbed.

"The latest lab report on evidence collected at Sullivan's home," she replied as she finished reading the second and last page.

"Anything interesting?" mumbled Salazar, his mouth full of doughnut.

"Mostly confirming suspicions we already had."

"Meaning?"

"They found traces of both wolf and human blood in the Rottweilers' mouths. The human blood didn't belong to Sullivan. That means someone else was in the house when the wolf killed him."

"That answers the riddle of the second gun..." Salazar licked sugar residue off the tips of his fingers.

Of the two guns found at the crime scene, one had been Sullivan's, but the other one hadn't shown any print and hadn't been fired.

"Only partially," said Samantha Lewis thoughtfully. "We still don't know why he left his gun behind, or why he brought a gun in the first place if he was planning to use his wolf as the murder weapon."

"He probably brought the gun as a backup and dropped it by accident as he fled the scene," suggested Salazar.

"Maaayybe. There are still way too many pieces that don't fit the puzzle, if you ask me. If the murderer brought the wolf as a weapon, why didn't the wolf leave with him through the door instead of busting a window to escape as suggested by the DNA evidence?" she asked, as much to herself as to Salazar.

They considered the question in silence a few minutes, but no obvious answer jumped out at them. Lewis started the car and began driving through the rain that still poured over the city.

"This whole case doesn't make any sense," said Salazar finally. "Even simple things like the shoes don't make sense."

"The shoes?" asked Lewis, surprised. "What shoes?"

"The shoes on Sullivan's shoe rack. That was on the first report from the crime lab—I thought you saw it."

"What are you talking about?" asked Lewis, irritated.

"One of the lab guys found a pair of black leather moccasins, size eleven, on the rack in Sullivan's hallway," explained Salazar.

"And that's important because—?"

"All the other pairs of shoes were size nine… Sullivan's size."

Chapter 36

The local ducks had come to investigate whether the newcomer had brought food with him and now they were vehemently quacking their disappointment at Peter Clemens, who was sitting on a bench facing the small lake.

Ivanov was now fifteen minutes late, and Clemens started to suspect the mobster's lateness was no accident. It was more likely Ivanov's petty way to affirm his status and show he did not fear him. *The idiot…*

A scent in the air interrupted his train of thought—Ivanov had finally made it. A minute later, the mobster showed up and sat next to Clemens while his bodyguard placed himself directly behind the bench. A couple more of Ivanov's hoodlums were standing by a tree a hundred feet away, watching the area.

"Good evening, Peter. It looks like we're going to have a nice night," said Ivanov in his light rolling Russian accent.

The rain had stopped a few hours earlier, and the sun had already dried the bench on which they were sitting. The ducks, having given up on Clemens, were trying their luck with Ivanov and Stan.

"Good evening, Dimitri. I am glad you could make it," replied Clemens in a tone devoid of sarcasm. He knew very well how much Ivanov disliked to be called by his first name in front of his men, and it was his way to remind him where he stood.

"What is this urgent matter you wished to discuss?" asked the mobster.

"I have a favor to ask of you," answered Clemens, using the word "favor" on purpose to flatter Ivanov. Most people would think long and hard before asking a favor from the mob, but Clemens knew he had little to fear from Ivanov's organization.

"I am listening," answered Ivanov benevolently.

"In the past, you've come to me on several occasions to help you with individuals that had become a nuisance to you." Expecting a reaction from his interlocutor, Clemens paused. Ivanov remained silent, however, and the wolf eventually resumed, "Well, today, I am asking you to do the same thing for me."

Ivanov contemplated the Alpha's request before answering, "And why is it that you cannot take care of this matter on your own?"

"If something were to happen to this particular individual, I would be under too much suspicion. I don't want the cops to be able to link me to this in any way," lied Clemens.

The ducks, tired of the parsimonious trio, chose this instant to return to the lake with exuberant splashes of water that barely missed Clemens and Ivanov.

"I see, and who is the mark?" replied Ivanov, not fully convinced by the argument.

Clemens handed him an envelope containing a picture of Michael Biörn. The photo had been taken by one of the surveillance cameras hidden around the Alpha's cabin. Along with the picture was a note with Michael's name and hotel address. Through an informant inside the Houston Police Department, Clemens had also discovered Michael Biörn was not a cop but a park ranger from Wyoming: a wildlife expert the Houston PD had called upon to help them with the recent series of murders seemingly perpetrated by wolves. In other words, Biörn had come knocking on his door under false pretenses. What a naughty thing to do.

"He looks like a big guy," commented Ivanov, glancing at the photo.

"He *is* a big guy… and dangerous too. Your men should take their assignment very seriously. It will probably require several of them to finish him off, and some heavy artillery too. Once they are done with him, I want them to bring me back his head," said Clemens, sounding utterly serious.

Ivanov turned towards Stan and asked him to give them some space. The bodyguard didn't seem particularly comfortable with the request, but he obeyed nonetheless and went to stand fifty feet from them.

"Is there something you are not telling me about this man, Peter?" asked the mobster in a voice low enough to prevent any eavesdropping. "Are we dealing with a mere human or something more?"

"I have told you everything I know about him," answered Clemens, and technically he wasn't really lying. Biörn's potential needed to be tested and Ivanov's goons were more expendable than his own wolves; this point was not mentioned to Ivanov, though. There was such a thing as being too honest, after all.

Chapter 37

Olivia Harrington looked older than her twenty-five years, but Michael thought the grieving probably had a lot to do with it. Few people looked their best five days after burying both of their parents.

Her brown hair, held behind her head in a French twist, gave Olivia a secretarial appearance that was further emphasized by the conservative-looking black dress she wore cut just above the knees. Michael didn't find her particularly pretty, but she had charisma, and charisma often trumped looks.

This trait reminded him of a now distant time... Isibel had possessed charisma, along with an uncanny inner strength. A woman needed inner strength to marry a praeternatural being... especially one like Michael. In the end, however, her inner strength hadn't been enough to save her.

Realizing he had not listened to a word Olivia had pronounced in the past thirty seconds, Michael made a conscious effort to drive the demons of his past out of his mind and focus on the conversation at hand. The young woman had called him the night before and asked if he would be available the following day to meet her for coffee. Her request had surprised him at first. Although he had told her how to get in touch with him in case she needed help with anything, Michael had not expected her to take him up on his offer. Here he was though, sitting across from her in a small *Tea Salon*—according to the inscription on the window—sipping on terrible black tea. The water used for the brew had clearly not been anywhere close to boiling temperature.

"Thank you for coming," she said, and Michael could tell by the sound of her voice that she meant it.

"It's my pleasure," he answered soberly.

Although the malfunctioning air-conditioning unit left the place feeling moist and stuffy, she had her hands wrapped around her cup of unsweetened jasmine tea as if she were trying to absorb heat from it.

"I understand my dad asked you to come to Houston to help him out with a case, is this correct?"

"Yes, it is."

"Is this case related in anyway with my parents' murder?" asked Olivia, looking straight into Michael's eyes. This would have been a dangerous thing to do under other circumstances, but Michael knew this was not a domination challenge; she was simply trying to gauge him.

"I'm afraid so. Your dad brought me in as a wildlife expert. He was working a case where a wolf was suspected to have been used as a murder weapon."

Olivia considered Michael's answer for an instant before asking, "And now that he's dead, are you continuing the investigation or are you going back home?"

"Your dad brought me in because I was a friend, but the detectives who took over the inquest don't seem eager for my help. As a park ranger, I have no legal attachment to the investigation unless they want me to," answered Michael, sounding apologetic.

"This isn't an answer to the question I asked," she retorted calmly, as if she were simply stating a fact.

Michael kept silent a few seconds before answering, "I'm not going back home."

Olivia seemed satisfied by his answer as her lip curled up in the half-smile he had already seen her display at the funeral. She took a sip from her cup and asked, "Will you keep me posted?"

"I will."

Chapter 38

Katia Olveda was about to enter her shower when she heard the doorbell. Her eyes went to the clock on the bathroom wall: 7 p.m. It couldn't be her friend Tania. Tania was not supposed to pick her up before 8:30… and she was always late.

Katia grabbed the white robe lying abandoned on the side of the bathtub and wrapped it around her naked body. She checked her looks in the mirror located directly above the sink and headed for the front door, which, as always, she opened without checking the peephole.

"What are you doing here?" she said with genuine surprise to the man who stood at her door.

"Is that a way to greet people, gorgeous? Aren't you going to let me in?" He pushed the door open and walked straight to her living room.

She closed the door and followed Peter Clemens to the bar where he was pouring himself a glass of scotch.

"Will you have something?" he asked, but she declined the offer.

"Now that you have your drink, Peter, are you going to tell me what you're doing in my apartment?" she asked, not trying to mask the impatience in her voice.

He looked at her with an aggravating smile and went to find a seat before finally answering, "This boyfriend of yours, the cop, are you still seeing him?"

"Do you mean David Starks?"

"Yes, I mean David Starks! How many cops are you fucking?" he asked crudely. "Aren't detectives below your pay grade anyway? I thought assistant DA's went for fancier things."

"Don't act all surprised when you're the one who ordered me to start seeing him in the first place," she replied, making a point for anger to be clearly noticeable in her voice. Truth being told, she found great satisfaction in the *assignment*, but she kept this detail for herself.

"Oh yeah… It had skipped my mind," he answered with a satisfied smile.

She noticed his eyes lingering over her not fully concealed curves, but she didn't particularly worry about it. Wolves typically mated for life, and she had never heard anything to make her think Clemens belonged to the few exceptions.

"Why are you asking if I'm still seeing him?"

"It turns out that your detective came knocking at my door."

"Really? What did he want?" she asked, genuinely surprised.

"He was looking for a couple of hunters who happened to be at the wrong place at the wrong time, but I don't believe that was the only reason for his visit."

"What makes you say that?"

Clemens finished his scotch in one gulp and got up to pour himself another one before replying, "He had a man with him, a Michael Biörn." He saw the flash of recognition in her eyes and added, "Do you know him?"

"We met briefly at the hospital when David got hurt. You wouldn't know anything about that *incident*, would you?"

"I don't," he replied, "but getting back to this Biörn person, what do you know of him?"

"Not a whole lot. He's a park ranger who came at David's old partner's request to investigate the Sullivan murder case. Apparently he too was attacked by a wolf, but I'm sure you have nothing to do with this either," she said sarcastically.

"Indeed I don't," answered the wolf. "But I have a vested interest in the case. If you learn anything about the cops' investigation, I want you to let me know immediately."

"Of course," she replied.

"I also want you to find out everything you can about Biörn. It's time for you to show me I haven't been paying you all these years for nothing."

Chapter 39

It was around four in the afternoon when Michael left David's beach house in Kemah.

Seeing David's cabin had reminded Michael of the long house he had built on the coast of Labrador an eon earlier. After King Jarl Eiríkr Hákonarson had outlawed the berserkers, Michael had migrated to Greenland, where he had spent two years in the so-called Middle Settlement, the smallest of the three Viking camps on the island. Despite the camp's isolation, it had still been too populated to Michael's tastes and, taking advantage of a wood gathering expedition, he had reached Markland—the region known today as Labrador. It had been his first landing on the American continent. Taking advantage of the relatively warmer summer climate, he had built his long house on the beach. Two centuries of watching icebergs float by in almost complete isolation—with the exception of the occasional skræling encounter—had finally managed to bring him the peace and tranquility that three decades spent wreaking havoc as a berserker had failed to deliver. He had not forgotten Isibel— how could he?—but her memory no longer haunted every waking hour. He had not forgiven himself for the tragedy, but he could, henceforth, contemplate his own reflection in a pond without wanting to heave.

Michael had been surprised at first to learn David owned a cabin on the beach—cops' salaries were apparently higher than he suspected— but the detective had answered his unspoken question by explaining he had inherited the house from his maternal grandfather. His mother had been an only child and, after her death, David had become his grandfather's sole heir.

Kemah was only an hour away from Houston, and shortly after he was attacked at his house in the city, David had decided to move to his beachfront property. A motivated assassin would probably be able to find him there, but he would at least have to work for it.

The two men had spent most of the morning going over the evidence they had collected so far. The detective had been able to access almost all the information available to Lewis and Salazar, the cops officially working the case, and, thanks to Michael's peculiar talents and Ezekiel's connections, they even knew things the others didn't.

They knew, for instance, that none of the wolves they had met at Clemens' during their visit had murdered Steve and his wife, or Chief Deputy Sullivan. They had not attacked David either. Michael had committed to memory the wolf scents he had found lingering at each crime scene and he was positive on that point. The ranger had not even detected the murderers' odors at all inside Clemens' cabin, but the wolf stench there had been so overwhelming that the assassins' scents could have been lost in the olfactory mayhem.

Three different wolves were responsible for murdering two cops and trying to kill a third one within the span of a few days, but so far Michael and David had been unable to link the hits to the local Alpha.

If a single werewolf had been responsible for all the attacks, Michael would have entertained the idea that the assassin was a lone wolf, not connected to the Houston pack… but Ez had told him there were no lone wolves in town. A single lone wolf could possibly have passed under the wizard's radar undetected, but not three of them—Ez was too smart for that.

The motel parking lot was almost empty when Michael pulled in around 5 p.m. Once in his room, he immediately headed for the bathroom. He was not used to Houston's constant heat and humidity, or the stickiness associated with it, and he wanted to take a shower before doing anything else. Before he had a chance to step under the shower, however, he heard the hotel door slam open.

He immediately stepped out from the bathroom into the living room to find four goons armed with machine guns. The total lack of expression on their faces indicated these men killed for a living: professionals devoid of the slightest shred of compassion. Before Michael had a chance to make a move, they started shooting.

Chapter 40

Unlike his lab, always kept spotless, the Chemist's living room looked like a war zone. Dirty clothes littered the floor, couch and loveseat. Cobwebs collected dust in every possible corner of the room, and every single piece of furniture was coated with an inch-thick layer of grime.

The Chemist was pretty sure there was a coffee table hiding under the piles of mostly finished Chinese take-out cartons and countless other food items at various stages of decomposition, but he could not remember what it actually looked like. When something started to smell too bad, Victor eventually trashed the offensive item, but that was the extent of the cleanup he was willing to do.

One of the first football games of the season was playing on the sixty-inch TV screen, but the Chemist, half asleep on the couch, paid no attention to it. His cell phone rang. Suddenly wide awake, he fumbled inside his pockets before finding the device buried under the latest addition to his empty pizza box collection.

When he saw the *caller unknown* message on the phone's LCD display, the Chemist felt a knot in the pit of his stomach.

"Hello?"

"Do you have what I requested?" said the voice on the other end of the line.

"Not quite all of it yet," replied the Chemist uneasily. "Manufacturing such a large amount requires time."

"You've had plenty of time already. People in your line of work typically understand the importance of timely delivery." The tone was sharp as a razor.

There was a pause during which Victor tried to come up with a reasonable excuse: one his interlocutor would accept. He had not been slacking, but the process was time-consuming. Short of working twenty-four hours a day, he simply could not go much faster than he already was.

"I do not have time for your pretexts," resumed the man. "I'll be checking on you shortly. In the meantime, I suggest you turn off that TV and get back to work. I am not paying you to watch football."

Before the Chemist had a chance to reply, the Alpha simply hung up.

Chapter 41

A shower of bullets poured out of the men's machine guns and drowned the room under a deluge of metal. Michael jumped to the side and successfully avoided the first volley, but the second caught him in mid-air and sent him rolling to the ground. He could feel the lead chewing his entrails and blood starting to pour out of the wounds riddling his midsection, but Michael Biörn was not easy to kill.

In a single motion, he reached for the wooden chair lying to his right in a corner of the room and, from a half-seated position, hurled it at his closest opponent. The piece of furniture's velocity projected the man into the wall, the impact shattering most of the bones in his back. The man slid to the ground in a seated position and sat motionless, back against the wall, blood sputtering out of his mouth to the beat of his dying heart.

Already back on his feet, Michael threw himself at his remaining enemies, but the fifteen-foot gap gave the thugs plenty of time to adjust their aim.

Michael felt the ground sliding under his feet as time seemed to slow down. Although his bullet-riddled head was on a collision course with the floor, he did not care. Isibel's face was the only thing on his mind. His wife had been dead for over a millennium, but her memory still haunted his dreams… and nightmares.

Michael Biörn was dead before his head hit the ground.

The three remaining assassins walked carefully towards him, weapons still trained on his body. Shattered glass from the TV screen and mirror was cracking under their shoes. They found his corpse on the other side of the bed, soaking in its blood. His face was a bloody mess, its aspect closer to the inside of a battered watermelon than to a human head.

While two of the assassins were pointing their guns at the dead man's head, the third one squatted to check his pulse. The way Michael had killed their partner with a simple chair had left a lasting impression in their mind, but when the man indicated to his companions that the 'bastard was dead', they all relaxed.

"Let's get his head and get the fuck out of here," said one of the men in Russian.

"I left the axe by the door," replied another one as he started walking to the door.

"That was a tough son of a bitch! The boss wasn't kidding around," said number one with a tone of professional appreciation, which was as close to respect as men like these could manage.

"No shit! Boris weighed easily two fifty and that chair sent him crashing against the wall as if he'd been a bloody roach," replied number two, sounding amused.

The third man came back with a fireman axe. He placed the sharp edge of the blade on Michael's throat before lifting it above his own head.

"Wait!" yelled number one. "Let's cover him with the shower curtain first or we'll all be covered with the bastard's blood."

"Good idea," replied number three, whose brain was clearly incapable of making such projections.

He soon returned with the curtain and used it to cover Michael's head and upper body. The curtain was transparent and therefore allowed the wannabe butcher to keep an eye on the dead man's throat. He once again lifted the axe above his head and brought it down on Michael's throat with all his strength. The blade was mere inches from its target when Michael opened his eyes and grabbed the axe handle in mid-air, effectively stopping the weapon. He had died many times before, but he always hated the coming back to life part. The whole being dead thing made it really difficult for him to prepare for action... and action was typically requested when he returned to the world of the living.

The butcher's jaw dropped in bewilderment, but before he had a chance to accept what he was seeing, Michael had wrestled the axe away from him and sent the curtain at the others' faces.

Still on the floor, he struck his unsuccessful executioner between the legs using the axe handle, incidentally projecting him upward at high speed. The man's squeal of pain and terror died in his throat a quarter second later when his head went through the ceiling, breaking his neck on impact.

Michael got back on his feet at the same moment his two remaining antagonists were freeing themselves from the curtain. Before they had a chance to even lift their weapons, he had decapitated the closest one with a single swing of his axe.

Although the other man had stepped back and was no longer within swinging distance, he was only able to pull the trigger once before the expertly thrown axe caught him square in the chest. He exhaled his last breath effectively pinned to the wall by the weapon.

Michael called 911 and headed for the shower. His body was healing fast and his face was almost back to normal already. He had to get rid of his clothes. They had been shredded to pieces by the bullets and were soaked in blood. It wouldn't do for the cops to find his intact body wearing these rags... it wouldn't do at all!

Giving a Viking an axe... what a stupid idea, he thought as he stepped under the shower.

Chapter 42

Bent over her cauldron, the witch was muttering incantations in a tongue strangely resembling Latin. Unobtrusively standing in a corner of the room, the Alpha observed the scene with a cold detachment.

The woman's dirty gray hair was falling onto her shoulders from under the brown piece of cloth tied over her head. She wore a shapeless black dress that fell to her ankles and obscured most of her silhouette. The dirty inch-long nails terminating her fingers were, with her face, the only visible parts of her body.

Although the day was still bright outside, twilight prevailed inside the room. Thick black curtains had been drawn in front of the only window, and the half dozen black candles spread out through the chamber provided the room's sole illumination.

The cauldron had been set on a small round table in the center of the room and not atop a wood fire as one might have expected under the circumstances. Why the old hag had to transfer the drug from the convenient sealed glass vials provided by the Chemist into her idiotic-looking cauldron, the Alpha could not fathom, but the woman was adamant on this point. The Alpha suspected the cauldron served the same purpose as the woman's long curvy nails and gray shaggy hair: satiating the witch's thirst for theatrics. Despite her taste for melodrama, she was the real deal. The Alpha had approached several witches before finding one able to solve his problem and he had had to eliminate just as many. Someone in his position could not afford to leave witnesses alive. People were prone to talking, and his secrets were not meant to be revealed just yet.

The hag raised her voice as she pronounced the last words of the incantation. The spell was now completed, and the drug safe to use, assuming one knew what one was doing, of course.

The Alpha left his corner to join the witch in the center of the room and help her with the painstaking exercise of transferring the drug from the mostly empty cauldron back into the sealed vials suitable for injection.

As they filled the vials, his mind wondered to the Chemist and his next delivery. This one would be significantly larger than the others, maybe even enough to fill the witch's cauldron to the rim. That would not happen though; the Chemist's next delivery was not to be transformed by the witch. The Alpha had other plans for it.

Chapter 43

Michael Biörn had barely stepped out of the shower when the first cops arrived. He grabbed a towel from the rack and wrapped it around his lower body as they reached the bathroom, guns in hand.

"Hands up," screamed one of them to Michael's attention.

Both officers were pointing their weapons at him as he lifted his hands up in the air while trying to look as non-threatening as possible. This was no easy task for Michael as his three hundred pounds of muscles looked anything but non-threatening. The bullets had been expelled from his body and were now littering the bathroom's tiled floor. Not a single scar remained from the ordeal.

"On the floor, face down," shouted the other officer, looking even more nervous than his partner. Once again, Michael obeyed, moving slowly to avoid rattling the officers' nerves even further. If one of them were to shoot him out of fear and the wound started healing under their eyes, there would simply be too much explaining to do.

More footsteps could be heard entering the hotel room as one of the officers handcuffed Michael's hands behind his back.

"I am the one who called 911," said Michael non-confrontationally.

"Which one?" asked the officer sarcastically. "There were a dozen calls made to report this blood bath."

"I called as soon as they were done shooting at me," answered Michael in an even tone.

More cops entered the bathroom at this moment to enquire about the situation. The smell of blood was thick in the air but Michael detected a scent he knew, and then immediately after a second one. The familiar odors were approaching rapidly; they would reach the bathroom any second now.

"What the hell do we have here?" asked Detective Lewis in an authoritative voice as she entered the room with Salazar on her tail. Before any of the uniformed cops had a chance to answer, she recognized Michael.

"Biörn! You've got to be shitting me!" she exclaimed. "Are you the one responsible for this mess?"

"What's your excuse for being on the crime scene this time?" asked Salazar defiantly. "I didn't see any paw prints on the bloody floor..."

"This is *my* motel room. I didn't think I needed an excuse to be here," answered Michael in his usual, controlled voice.

Salazar tried to think of a clever comeback, but couldn't. So he simply acted as if Michael hadn't spoken at all.

"Get him on his feet, and bring him in the other room," ordered Lewis.

When Michael was brought into the bedroom, he noticed a couple more officers were standing watch outside. A small crowd of inquisitive patrons had formed in front of the room and were trying to get a peep at the butchery.

"You have some explaining to do, Biörn, and I would advise you be convincing if you don't want to spend the rest of your life behind bars," said Lewis in a matter-of-fact voice.

Michael was about to open his mouth when David Starks entered the room.

"Are you all right, Michael?" asked David, sounding concerned.

"I'm fine."

"What in heavens happened here?"

"The suspect was about to answer that question for us, Starks. What are you doing here anyway?" interjected Lewis.

"Michael's a friend. When I heard over the radio there had been a shooting at his motel, I got worried and came over to see for myself."

"You're friends with this guy?" asked Salazar doubtfully.

"I am. Why? Is that a problem?"

Salazar just shrugged his shoulders in answer.

"Can we get back to business now?" asked Lewis in an irritated voice. "Mr. Biörn was about to tell us his story."

All turned their attention to Michael who, standing half-naked between two cops, was expecting the towel wrapped around his hips to drop to the floor at any moment now.

"Could I please sit, or put some pants on first?" asked Michael.

"Sit him on that chair," said Lewis to the officers standing on each side of him. They obeyed, and Michael started telling his story, omitting only the details that would raise the most questions—such as his resurrection or the total absence of wounds on his body. The cops listened attentively without interrupting him. When he was done, Salazar asked, "If I understood everything you said, you expect us to believe you were attacked by four men with machine guns and an axe and managed to escape without a scratch while killing all your attackers?"

"The proof of the pudding is in the killing," commented David humorously, but, beside the two uniformed cops surrounding Michael, nobody smiled at the joke.

"Yes, that's correct," said Michael in answer to Salazar's question.

"Do you know what the statistical probability of someone surviving this type of encounter is?" asked Lewis to Michael. "Do you really expect us to believe your story?"

Michael remained silent, but David came to his defense. "Did your statistical calculation take into consideration that Michael was ex-special forces and carries more muscle than all of us in this room combined?"

It was Lewis turn's to remain silent this time.

"Fine," said Salazar, "say we believe your story. Please tell us why there are a dozen case-less bullets lying on the bathroom floor?"

All turned inquisitive looks towards Michael who answered, "I can't answer that question. I found them there when I entered the bathroom to go shower. I have no idea how or when they got there."

This was not a convincing argument, but the truth was even less convincing. As long as his torn bloodied clothes hidden inside the bathroom ventilation duct weren't found, he might just get away with his lie. He had also taken the time to grab another set of clothes and soak them in blood before dropping them on the bathroom floor as supporting evidence of his tale.

"You really take us for morons, don't you?" said Lewis, visibly pissed off.

"And who bothers taking a shower immediately after killing four men?" added Salazar.

"Someone who doesn't like to be covered with other people's blood...?" offered Michael.

David Starks smiled at the comment, Lewis shook her head in exasperation, and Salazar just stood there with a blank look on his face.

Chapter 44

It was approaching ten o'clock, and night had now fallen over the city. Salazar, Lewis and Starks were standing outside in the poorly lit parking lot, still talking to Michael, who had retold his story three more times and answered a throng of questions from the suspicious detectives before they finally agreed to remove the handcuffs and let him slip into some clothes.

Michael knew the detectives had not bought his entire story at face value, but Lewis and Salazar had to admit he did not look like the aggressor in this mayhem. The fact that one of the dead bodies belonged to a gangster with known affiliation to the Russian mob did not hurt either.

In the meantime, more cops had shown up on the scene, shortly followed by the forensic investigators. After photographing the room and bodies from every conceivable angle, the forensic team had moved on to dusting the room for prints. In the process, they had collected a multitude of potentially interesting pieces of evidence for genetic and other analyses. Of course, the fact the crime scene was a motel room was going to significantly complicate their work. Most of the genetic evidence collected was bound to belong to previous patrons or the motel staff.

"I don't know what you did to piss off these guys, Biörn," said Lewis in a more courteous voice, now that she had calmed down, "but if the mob is involved, killing these four won't make your problems go away."

"They'll come back for you, and next time you won't be as lucky," added Salazar, who liked to state the obvious.

"I am going to ask the manager to move me to another room for the night, and tomorrow I'll look for a different hotel."

"That's a good idea," commented David Starks. "I can help you with that."

"What are you still doing in town anyway?" asked Lewis suspiciously. "Now that Harrington is dead and the case was handed over to us, you have no reason to stick around."

"I like Houston, and I have some unfinished business to attend to."

"Make sure your business doesn't interfere with our case, or I'll have you arrested, as sure as my name's Samantha," she threatened.

Michael nodded and started heading towards the reception to request a different room for the night. He came back a few minutes later to find Sheila Wang in the midst of a voluble discussion with the detectives.

The journalist was prying into the incident, but was going nowhere fast with the cops, who mostly ignored her questions.

"Does this have anything to do with the recent police officers' assassinations?" he heard her ask David Starks, who simply answered, "It's too early to tell anything for certain, but nothing seems to support that hypothesis."

Sheila suddenly recognized Michael who had rejoined the group and welcomed him with a "My savior!", which drew questioning looks from Salazar and Lewis.

She answered their unspoken question by explaining how Michael had neutralized the thief who had stolen her camera. She was staring at Michael with hungry eyes that reminded him of the type of look a wolf would give a tasty lamb. She was an experienced reporter and she knew Michael was more likely to let interesting bits of information slip out than the detectives were.

"Short of arresting this one," started Salazar, nodding towards Michael, "we've done everything we could do this evening. Let's go home, Lewis, we'll get back at it tomorrow."

She agreed, and the two took their leave. They were about to reach their car when Lewis turned around and headed for one of the officers in uniform. She talked with him for a few seconds before returning to Michael.

"I asked one of the officers to stay on this parking lot tonight. Just in case the mo—" she stopped in mid-sentence remembering who Sheila was, "—just in case."

"Thank you," answered Michael, as Lewis turned around and headed once more towards her car.

"It's about my bedtime as well," said David. "Do you think you can handle Lois Lane on your own?" He looked pointedly at Sheila.

"Let's hope," answered Michael.

"All right, I'll talk to you tomorrow then."

Michael and Sheila were left alone in the parking lot. Alone... with the dozen remaining officers, the coroner's team picking up the bodies, the forensics experts still at work and the nosy patrons whose number had dwindled down to five or six.

"Were you involved in the shooting?" asked Sheila in a concerned voice. She was wearing a low-cut blouse designed to show as much cleavage as one could afford without looking vulgar. Michael, who was typically an oak when it came to women, was trying his best not to stare at her chest; but it was harder than he would have suspected. Sheila, with a concerned look on her face, pretended not to notice.

"I was the target," answered Michael after a moment.

The journalist's look of concern turned into a mixture of surprise and outrage. *She would make a very fine actress*, thought Michael, but he kept the remark to himself.

"Would you like to talk about it over a cup of coffee? I know a nice little place not three blocks from here," she suggested.

"Why not?"

Chapter 45

The sun was shining brightly outside Dimitri Ivanov's office. Had it not been for the tinted glass windows, it would have blinded the two detectives standing on the other side of Ivanov's desk.

Lewis and Salazar had found out that not one but two of Michael's failed assassins had ties with the Russian mafia, and they had decided to go kick the hornets' nest to see what came out. They had, therefore, found their way to Ivanov's office in downtown Houston and knocked on the door.

"To what do I owe the pleasure of your visit, Detectives?" asked Ivanov pleasantly in his slight Russian accent, brushing an imaginary speck of dust off the sleeve of his Yves Saint Laurent suit.

"We are working on a case, and we were wondering if you would mind answering a few questions for us," replied Lewis in the same pleasant tone.

"Anything I can do to help the police…" answered the mob boss in his fakest voice.

"There was an altercation last night in which four men lost their lives, and we have reason to believe that you knew these men."

"What are their names?" asked the mobster, looking concerned.

Salazar read the names from a piece of paper he pulled out of his pocket, while Lewis kept her eyes trained on Ivanov, hoping his facial features might betray some involuntary reaction. The mobster remained impassive at the enumeration, however, and simply commented, "I am afraid none of these names sound familiar."

He had sent his men after Biörn but they had failed to report to him. His men's silence had forced him to send someone inquiring at the motel late in the evening. The envoy had returned with worrying news. He had found cops snooping all over the motel parking lot and going in and out of Biörn's room. The envoy had been unable to gather more information, but the detectives had just confirmed what Ivanov already dreaded.

"What happened, exactly?" he asked calmly, perfectly hiding his rising wrath.

"They tried to kill a man in his hotel room, but met with some resistance," offered Lewis.

"Is the man all right?" asked Ivanov, falsely concerned.

"Not even a scratch," replied Salazar.

This time a shadow passed over Ivanov's face. It was only there for an instant, but Lewis did not miss it. She wished Salazar had not mentioned Biörn was still alive—it would have been a lot safer for the ranger if Ivanov had believed him dead—but at least they now had confirmation that Ivanov was behind the failed assassination.

"That's a lucky man," said Ivanov with a forced smile.

"Lucky indeed," replied Lewis with a genuine smile.

"Well, Detectives, if you have no further questions, I need to get back to work," said Ivanov before adding, "Stan, will you please see the detectives out?"

The bodyguard nodded and held the office door open for Lewis and Salazar to take their leave.

Lewis turned towards Ivanov as they were departing and said, "In case our lucky friend became the target of another assassination attempt, rest assured that your office will be our first stop."

She was smiling her nicest smile when she added, "Tell your boys to play nice, because we'll be watching."

Chapter 46

Peter Clemens' cell phone chimed, announcing the arrival of a new text message in his inbox. He picked up the phone from the coffee table where he had left it and read the message:

We need to talk right now, usual means.

Although the inscription "*Sender unknown*" was displayed on the caller ID, Clemens knew exactly who had sent the message, and what he meant by "usual means". These last two words could only imply two things. One: Ivanov had something very urgent to tell him which could not suffer any delay; or two: the mobster was very pissed off and could not stand the idea of waiting a few hours for a meeting in person. Given the circumstances, option number two was the likeliest. Ivanov always preferred interacting in person; mobsters usually did. It was much easier to judge your interlocutor face to face than over the phone or worse via email.

Clemens walked to his study and sat down in front of his desktop computer. He logged into the usual chat room under the username *Blondie-TX* and found the private chat room hosted by *Isaac_Steinman*, Ivanov's nickname on the site.

"*What did you want to talk about?*" typed Clemens before pressing the send button.

The answer came within a few seconds. "*I sent four men after M.B. They were packing heavy but they are all dead, and he did not get hurt. What did you send us after?"*

Clemens could sense Ivanov's anger pulsing through his typed message and found himself wishing he were face to face with the mob boss at this instant. Ivanov's fury would have entertained him, and now that his fears had just been confirmed, he could have used some divertissement.

"*I warned you about him,*" typed Clemens. "*Don't blame me for your men's incompetence.*"

"*Tell me why you asked me to take care of this man. Why didn't you do it yourself? I want the truth this time! No more bullshit!*" replied the mobster in a demonstration of bravado that surprised the Alpha. Ivanov was a respected mob boss used to ordering people around, but he had not tried this tone with Peter in a long time. Ever since that afternoon twelve years earlier, he knew better.

Ivanov had lived in the blissful ignorance of the praeternatural world at the time, focused on ascertaining his newly found position of power at the head of the Russian organization. One of the ways he had planned on doing that was by increasing his racketeering revenues. Little did he know that the world as he knew it was about to collapse the day he sent a group of collectors to a small law firm ran by a certain Karl Wilson. His goons had scared the office staff half to death before leaving with the cash from the safe and the promise to return a month later, but they had never been back. The same afternoon, Clemens and Karl had dropped by Ivanov's office unannounced. Only three other wolves had accompanied them, but their demonstration had been compelling enough to convince Ivanov of his mistake and of the value a business relationship with the Houston pack represented. Seeing a man changing into a wolf in front of one's very eyes had a sobering effect, even on a Russian mob boss.

"*I told you all I knew already, and I do not like your tone. It would seem I'll have to handle this matter without your help. Do not expect favors from me in the immediate future, and do not contact me again regarding this matter.*"

Clemens clicked on the Send button and disconnected from the chat room before Ivanov had a chance to reply. He was not the least concerned about Ivanov's wrath. What was the boss going to do? Come after him? Unlikely… and if he was stupid enough to try, the Houston pack was more than a match for Ivanov's organization.

The Alpha, however, was more concerned with Michael Biörn. In spite of what he had told Ivanov, he knew his men were professionals and were more than able to deliver on this type of assignment. The fact Biörn had survived the attack unscarred was an indication of the man's power.

Biörn was definitely a praeternatural being, Clemens had known that the instant he had seen the guy. Now he had confirmed Biörn was a

dangerous predator, and since he was not a wolf, there were limited possibilities left. Peter Clemens was pretty sure he knew what Biörn was, but
there was one problem with this answer: his kind had been extinct for
nearly two centuries.

Chapter 47

The rain was falling hard and bouncing off the pavement all around
David Starks. He increased his pace, walking towards his favorite
coffee shop for his morning fix of caffeine. The streets of downtown
Houston had already started flooding under the relentless assault of the
weather. In some places, the water was overflowing onto the sidewalk,
making it difficult for the handful of pedestrians to keep their feet dry.

David pushed the door open and stepped briskly into the shop. He
ordered a large black coffee, and paid for it. He was trying to summon
enough motivation to brave the elements once again when a newspaper
abandoned by a customer on one of the tables caught his eye.

It was the morning edition of the Houston Post. On the first page, a
close-up picture of a growling gray wolf, fangs showing, was preceded
by the title "KILLER WOLF IN HOUSTON, by Sheila Wang."

"Here comes the unwanted publicity," he thought, sitting down at
the table in front of the paper. He was not particularly surprised the press
had finally gotten a hold of the story. As a matter of fact, it was a miracle
it had taken them this long to find out.

The article was concise, well written and mostly factual, which was
not a given for a news piece in this day and age. There was, of course, a
small amount of speculation as to the motives of the murders, but nothing much.

In essence, Sheila Wang was informing the public of the recent series
of murders targeting police officers, while insisting at length that in every
case a wolf had been used as the murder weapon. The fact she had used
the singular 'wolf' instead of the more appropriate 'wolves' indicated her
source at Houston PD did not have access to the lab reports.

The article also recounted the attack on Michael Biörn, the wolf expert brought in by Houston PD as a consultant in the case, and the fact
that at least two of the assassins had known ties with the Russian mafia.
From there, Sheila more than alluded to the seemingly obvious conclusion that the mob was behind the murders, and that Biörn had likely been
targeted because he posed a threat to their organization.

The chick has balls, thought David as he folded back the paper and
grabbed his untouched cup of coffee. Accusing the cops of hiding a series of sensational murders from the public was the type of thing one
could expect from a journalist, but going after the mob was a different
ballgame altogether.

The Russian mafia did not like publicity, and Sheila Wang was too smart to ignore that. Making accusations against the mob in a newspaper article amounted to a war declaration, and most reporters did not dare swim in these troubled waters.

Chapter 48

Michael had just completed his leisurely stroll around Elm Lake, an eighty-acre body of water located in the center of the park, and was walking towards a picnic table facing the lake's east shore.

Situated forty-five minutes south of Houston, Brazos Bend State Park was as remote and wild a place as one was going to find so close to the city. It had been many years since Michael had first visited the park, accompanied by Steve Harrington and his two daughters. Olivia had been just a kid at the time and her sister Lucy barely a toddler.

The park was virtually deserted on this Tuesday morning, and Michael had encountered many more alligators than he had humans. After hours of continuous rain, the sun had finally deigned to come out, and the reptiles could be found sunbathing all around the lake.

The temperature was steadily rising from the low seventies where the storm had dropped it, but it still hadn't reached the mid-nineties forecasted for the afternoon. The humidity was on the rise as well, and Michael's shirt was soaked with sweat, but he scarcely noticed it.

He had reached the picnic table still lost in his thoughts and had sat on the bench, facing the lake. He pulled out a notepad and a pen from a small backpack and placed them in front of him on the table. He then got out a large bottle of water and proceeded to drain it in a single gulp. His thirst partially quenched, he grabbed the pen and started a list of the facts and evidence he had collected so far:

> *1) Deputy Chief Sullivan and his two Rottweilers were killed at home by Wolf-A, who escaped through a window. Window broken from the inside indicates escape point and not entry way.*
>
> *2) Two guns were found on the floor in Sullivan's living room, but only one set of paw prints.*
>
> *3) Steve and Marge Harrington were killed in their home by Wolf-B, who too escaped through the window. Same observation as above for the window.*
>
> *4) David Starks attacked at home by Wolf-C, who was shot repeatedly by the detective but managed to escape...*

Michael stopped writing, suddenly wondering about the windows. Why had they all been shattered from the inside? It was the case at Sullivan's, at the Harringtons' and even at David Starks', although he had survived the attack.

This peculiar detail about the windows bothered Michael particularly. He simply could not find any logical reason for the wolves' *modus operandi*.

It seemed as if every attack was designed to follow the exact same pattern as the others, and he could find no reason for this. No reason unless someone was solely trying to draw attention away from more important details by orchestrating a needlessly sophisticated mise-en-scène around the murders.

Not finding any immediate solution to this puzzling question, Michael returned to his list:

> 5) There is an active Wolf pack in Houston whose association with the mob is likely.
> 6) I was attacked by the mob shortly after visiting Peter Clemens, the Alpha, at his house in the forest. Possibly the pack headquarters.

He was trying to think about what else was missing on his list when he suddenly remembered the sheriff deputy at Steve's funeral and added:

> 7) At least one Wolf has infiltrated the local police, possibly more.

He looked down at his list for a minute, trying to decide if anything else needed to be added, but decided against it. These were the facts so far; everything else was pure speculation.

Chapter 49

The restaurant was nice, an upper-class Italian establishment in Houston's River Oaks area, but Samantha Lewis would have preferred being at home playing with her two kids. Instead, she was sitting at a table in a small private dining room in the company of her partner, Detective Salazar, and Executive Assistant Chief of Police Thomas Maxwell.

Maxwell had called Salazar earlier in the afternoon to invite both of them for dinner. Lewis and Salazar had both been in shock after the call, wondering why in heaven the Houston PD second in command would want to have dinner with them.

After a few minutes of chitchatting, which had allowed them to look at the menu and place their order, Maxwell had finally come to the point of the meeting. It hadn't really surprised the detectives when the assistant chief had brought up the wolf case they were working on. The case had made the first page of the Houston Post that morning, and, since they had had plenty of time to ponder the reasons of their summoning during the day, the detectives had reached the only logical conclusion: the wolves had started to make noise in the city's higher circles.

"...now that the media have jumped on the case, you can be certain they won't let it go..." Maxwell was saying.

Lewis' first impression of Thomas Maxwell caused conflicting feelings in her. The man was handsome, athletic, polite, well mannered, and had plenty of charisma. He had to be in his early fifties but seemed to be in a better shape than most men half his age. He talked to the detectives as if they were old buddies and tried his best to act as if there were not five pay grades separating them. Despite all his efforts, however, Lewis still felt uneasy in the man's company. There was something about the way he looked at them which worried her: something she couldn't quite figure out.

"…the chief asked me to keep him informed of all developments in this case, no matter how small they might be," said Maxwell. The chief of police was currently out of town on vacation, but the detectives did not need to know this. The Alpha's order had been clear: take control of the investigation and do whatever it takes to protect the pack's secret existence.

Of course, the series of gruesome murders was not exactly Maxwell's idea of keeping a low profile, but the Alpha knew what he was doing. He never did anything without a good reason, and Maxwell wasn't about to question his motives.

Salazar, falling over himself to please his superior, replied, "Of course, sir, as soon as we have additional information we'll let you know right away."

They had already told the assistant chief all the details of the case, and where the investigation was taking them so far. Maxwell had seemed pleased to hear about the Russian-mafia lead, almost relieved.

"I do not have to stress the importance of keeping this investigation away from the public eye. The fewer people trusted with the details of this case, the better. This will maybe allow us to avoid crucifixion by the media," said Maxwell in a low confidential voice.

Chapter 50

No light was visible inside the apparently deserted house. The night was clear and the trees bordering the clearing where Clemens' cabin had been built danced to the howling song of the wind. The light reflected by the half-moon caught the frames of the towering giants and projected their trembling shadows in the driveway where Katia had parked her car.

Katia got out of her vehicle and walked to the main entrance. She was not easily frightened, but she had to admit the atmosphere was a bit unnerving. She rang the bell, waited thirty seconds and rang it again, but nobody came to the door, although she was pretty sure Clemens hadn't gone to bed yet. For one thing, he had been the one requesting her to come. On top of this, there were five cars parked in the driveway in addition to hers. It looked like Clemens was having a small gathering, but if that was the case, where the hell was everybody?

She tried the door and found it unlocked. She pushed the door open, but before she had a chance to step inside the house, she sensed a presence at her back. She pivoted quickly to find a large white wolf less than ten feet away from her. The beast was majestic. Its coat was as close to immaculate as one could be, with only a few muddy spots spoiling the otherwise perfect fur. It moved with an almost hypnotic animal grace, emitting a low growl as it advanced towards Katia with the slow pace of the hunter who knows its prey has nowhere to run.

Katia should have probably been terrorized, but she had no reason to believe the beast's apparent hostility was anything other than bluff. She had recognized Isabella's wolf form and was fairly confident Clemens' wife wouldn't dare to hurt her without her husband's express consent. Yet as the beast got closer, Katia suddenly found herself panicking. What if the aforementioned consent had been given? What if she had willingly answered the Alpha's summoning only to realize too late she'd been summoned to her own execution?

As the wolf finally closed the last paces separating them, Katia felt her muscles tensing. She would not go down without a fight, but she knew she was no match for Isabella. The wolf mouth opened up into a gaping black hole as it moved towards the assistant DA's throat. Katia could smell the beast's breath, a nauseating stench. The monster's jaws closed an inch away from Katia's jugular as a booming laughter rose from the trees.

Peter Clemens stepped out in the open followed by nine wolves. He was completely naked and looked filthy. His body was coated with dirt, and dried blood was clearly visible all over his face and torso.

"I hope we didn't make you wait?" he said, not even trying to sound sincere. "We were on a hunt and lost track of the time."

"I blame it on the wild boars," said Karl who had just morphed back into his human form. "They're just too much fun to go after."

"Unlike some, the boars know how to put up a fight," said Isabella, who had also regained her human body. She was still standing against Katia, her bare breasts practically shoved into the assistant DA's face.

"Enough chitchat," said Peter. "Katia did not come here to hear our hunting stories."

The wolves had all regained their human form and gone to freshen up in Clemens' many bathrooms. After a voluntary transformation, werewolves could return to their man form at will in only a few seconds. The initial morphing into the wolf form was the tricky part. Newly turned werewolves went through excruciating pain during the first few months of their new life. The morphing was always involuntary at first and could take as long as twenty minutes in some cases. If one was not in the right state of mind, the muscular and skeletal transformation was so traumatic for the body that the pain was almost unbearable. With practice though, the process became easier and eventually painless. An experienced wolf with good control over his body could morph in less than six seconds;

Clemens could do it in four.

Clemens and his beta, Karl, had been the first ones to return to the living room where Katia awaited. Isabella had arrived shortly after, wearing a see-through black gown that showcased her lengthy muscles. Katia caught Karl discreetly eying the curves of the Alpha's wife and wondered if Clemens had noticed. Katia and Karl had shared a brief relationship, but they were now making a point to ignore each other.

"Can I offer you something to drink?" Clemens asked Katia.

"A glass of water will do, thank you."

"Darling, Karl, anything for you?" enquired Clemens as he walked to the bar located in a corner of the living room.

Karl and Isabella both declined the offer and Peter returned from the bar with a glass of water for Katia and a glass of scotch for himself.

"So, tell me, what have you learned about the case and Michael Biörn since our last meeting?"

"Not a whole lot. The cops don't have a suspect so far and therefore the DA's office has not been asked to provide an assistant for the prosecution. That means all my intel comes from Starks and I have to be careful with him, he's a smart man. If I ask too many questions, it will raise suspicions—"

"Good! Now that we've heard your excuses, tell us what you know exactly," interrupted Clemens.

"I know the cops assigned to the case are Detectives Salazar and Lewis. I know they don't like Biörn all that much for some unknown reason. And I know the Russian mob tried to assassinate Biörn in his hotel room three days ago," answered Katia in a calm voice, for she knew better than to show fear in the presence of three wolves.

"Now, that's interesting," replied Peter. "Give me some details about the assassination attempt."

"The details are murky to say the least and the cops don't buy Biörn's version of the story, but what is sure is that four men armed with machine guns stormed his motel room Sunday late afternoon and left in body bags."

Katia gave as many details about the incident as she had to offer, which seemed to satisfy Clemens' expectations.

"Now can you tell us why Biörn and your boyfriend came knocking at my door under a false pretense last week?" asked Clemens.

"I can tell you all I know, but it isn't much," started Katia.

"I am shocked!" interrupted Isabella, her voice dripping with sarcasm.

"Carry on," invited Clemens, while giving his wife a look that meant she was to shut up from now on.

"I believe the idea came from Biörn. He knew Harrington, Starks' old partner. Harrington was investigating the death of Chief Deputy Sullivan and had asked Biörn to come and help him with the case. When

Harrington and his wife were murdered by a wolf two weeks ago, Biörn decided to stay in Houston to investigate and he recruited Starks to help him out." Katia took a sip of water.

"That still doesn't explain how they found me," replied Clemens.

"I'm not sure either. I know your name was brought up by Biörn. As far as I know, Starks had never heard of you before meeting Biörn."

Chapter 51

The news network staff meteorologist was announcing a likely relief in the rain pattern of these last few weeks. Apparently, the tropical depression responsible for the deluge Houston had been experiencing lately was moving west. Michael was finishing getting ready and not paying close attention to the TV. He had only turned it on in case the wolf attacks had been picked up by the local TV networks, but so far it didn't seem to be the case.

The knock on the door caught him off guard; he wasn't expecting anyone. Immediately alert, he smelled the air for any indication of danger. The motel door was well insulated and almost completely masked the visitor's odor, but as he got closer to it, he finally identified the faint scent. He opened the door to find Olivia Harrington carrying two large paper cups and a white paper bag.

"I brought you breakfast," she announced with a smile. "May I come in?"

Michael stepped aside to let the young woman through and closed the door behind her.

"Sorry to barge in so early, but I wanted to catch you before you took off for the day," said Olivia, not sounding particularly sorry.

Michael had given her his new contact information after relocating to this motel following the assassination attempt against him three days earlier, but he hadn't thought she'd show up at his door. This was the second time she had surprised him, and he was debating whether he should start being annoyed about it.

Olivia sat at the room's only table and started taking scones and blueberry muffins out of the bag.

"I got you black tea with honey," she told Michael, who still hadn't said a word. "Are you going to sit down with me or just make me feel awkward?"

Michael sat down on the opposite side of the table and tried a sip of the tea. It could have used a bit more honey, but it was drinkable.

"Thanks for the breakfast," he said finally. "But I assume there's another reason for your visit."

Olivia was nervously playing with one of the napkins she had brought, twirling it between two fingers and then straightening it out again. At last she looked up to meet his eyes and said, "I want to help."

Michael was fairly confident he understood what she meant, but he acted as if he didn't.

"And with what would you like to help?" he asked.

"With your investigation," she replied, sounding hesitant.

"It's a bad idea and I can't let you do that," replied Michael in a tone which did not invite any rebuttal.

"Both my parents were murdered, and I don't know why. I don't understand any of this. They were killed by a wolf in the middle of the country's fourth largest city, and the mob may or may not be involved… The whole thing just doesn't make the slightest sense," said Olivia, all hesitation now gone from her voice.

"I agree with you, but you have to let professionals take care of this, Olivia. This is not the type of business in which a college kid should be involved."

Any individual with even an ounce of emotional intelligence would have known not to call Olivia a "college kid," but not Michael. On the best of days, he was already relatively limited in the social skills department; finding the right words to dissuade a distraught young woman whose parents had just been brutally murdered was simply too much to ask of him.

"I didn't come here to ask for permission, Michael," she retorted in a combative tone. "I was just offering you my help, but if you refuse it, I'll seek my parents' killers on my own."

Michael was getting more annoyed by the second and still did not know how to handle the spirited young woman. "Your dad would kill me if he knew I let you in on this. It is simply too dangerous for you and I won't have it." He tried to sound definite.

"Suit yourself, Michael." Olivia got up. "Enjoy your breakfast," she added as she opened the door and left, but she didn't sound like she meant it.

Chapter 52

Nine o'clock on a Wednesday morning was not Memorial Park's busiest hour, but it still meant a few hundred joggers and walkers were circling the main loop around the park. Sheila Wang, however, preferred jogging the quieter mountain-bike trails inside a small wooded area on the edge of the park. She jogged religiously three times a week, always at the same time, and always on the same trails.

She was finishing her last lap of the day when she noticed two men standing under the small foliage arch which marked both the entrance and the exit of the wooded area, the only path leading to the lot where her car was parked.

As she got closer, she noticed the men were speaking in a foreign language. By the time she was close enough to realize it was Russian, it was already too late. The two men, who had been dutifully ignoring her up to that point, came towards her in one coordinated motion, catching her off guard. Before she had a chance to react, one of them grabbed her by the wrist in a vice-like grip. Sheila reflexively started screaming for help, but the second man was already behind her. She felt his immense left hand pressing on her mouth and nose, effectively preventing her from screaming and breathing at the same time, while his right arm wrapped around her arms and torso to immobilize her entire upper body. The first man released his grip on her wrist and took a few steps back, seemingly admiring the scene.

Panic quickly overtook Sheila. The mountain-bike trails were completely deserted this time of the day, and she was fairly certain nobody could have heard her short-lived cry for help. She knew all too well why these men were after her, and she knew her chances of surviving the encounter were slim at best.

The lack of oxygen was starting to make her dizzy, and she realized she had to calm down and find a way to breathe lest she die of asphyxiation before the goons had a chance to do anything else to her.

The man holding her had probably come to the same conclusion for he lowered his hand to free her nose while still preventing any sound from leaving her lips. Sheila inhaled deeply as the man facing her started to speak. "You been a naughty journalist... You know what happen to naughty journalist?" His Russian accent was so thick she could barely understand him. "They die..." said the man, smiling as he pulled out a hunting knife from a holster he carried in his back.

He took a step towards her, still flashing a sardonic smile. Sheila's eyes were trained on the blade. She was sweating now and feeling nauseous too. The man took another step, dangling the knife in front of her. He was only a couple feet away from her when she threw her right foot as hard as she could in the direction of his genitals. The man, who had reflexively shifted his balance, caught her foot inside the thigh. The kick wiped away his smile, and he now looked more pissed than in pain.

"You pay for that, little bitch," he said in a threatening voice before punching her in the gut as the other man tightened his embrace around her. The blow hit her liver, driving the blood away from the organ. Her legs went limp and she would have collapsed to the ground if the other hoodlum had not been holding her. The man slipped the blade under her jogging shirt and cut it open from top to bottom before doing the same thing with her sports bra. Sheila had regained minimal strength by now and started fighting back again, but it only brought her another punch to the gut. The second man let her collapse to the ground this time. Before she had a chance to try and call for help, the two mobsters started furiously kicking her head and body. Soon, everything went dark around

Sheila Wang.

Chapter 53

A grumbling sound loud enough to shake the hotel's foundations rose from Michael Biörn's empty stomach. The scones and muffins Olivia had brought for breakfast were long digested, and the hungry organ demanded its dues. Michael looked at his watch. Eleven forty: time to get going if he didn't want to be late for his lunch with David.

He grabbed his car keys and headed for the door. His hand was on the handle when he remembered the room's key card still sitting on the bedside table. He walked back to the bed, grabbed the card and stuffed it in his jeans' back pocket before leaving the room for good this time. Thirty seconds later, Michael was racing down the streets of Houston.

As soon as Michael's car was out of sight, a vehicle parked on the other side of the street relocated to an empty spot three doors down from Michael's bedroom. The driver promptly exited her car and walked straight to Michael's door. Using a pass key card stolen a couple hours earlier from the room service cart, Olivia Harrington let herself inside Michael's room in search of usable information. She did not need his approval to help catch her parents' killers.

Chapter 54

A chain Italian restaurant wasn't Michael Biörn's idea of fine cuisine, but he had not been the one picking the place. At least it was affordable. A definite bonus since he'd ordered half of the menu, and still had doubts it would suffice to tame his hunger.

Michael had been surprised to find David in the company of Katia Olveda when he arrived at the restaurant, but he hadn't mentioned anything. The assistant DA was wearing a flattering white blouse and dress pants which managed to make her look professional and sexy at the same time.

"David told me what happened last Sunday. I am so glad you did not get hurt, it was quite the miracle from what I heard," said Katia after the waiter departed.

"I was very lucky," said Michael simply.

"If every victim was as *lucky* as you were, Katia and I would be out of a job," replied David, smiling.

"David mentioned you used to be an army ranger. The training must have come in handy Sunday night."

"It did," retorted Michael, not bothering to develop further on her statement.

Feeling it was time to change the subject, David asked, "So where's your new motel?"

"At the corner of Rankin and Imperial Valley, not far from the airport," answered Michael.

Katia made a mental note of this before orienting the discussion towards his job as a park ranger, and how he came to be so familiar with wolves.

Katia took her leave as soon as her lunch was finished, leaving David and Michael alone and free to talk at last.

"Sorry about that… She called me an hour ago and insisted on having lunch, so I told her she could join us," apologized David.

"No problem. It didn't bother me," replied Michael honestly.

The discussion was interrupted by the waiter bringing coffee for David and two desserts for Michael who hadn't been able to choose between the tiramisu and the cannoli. Michael started on the cannoli as David was saying, "What we need is a link between Clemens and Ivanov. The fact you got attacked by the Russians a few days after visiting Clemens is definitely more than a coincidence, but that's not going to be enough for a judge."

"Especially since we don't have anything linking either one of them to Steve's murder!" said Michael, attacking the tiramisu.

"We know for a fact Clemens is behind that." David sounded convinced.

"I don't know about 'knowing for a fact', but it sure looks that way."

"I don't really care what Clemens goes down for, as long as he pays," started David before lowering his voice to add, "I heard from an informant that Ivanov was expecting a large cocaine delivery Friday evening."

The statement caught Michael's attention. He replaced his spoon on the plate that still held half a piece of tiramisu and asked, "Do you know where?"

"Port of Houston. I wouldn't be surprised if Ivanov had asked Clemens to help guarantee the shipment's safety."

"Is your source reliable?"

"Most of the time…"

Michael pondered the information as he finished his tiramisu. "Maybe we should go check it out for ourselves," he said finally.

"I was just going to propose that," said David with a smile. "We can go take a look, just the two of us. To assess the situation if you will…and we can call backup as needed. What do you think?"

"You are reading my mind."

As they were exiting the restaurant, David took a phone out of his pocket and gave it to Michael who just looked at it as if he had never seen one before.

"I'd like you to keep it with you," said David.

"I don't do cell phones." Michael handed it back to David.

"Listen, Michael, given the situation, I believe it would be useful to both of us if we can be reached at any moment." David spoke in what he hoped was a convincing but non-commanding tone. He knew praeternatural creatures did not typically take orders well. There was always some type of power play involved.

Michael considered the argument for a minute before shoving the phone into his pocket.

"You're right."

Chapter 55

The ground under her feet was spongy and wet and the air smelled of damp wood and decaying vegetation. It had been years since Olivia last visited Sam Houston National Forest. She had been a junior in high school at the time and had come with a boyfriend on a day trip. She remembered it vividly; it had been a sunny, merry day.

The circumstances of today's trip to the forest could not have possibly differed more from those of her last visit. She had found Peter Clemens' name and location jotted on some list Michael Biörn had kept in one of his hotel room's drawer. The whole list had been cryptic to say the least, stating among other things that the police had been infiltrated by wolves, and referring to Clemens as the Alpha… Since Clemens' name and location were the only lead she had so far, she had decided to come and take a look at the alleged "pack headquarters".

She wasn't really sure what she should be looking for… cages, a pen filled with murderous wolves in the backyard, or what?

She had parked her car on one of the trailhead parking lots a couple miles from Clemens' cabin and had followed the dirt road that led to it. She walked alongside the road, thirty feet into the woods, less chance to be noticed that way. She wore hiking boots, shorts, a lightweight shirt and a small backpack containing water, a camera, and binoculars. In addition to being functional, the attire made her look like any other hiker roaming the woods.

The road was now opening onto a clearing with a house in the center—presumably Clemens'. There was no car in the driveway and no visible sign of life inside the house, but Olivia decided to stay under the cover of the trees, just in case. She pulled out the binoculars from her backpack in the hope of using them to peer inside the house, but the windows were treated and didn't allow anything but light to penetrate their impervious barrier.

Frustrated, Olivia decided to check out the house perimeter in hope to find some clue of wolf activity. She replaced the binoculars in her pack and started slowly circling the house while carefully staying a few feet outside the outskirt of the clearing.

She completed her circle and found herself on the other side of the dirt road without finding the slightest indication of the presence of wolves. Whatever reason Michael had for believing this place was linked to the wolves' attacks had to be inside the house, and therefore out of her reach.

Her train of thought was interrupted by the sound of a car coming up the dirt road. She slowly retreated a few steps deeper into the woods and crouched down. Her heart was racing, and she could feel sweat from her armpits running down her body. As the driver parked the vehicle in the driveway, she felt a wave of relief shortly followed by a feeling of disappointment. The car belonged to a cleaning company. The "Houston Dirt Removers" according to the sign plastered on the driver's door. She probably did not have much to fear from the hundred-pound woman who had gotten out of the car and was now pulling a vacuum cleaner out of her trunk, but she wouldn't learn anything useful from her either. Olivia simply needed to get inside the house. There was no way around it.

Chapter 56

It was nearing 10 p.m. and the cleaning lady was long gone when Katia arrived at Clemens' house. An underling she didn't know had answered the door and he led Katia to the living room where Peter, his wife Isabella and the pack's second in command, Karl Wilson, were debating the upcoming mid-term elections. They all had drinks in their hands, a beer for Karl and scotch for the Clemenses. Another beer stood on the coffee table in front of an empty chair. The underling grabbed the bottle from the table before returning to his seat, leaving Katia the only standing person in the room. This would have been awkward in any situation and was even more so amongst werewolves for whom a lower stance was a sign of submission, but Katia was no threat to them, and they did not care whether she stood or lay down on the hardwood floor.

She had been standing there a good minute before Peter stopped ignoring her and finally acknowledged her presence. "Katia, grab a drink and come sit with us, we're all eager to hear what you have to say," he said, with a benevolent smile on his face.

Katia went to the bar and poured herself a glass of water before sitting in an empty chair facing the couch where the husband and wife were sitting.

"I heard you were able to gather a bit more information about our Michael Biörn," said Peter.

Katia took a sip from her glass before answering, "As you already know, he is a park ranger in Yellowstone National Park and he's in Houston at the request of the now deceased Steve Harrington, the Houston PD lieutenant who was in charge of Chief Deputy Sullivan's murder investigation."

She paused for an instant and took another sip from her glass. She didn't like to be in this house. This place was dangerous for both her career and her life, which was why she only showed up late at night, when her presence was the least likely to be noticed. She would have much rather been in David Starks' bed, but she didn't have the choice. What the Alpha wanted the Alpha got, and she was not in a position to argue.

"Biörn has been a ranger in Yellowstone since ninety-four," resumed Katia in a slightly trembling voice that betrayed her nervousness. "Prior to that he was an army ranger, which is where he met Steve Harrington. Apparently the two of them got in hot water in Somalia and were the sole survivors of their recon team."

"I am shocked the Somali army could not take Biörn down," interrupted Karl sarcastically.

Katia shot him a murderous look to which he replied with a smile that looked more threatening than friendly. Karl had never forgiven Katia for rejecting him. They had dated for a few months and he had been the one who had introduced her to Clemens. She had known from the very beginning of their relationship that Karl was different. One evening, she had been invited to a gathering at Clemens' cabin and she had been shown the true nature of the wolves. She had displayed all the signs of hysteria before Isabella and another woman had finally managed to calm her down. Karl had been in love with Katia and had wanted to take her as his mate, but he had been forced by Clemens to reveal his secret to her before proposing.

In a state of panic, Katia had rejected him, which was when things had gotten complicated. Since she knew their secret, and refused to join them, she should have been executed, but Clemens had anticipated her refusal and had come up with an alternative.

He had never understood what the two of them were doing together in the first place. Karl was well built and had the magnetic charisma usually associated with werewolves, but Katia was still out of his league. They also disagreed on most issues and had opposite tastes in just about everything. Clemens had therefore predicted Katia's rejection and agreed to Karl's request only because he saw the value of having a mole in the District Attorney's office.

After rejecting Karl, Katia had been offered a choice between death and becoming a spy for the pack. She had chosen spying.

"I could not find any trace of him prior to eighty-nine when he joined the Army," resumed Katia in an apologetic voice. "Without an open investigation against him, I cannot access the type of documents I would need to run a full background check. So I'm afraid this is about as much as I can tell you from a background standpoint."

"What else can you tell us besides background then?" asked Peter in a slightly irritated voice.

"He befriended David Starks, the cop I am dating," she added, with just enough emphasis on the word "dating" to tick Karl off. "I had lunch with them yesterday, and I can tell you which motel he's staying at."

"Now that's the type of information we can use," answered Clemens with a grin.

Chapter 57

At two in the morning, the Port of Houston was about as deserted as it would get. David and Michael had been walking quietly from dock to dock in a furtive search of the vast premises for the better part of the night, and they were starting to wonder about the veracity of the information David had received.

As they were heading towards dock seven for the second time of the evening, Michael stopped David with a peremptory gesture of his hand.

"We have some activity over there," he said, pointing vaguely ahead of him.

"I don't see anything," answered David in a low voice.

"Neither do I, but they're there all right, at least a half dozen men."

"Are you telling me you can smell them?" asked David, but Michael simply ignored the question: a silence the detective interpreted as a yes.

"Let's walk around these containers," whispered Michael. "That should give us a view of the dock without being too much in the open."

The two men walked silently towards a grid formed by forty-foot-long shipping containers facing dock seven. As they stealthily made their way through the maze of containers, voices started to invade the silence of the night. Faint at first, the voices quickly grew into full-blown discussions in a language Michael identified as Russian.

The last row of cargo containers stood parallel to dock seven, about twenty yards from the water. Crouched to the side of one of them, Michael and David were hiding in its shadow projected by the dock's dim lighting. Their position offered a vantage view of the bustle both on and off the docked cargo ship. Men could be seen walking back and forth along the vessel, while others paced up and down the ship's main bridge. Most of them carried Kalashnikov assault rifles, easily identifiable by their curved magazines.

"They are waiting on a truck," whispered Michael in David's ear.

"You speak Russian?" asked David, the whispering mostly masking the surprise in his voice.

Michael simply nodded in answer. Ten centuries was more than enough time to fully master a good dozen languages, and Russian was not as difficult as people thought. Chinese and Arabic, on the other hand...

"I am not seeing any wolves," said Michael in the same low voice.

"Could you recognize them from here?" David sounded slightly doubtful. Michael, unperturbed, nodded.

"Shit!" swore David under his breath. "So much for linking Clemens to the mob... We should call for reinforcement now. If the wolves aren't around, there is no point tackling this on our own."

Michael agreed, and they started retreating to a safe distance in order to call for backup without running the risk of being heard by the sentinels. As they approached the third row of containers, two men suddenly appeared in front of them, their Kalashnikovs aimed at Michael's and David's chests. The men had been downwind from their position and Michael had not picked up their scent.

Moving at a speed no mere human could have ever matched, Michael shoved David to the side before rushing towards the two Russians. A bullet grazed his right arm and another pierced his left side before exiting through his back, but that did not even slow him down. Within one second, Michael was on the two men. He grabbed the two guns simultaneously by the barrels and ripped them out of the men's grips. The motion sent the sentinels flying forward and before they had a chance to spin around to face their assailant, Michael grabbed both their heads and smashed them together. He had meant to simply knock them out, but the sinister cracking sound the heads made on impact told him he still needed to work on his restraint.

He walked towards David who was just getting back on his feet after being projected ten feet to the side.

"Are you OK?" he asked.

"I feel like I was just hit by a train, but I don't think I have anything broken."

The gunshots had raised the alarm and the steps of running men could be heard getting closer by the second.

"Call for backup and hide," ordered Michael, picking up the two rifles from the ground. "I'll slow them down."

He handed a weapon to the detective. "Do you know how to use this?"

David nodded and grabbed the weapon.

Chapter 58

The room was dark, and Sheila Wang did not realize right away she was not lying in her own bed. Her head throbbed painfully with each heartbeat, and her jaw ached terribly when she tried opening her mouth.

Now that she thought of it, her entire body was in pain.

She suddenly became aware of a faint green glow originating some-where on her left and she tried turning her head towards it to investigate, but something prevented her. Had she been in a car accident? She could not remember anything like that, but maybe she was suffering from am-nesia...

At the price of a painful intensive effort, she rose on her right elbow and slowly turned her upper body towards the light. The glow was com-ing from a hospital monitor whose wires disappeared under her sleeve. She followed the wires to find a couple of electrodes attached directly to her chest. This discovery confirmed the suspicion that had been slowly seeping through her subconscious. "I am in a hospital."

And then she remembered it all: her morning run at Memorial Park, the two men who had ambushed her, her sports bra being cut off her, and the beating... In a sudden panic, she wondered if they had raped her. She could not remember anything about it, but they could have done it after she had passed out... The anxiety attack replaced the pain with a heavy weight on her chest, so she could barely breathe. She felt as if someone had placed her lungs in a vice and were squeezing the oxygen out of them.

She fumbled for the call button invisible in the room twilight, finally found it, and pressed it continuously until a nurse appeared in the room, a concerned look on her face. With graying hair falling onto light-blue scrubs, the woman looked to be in her mid-fifties.

"You've finally woken up," she said, with a well-practiced sympa-thetic smile.

Sheila tried to speak, but the words choked in her throat. Her mouth was as dry as a desert and the pain in her jaw prevented her from articu-lating any sound.

"Calm down, sweetie," said the nurse. "Your jaw was dislocated and it is going to be painful for the next few days."

Sheila swallowed and the pain caused by the effort brought tears to her eyes.

"Don't try to speak, I'll tell you what's going on and if you still have questions after that, you'll write them down," said the nurse, who had clearly had some experience with patients coming out of comas. Sheila closed her eyes for a second to indicate her agreement.

"The doctor is on his way; he'll come and see how you are doing. You were brought here in a coma Tuesday morning. It is now Friday night, so you were only out for a little over three days. That's usually a good sign," said the nurse with a warm smile. "A runner found you un-conscious in Memorial Park and called an ambulance. It would seem that you were attacked, but you have only a couple of broken ribs and a dis-located jaw to worry about; everything else is superficial."

The nurse must have seen the anguish in Sheila's eyes, because she quickly added, "We have no reason to believe you were sexually abused. No bruising in that region and the rape kit didn't show anything at all."

Chapter 59

The maze of shipping containers offered a multitude of aisles to run around but practically no place to hide, so Michael and David had little choice but to shoot whoever decided to show up in their line of sight while hoping they would not get shot first. Short of a focused fire on his neck resulting in his beheading, the Kalashnikovs' 8 mm rounds would not kill Michael, but they still stung worse than a swarm of hornets.

After calling for reinforcements, David had quickly realized there was no way out of the maze and had decided to return to Michael's side. They were now lying on the ground next to each other but facing opposite direction in an alley near the center of the containers' lot. The wind prevented Michael from detecting enemies coming from the north, while the grid of cargo containers made it difficult to pinpoint the exact location of the men coming from the dock located at their south.

Another man appeared in front of David and was immediately shot in the head. Michael had been pleasantly surprised to discover David's marksmanship. The detective's aim was both swift and accurate, which was a definite bonus in their current situation.

"Time to move," announced Michael in a whisper.

The two men stood up and, back to back, slowly started heading for a different location. The sound of gunshots and the accumulation of bodies were a dead giveaway of their location, and the two had to move each time another thug fell under their bullets. Michael, being substantially more bulletproof than his comrade, always led the way while David covered his back. He had been shot one more time, this time in the leg, but it was the only wound that still trickled blood. His arm had already fully healed, and his side was well on its way.

The truck had showed up on the dock in the middle of the mayhem and was now being loaded by a couple of Ivanov's associates while the others were focusing their efforts on the man hunt, of which Michael and David were the coveted trophies.

Michael led David towards the western edge of the labyrinth in the hope of finding a way out, but as they got closer, he started smelling trouble in that direction. Had he been alone, Michael would have forced his way out of the maze using the shortest route, but since this strategy would have drastically increased the chances of getting David killed, he had decided against it.

The voices were getting closer and coming from all directions. This time they were effectively surrounded, and the net was closing on them fast. The first row of belligerents appeared in front of Michael a second later. Three men armed with assault rifles opened fire at the same time Michael did. He caught three bullets in the abdomen while mowing his opponents down with a semicircular motion of his own weapon. As the bullets were finding their way into his stomach and liver, Michael fell on his knees in pain. He could still hear Ivanov's men coming from all directions as he stumbled back to his feet, grabbed David under the arms, and told him, "Lie down and be quiet." A second later, the detective was airborne.

David landed on his butt on top of one of the containers before he even realized what was happening. He quickly came out of his flight-induced stupor and rolled to the center of the container as the mobsters rushed Michael from all sides.

Michael's gun was out of ammo and he decided to use it as a club, which, in his hands, was just as lethal a weapon. He was surrounded by six of Ivanov's men who had dropped their weapons for fear of shooting each other in the crossfire and were now holding knives. The pain in Michael's stomach was slowly subsiding as the organs were working hard to regenerate themselves. The effort cost him a huge amount of calories, however, and this came at a price: slower reflexes and a significantly weakened state.

The thugs all rushed him at once and Michael had to draw on a thousand years of warfare experience to avoid the blades of his opponents, while bashing their heads open with powerful swings of his improvised club.

Sirens could be heard in the background, but it was not a sound of relief for Michael Biörn, who did not want to have to deal with the cops yet again. With the last of his enemies lying slain at his feet, Michael called for David, "I have to head out before the cops get here."

David's head appeared from above the container to ask "Why?" in a dumbfounded voice.

"Because my clothes are riddled with bullet holes, soaked in blood, and I will have no wounds to show for it by the time they get here," replied Michael before sprinting away, albeit at a much slower pace than he would have managed had he not been shot six times in the past fifteen minutes.

Chapter 60

Although the temperature outside had already reached a toasty ninety degrees, inside Clemens' house the climate was not nearly as warm. The temperature had seemed to drop twenty degrees at Ivanov's arrival, and the six men of his escort had a lot to do with the atmosphere of passive hostility that prevailed in the room. The mob boss had decided six body guards was a high enough number to be taken seriously, but small enough to not be interpreted as a declaration of war.

Truth being told, Ivanov's men and the large calibers they were no doubt packing would have made Clemens take notice had he himself not been accompanied by three of his wolves in their man form. Ivanov, who had hoped to catch Clemens off guard and alone by arriving unannounced, was not pleased with the balance of power in the room.

"You have to stop him!" said Ivanov vehemently. "You are the one who brought him into our business—"

"We've already had this discussion, Dimitri," interrupted Clemens with authority. "I cannot be held responsible for your men's incompetence."

"You sent us after a…" But Ivanov did not finish his sentence. The expression on Clemens' face left no room for interpretation. Certain matters were not to be discussed in front of non-initiates, and the six goons he had brought with him definitely belonged to that category.

"How do you know it was Biörn who attacked you last night?" asked Clemens.

"I showed his picture to one of my men who took part in the fight and managed to escape before the cops arrived to steal the dope away from me." Ivanov sounded irritated.

The tension between the two men was contagious and placed everyone in the room on edge. Inch by inch, the mobsters were slowly moving their hands closer to their guns, while the wolves, fully aware of their opponents' intentions, waited on a sign from their Alpha to pounce on them and shred them to pieces.

Clemens pondered the situation in silence for an instant before saying decidedly, "We will take care of Biörn for you. You can consider him dead."

As the Alpha saw relief wash over Ivanov's face he added, "We can discuss payment for our service once the job is done."

Chapter 61

The Clemenses' house was as big on the inside as it looked from the outside. It was decorated in a rustic style that fitted perfectly with the wooded surroundings and conferred to the house an atmosphere of extra temporal comfort.

Olivia had applied for a job with the Houston Dirt Removers the day after her visit to the woods surrounding the Clemenses' house. She had been in luck. The company was hiring, and they had hired her the same day. She had spent the next few days cleaning houses all over town. It was not exactly what she had gone to college for, but the gamble had paid off. After a bit of flirting with the guy in charge of assignments, and a lot of lying about the part of town she was from, she had been sent to the Clemenses' residence, which was supposedly very close to her place. She had been surprised and disappointed to see a woman answering the door. She had not expected anyone to be home and had thought she'd be free to search the house in peace without having to worry about someone walking in on her at any moment.

For the most part, the woman who had introduced herself as Isabella Clemens was doing her best to avoid the rooms Olivia was cleaning, but the threat she posed was nonetheless omnipresent. If she walked in on Olivia sticking her nose where it did not belong instead of industriously scrubbing the floor or the windows, her career as a maid would be short-lived, and the consequences likely dire. If these people were responsible for the death of her parents and the attack on David Starks, they wouldn't think twice about eliminating a potential threat. Olivia found reassurance in the fact she could probably get the better of Isabella Clemens in a fight if it came to that—but in that respect, she was very wrong.

After finishing the kitchen, Olivia moved to a large office whose walls were lined with mahogany bookshelves. Old books covered the shelves, many of them written in languages and even alphabets she did not recognize. Some of the covers had cabalistic scribbling which looked to her like Elvish, except that Elvish was a language invented by the fantasy writer J. R. R. Tolkien and had no historical meaning. In addition, many of the books looked like they predated Tolkien by quite some time.

A dark mahogany desk stood in the middle of the office; the ornamental hand carving was of the finest quality, and a clear indication of the value of the piece of furniture. One thing was for certain, the Clemenses had not suffered too much of the recent recession. The desk had a total of seven drawers, three on each side and one in the center. Every one of them was equipped with a keyhole, but only two of them were actually locked.

From behind the desk, Olivia had a good view of the living room through the wide opened double French doors of the office. She was pretty sure Isabella Clemens was upstairs but it was hard to be certain, as the woman moved so quietly it seemed as if she glided over the floor like a ghost. So far, Olivia had not found anything truly suspicious. She had picked a couple of long hairs from the living room floor, but they could have belonged to a dog just as well as a wolf…

She drew in a long breath before slowly and very quietly pulling a small lock-picking kit out of her back pocket. Her dad had taught her the ancient skill when she was just a kid. She had not practiced it in some time, but she was confident she could still do it. She threw a glance towards the living room to reassure herself it was still empty and started working on the lock. The lock was ancient but surprisingly difficult to pick, and it took her a good five minutes to finally unlock the first drawer, which contained a dozen manila folders labeled with what looked like family names. The first one, titled Ivanov, contained a few pictures, a list of properties and some verbiage Olivia did not have time to read. The second file on the pile immediately caught her attention. It was labeled Biörn. She opened it to find a close-up picture of Michael, but did not get a chance to take a look at the remaining documents as from the corner of her eye she saw Isabella's silhouette back in the living room. Olivia immediately replaced the folder in the drawer before quietly shutting it just as Isabella was coming through the door.

"Is this going to take you much longer?" Isabella sounded displeased. "The other girls don't usually take this long."

"I'm sorry," apologized Olivia. "I'm new at this job and it takes me a bit longer. I'll be out of your way in thirty minutes at most."

Isabella checked her watch, sighed heavily, and left the room without saying another word, but since she seemed intent on staying in the living room, Olivia did not dare to reopen the drawer and just busied herself dusting the bookshelves.

Chapter 62

When Michael got back to his motel in the middle of the afternoon, a dark blue Austin Mini with tinted windows was stationed in front of his door, forcing him to park a few spots down from his room.

Michael was frustrated with his investigations and was running out of leads to follow. Actually, he had officially run out of leads after the Port of Houston stakeout, which had ended in a bloody confrontation with the Russian mob. David Starks was still explaining the exact circumstances of the incident to his superiors. According to his version, it had been a settling of scores between mobsters, but it was a tough sell, and they weren't really buying! Michael had been in Houston almost a month already, and he was still nowhere close to linking the Houston pack to the death of his friends, or anyone else for that matter. Maybe he was wrong about Clemens and his men, maybe they had not done it after all...

He pulled his key out of his pocket and was about to unlock the door when a woman stepped out of the Mini. Michael's nose told him the young woman standing in front of him was Sheila Wang, but it took a minute for his eyes to actually agree. Her usually olive skin was mostly purple and turning yellow in some places, notably under the eyes. She was wearing a white plastic corset above her clothes and walked with a limp.

"Sheila? What happened to you?" he asked, bewildered.

"Long story," she answered with a forced smile. Her pronunciation was off too. "May I come in?" She was trying to appear peppy in spite of the fact she sounded like someone with a hot potato in her mouth, but Michael wasn't fooled. The smell of fear emanating from her body was unmistakable and Michael had to concentrate to keep his predatory instinct in check. Predators could sense fear, and it triggered some of their most primal instincts, such as a thirst for blood.

He invited her in and poured her a glass of water after she declined his offer of tea. The motel room furnishing being Spartan, he let her sit on the bed while he took the only chair present in the room and sat facing her.

"You have to leave," she said before he had a chance to open his mouth.

"I beg your pardon?"

"You have to leave, Michael, or they'll kill you," she repeated, sounding both convincing and scared.

"What are you talking about, Sheila? You're not really making any sense," replied Michael soothingly, hoping his voice would calm her down. "We're in no hurry. Why don't you start from the beginning? By telling me what happened to you, for example..."

"I was attacked," she uttered in a low voice, tears coming to her eyes.

"Who attacked you?"

"The Russian mob... I wrote an article about—"

"I read it," interrupted Michael. "Detective Starks told me about it the day it came out."

"Well... the next day, I was running in Memorial Park and I was attacked by two men who spoke Russian and told me very convincingly to not put my nose in their business," she managed to say, mostly intelligibly. The pain caused by her talking was visible on her face.

"I have a dislocated jaw..." she answered apologetically to Michael's inquisitive look.

"What else did they do to you?" he asked, trying hard to battle the internally growing rage that gnawed his guts. He viscerally hated thugs who went after defenseless women almost as much as he loathed werewolves.

"Not much... a couple of ribs... I lost consciousness while they were beating me up, but according to the doctors I wasn't sexually abused."

The tension in Michael's muscles relaxed a little at the news, but he was still picturing Sheila on the ground overwhelmed by her aggressors. He had to drive the image out of his head, or the anger would make him lose control. He took a deep breath and tried to focus on the moment. He realized he simply could not stomach the idea of Sheila being in distress and wondered what that was about. He had not felt this angry in ages. Even Steve's death had not triggered such a reaction in him.

"These people mean business, Michael. Whatever is going on with the wolves' killings, the mob is involved and they don't want anybody snooping around in their affairs," she said in an agitated voice.

"You might be right, but the mob doesn't get to decide when I leave or where I go."

"Don't be obtuse, Michael. You're no match for these people. You were lucky last time, but it won't happen again. Take it as a sign to leave this city and forget about it," she said vehemently.

Michael didn't feel offended by her remark. From her point of view, she was perfectly justified in her logic and had no reason to suspect things were the other way around… That the mob was no match for Michael.

He was about to tell her she'd better worry about her own safety when the phone rang. Still sitting on his chair, he extended his arm and picked up the phone.

"Michael?" asked the voice.

"Yes?"

"It's me, Starks. You have to get out of there… Quickly!"

What was it with all of them today? wondered Michael. Why did everybody want him to leave town all of a sudden?

"What's the matter?" he asked. "Why should I leave town?"

"I'm talking about your room, Michael. You need to leave your room now. The pack is after you. They'll be at your door any minute now. You need to get out right away," answered David frantically.

"All right!" Michael hung up the phone. He stood up, grabbed Sheila by the hand and pulled her off the bed. "Trouble is on the way. We need to go now!"

She looked at him with terror in her eyes and nodded. As they passed the threshold of the room, two cars were already pulling into the motel parking lot. Michael immediately recognized his ancestral enemies as the vehicles' occupants.

Chapter 63

The wheels had been set in motion; the confrontation was now unavoidable. In a few minutes, Michael Biörn would be facing the Houston pack, or at least a sizable portion of it.

The Alpha had a grin on his face. There was no positive way to be certain of the outcome of the battle, but one thing was sure: his enemy would be badly wounded at the very least. This thought was satisfactory in itself, but not as satisfactory as attending the battle would have been. Unfortunately, being present for the confrontation was a luxury he could not afford. The risks were too high; he could not afford to jeopardize this long planned enterprise so close to reaching the objective.

Biörn's intervention at the Port of Houston had gone beyond expectations. Ivanov had lost many men in the encounter and was now significantly weakened. Biörn had been, against all expectations, useful to the Alpha's plans, but he was also a serious liability, and the time had come to take this variable out of the equation. He should have stayed hidden in his park, kept his nose out of wolves' business. He had brought this on himself, and it was time to face the consequences.

Chapter 64

Sheila Wang's piece had opened the floodgates to a sea of articles focusing on the wolves' attacks. Every newspaper and tabloid in the state had the story on its front page, and the case had become national news. The articles were, for the most part, unsubstantiated and simply presented the few known facts of the case over and over again in different literary dressings in hope the reader would not notice the total absence of original details. Fortunately, most readers didn't, and as was often the case in modern news reporting, the journalists' interpretation of the anorexically thin factsheet filled most of the columns and airtime.

Detectives Lewis and Salazar, the main victims of the journalistic frenzy, started to more than resent their assignment to the case. In addition to being harassed on a daily basis by reporters hunting for a scoop, they were under constant pressure from their hierarchy, in particular Thomas Maxwell, the Houston PD second in command, who demanded to be kept informed of absolutely everything related to the case.

"That's it... I'm done!" said Salazar, slamming the phone receiver back on its base. "If I get one more call from a journalist regarding this business, I'll set up a secret meeting with them at the Zoo in front of the wolf exhibit, and when they show up, I'll throw them inside the pen!"

"Can I help?" asked Lewis eagerly.

"I was hoping you'd offer."

The department was almost empty. Most of their colleagues were in the field inspecting crime scenes or following leads, but Salazar and Lewis had no lead to follow and their most recent crime scene was almost a month old and had undergone more inspecting than one could possibly conceive. Due to the high profile of the case, all their other pending assignments had been redistributed to other detectives and they were therefore stuck with a case that was going nowhere fast.

"Why won't the journalist drop it?" asked Lewis, not really expecting an answer from her partner. "It's been almost a month since the last killing; don't you think people would get tired of it?"

"Maybe we should re-interview Biörn," proposed Salazar half convincingly. "Harrington seemed to think he could help..."

"Beats me why," answered Lewis vehemently. "I don't see how a park ranger can be of much help in a murder investigation..."

"He's a wolf specialist, maybe he could find leads we wouldn't think of..." offered Salazar tentatively.

"Maybe... but doubtful. We don't enroll the help of a gun dealer every time a body turns up with a bullet in the head…"

Lewis was proud of her argument, even though she realized Salazar might have a point.

"Do you have a better suggestion?" he asked, a bit ticked off.

She tried hard to come up with something, but to no avail. They had been going round and round checking and rechecking every possible shred of a clue, following anything remotely resembling a lead, and had gone absolutely nowhere.

"I guess your idea is as good as any," she finally conceded. "The mob has tried to kill him after all, and we still don't know why."

The investigation of Michael Biörn's attempted assassination had been assigned to a different team, but Lewis knew from the detectives in charge of the case that the motive behind the attack was still unknown. They were pretty sure Ivanov was behind the failed assassination attempt, but they could not find any evidence. The cops hadn't had any more luck linking the Russian mobster with the Port of Houston drug bust that had taken place a few days earlier. Charges simply never stuck to the man. He was slick as an eel and just as slimy.

Chapter 65

Michael lifted Sheila and in two strides carried her back into the motel room. He dropped her there, not too carefully, and returned to the door to lock it.

"Go lock yourself in the bathroom," ordered Michael, but Sheila just stood there, bewildered and unable to react.

"Now!" he yelled. She finally snapped out of her indolence and limped her way to the bathroom. She closed the door behind her and, to her dismay, noticed there wasn't a lock on it. Not that it would have made any real difference; the door was paper-thin and she could have kicked it in herself if she wanted.

Inside the bedroom, Michael had stripped naked in a second and was morphing. After a millennium of practice, he had the transformation down to a science. The process was both quick and almost painless, almost… Five seconds later, the transformation was complete, and when Clemens' wolves smashed the door open, they found an 800-pound bear standing in the middle of the room. The look of surprise on the face of the first man to walk through the door was short-lived, as the bear closed the distance in a single stride and snapped his gigantic jaws shut on the man's neck. Vertebrae and spine snapped under the pressure, and blood spurted out of the severed carotid artery as the detached head fell to the floor with a muffled sound.

The remaining members of the execution squad, seven men total, had fanned out inside the room and were surrounding the werebear.

Some of them had started to morph into their wolf form, while the others focused on distracting the beast.

The bear stood about eight feet tall. With his two-inch claws and his flattened face, he resembled a large grizzly bear, but some features, such as the hump on the back and the rounded ears, were missing. An expert would have been unable to assign the animal to any of the known species of bear.

One of the assassins grabbed the metal chair and hurled it at the back of the beast with enough force to knock out a large sumo wrestler. The chair simply bounced off the animal, who immediately spun around, dropped on all fours, and charged the chair thrower, who barely escaped the assault by ducking to the floor.

Four of the werewolves were now in their wolf form and, as if answering to a silent signal, threw themselves at their opponent in a perfectly synchronized motion. Their fangs sank deep into the werebear's side and hind limbs, and he roared in pain and anger. He lifted one of his front paws and thrust it into the flank of the wolf whose teeth were locked on his side. The sharp claws pierced the animal's flank as if it had been a simple balloon and came out on the other side covered in guts and blood. The animal released his bite immediately and fell on his side, whimpering in pain and barely moving.

All the werewolves had now morphed and Michael was facing six of the monsters. Three of them were still chewing on his back legs, seriously reducing his mobility. In a quick motion, his fangs closed on the rear end of one of the wolves and with a powerful pull, ripped him off his back leg and threw him against the bedroom's brick wall. The wolf hit the wall violently and slipped unconscious to the ground, leaving a bloodied mark along the wall.

Michael was now standing on his back legs as the two wolves who had not taken part in the fight simultaneously jumped at his throat. He had seen them coming, however, and swatting with his front paws as one would swat at flies, he caught the werewolves in mid-air and crushed their skulls one against the other. Regular wolves would have died on impact, but werewolves were a lot more resistant and they simply fell to the ground unconscious. The three wolves still standing were now circling their erect prey, who had a good four and a half foot advantage on them.

A bear's back claws weren't typically very long, but Michael's were, and in a display of bravado, he sank the claws of his right foot deep into the throat of one of the unconscious wolves. He then kicked his foot free of the limp body, which went flying towards one of the circling wolves and caught him on the side. Taking advantage of the distraction caused by the impact, Michael hurled himself at the wolf closest to him and closed his fangs on the animal's throat before shaking its head free of its body.

The two remaining wolves decided the odds were now against them and fled through the destroyed door. Not wasting an instant, the bear walked to the injured wolves scattered throughout the bedroom and, using his powerful jaws, beheaded every single one of them. Satisfied his enemies could no longer recover from their injuries, Michael changed back into his human form.

It was only after he recovered his human appearance that he noticed Sheila, standing by the bathroom door, staring at him. He immediately recognized the look on her face: a mixture of terror and bewilderment. Isibel had looked at him with the same eyes that night, an eternity ago... It had been the last expression Michael had seen on his wife's face, the last time he had seen her alive.

Chapter 66

The Alpha slowly pressed the piston and felt the cool liquid flow into his veins. The first effects were immediate. He started sweating and felt his entire body warming up as the drug invaded it, a bit deeper with every beat of his heart. Soon he started feeling nauseous, but this would only be temporary. Every drug had unpleasant side effects, and this one was no exception. The drug's benefits far outweighed its negative effects, and the Alpha regarded the temporary discomfort accompanying the injection as an investment whose dividends would soon be paid out.

His cell phone rang and he answered. The voice he heard on the other end of the line belonged to Axel Thompkins, the Houston pack fourth in command. Thompkins was an African American who had been called by many other names over the past two hundred years he had spent living in the United States.

"We failed," said Thompkins. "Biörn is still alive and the last time I saw him, he looked in pretty good shape."

"What happened?" asked the Alpha, irritated.

"You were right. He's a werebear, and a big one too," answered Thompkins in a matter-of-fact voice. "He was about to leave with some girl when we drove into the motel parking lot. He saw us and went straight back to his room. He had already morphed by the time we walked into the room."

He paused to give the Alpha a chance to react, but the Alpha remained silent and Axel continued his story.

"We attacked him in waves, but he was too strong and knew exactly what to do to defeat us. We weren't his first wolves," explained Thompkins.

"How many of you escaped?"

"Only two wolves, including myself, but the witch managed to get out of there as well. A couple of the wolves were not yet dead by the time we fled, but I wouldn't hold my breath. I'm sure he has finished them off by now."

"Me too," replied the Alpha. If Biörn had remained alive all these years, it was probably not due to a sentimental nature. The fact that Thompkins decided to escape instead of keeping up the fight was speaking volumes in itself. Axel Thompkins was one of the rare members of Clemens pack to have been born a werewolf, and, as every full-blooded wolf he was both dominant and powerful. Not the type of wolf to back out of a fight if there was even a small chance to win it.

"So you're telling me that we have six dead wolves rotting in Biörn's motel room right now?" asked the Alpha.

"I am afraid so," replied Thompkins apologetically.

"Great!"

Chapter 67

Sheila looked petrified, her expression a mixture of terror and disbelief. "Sheila?" said Michael softly, but he did not obtain any answer. He grabbed his clothes and moved away from the doorway where he could be seen from the parking lot. He would have liked to wash up, but he did not dare leave Sheila alone, for fear she'd take off on him. Using his hands, he wiped off the fragments of flesh and organs that still caked his body in places and proceeded to put his clothes back on while watching Sheila from the corner of his eye. His pants and shirt soaked up the blood that covered a good part of his body and hadn't had the time to dry out yet. A part of his subconscious complained about yet another ruined outfit, but his active focus was on Sheila, whose expression had changed ever so slightly in the last thirty seconds.

"Are you OK?" he asked, not really expecting an answer. She looked at him, and all he could see in her eyes was fear.

"I won't hurt you," he told her, trying to sound as convincing as possible. "I'm one of the good guys."

She did not dare look at him in the eyes. "What are you?"

"I will explain everything, but now is not the time. I need to call for help. We can't leave dead werewolves lying around for everyone to see."

"Werewolves?" she whispered, but he didn't reply, simply picked up the phone and dialed the number Ezekiel had given him a few weeks earlier.

The wizard picked up at the second ring.

"Troubles?" he asked without preamble.

"Dead wolves all over my hotel room. Looks very messy," replied Michael without humor.

"I'll be over in a jiffy."

The line went dead and Michael pulled the cell phone David had given him from his pants pocket and dialed the detective's number.

"Michael! What's up?" said the voice of David Starks.

"We couldn't escape. They caught us in the parking lot."

"Us? Who's with you?" asked David, surprised.

"Sheila."

"Wonderful! Are you both OK?"

"More or less… I need you to come and pick her up. She's not safe here, and I don't want to leave her alone. When can you be here?"

"I'll be over in thirty minutes," answered David.

Michael replaced the cell phone in his front pocket and turned his attention on Sheila who was still looking at him, not daring to move a muscle. She would probably have bolted out of the room had she been closer to the door, he thought. He stood between her and the only way out of the room, however, and she did not dare try her luck.

"Why haven't the police arrived yet?" asked Sheila in a trembling voice. "A bear just battled werewolves in the middle of Houston with a door wide open on a busy parking lot. People should have called 911 fifteen minutes ago…"

"Because nobody saw a thing…" said Ezekiel with authority as he walked through the door. "They had a witch with them!"

The wizard wore his eternal pointy hat and was wrapped in the same gray cloak Michael had seen him wear for centuries. Wizards, apparently, did not wear out their clothes very fast.

After what she had just witnessed, the arrival of a man dressed in what looked to Sheila like a Halloween costume of Gandalf the Grey from *The Lord of the Rings* only seemed to thicken the surrealistic aura that had suddenly swathed her life.

"I suspected as much," replied Michael. "I can still feel the residual magic in the air, and it doesn't feel like fae magic… "

"The spell is fading fast, but it was good enough to make the entire room unnoticeable. To novice eyes, the door even looks intact from the outside," explained Ezekiel.

Sheila had started to recover from the shock and looked a little more like herself than she had a few minutes earlier.

"Who… who are you?" she asked.

"The name is Ezekiel, wizard of the second circle," replied Ez in a booming voice meant to be intimidating. The trick worked on the journalist who decided not to press her questioning further. Clearly she was surrounded by dangerous lunatics and her survival resided in them paying the least possible amount of attention to her.

"Thank you for coming so fast, Ez," said Michael with gratitude.

"No need to thank me, old friend," said the wizard in a warm voice. "I only did what you would have done for me were our places switched around."

Michael knew the statement was true, but still he felt fortunate to have a friend like Ez on his side. The Houston pack obviously had witches on payroll, but he had Ezekiel, one of the most powerful wizards alive.

"That's a lot of wolf pieces for a single room," said the wizard, looking around and using the same voice one would use to appraise a piece of real estate. "It looks like someone had too much fun," he added, looking at Michael, who simply ignored the remark.

The wizard took a small leather pouch out of an inside pocket and untied the leather laces that kept it shut. Inside was a bright blue powder, which he proceeded to sprinkle over the wolves' bodies while chanting in a low voice words Sheila could not understand but that seemed to rhyme. As he did so, the corpses started shimmering and slowly became transparent. A few minutes later, the carcasses had all disappeared, together with the blood and body parts that had maculated the room.

This was too much for Sheila, who passed out and fell to the ground before Michael could catch her.

Chapter 68

The cars kept rolling into the already overcrowded driveway. The newcomers were now parking under the trees edging the forest clearing where Clemens' cabin had been erected.

Inside the house, the wolves were agitated, although they ignored the reason of their summoning. The pack was feeding off the Alpha's mood, and Clemens' mood was not good.

The whole pack typically met at Clemens' a couple times a month for scheduled meetings, but this time the summoning had come late in the afternoon for the same evening. Something was definitely going on.

The pack's gatherings took place in the second story of the house, in a room large enough to comfortably host fifty people. There were plenty of seats for everybody, and they were arranged by groups of five or six around coffee tables. One of the walls was equipped with a retractable projection screen hidden in the ceiling when not in use, but which was now ready for operation.

"I believe everybody is here, so we'll get started," said Clemens, standing in front of the screen.

There were thirty-eight wolves present in the room including Clemens and his wife, which meant a few wolves were missing, but nobody voiced their observation. Every member of the pack was intrinsically aware of his pack mates and able to tell without even looking who was missing. The Alpha's senses were, above all, tuned to the frequencies of his subordinates, and if he said everyone was present, that meant nobody else would be coming.

The room lighting was dimmed and a close-up photo of Michael

Biörn appeared on the screen behind Clemens.

"This man's name is Michael Biörn and he is the enemy," started Clemens, his voice crisp with contained rage. "Today, he killed six of our brothers in a single confrontation."

A muffled rumor could be heard in the room as the wolves started speculating between themselves as to what the revelation implied. There were very few things out there capable of dispatching six werewolves at once. It would, at the very least, have taken a vampire of the strength the world had not seen in many centuries. Even among the Supernatural beings, few had the strength to pull something like this. An elf lord, a wizard of the upper circles, or a particularly powerful warlock, maybe. The list was short.

"What is he?" asked Rachel, a woman of about five feet and a hundred pounds, who had the reputation to make up in viciousness what she lacked in strength.

"He's a werebear," answered the Alpha, with pronounced emphasis on the last word.

The rumor in the room grew by an order of magnitude as the wolves expressed their surprise and disbelief.

"But werebears are extinct!" exclaimed Rachel.

"The last one was killed in Spain over two centuries ago," added another wolf.

"Axel," said Peter Clemens, looking at the pack's fourth in command.

Axel Thompkins rose from his chair, one of the closest to the screen, and turned towards the audience. "I fought him in the company of our fallen brothers not four hours ago. He is definitely a werebear, a grizzly type I believe, and he is big, very big."

"How big?" asked a voice from the back of the room.

"I'd say at least seven hundred pounds, possibly eight hundred," answered Thompkins.

"How can he be so big? He'd have to weigh like five hundred pounds in his human form…"

"No! Werebears are different from us," corrected Clemens. "Whereas our body weight typically increases by fifty percent during morphing, the werebear's mass jumps up a hundred and fifty percent. They are therefore two and a half times bigger as bears than they are as humans."

"How do we kill it?" asked Rachel in a cold and calculating voice.

"The same way we kill all praeternaturals… We chop his head off!" replied Clemens.

"What are we waiting for?" asked Clemens' wife Isabella, whose comment sparked a throng of agreeing hollers.

"Quiet!" said Clemens imperatively. "He caught us off guard today. Shame on us… shame on me! But I'll be damned if I make the same mistake twice."

No sound came to interrupt the Alpha's statement this time.

"We will smite him with all our might, when he expects it the least. We'll hit him with such an overwhelming force that he won't stand a chance."

Cheers erupted in the room as Clemens continued, "But today is not the time. He has no doubt vacated his motel and we need to locate him first. Then, we need to prepare for the kill…"

Chapter 69

Ezekiel had taken his leave by the time David Starks arrived at Michael's motel. Sheila had recovered from her fainting spell and was sitting on the bed still looking slightly dazed. At her request, Michael had explained a few things about werebears and werewolves, but even though she had seen them with her own eyes, her brain refused to accept their reality.

David knocked on the door that the wizard had returned to its original dilapidated but one-piece style, and Michael opened the door.

David stepped through the entrance and took a look around him.

"It doesn't look like there was much of a struggle in here," he commented, surprised.

"I had a friend come over to do a bit of cleaning," explained Michael cryptically.

"I didn't know you had friends in town," said David.

"I do."

"Should I even ask?"

"I'd rather you didn't…" answered Michael matter-of-factly.

"All right," said David skeptically. "How many of them were they?"

"Eight werewolves and a witch."

David looked Michael in the eye, just for a second, "And you killed all of them?" he asked dubiously.

"Only six wolves, the rest escaped…"

Sheila, who could not believe the tone of the discussion, finally intervened. "You seem to find all this perfectly normal," she said to David, sounding bewildered. "What's wrong with you? You're a cop, for God's sake. When someone tells you about werewolves and witches you're supposed to send them to a shrink, not believe them!"

"What are you planning on doing with Lois Lane?" asked David to Michael, purposefully ignoring the journalist's intervention, but before Michael had a chance to reply, Sheila chimed in, "Asked the detective to the bear!"

"Bear, hey? I hadn't heard of that type before…" said David, sounding impressed.

Michael simply shrugged. "There is a first time for everything…"

"So, what about her?" repeated David.

"I need you to take her away from here. It isn't safe for her to be around me, and I can't really trust too many people in town."

"You two do realize I am still in the room, right?" asked Sheila sarcastically.

"I'm sorry, Sheila," said Michael. "But you are in danger and you need to take the situation seriously."

Although she had regained her natural combativeness, she hadn't forgotten the wolves, or the bear, or the wizard with his pointy hat. She had fallen back into aggressiveness and sarcasm as a defense mechanism because she refused to face reality.

"What are *you*?" she finally asked David.

"I'm afraid I'm just a cop," he answered, smiling.

"But you believe in monsters?" she asked suspiciously.

"I have seen things. Just like you… Things one cannot ignore."

She remained silent for a moment, and Michael took advantage of the opportunity to do a bit of lecturing. "I know you're a journalist, Sheila, which means you will want to write about what you've seen as soon as you start accepting it yourself. This cannot happen; you cannot write a word about this. Do you understand?"

She looked at him defiantly. "Or what? Are you going to kill me too?"

He stared at her with a surprised look on his face for a minute before answering, "I'm one of the good guys, Sheila, I would never hurt you. But as you have seen for yourself, there are some bad guys out there, and I assure you they won't hesitate to kill you to keep their secret."

It took him an additional twenty minutes to convince Sheila to leave with David before the bad guys came back, but in the end she accepted.

"What are you going to do?" asked David, a hand on the doorknob.

"I am not sure yet," replied Michael. "I need to think this through."

Chapter 70

The car stopped in front of a brick veneer one-story house that looked cute and unassuming at the same time. A cookie cutter house surrounded by enough other styles of cookie cutter houses that there weren't two identical homes on any given street of the neighborhood. This created the illusion you owned an original house when, in reality, there were two dozen homes identical to yours in the subdivision.

Michael checked the address David had given him and got out of the car. He had been surprised to find himself driving to suburbia this morning, to a city called Sugar Land, located southwest of Houston. He would have expected her to live within Houston proper, to be an *inner looper,* as the locals called those living within the Interstate-610 belt that surrounded the heart of the city.

"I believe we need to talk," said Michael as soon as Sheila Wang opened the door. She was wearing a pair of light pink, tight-fitting cotton shorts and a white tank top that stopped just above the shorts waistband. No makeup was visible on her still bruised face, and Michael rightly concluded he had caught her fresh out of bed.

He could smell fear on her, and knew he was the one causing it. He could also detect a hint of excitement; Sheila was a reporter and she simply couldn't silence her natural curiosity.

She only hesitated a second before stepping aside and let him through the door. He noticed that she had not locked the door but simply shut it... an easier escape route, he assumed. The smell of fear emanating from Sheila grew stronger, and Michael also started smelling fresh perspiration, but as they entered the kitchen, these odors were quickly diluted with the aroma of brewing coffee and fresh toast.

The house had an open floor plan, where the kitchen and living room were only separated by a bar-height counter equipped with bar stools on the living room side. Michael pulled up a stool and sat at the bar while Sheila went to stand against the fridge. By doing so, she was placing a counter and a good eight feet between herself and Michael; one didn't have to be too observant to get the message.

"Would you like some coffee?" she asked in a cold voice. Her pronunciation was a lot better than it had been the day before, but still not perfect.

"I don't drink coffee, but I'll take tea if you have honey," he replied, before adding cheerfully, "You sound like your jaw is getting better."

Ignoring his last remark, she opened a cupboard and started rummaging through it. She pulled out a jar containing a honeycomb half submerged in liquid honey and placed in on the bar in front of Michael.

"I thought the whole bear and honey thing was a myth."

Michael thought he detected a touch of wryness in her voice. Wryness was good! It beat fear by an order of magnitude...

"It's not," he replied, smiling. "But I'm not truly a bear either, as you may have noticed..."

She gave him a look that stated *I beg to differ,* as she started boiling some water for his tea.

"After what happened yesterday..." Michael started hesitantly, "you probably deserve some explanations."

"I would say so indeed!" replied Sheila vehemently.

"I don't have this type of discussion very often, you see," he said, looking sheepish. "I usually try to keep a low profile... stay under the radar, if you know what I mean."

"I believe I do. Please do go on." Sheila spoke half sarcastically, half encouragingly.

Michael looked particularly uncomfortable, both figuratively and literally. The bar stool had been designed for a normal human being; beneath him it looked like a replica belonging to an oversized dollhouse.

"I don't really know where to start…"

"Maybe you could start by telling me what you are exactly, and what those things that tried to kill you were?" she offered in a slightly less sarcastic voice.

"What I am has many names, which vary with time and geography. In this country, today, I would be best described as a werebear."

The kettle started emitting a high-pitched whistle, but Sheila didn't seem to notice.

"And what is exactly a werebear?"

Michael got up and walked around the bar to the island in the center of the kitchen to remove the kettle from the stove.

"A werebear is a praeternatural being, similar to a werewolf," he started, as he poured the hot water into a mug containing a bag of black tea and a spoon Sheila had set on the island by the stove, "except that his animal form is bearlike."

Sheila was listening attentively, so he continued his explanation as he returned to his undersized seat. "We spend most of our time in our human form. Although even in our human form, we are never entirely human—"

"What do you mean by that? Is it just a disguise? Are your thoughts completely alien? Do you eat raw meat?" she interrupted, as her journalistic training kicked into gear.

"Very few people are in the know, Sheila, and those who do know are bound to secrecy," he said, looking at her so intently that she dropped her gaze. "I am about to tell you things that could get you killed if you were to go around repeating them. Do you understand me?"

She nodded slowly, acquiescing. Then she poured herself a cup of coffee to which she added sugar and milk and went to the living room, where she sat on a black leather loveseat.

"Maybe you should move to the couch," she said, extending a hand towards the empty sofa located at a ninety-degree angle from the loveseat. "You look like a G.I. Joe on a Lego stool sitting on that thing…"

Chapter 71

Michael accepted Sheila's offer and moved to the empty sofa, bringing his tea mug along with him.

"What I meant was that even in our human form our senses are different, our instincts are different. We face a constant struggle between our humanity and our bestiality."

"And sometimes your humanity loses the battle?" she asked in a whisper.

"Sometimes..." he answered, his mind projected a millennium in the past, reliving the events which had cost him his wife, Isibel, and so much more. He had woken up in his human form, covered in blood, with no recollection of what had happened... until he saw the body.

Sheila saw the change in his eyes, and could tell he was no longer with her. She waited what seemed like an eternity but was only a minute for him to come back to the present world. When his eyes were once more focused on her she asked, "And what happens when the animal wins the battle?"

"Bad things," he answered after a few seconds, "but you don't have to worry about that, not from me at least. As one grows older, one learns to control the beast within. I have not lost control to my bear side in a very long time."

"What exactly do you call a very long time?" she asked skeptically. "Are we talking years or hours? Because yesterday, at least from where I stood, it didn't look like your human personality was in much control..."

"If my human form had not been in control yesterday, you would be dead. I morphed and killed those men because I did not have a choice. They would have killed both of us without hesitation. I could not allow it."

"Alllrriight..." she said, not completely convinced. "So when was the last time you lost control by accident?"

"During the winter of 978," he replied placidly.

"What do you mean? September 1978?"

"No, 978 is the year."

She stared at him, clearly not convinced. "You're telling me that was over a thousand years ago?"

"Yes, that's what I am saying," he answered stoically.

She was ready to call him a liar, or worse a lunatic, but then she remembered the man's transformation into a bear and thought better of it. The man might very well be a lunatic, but then so could she be!

"How old are you exactly?" she asked, trying not to sound too suspicious and failing miserably.

"I was born in the country now called Norway in the year 956."

"OK, so you are a thousand years old, give or take. And you are what you are because you got bitten by a bear on your way back from pillaging a school as a young Viking, right?" she asked dubiously.

"Nothing bit me, bear or other. I was born that way. My parents were both werebears, and against all odds, they transmitted their curse to me."

"Why do you say against all odds?"

"Because werecreatures usually suffer from fertility issues. It is very rare that two werebears, or werewolves for that matter, manage to conceive. They typically have children with humans, but in that case the kids usually turn out human."

Sheila was now sitting on the edge of her seat and the smell of fear was no longer present on her.

"But where do werecreatures come from? I mean initially, how were they created?"

"No one knows…"

"And you're not curious?" she asked, sounding slightly bewildered.

"Of course I'm curious, but that's not the type of information you can find online. And if I may say so, nobody knows for a fact where humans come from either…"

She contemplated his reply for a minute before answering, "Touché… although the theory of evolution offers some pretty compelling evidence."

"Not about where the very first species to evolve came from…"

"Fine! But this isn't the subject of our discussion. How do you transform? There was no full moon last night…"

"That's not how it works," he replied, placing his empty mug on a coaster on the glass end table to his right. "The folklore legend about men turning into werewolves under a full moon is based on a simple but misinterpreted fact. The full moon is the time of the month when morphing is the least painful. For this reason, werebeings tend to morph more often during that time. As a result, in the middle ages, werebeing-caused mayhem peaked significantly at the full moon, so folks erroneously concluded that the full moon was required for the morphing process."

"So what you're telling me is that all the old folktales about monsters are actually factual and not due to overactive imaginations?" Her voice was dripping with skepticism.

He did not hold her incredulity against her. He had been a werebear for over a millennium, and he still had a hard time believing some of the things Supernatural beings could do. He had witnessed Ezekiel do things that would make a man turning into a bear look like the most natural thing in the world.

"A few stories are completely bogus, and the others are draped in so much exaggeration that it's hard to tell the truth from the fiction, but there is often a hint of truth in the old tales."

"All right, just tell me if these are real or fake," she said defiantly. "Vampires?"

"Real… unfortunately," he replied seriously. She hesitated to ask a follow-up question and finally decided to move on.

"Witch, wizard, sorceress, etcetera?"

"Real."

"Faeries?"

"Real… although their family has many subcategories and some of them, like the orcs, are purely fictional."

"Bogeymen?"

"You're just being silly now," he said with a smile, as his phone started ringing loudly inside his pocket.

"Are you going to answer that?" she asked, when, after the third ring, he had not made a move to pull his phone out.

"No. Whatever it is, it can wait." He had spent his whole very long life without a cell phone and wasn't about to turn into one of those ill-mannered phone junkies, the type who answered their phone at the first ring under any given circumstance. The voice mail picked up after the fourth ring and the phone fell silent.

"What about the monsters who attacked you last night? They were werewolves, right?"

"Yes."

"But they looked like regular wolves, just way bigger. I thought were-wolves walked around on two legs, you know, like in most movies…" This time she spoke with more surprise than skepticism.

"Only in movies. In real life, they look just like what you saw."

She filed the information in her mental database and moved on to her next query. She was no longer in skeptic mode; she had switched to her investigative reporter mode.

Chapter 72

The clock on the dashboard indicated quarter past twelve when Michael got back in his car—no wonder he was getting hungry.

He had spent the entire morning answering Sheila's questions on praeternatural beings, and they had barely touched the tip of the iceberg. He hoped for her sake that she would be true to her word and not try to publish anything she had learned. Her life depended on it. The praeternatural and supernatural beings did not like publicity. Humans who had learned too much and could not keep quiet did not live long happy lives.

Sheila had also questioned him relentlessly about the series of murders targeting police officers. On that subject, he hadn't had much to tell her though. All signs indicated werewolves were involved—which in Houston meant Clemens—but that did not prove the wolves were behind the whole thing. Clemens could simply be the muscle and not the one pulling the strings… but in this scenario, who was the puppeteer? Ivanov was an obvious suspect, but maybe a bit too obvious. In addition, the Houston pack had not been present to protect the drug shipment at the docks, which seemed to indicate Ivanov did not routinely rely on Clemens' wolves for protection.

Michael was about to put the car in gear when his phone rang again. He tried to reach for it inside the front pocket of his pants, but his seated position and the size of his hand prevented his fingers from retrieving the device. In the end, he had to get out of the car to extricate the phone.

"Hello?"

"Michael?" said the voice of Olivia Harrington.

"Hello, Olivia."

"I need to talk to you, Michael," she said anxiously.

"I'm listening."

Olivia had initially thought of going to see Michael in person, but what she had to tell him had good chances of alienating the man, and she preferred doing that over the phone.

"Clemens is coming after you," she blurted out without preamble.

"What?" he replied in shock. "How do you know that name?" He didn't mention that Clemens' pack had come after him the day before.

"The details don't matter," she said dismissively. "What matters is that he is coming after you, and I want you to know about it so as not to be caught off guard. I am sure he is the one who killed my parents."

Michael remained silent for an instant.

"Of course, if you prefer fleeing... I would understand," she added unconvincingly.

"Olivia, you need to tell me where you got this information," he said with authority. "I am a lot more concerned about you than I am about myself at the moment. How do you know all this?"

She pondered her answer for a moment before deciding to tell the truth. "I found a file with your name on it locked inside his desk drawer."

Michael couldn't believe what he was hearing, "How did you get access to his house? What was in this file?"

"I only saw a picture. His wife came into the room and I had to put the file back in place before I had a chance to read anything from it," she replied with obvious disappointment.

Under different circumstances, Michael would have been relieved to hear she hadn't had a chance to read the file—whatever was in it probably wasn't something he'd want Olivia to know—but he was too flabbergasted by her snooping inside Clemens' house to feel thankful.

"How did you get inside his house, Olivia?" He struggled to keep anger out of his voice and only partially succeeded.

"I took a job with the company that cleans it, and I talked the guy in charge of the assignment into sending me there," she answered, clearly proud of her accomplishment.

"You are *never* to return to his house, Olivia. Do you hear me?" retorted Michael, no longer trying to keep his anger in check. "This man is more dangerous than you could ever imagine. If you had been caught, you'd be dead or worse right now."

"What's worse than dead?" she asked defiantly.

He almost answered her but caught himself in time.

"How did you know who was cleaning his house, how did you know the man?"

She considered telling him she found the address while snooping in his own motel room, but decided against it. In some cases, honesty simply wasn't the best option.

"It's not important."

"It absolutely *is*! I cannot protect you if you don't tell me the whole story," he replied vehemently.

"I don't need your protection Michael. I only need you to catch my parents' murderer," she answered. Now it was her turn to be angry. "I'm not some child you need to worry about."

"Go back to school, Olivia. I'll call you when I find something," he said in a non-confrontational tone.

"I'll go back to school when I goddamn choose," she retorted, hanging up.

Chapter 73

It was the middle of the afternoon when Michael walked through the door of the Houston PD main office downtown. He walked decisively to the front desk where the officer on duty greeted him with an automatic, "How may I help you?" despite the obvious uneasiness he felt in the presence of Michael's impressive physique.

"I am looking for Detective Lewis," Michael answered. "She's expecting me."

"Fifth floor," replied the officer with a hint of relief in his voice.

Michael thanked him, walked past the elevator and headed for the stairway.

The phone call he had missed while visiting Sheila had been from Detective Samantha Lewis. Only three people had Michael's cell phone number, and Samantha Lewis wasn't one of them. Michael doubted Olivia or Sheila would have given the number away to the detective, so that left only David Starks as the culprit.

Samantha Lewis' voice had been unusually friendly on the message she had left, asking Michael if he "would be so kind as to return her call". He had met Lewis and her partner twice since he had arrived in Houston, and she had been anything but friendly on those previous occasions.

Out of sheer curiosity, Michael had decided to return her call to find out for himself what this change of attitude was about. He had been more than surprised when Lewis had come just short of apologizing for her past behavior and had requested his help as a wildlife expert.

He landed on the fifth floor without breaking a sweat and asked the first officer he met where Lewis' office was. The man pointed him in the right direction and a minute later Michael was in the detective's office, sitting in a chair which was, in fact, even more uncomfortable than it looked.

Salazar and Lewis shared a small windowless office furnished with cheap-looking metal furniture. The carpet had been a shade of taupe in a remote past, but now the stains of coffee and other unidentifiable substances covering it formed an uneven pattern best described as filthy.

"Thank you for coming, Mr. Biörn," said Samantha Lewis as soon as he had sat down. She was facing him from the other side of her desk while Salazar stood against the wall behind her.

"As I explained over the phone, we would like to ask you a few things in your capacity as wolf expert," she said in a soft voice ill-fitted to her personality.

Michael managed to suppress a smile. "Should I understand that you no longer consider me a suspect?"

"You have a knack for being at the wrong place at the wrong time, and we know you can kill an entire mob execution squad and walk away unscathed," started Lewis in a scolding voice which suited her better than the honeyed tone she had used earlier. "You definitely qualify as a suspect, Mr. Biörn."

"We just don't think you are a suspect in the case we are working," intervened Salazar.

"I see," answered Michael neutrally. "So what can I do for you?"

"Well, you see, Mr. Biörn, we have received various forensics evidence which seem to corroborate your opinion regarding the wolf attacks," said Lewis. "There would seem to be several distinct wolves responsible for the killings after all."

She expected some sign of condescension to come from Michael, but he simply kept silent, his face an unreadable mask.

"We have a hard time explaining this fact," said Salazar. "When wolves go after police officers in the heart of Houston, we are clearly dealing with assassinations. This point at least is clear."

Michael nodded in agreement but did not offer any comment.

"When Harrington and Starks were in charge of this investigation, they were favoring the organized crime hypothesis," explained Lewis in a matter-of-fact voice. "But this was before the wolves' attacks. Now, with the wolves coming to complicate the case, we don't understand why the mob would have changed their *modus operandi*."

Salazar stepped forward to sit on the corner of Lewis' desk, not three feet from Michael.

"I don't suppose you expect me to give you an explanation for this?"

"Of course not," replied Lewis. "But could you tell us if there would be any reason for three different wolves to be used in these attacks? Why can't they use the same wolf every time?"

Michael of course knew the answer to that question but could not give it to the detectives without raising more questions: questions of the type he definitely couldn't answer. There was more than one wolf involved simply because there was more than one killer.

"I can't think of a good reason for that," he answered unconvincingly.

"How hard would it be to train three wolves to kill humans?" asked Salazar.

Michael thought about the question for a minute before answering, "It would be pretty difficult. For one thing, wolves aren't dogs; they're not easy to approach, let alone train. In addition, wolves do not typically attack humans, they are naturally scared of us. Turning a wolf, or several for that matter, into killers would require a lot of time and effort. The easiest way would be to raise them from pups for that purpose."

"That sounds like too much trouble for the mob to bother with," said Salazar pensively. "They usually have a more direct approach."

Lewis looked at Michael. "Although I would tend to agree with my partner, we have to live with the fact that you, the wolf expert, were attacked by a mob delegation." She looked questioningly at Michael, who wasn't displaying any sign indicating that he'd even heard the question.

"Do you have any explanation to offer for this?" she asked finally, slightly irritated.

"Not in the least. Are you positive these were mobsters and not random thugs?" he asked innocently.

"Don't fuck with us, Biörn!" warned Lewis threateningly. "We know you're not telling the whole story, but since we found nothing implicating you in this mess and since Harrington trusted you enough to ask for your help, we are not holding it against you... yet! But don't push your luck..."

Michael got up to stretch his legs and looked down upon the two detectives, who were still seated.

"I honestly don't know why these guys tried to kill me," he answered authoritatively—for he was telling the truth, mostly. "I would be happy to help you as best I can with any question you might have regarding wolves. But if you try to use my offer as an excuse to question me on unrelated matters, I will walk away."

Chapter 74

Jack had a grin on his face when he shut his cell phone and replaced it in his pocket. Ever since the debacle at Chief Deputy Sullivan's where he had left bloody paw prints and pieces of shredded Rottweiler all over the floor, Jack had had no contact with the Alpha. A painful punishment since Omegas craved praise and recognition from their Alpha and suffered when kept outside pack business.

Jack had been tempted to contact the Alpha numerous times over the past month, but he had never dared act on his impulses. Every member of the pack knew the rule: extreme emergencies aside, contact was to be initiated by the Alpha exclusively. Since no emergency had emerged, Jack had been condemned to suffer alone and in silence, waiting patiently for the pack leader to contact him.

But this time had passed; Jack was now back in the Alpha's good grace and he had been trusted with a most important mission. A mission he would execute with perfection to prove the Alpha he had placed his confidence in the right wolf.

The mark this time was a woman. Jack had never killed a woman before, but it made no difference. One way or another, the bitch had crossed the Alpha and it was all that mattered. The fact the woman needed to die simply because she had witnessed things she shouldn't have had not been mentioned. Jack had not been told anything, and he had not asked. It had never been his place to ask questions. All he knew was that within the next twenty-four hours, Sheila Wang would be dead.

Chapter 75

In spite of Michael's warning, it had not taken Sheila long to start writing another article. She had spent the better part of the afternoon in front of her computer and was now proofreading her piece. She felt slightly uneasy about ignoring Michael's advice, but only slightly. After all, the article did not even mention werewolves… or were-anything, for that matter. It simply related the aggression towards her in the park and drew obvious conclusions as to who was behind the attack. All in all, wolves were merely mentioned in passing, not enough to seriously upset the "praeternatural community" as Michael had called it.

The Russian mob, on the other end, had not been spared by her quill. Dimitri Ivanov's name was mentioned no less than four times in the one-page article and never in flattering terms.

Sheila re-read her last paragraph for the fourth time, making sure all t's were crossed and all i's dotted. *That will teach them to try and intimidate me*, she thought as she hit the Save key. It was now time for the truly difficult part. Writing an antagonistic article against the mob was one thing, publishing it was another. As long as the piece remained comfortably nested on her hard drive, no harm was done, but as soon as she pressed the Send key, the article would be on its way to her editor-in-chief and in the paper the following day… and from there, all hell would break loose.

She stood up from her computer and paced the length of her living room a few times to stretch her legs. She had spent several days in the hospital after her last article targeting the mob and still had broken bones to show for it. What were they going to do to her next time? Sheila was a brave woman, but that did not mean she had no fear. She knew full well the distinction between the two; being brave implied overcoming one's fears, while being fearless was a luxury reserved to foolhardy idiots... and Sheila was no idiot. Despite the risks, she was too young a journalist to let herself be intimidated by bullies, even bullies who used killer werewolves to do their dirty work. If she backed out of the story just because she was scared of reprisals, she might as well change careers right away and not bother. Sheila did not know any Pulitzer Prize winners personally, but she was pretty sure none of them were of the type who surrenders at the first roadblock encountered.

She sat back down in front of her computer, took a deep breath and pushed the Send key. *Alea iacta est,* she thought.

Chapter 76

Located in the heart of the city, halfway between Memorial Park and the downtown area, River Oaks was Houston's most exclusive neighborhood. Dimitri Ivanov's private residence, one of the largest in the area, occupied the center of a three-acre lot bordered by a ten-foot wall.

Surrounded by row after row of Texas oak trees, the house was virtually invisible from the street, despite being the size of a small castle. To a passerby, the property was indistinguishable from others in the neighborhood, but a more acute observer might have noticed that the state of the art cameras perched atop the surrounding wall were both more numerous and less stationary than those watching over neighboring estates. In addition to the sophisticated video surveillance system watching over the entire park, the grounds of the property were walked twenty-four hours a day by armed guards with Dobermans and German Shepherds. All in all, the mob boss was well protected.

Ivanov was in the habit of getting up slightly later than usual on weekends, and although it was nearing ten o'clock, he was still drinking his morning coffee in front of CNN when Igor Petrovich entered the drawing room and dropped the latest issue of the Houston Post on the coffee table in front of him.

"You'll want to read this." Petrovich pointed at an article on the front page. "It continues on page two."

Ivanov grabbed the paper and started reading the article entitled: *"Two broken ribs and a dislocated jaw courtesy of the mob. By Sheila Wang, investigative reporter."*

He read the entire piece without saying a word, but a throbbing vein on his forehead betrayed his anger to Petrovich who recognized the sign. Once finished, he closed the newspaper, folded it in two and handed it back to his second.

"The bitch doesn't learn," said Petrovich in a matter-of-fact voice devoid of emotion. "What do you want to do about her?"

Ivanov remained silent for a moment weighing the possibilities in his mind. The journalist had gone too far this time. She had been warned to keep her nose out of his business, and she should have listened, for one warning was all she would get. Naming him in her article was a mistake she would not live to regret. Unlike her first article, this one was not about the wolves but about his own organization. The wolves were just a side-note this time, not enough to threaten Clemens. It was therefore unlikely the wolves would save him the trouble by dealing with the nosy bitch themselves.

"Have Vadim take care of the problem," said Ivanov in a command-ing tone. "Tell him to get it done today. I want to see her name in to-morrow's paper as well, but this time in the obituary section."

Chapter 77

To most Houstonians, fall constituted the best season to be outside. After five or six months of a stifling heat called summer, mid-Octo-ber, with its average high typically in the low eighties, brought much an-ticipated relief to wildlife and people alike.

With a cloudless sky, a temperature of seventy-six degrees and a hu-midity of only 64%, the day was as perfect as they got, and David Starks had taken this opportunity to go for a run on the beach. He had been jogging along the water for over an hour when he found himself staring at his beachfront property, back where he had started.

The house was built on piers and stood fifteen feet off the ground. The back patio was furnished with a two-seater porch swing, a couple of reclining deckchairs and a wooden patio table and chairs set.

David's eyes were drawn to the silhouette sunbathing on one of the deckchairs. He spent a few minutes contemplating Katia Olveda's flaw-less curves from a distance before heading for the stairway that led from the beach to the patio. The sound of his footsteps had been muffled by the sand and he decided to climb the staircase as quietly as possible in an attempt to surprise his lover. He landed on the patio deck without a noise and slowly tiptoed his way to Katia's chair. She was wearing a yellow bikini that covered very little of her eloquent figure. Her eyes were closed and her chest heaved up and down in slow motion, but as David bent over her with the intention of kissing her lips she said, "You're out of coffee darling. Will you be a sweet and go fetch me some?"

The closest coffee shop was only two blocks away, and David

decided to walk there in order to stretch his legs after the eight-mile jog.

He was walking back holding a tray with Katia's cappuccino and his own caramel macchiato when he passed in front of a newspaper box which caught his attention. In the box window, the front page of the Saturday edition of the Houston Post featured an article by Sheila Wang. After reading the article's title, David knew he had to buy the paper.

He placed the required change inside the box slot, opened the door, and grabbed a copy. He had read the entire piece by the time he made it back to the house.

Chapter 78

It was 2.47 a.m., and with the exception of a stray cat on its nightly stroll, the street was entirely deserted when the black SUV rolled to a stop in an alley adjacent to Sheila Wang's house.

Two men climbed out of the car and started walking in silence towards her house. When they reached the street corner, Vadim turned towards his accomplice and said in a hushed voice, "Stay here and stand watch. I have my phone on vibrate, call me if you see anything unusual."

The house's front door was in a recess and invisible from most of the street. Vadim drew a glasscutter equipped with a suction cup from one of his jacket's inside pockets and proceeded to cut a circular piece of glass from the viewing window in the door. He then delicately tapped on the scored glass, which yielded readily but remained attached to the suction cup. Vadim passed his hand through the opening in the window and quickly unlatched the door. An instant later, he was inside the house, gun in hand.

His weapon was equipped with a silencer, but he did not intend to use it. His instructions were to make her death look like an accident; Vadim knew how important pleasing Ivanov was to his own wellbeing.

Gas explosions were always a popular choice in his line of work for obvious reasons. For one thing, the mark had little chances to survive the mayhem created by the blazing inferno. As an added bonus, the blast generally erased all clues the assassin could have accidentally left behind. Since Vadim was not a very imaginative man, he had decided the accidental gas leak was the way to go.

As he walked cautiously towards the gas fireplace, he heard a muffled sound on his left. He immediately spun his gun towards the noise, but the other man was already on him, effortlessly driving his knife through Vadim's left temple, killing him instantly.

Jack had been about to enter Sheila's bedroom when he had heard the man's glasscutter scoring the window. He had quickly retreated to a dark corner of the living room, waiting for the situation to develop. He hadn't known the man, but he had immediately noticed the gun in his hand and had decided to treat him as a threat. In retrospect, maybe this had been a mistake. The fellow's behavior had not been that of an honest man, and if he had been sent to kill the woman, Jack could have avoided getting his hands dirty by letting the other man do the work... It was too late now anyway! He needed to get back to his mission and get the hell out of this place. He had the uneasy feeling the Alpha was going to be unhappy with him once again.

A muffled vibration interrupted his line of thoughts. After investigation, he found out the noise came from the dead man's front pocket; his phone was vibrating. Jack ignored the ringing phone and walked into Sheila's bedroom.

He was a wolf and wolves knew how to be silent when they had to, so she was still deeply asleep when he reached her bed, knife firmly clasped in his right hand.

Chapter 79

After a long drive through the dimly lit streets of Houston, Michael returned to his hotel shortly after two in the morning. The drive had been an attempt at finding sleep, but after driving around town for a couple hours, he still wasn't feeling any sleepier. His mind was too busy thinking things over for him to get any rest. If only he had been making headway in his investigation, he would at least be restless for good reasons, but his investigation was going nowhere.

Michael had not heard from David Starks in a few days, and he was taking this silence as a sign the detective's enquiries were not progressing any faster than his own. He still didn't know for a fact who was behind Steve's murder, and, to further complicate matters, he now had Olivia and Sheila to worry about. If these two did not learn to keep their noses out of Clemens and Ivanov's business, they wouldn't live to be very old.

Michael was an old bear, both literally and metaphorically, and he did not typically worry too much about the wellbeing of strangers, but he was strangely fond of these two women he barely knew. He could easily find an excuse regarding Olivia. She was the daughter of his freshly murdered old army buddy, and he had good reasons to care about her. He had more difficulties rationalizing his feelings towards the journalist, however...

It was getting really late, and if he didn't get some sleep fast he'd be tired and unproductive all the next day, so he did what he almost never did and turned on the television. To him, watching television was as unappealing as a trip to the dentist and twice as painful. He had read somewhere that doing something boring helped a restless mind find sleep, and watching TV was the most mind-numbing thing he could imagine.

If daytime television was unattractive in the first place, nighttime TV was its uglier sister. After flipping through the thirty-six channels offered in the room three times in four minutes, Michael started watching a cooking show... that is, until the chef decided to add ketchup to the sauce he was preparing. Michael, who had lived in France during the birth of modern cuisine and still owned an original copy of *Le Cuisinier François*, the founding text of modern French cuisine, refused to stand for this type of behavior. He flipped through another twenty programs in a thirty-second span before landing on the rerun of the local news. He would have kept flipping through the channels if a name had not caught his attention. The anchorwoman was talking about Sheila Wang.

Chapter 80

Sheila looked peaceful lying asleep in her bed. She was sleeping on her side, facing the bedroom door. A lock of her raven hair, resting on her cheek, vibrated gently in time with her soft breathing.

Jack felt slightly turned on at the sight of his defenseless pray resting, unaware of her imminent fate. Although it wasn't part of his orders, for an instant he wondered if he shouldn't have a bit of fun before completing his task.

Bent over the journalist's bed, his mouth displayed an ugly grin when his nostrils started flaring. For half a second, he wondered if he wasn't imagining the odor before deciding it was definitely real. He was not familiar with the scent, but he knew exactly what it was; he had been warned. Without a sound, but not painlessly, Jack morphed into his beast form.

Pressed by time, the wolf hadn't had a chance to strip out of his clothes before morphing, and it was a werewolf wearing a ripped-off shirt and saggy blue jeans that jumped at Michael's throat as soon as he entered the bedroom. Michael, who had sensed the enemy's presence before entering the room, had anticipated the attack. He received the wolf with a punch to the muzzle, which sent the beast flying across the room. Jack fell short of hitting the opposite wall and somehow managed to land on his feet.

The commotion had woken up Sheila who was now sitting up in her bed screaming, for her human eyes only picked up glimpses of shadows moving around the dark room.

Michael was struggling to maintain control over his inner beast, fighting his instinctive urge to transform. Over the past ten centuries, he had learned to master the process and was now able to morph in a few seconds, but it would still offer a window of opportunity to his opponent, a chance Michael was not willing to take. The presence of a distressed Sheila made his internal struggle more difficult than it should have been. He had to fight harder than ever to maintain his anger in check instead of letting it spill over him.

The wolf was on the other side of the bed, his mouth opened in a growl displaying sharp, inch-long fangs. Jack knew he was outmatched and would not be able to defeat the bear one on one, but that did not necessarily mean he could not accomplish his mission. His main target was sitting defenseless on the bed, a mere six feet away from him—a distance he could close in a single pounce. It would take only a second to tear her throat apart and let her bleed to death.

The stench of her fear was overwhelming and appealed to his most basic instincts. Wolves had fast reflexes, faster than bears; if he were lucky he might even be able to fulfill his mission and escape before the bear could catch him... At any rate, Jack could not stomach the idea of disappointing the Alpha one more time. His decision was made: failure was not an option.

The werewolf pounced on the bed and in a second his jaws were closing on what should have been Sheila's throat but was nothing but air. Michael, guessing the wolf's intention, had grabbed the woman's hand and jerked her out of harm's way. In an instant, he was on the wolf. Grabbing the beast by the head in one hand and by the neck in the other, he beheaded it in a single powerful tug.

Sheila was still screaming hysterically when Michael flipped on the light switch to cast a painfully bright light on the morbid scene, but to his amazement, the scene was not at all what he had expected. Instead of a dead werewolf, the beheaded corpse of a dead man was lying on the bed. Werewolves never turned back into their human forms after their death under normal circumstances, and this had definitely been a werewolf. Michael had caught his scent while crossing the living room—an odd fact in itself since he should have smelled the beast as soon as he had stepped inside the house. Even stranger, in death the man had not only regained his human form, he had also totally lost his wolf scent, a scent Michael had recognized from the crime scene at Chief Deputy Sullivan's.

Michael stared at the corpse for an instant, puzzled, before kneeling beside Sheila. It took what seemed to him an eternity but was, in reality, only mere seconds for Sheila to finally recognize him and stop screaming.

"Are you OK?" he asked, but she did not answer. Taking her silence as a yes, he walked to the Chinese broadsword hanging on the wall above the bed, detached it from its anchor and started hacking at the wolf neck before dropping the sword on the bed. The beheading would be a lot easier to explain if it looked like a sword had been used in the process.

Sheila was staring at him still in shock, not comprehending the purpose of his action and wondering, not for the first time, if she was dealing with a dangerous psychopath, when she heard running footsteps approaching.

Accustomed to the procedure by now, Michael lifted his hands high in the air before the cops even entered the room. Sheila's screams had not gone unnoticed by the usually quiet neighborhood, who had called in the cavalry.

Chapter 81

Sitting in a recliner, the Alpha was watching the morning news on TV. He was in a foul mood. Jack had failed him for the last time during the night, and the pack leader felt sick to his stomach at the idea that one of his wolves was gone for good, murdered by a thing which should have been extinct for hundreds of years.

He had received the call around 3 a.m. and had been unable to go back to sleep. He had spent a couple of restless hours tossing around on his bed before finally getting up. After a long walk, he had returned to the comfort of the living room where he had turned on the TV to find out how much the media already knew.

He had sent Jack after Sheila Wang in the hope of silencing the most dangerous journalist out there—the one who knew the most about what was going on, which, although very little, was already far too much for his comfort. Now Jack was dead, the bitch was still alive, and the media circus was going to jump on the story like ants on an abandoned picnic basket. The irony of the situation was not lost on him.

After flipping one more time through the various local and national news networks without hearing the night's events mentioned once, he was about to turn off the television and go fetch the morning papers when a headline caught his attention: *Chief Deputy Sullivan's replacement announced.* He immediately increased the volume and listened attentively to the anchorwoman announcing the nomination of Paul Garber at the post of chief deputy of the Harris County sheriff's department.

The Alpha grabbed the remote control and sent it flying towards the wall above the TV. Missing the screen by mere inches, the remote exploded in pieces on impact, leaving a very noticeable scar on the drywall. He then got up and with his bare fist punched another crater next to the one left by the remote.

The Alpha took a deep breath, pulled his fist out of the beat-up wall, walked to his cell phone, and hit speed dial number four.

"Hello," answered Major James Fanning after only two rings.

"What happened?" asked the Alpha angrily. "Who the fuck is this Paul Garber?"

"He was brought in from the Fort Bend sheriff's department. He was a major there," answered Fanning in a tentative voice.

"You were to get the job, James, not this Garber bastard! What happened?" asked the Alpha, still boiling.

"Politics happened, what do you think?" replied Fanning defensively. "It's not as if anyone asked for my permission before giving the post to another guy…"

"How long have you known?"

"I heard last night. I was going to call you this morning. You just beat me to it," replied Fanning in an ill-assured voice.

"We'll talk about this later," added the Alpha, before hanging up.

Chapter 82

Andrei was standing in the middle of Ivanov's home office, looking as sheepish as a six-year-old caught stealing candy from the pantry. Across the desk, a red-faced Ivanov was fuming. His bodyguard, Stanislas, stood at the door wearing his usual poker face. Igor Petrovich, Ivanov's second, was sitting in a comfortable-looking armchair at the right of Andrei and was currently directing the questioning.

"Humor me one more time, Andrei, if you will. How come you didn't go and help Vadim when you saw Biörn walking into the house?" asked Petrovich in a disgusted tone.

"I called his cell to warn him, but he didn't pick up, or get out of there…" replied the henchman uneasily.

"Maybe you waited a bit too long before calling…"

Andrei was fidgeting nervously with his hands, wishing he were anywhere but here. He was going to answer that he had called as soon as he had seen Biörn come out of his car when one of the disposable cell phones on Ivanov's desk started ringing. The mobster checked the caller ID before answering.

"Did you learn more about our problem?" asked Ivanov impatiently.

No one else in the room could hear the man on the other end of the line, but he must have answered in the affirmative for Ivanov started listening intently to what he had to say, occasionally answering with a monosyllable.

"I see," said Ivanov after a few minutes. "Thank you for calling and don't hesitate to call back if anything else comes up."

He replaced the phone on the desk. One could tell by the throbbing vein on his forehead that the call had not appeased him in any way. Petrovich was staring inquisitively at his boss while Andrei looked like he was trying to blend in with the carpet. They all stood there in silence for a while before Ivanov finally spoke. "Vadim did not react to Andrei's warning call because he was already dead by the time Biörn walked into the house."

"Do you mean to say that the bitch killed him?" asked Petrovich dubiously.

"No. According to one of my cops on payroll, another man was in the house. That's who killed Vadim."

"Was he a cop? Was he there to protect Wang?" asked Petrovich, trying to understand.

"No. He was apparently there to kill the journalist, and I have good reasons to believe he was one of Clemens' men," answered the boss, trying to keep his rage in check.

Vadim's killer had been decapitated by Biörn, and this detail had immediately raised an alarm in Ivanov's mind. Why would anyone chop someone's head off when there were a thousand easier ways to kill a man? But the answer became obvious if the killer had not been a man but a werewolf...

"How do you know that was one of Clemens' men?" asked Petrovich disbelievingly. "Why would he be after Vadim?"

"Never mind how I know," replied Ivanov impatiently. "It is time for us to find out what Clemens is up to. Andrei, go back to watch Clemens' house and let me know everything that happens there. Igor, hit every informant we have. I want to know about any recent unusual activity, and I'm not only talking about drugs, I mean prostitution, gambling, weapons, the whole nine yards. I want to know if there is a new gang in town trying to play in our field, and I want the information yesterday!"

Chapter 83

Michael was strolling along the bayou in downtown Houston. The bayou shores had been converted into a nature walk, which, if one managed to tune out the surrounding clamor of the city, offered a restful if not peaceful saunter along the water.

Michael's train of thought kept going from Ivanov, to Clemens, to Sheila, without ever following thoroughly a single line of thought. His incapacity to stop the violence left him feeling helpless: a disgusting sensation. In spite of all his strength and power he was unable to protect the people he cared for. He had arrived barely on time to save Sheila, and it had been nothing but sheer luck. What would have happened if he had arrived a couple minutes later, or if he hadn't turned on the TV and learned about her article? He did not want to think about this possibility but could not help it.

Sheila was now at her house under the guard of two Houston PD babysitters, but the cops could not protect her forever, and Michael seriously doubted their capacity to deter a werewolf attack. He was the only one who could stop the violence, but first he needed to understand the situation and motivations behind it.

Lewis and Salazar had shown up at Sheila's twenty minutes after the first cop car and had taken charge of the situation. Michael had then woken up David Starks with the news before returning to Sheila's side.

His motivation for staying close to the journalist during the cops questioning was not purely sympathetic; he also wanted to make sure the shaken-up young woman did not accidentally reveal embarrassing information.

He pulled out a folded sheet of paper from his right back pocket and unfolded it carefully to avoid ripping the already abused document. It was his fact list. He had spent countless hours staring at the list over the past week and had added relevant pieces of information to the document as they became available to him. The list currently counted ten items:

1) Deputy Chief Sullivan and his two Rottweilers were killed at home by Wolf-A, who escaped through a window. Window broken from the inside indicates escape point and not entry way.

2) Two guns were found on the floor in Sullivan's living room, but only one set of paw prints.

3) Steve and Marge Harrington were killed in their home by Wolf-B, who too escaped through the window. Same observation as above for the window.

4) David Starks attacked at home by Wolf-C, who was shot repeatedly by the detective but managed to escape...

5) There is an active wolf pack in Houston whose association with the mob is likely.

6) I was attacked by the mob shortly after visiting Peter Clemens, the Alpha, at his house in the forest. Possibly the pack headquarters.

7) At least one wolf has infiltrated the local police, possibly more.

8) Sheila was attacked by Ivanov's henchmen after writing an article hinting at a connection between the mob and the wolf attacks.

9) Clemens keeps a file with my name on it in his desk.

10) Clemens sent his wolves to try and kill me.

He pulled out a pen from his shirt pocket and, using his knee as a table, added a line at the bottom of the list:

11) Wolf-A was killed by me while trying to kill Sheila. He had previously assassinated a known associate of Ivanov, presumably sent to kill Sheila as well. Strangely, Wolf-A morphed back into his human form after his death and the wolf scent had completely disappeared from the body.

In spite of the strongly suspected business association between Clemens and Ivanov, the facts were pointing against them working together in this specific instance. Why would they both send a hitman to kill Sheila if they had agreed on the hit in the first place? It simply didn't make any sense. The fact that Ivanov's assassin had been killed by Clemens' wolf was a clear indication that the two organizations weren't as close as he and David had previously suspected.

Ivanov's motivations for silencing the journalist were clear. His name had been mentioned multiple times in Sheila's latest piece and since she had ignored the mobster's not too subtle previous warning, he had decided to deal once and for all with the problem.

Clemens' motivations, on the other hand, were less obvious. The wolves' attack had barely been mentioned in Sheila's latest article, and there was a good chance Clemens did not even know Sheila had been in Michael's bedroom when his wolf had shown up to kill him. So why did he want her dead if, as far as he was concerned, she knew nothing about him? Unless Wolf-A was not one of Clemens'... but that possibility sent his head spinning. The pieces of the puzzle definitely did not fit together.

Chapter 84

Aside from his occasional customers, the Chemist never had any visitors. He lived in quasi-isolation, only getting out to stock up on essentials—toilet paper, soap or bourbon—when his supplies were running low. He hardly ever talked to anyone, and the Chinese food delivery guy was the closest thing he had to a friend. As a result, he benefited from one of the lowest phone bills in the country, only calling to order food or, more rarely, to take commands from his various employers. So, when the phone rang, the Chemist knew exactly who was calling him. He had been expecting the call all day and for once was glad it finally came. He had been receiving the same call daily for the past two weeks, but this time was different: this time he had what the other man had been asking for so persistently.

"Hello?"

"I hope for your sake you have some good news for me, Victor," answered the Alpha's voice on the other end of the line. "My patience is running extremely thin."

"I do. I just sealed the last drum, sir," answered the Chemist in an ill-assured and slightly quivering voice.

"I will send my man to pick up the drums tomorrow," replied the Alpha in a business-like tone. "How many are there?"

"There are eleven five-gallon drums, sir,"

"Good," the Alpha answered in a neutral tone. He was about to hang up when the Chemist, who had finally gathered his courage, added, "Please make sure your man brings my money with him."

The Alpha did not bother answering and simply hung up.

The Chemist was shaking slightly and his pulse was racing. He hated doing business with this particular customer, but the money was too good to pass up. He also knew he wasn't dealing with the type of man who would take no for an answer. Since he was forced to do the work, he might as well get paid for it...

Victor settled back down in front of his TV program wondering what these people were going to do with his product. In its current state and in such an amount, it could kill off an entire city block. For the first time, Victor considered the possibility that these men belonged to a terrorist organization... but he quickly dismissed the thought. His previous shipments had been delivered in injectable vials—hardly a convenient way to poison a large group. What the hell were they doing with the stuff?

Chapter 85

The investigation was not progressing at the pace Detective Samantha Lewis would have liked. As a matter of fact, it was not progressing at all, but this was about to change. For the first time since the beginning of their investigation, Lewis and Salazar had finally caught a break.

The DNA analysis of a blood sample taken from the body of the man Michael Biörn had executed at Sheila Wang's over the weekend had just come back from the lab. According to the report, the same DNA had been found in the mouth of one of Chief Deputy Sullivan's Rottweilers.

Samantha Lewis was still poring over the report when Salazar entered the office carrying a steaming cup of coffee in one hand and a raspberry cheese Danish in the other.

"Have you already seen this?" asked Lewis, pointing at the report, but Salazar's mouth was now filled with Danish and he simply nodded.

"And what do you think of it?"

Salazar chewed a few more seconds before answering, "What is there to think? We know the guy who, most likely, brought the wolf that killed Sullivan, and also tried to do the journalist in. The only certain conclusion I can draw from this is the man was a killer… everything else is conjectural." He sounded slightly annoyed, but Lewis knew his animosity wasn't directed towards her; he was simply as frustrated with the case as she was.

"Why do you think he was after Sheila Wang?" asked Lewis.

"Not the faintest idea. Ask me about Vadim, and I'll tell you he was sent by Ivanov to get rid of an irritating journalist who should have kept her nose out of the mob's business. But about that guy… it beats me!"

"Same here," replied Lewis. "And why did he kill Vadim? If they were both sent to kill the journalist, why would they kill each other?"

Salazar pondered the question an instant, taking advantage of this opportunity to finish up his pastry. "I suppose they could have stumbled upon each other, got scared and started fighting…"

"There was no sign of struggle, but that doesn't mean much… The fight was probably short-lived." Lewis got up to go fetch herself a cup of coffee.

She came back a minute later, sipping on a mug of what looked like slightly off-white liquid. Samantha Lewis did not drink her coffee with milk, she drank her milk with a hint of coffee.

"At least we know the guy's identity now: Jack Moore, according to his driver's license. That's a lead…" she said, more cheerfully than she really felt as she sat back behind her desk.

"Hasn't done us much good so far... We know he's a mechanic and has no known affiliation with organized crime. Aside from a couple parking tickets, his file was more virgin than my fifteen-year-old daughter."

"Aren't you always the cheerleader? At least that gives us somewhere to start. We can go to the garage he used to work at and ask questions. It beats staying here drinking coffee and eating doughnuts!" replied Lewis scornfully.

"It was a Danish, not a doughnut!"

"Whatever!"

They sat in silence for a few minutes, each doing their own thing before Lewis said, "It sure is strange to find Biörn around every fresh body…"

"It's more than strange, but until we can link him to any wrong doing, there is not much we can do about it." Salazar sounded pensive. "But since so far he's only been taking the garbage out, and in apparent self-defense moreover, I can't really say I'm eager to put him behind bars."

Chapter 86

"You don't understand, Ma'am. We have our orders. We are to stay inside the house at all times," said the officer in a confused voice. His partner was looking at him uneasily, neither one of them comprehending why Sheila wanted them out of the house when the sole reason for their presence in the first place was to assure her protection. Only three days ago, the woman had been the victim of a double assassination attempt and now she wanted to send the cops assigned to her protection packing.

The officer suspected that her sudden decision was driven by the recent arrival of Michael Biörn, but the man didn't even carry a gun. What was he going to do if the mob sent more assassins after Sheila? Chop them to pieces with his sword? He'd been lucky once, but that wouldn't happen again, especially not if they sent a whole squad after her the next time around.

"I understand your orders, and I most definitely appreciate you watching over me these past few days. But I can't live like this, with police officers babysitting me day in and day out," said Sheila in a conciliatory tone. "Tell your commanding officer that I kicked you out. The law forbids you to stay inside my house against my will without a warrant, and since you don't have one… you have to go."

"But Ma'am—"started the second officer, as Sheila walked to the door, unlocked it, and held it wide open for the officers to take their leave. Reluctantly, the two cops complied and left the house.

Sheila returned to the living room where Michael was waiting, sitting in a black leather armchair. She walked to the loveseat located at a ninety-degree angle from his seat and settled on the side closest to him. Her demeanor and determination reminded Michael of a Potawatomi woman he had known while fighting alongside the natives during the Northwest Indian War. The same petite body, the same feistiness and obstinacy... She had survived the war against the United States only to be killed by a vampire three months after the conflict had ended in 1795. Alcoholism and smallpox weren't the only gifts the Europeans had brought with them to America. Vampires had also been part of the package.

"Are you sure this was a good idea?" Michael motioned with his head towards the door.

"No, but I couldn't take it anymore. In addition, I feel much safer with you around than with those two gentlemen. We both know they couldn't do much against those who want to kill me..." she added in a conspiratorial tone.

"They could have done something against the mob. You apparently made a lot of enemies these past few days."

"True, but unlike them, you can protect me from both."

Michael considered her last statement for a moment before answering, "I might make a more efficient bodyguard than those cops out there, but if it weren't for me, you probably wouldn't *need* a bodyguard..."

He was also thinking that the cops were soon going to arrest him with or without evidence if the bodies kept piling up around him. His providential arrival at Sheila's the night of the assassination attempt had been nothing short of a miracle. After hearing about her new article on the news, he had rushed to her house and had made it just in time. He had told Lewis and Salazar so, but although for once he had been telling the truth, the detectives hadn't seemed to be buying it. Cops did not believe in miracles.

"The mob attacked me in the park long before I ever came to see you and accidentally witnessed your dirty little secret, Michael. So your point isn't really valid. Unless, of course, you mean to tell me you are the one behind the werewolf attacks?" she retorted.

In spite of the woman's aggravating way of contradicting every point he made, Michael did not get upset by her. There was something about the way the corner of her mouth pointed slightly upward after she made a point that prevented him from getting irritated.

"At any rate, I don't live here, Sheila. No matter how long I stay with you, I will have to go back to my motel sooner or later, and then you'll be without any protection at all," he replied in a slightly lecturing voice.

"About that," she said, trying not to smile, "I was thinking maybe you could move in with me for the time being. I have a spare bedroom and it would be cheaper for you than staying in those sleazy motels. That way you'd save money while protecting me... two birds with one stone, as they say."

Before Michael could object, she jumped out of her seat and started walking towards the kitchen. "I'll prepare some tea. No milk, no sugar, and twelve spoons of honey, right?" she asked without looking at him.

Chapter 87

Katia Olveda was in the elevator of the government building that harbored the DA's office when her phone chimed, indicating the arrival of a new text message. She was still absorbed by her reading as she stepped out of the elevator onto a virtually deserted office floor. *Interesting*, she thought, replacing the phone in her purse before realizing the unusual vacancy of the office. She wondered for an instant why the place was practically empty before noticing voices coming from the break room.

She walked towards the room and squeezed through the door past a couple of administrative assistants absorbed in an animated discussion. The two women fell silent and Katia felt their stares burning a hole in the back of her head. *Strange*, she thought, not turning around to confirm her impression.

The break room contained a TV and the majority of the thirty plus people crammed into the room was absorbed by the special news report airing on television. The others just stared at Katia, which started to irritate her mildly.

It only took a few seconds for her to realize what the news was about: John Macfly had been gunned down an hour earlier on his way to work. A motorcycle had stopped next to his car, and the driver had shot him twice in the head before fleeing the scene. The killer had been wearing a dark visor and no identification had been possible.

John Macfly had been the Harris County's most senior Assistant District Attorney and had been well positioned to win the upcoming election to replace the soon to be retired DA.

Katia suddenly understood why the whole room seemed to be looking at her. With Macfly out of the picture, she had just become the most logical and likely candidate for the DA's position.

She stormed out of the room, ignoring the insistent and intent looks of her coworkers, and went to lock herself up in her own office. She needed time to think. She was pretty sure she knew who was behind the hit, but she had not been warned about it. You'd think he would have bothered telling her... There wasn't much she could do about it now. Complaining was useless and would not help her case anyway. The prospect of becoming the city's new DA wasn't too displeasing either; she just wished he had warned her about his intention, that's all.

After a few minutes thinking things over, she grabbed her cell phone and dialed Clemens' number. Clemens sounded busy and the call only lasted a minute or two. Katia delivered the contents of the text message she had received a few minutes earlier that had disclosed Michael Biörn's current location, before she was quickly dismissed by the Houston pack Alpha.

At no point during the conversation was Macfly's death mentioned by either party.

Chapter 88

After getting off the phone with Katia Olveda, Peter Clemens wasted no time in rallying his troops. He sent a mass text message summoning his wolves, and with the exception of two of them who were out of town, the whole Houston pack had made it to his house by the time the clock struck noon.

It had been almost a week since a small pack delegation had first fought Biörn. The confrontation had proven fatal for six of his wolves, and Clemens had since spent every waking hour thinking about Michael Biörn's imminent death.

While he had been right regarding the true nature of their opponent, Peter had underestimated Biörn's power, and the pack had paid dearly for this mistake. Not a single one of his wolves had even hinted at the Alpha's responsibility in the death of their brothers, but it did not matter to Peter Clemens who felt guilty nonetheless. Killing Michael Biörn would not erase the guilt from Clemens' conscience, but hanging the werebear's head as a trophy in the living room would go a long way towards easing the pain.

Peter Clemens had to raise his voice in order to carry above the loud grumbling that prevailed inside the second floor assembly room where the pack had gathered.

"You all know why we are here," started the Alpha in a commanding voice. "I was informed this morning of the whereabouts of our hereditary enemy. Our kind fought his kin for millennia until we finally prevailed a few centuries ago. We believed we had exterminated the bears, but we were obviously wrong… At least one of them has survived."

The grumbling started growing louder again as the wolves debated between themselves whether Biörn was the sole survivor of his species or just one of many. When Clemens' booming voice started once again, they all fell silent.

"This bastard killed six of our brothers, and for this we will make sure he suffers before he dies. But let us not repeat the mistakes of our fallen comrades. Let us not underestimate our enemy. Not one of us would have a chance against him alone, not even me. We need to work as a pack, bring him down as a pack, and slowly kill him as a pack!"

Clemens paused an instant to let his words seep into his wolves' minds.

"Where is he?" asked a wolf in the back of the room.

"He has spent the morning at the journalist's house, and according to my source, he was still there fifteen minutes ago. We will take this opportunity to kill two birds with one stone. Sheila Wang has become a problem and needs to be silenced once and for all."

"Won't he be expecting us?" asked another wolf.

"It's unlikely," replied Clemens. "But Wang lives in a residential area and we cannot go through the door in our wolf form. We'll have to shift inside the house, and at this point we will be vulnerable. This is why we need to storm the house as a group."

The particulars of the offensive were explained and re-explained in details to the pack until everyone understood his role. It was one o'clock when they finally left Clemens' property in a nine-car convoy.

Chapter 89

"Would you like some wine?" asked Sheila as Michael walked back from answering the door carrying two extra-large Hawaiian pizzas.

"No, thank you. I'd better not drink if I want to keep my ideas sharp." He put down the two pizza boxes on the kitchen table. "I'm a lightweight when it comes to alcohol."

Sheila gave him a dubious smile before pouring herself a glass of Pinot Grigio.

"The cops are gone by the way," said Michael. "They probably got tired of watching your front door without any way to be sure you were still alive inside."

Sheila pulled a slice of pizza from the top box and placed it on the plate in front of her. "Good riddance," she answered, before sinking her teeth into the pizza. "As I told you this morning, you are much better company."

Michael noticed the compliment, but he chose to ignore it. He had the feeling Sheila might be flirting with him, but he was so out of practice in that department that he couldn't tell for sure whether it truly was the case.

They had spent the whole morning talking, about the case mostly, but not exclusively. The journalist had asked a multitude of questions regarding what she referred to as his gift. She had even tried prying into his personal past, but Michael had shut like an oyster and had remained silent a long while after she had asked if he had ever been married. His silence had been more eloquent than any words could have been. Sheila had rapidly changed the subject, but not rapidly enough. She had managed to make him think about Isibel once again, and this was a part of his past Michael definitely did not want to think about. He had finally come out of his prolonged silence after a couple minutes, and she had carefully avoided mentioning anything remotely related to marriage from that point forward.

"I've been meaning to ask you," said Sheila, opening the second pizza box—Michael had made quick work of the first one—"why didn't you change into your bear form when the wannabe assassin turned into a werewolf the other night?"

"Time was one factor," answered Michael. "It takes me a few seconds to morph and I wasn't sure how long I had before he killed you." A fugitive smile of appreciation passed over Sheila's face, but Michael was too oblivious to notice it. "In addition, a single wolf is not typically a big threat to me. A pack is a different story, but a lone wolf doesn't have the mass or the strength to go one on one against me."

Sheila was about to ask him how much stronger than a wolf he really was when Michael's cell phone started ringing. He looked at the caller ID, wondering if David Starks was trying to reach him, but he was shocked to see Ezekiel's name on the tiny screen.

For one thing, Michael was certain he had never entered Ez' number in the cell phone David had given him, but that was beside the point; these sorts of tricks were no more difficult to Ez than uprooting a sapling was to him.

"Hello, this is Michael," he finally answered.

"Way to state the obvious, my friend," replied the wizard's sarcastic voice. "What are you guys up to?"

"Having lunch," replied Michael without asking how Ez knew he had company. "Do you care to join us?"

"Naah, I hate pineapples on pizza. It's just wrong! I was just calling to make sure you had plenty to share because I heard the whole Houston pack was coming to join you for lunch."

The statement caught Michael off guard and it took him a second to grasp the implications of the tip.

"I assume the information is reliable?" he asked finally.

"I wouldn't bother calling otherwise."

"How long do we have?"

"They should reach your current location in the next forty-five minutes or so, but I wouldn't stick around to verify the accuracy of my prediction if I were you."

"Thank you for the warning, Ez, I owe you one."

"You owe me a lot more than that, but who's counting?" retorted Ez.

Michael replaced the cell phone inside his pocket and turned to Sheila. "Pack a bag with a toothbrush and clothes for a few days. Be quick about it, we need to be out of here in five minutes."

Chapter 90

The front and back door of the house were kicked open within a fraction of second of each other. The Houston pack stormed Sheila's house in a perfectly synchronized offensive. Once inside, the wolves immediately morphed before spreading out like a tidal wave through every single room of the one-story habitation, but to no avail… Biörn and the girl were gone.

A small group was sent to check out the attic, but besides a couple of dusty boxes not nearly large enough to hide the bulk of the 300-pound giant, the place was empty.

"It looks like they are gone," said Karl Wilson, the pack second in command, in what seemed like a painfully obvious assertion. Clemens cast him a dark glance but did not say anything. Instead, he grabbed his phone and dialed Katia Olveda's number.

The assistant DA answered on the fourth ring. "Hallo? This is Katia."

"Biörn is gone," said the Alpha in a voice shaking with anger. "Do you know his current location?"

"I don't," replied Katia in a cool voice. "He was at the journalist's all morning, but it's hard for me to enquire again about his whereabouts without raising suspicions…"

"I trust your lying skills can overcome this obstacle, Katia. Get me the information I need." Clemens spoke threateningly.

"I'll see what I can do. I'll call you back in a few minutes."

The pack left the house as quickly as they had come in, and they were already exiting the subdivision when Katia called Clemens back.

"I tried obtaining his location for you, but no one seems to know where he is," she said slightly apologetically. This was not a completely true statement, however.

Chapter 91

Dimitri Ivanov walked out of the racquetball court a few steps ahead of his defeated opponent to find Igor Petrovich waiting for him beside the always silent but highly deadly Stanislas Erzgova.

The mob boss grabbed the towel his lieutenant was holding out for him and started mopping his sweat-covered forehead and neck. Ivanov was an excellent racquetball player, but the fact that few of his opponents were stupid enough to try and actually beat him did not hurt his winning record.

"We concluded our investigations," announced Petrovich without preamble.

"And what did you find?" enquired Ivanov, replacing the racquet into his gym bag.

"Not much, boss. Everything seems pretty normal. No new girls on the street, no new bookmakers, no drugs we can't account for. We even looked into the gun market, and only found the usual suspects."

The three men started walking towards the locker room, which, like the rest of the gym, was deserted. Ivanov owned this particular club, and the place only opened when the mob boss did not feel like using the facility. As a result, the place was not doing particularly well financially, but this was the least of Ivanov's concerns. The fitness business was not where he made his money.

"If Clemens is selling something other than his services, it's not in the greater Houston area, or at least it's not illegal," concluded Petrovich.

Stanislas went to check the showers for potential threats. Upon his approval, a naked Ivanov stepped into the closest shower stall and drew the curtain.

"There is still something fishy going on," said Ivanov, stepping out of the shower a few minutes later with wet hair and a towel wrapped around his midsection. "Have we looked to see if they are selling products outside Houston?"

"This isn't easy to check, but as far as we could tell, they aren't. The only thing remotely unusual we could find concerned Victor Grey."

"The Chemist?" asked Ivanov surprised.

"Yes, the Chemist."

"What the fuck did he do? I thought the little shit was dead or retired or something…"

"He hasn't done anything as far as we can tell, but his finances are a bit healthier than they should be for a retiree, if you know what I mean."

Ivanov was dressed and ready to go by now. He closed his gym bag and handed it to his lieutenant who accepted the burden without trying to pass it onto Stanislas. He had tried doing that once before, but Ivanov had chewed his ass to pieces. Stanislas was a bodyguard and as such, couldn't afford to have his hands busy carrying bags when he could be required to draw his gun at any time.

"I think it's important we find out exactly what new source of income our old friend found to supplement his retirement fund," said Ivanov as they exited the gym.

Chapter 92

Michael placed Sheila's suitcase next to his own in the trunk of the rented Chevrolet and walked back to the house where David and Sheila were amiably chatting around the kitchen table.

After Ez' warning, Sheila and Michael had spent a good part of the day strolling around a local State Park, trying to figure out what to do and, more particularly, where to go next. Troubles seemed to follow the two of them no matter where they were, and they were starting to run out of places to hide. After considering their options, they had decided to accept the hospitality David had graciously offered and had headed for the detective's beach house where they had spent the night.

Although David had had his problems with the wolves as well, his troubles hadn't followed him to his beachfront property. It was highly unlikely the pack had not figured out by now that David owned a house on the beach, but since no other attempts had been made against the detective's life in the past month, it seemed Clemens or whoever was behind the attacks had lost interest.

Their interest in Michael, however, was at an all-time high. How quickly the pack had found out Michael was at Sheila's was particularly worrisome. Michael hadn't told anyone he was going there, not even Olivia Harrington or David Starks. He supposed the pack could have been watching Sheila's house, but he hadn't noticed any wolves around the place and he could typically smell them from a mile away.

"Would you like more tea?" asked David as Michael entered the kitchen.

"No, we'd better get going if we don't want to miss our flight."

Sheila finished her last sip of coffee, got up and extended her hand towards David. "If I'd been told a month ago that I would spend the night at your house, Detective, I would have never believed it," she said with a smirk, shaking his hand. "Thank you very much for your hospitality."

"The pleasure was mine," replied David, smiling. He turned to Michael. "I will keep you posted on anything new happening here, just make sure you don't trash your cell phone as soon as you get back to your wildlife paradise. I need a way to contact you in case of emergency."

"I won't. And try to keep an eye out for Steve's kid, Olivia. I'm afraid she's asking for trouble."

"Will do, don't worry."

"OK, time to go. Thanks again for last night," said Michael.

They walked out to the car and Michael squeezed himself behind the wheel of the Malibu.

"Are you sure you don't want me to drive?" asked Sheila. "You look like a freemason in a tiny car parade."

Michael ignored the mocking tone. "I'm sure."

Fifteen minutes later, they had reached I-45 and were on their way to the airport. Michael had been in Houston for over a month and had hardly made any progress toward breaking the case, but he didn't really need to be in the city to stay on the case anyway. He simply needed to start thinking harder; he needed to understand the hidden part of the problem. For he was more and more convinced he was missing an essential element, the key to decipher the apparently senseless series of events that had occurred in the past few weeks. Any new pieces of information could be fed to him by David Starks, and there would always be time to go back and deal with Steve's murderer once the bastard had been identified with certainty.

After weighing their options, they had decided to go to Michael's house in Yellowstone until the dust settled down a bit. This option presented numerous advantages. For one thing, a pack of werewolves would not go unnoticed in the park. If he had to fight the entire Houston pack, Michael preferred the confrontation took place on his own turf, where he would have the advantage of knowing the terrain. He was also sick and tired of sleeping in those lousy motel beds and was looking forward to sleeping in his own bed for a while. It had been easy to convince Sheila to come with him; her life was clearly being threatened in Houston, and she would be a lot safer in the middle of Yellowstone National Park where Michael's cabin was located.

There was only one problem with the plan: his cabin only had one bed.

Chapter 93

It was ten past four, which meant the man was already ten minutes late. Olivia was playing with her cell phone. It was a way to kill time as much as to avoid making eye contact with the other patrons of the distinguished diner where she was sitting waiting for the guy. The diner was not in the best part of town, and the lustful glances in the eyes of some of the surrounding customers did not make her feel any more comfortable. She had never thought of herself as particularly attractive, but it probably didn't matter for men like these.

A twenty-something-year-old male, dressed like a professional rapper, stepped into the diner and, after surveying its occupants, walked over to her table. "Olivia?"

She nodded and he sat on the other side of her booth. Gang tattoos were visible on the man's forearms and neck. Not exactly the type of individual Olivia typically gravitated around.

"Do you have the money?" he asked in a low raspy voice. She nodded and reached inside her purse.

"Pass it under the table," he added quickly in the same hoarse voice. She complied with his request and handed him an envelope containing a thousand dollars in fifties. The man counted the money discreetly and placed the envelope in the inside pocket of his jacket before pulling out what looked like a dirty rag. He passed her the package under the table in a cautiously casual motion.

The object was heavier than she had anticipated. She carefully unwrapped it on the seat between her and the wall to discover a thirty-eight special.

"It's loaded," said the guy, "but if you need more ammo, it's extra."

"This is all I need," replied Olivia.

She had made up her mind a few days ago and the voicemail Michael Biörn had left on her phone had only reinforced her decision. Michael was on his way back home. He had given up on catching her parents' murderers. The man was not what she had thought him to be... he did not care about justice.

Since nobody cared besides her, the onus was on her to see that the man behind her parents' assassination paid for his crimes. She already knew where he lived. As a matter of fact, she was scheduled to clean his house the very next day... and now she had a gun. Peter Clemens' hours in this world were numbered.

Chapter 94

Upon landing in Bozeman, Montana, the two had picked up Michael's car from the airport's long-term parking lot and driven straight to a clothing store. With the average temperature for October in Yellowstone thirty degrees cooler than in Houston, Sheila had nothing in her hastily packed suitcase to protect her from the biting wind and forecasted snow.

Michael had first set foot in what would later become Yellowstone National Park in August 1805, three months after leaving the Lewis and Clark expedition and a full three years before John Colter visited the area. Michael had been skirmishing with a pack of werewolves in a part of the Indian Territory now known as Michigan when he had heard about a group of explorers getting ready to depart for the unclaimed land lying west of the Louisiana Purchase. Partially to protect his Potawatomi friends from being caught between him and the werewolves, and partially to answer the call of the wild, Michael had joined the Lewis and Clark expedition in St Charles, Missouri during the spring of 1804, and had remained with the group all the way to Montana.

Shortly after reaching Eastern Montana, Lewis had shot a grizzly bear dead without provocation, and Michael had decided to leave the expedition before his rage overpowered the control he held over his beast. He had wandered aimlessly in a southward direction for three months before finally reaching the yet non-existent borders of the future National Park.

Two hundred years later, finding food readily available inside the park was almost as tricky as it had been in 1805—especially from November to April when the park was mostly closed to tourists—so Michael and Sheila's second stop had been for groceries at a wholesale store. With the amount of food Michael engulfed, he tried to shop at wholesale stores as much as possible. Under normal circumstances, when his stocks were getting low—or even when they weren't—Michael would morph and go on a hunting trip inside the park: a luxury a human could not afford since hunting was strictly forbidden inside National Parks. A successful expedition could provide him with enough calories to go a week without eating, but with Sheila around, this option was out. He didn't think the journalist was quite ready to witness something like this.

They had finally made it to the cabin a couple hours after nightfall. Michael had graciously offered to sleep on the couch, but Sheila had rejected the offer. The couch looked barely big enough for her and she wasn't cruel enough to make him spend the night on it.

Michael had spent the next morning catching up with his boss, Bill Thomason, while Sheila had dusted and generally cleaned the cabin, which had been in dire need of the attention. For lunch, she had cooked a sixteen-egg omelet with two pounds of ham and a mountain of potatoes, which Michael had swallowed faster than she could put on lipstick.

Once lunch was over, he offered to take her on a walk in the forest surrounding the cabin and she accepted, glad for an opportunity to get out and discover the park's hidden beauties.

Sheila had visited Yellowstone with her parents when she was fourteen, but that had been twenty-four years ago, and she didn't remember a whole lot aside from Old Faithful and the view from the edge of the Grand Canyon of the Yellowstone River.

"Here, strap this on your belt," said Michael, handing her a canister the size of a large deodorant spray.

"What is it?"

"Bear spray. You have to carry it in case you stumble upon unfriendly grizzlies or, more rarely, an aggressive black bear."

She looked at him incredulously for an instant. "Are you telling me *you* need to carry this?"

"I don't… but it's part of the disguise. As long as I'm around you won't need it. There is nothing in this park that would dare come after me, even in my human form. But if you go on a walk alone, you should always carry it with you. There is no point surviving werewolf killers to finish up as a grizzly snack."

Sheila strongly agreed with the statement and promised herself she would never go explore the woods without Michael around. The journalist had no problem carrying investigations into the roughest part of the city, or talking to highly disreputable individuals, but she was outside her comfort zone in a wild-beast-infested forest.

The walk was particularly pleasant. The temperature had dropped to the low forties overnight, but her newly acquired sweater, gloves and jacket kept her quite comfortable. Michael was not even wearing a sweater on top of his hiking shirt, but this was not unusual for people living in this part of the country.

They hiked a three-hour loop around the cabin, which took them across meadows filled with elk and bison herds, small geysers, hot pools, two wolves on a stroll, and a black bear who took a look at Michael, turned around, and sprinted in the opposite direction.

By the time they made it back to the cabin, Sheila had wrapped her hand around Michael's. He had not encouraged the initiative, but he hadn't done anything to discourage it either. From their entwined fingers was rising a comforting warmth Michael hadn't felt in an eternity.

Chapter 95

When Olivia arrived at the house, the place was deserted with the exception of Isabella Clemens, who was in the living room reading a magazine with the television on. She got up at the maid's arrival and went to lock herself up in front of the computer in her husband's office, barely acknowledging Olivia's presence.

No worries, cunt, I hate you more than you hate me and you don't even know it, thought Olivia, putting down her cleaning accessories.

She felt a mixture of disappointment and relief when she observed that Peter Clemens did not appear to be home, but cleaning the house would take her a few hours and he was likely to come back before she left. At least she hoped so.

She grabbed a duster and got to work dusting the living room before moving to the dining room. She had dusted and tidied up the entire first floor and was working on cleaning the kitchen counters when Clemens walked in, accompanied by Axel Thompkins, the number four in the pack's chain of command.

The two men were in the midst of an animated discussion, which came to an abrupt stop when they noticed Olivia scrubbing the stove. Even though today was Thursday, they had clearly not expected the cleaning lady to be around. Olivia was too nervous to take pleasure in the two men's frustrated faces though.

The thirty-eight special was weighing heavily inside her pants pocket, but thanks to the baggy pants and loose blouse of the Houston Dirt Removers' uniform, the gun was invisible to anyone who wouldn't know where to look.

The two men disappeared up the stairs, and Olivia tried calming down her heartbeat by taking deep slow breaths. Although her father had been a cop all his life, she had never shot a gun before. She knew about things like the safety and the recoil from television, which was why she had bought a gun she could handle and not something like a forty-four caliber which would have ripped her arm out of its socket after firing the first round.

Her hands were shaking as she started tiptoeing her way up the stairs, a futile precaution given the wolves' sense of hearing, but Olivia was unaware of that point. The two men were staring at her from their respective armchairs when she entered the pack's meeting room. She had brought with her a bucket full of cleaning detergents and rags to justify her presence, and the men, visibly irritated by her arrival, resumed their discussion in low voices as she started slowly dusting her way towards them.

The room was sufficiently vast and furnished with enough seats to accommodate the whole pack, so it took Olivia a few minutes to close the thirty feet that separated her from her target. When she had done so, she stood five feet behind Clemens, dusting yet another coffee table. The two men had dropped the secretive talk and were chatting about football, not paying the least attention to her. She grasped the gun inside her pocket and slowly drew it out before flipping the safety to the off position. She then deliberately walked around the armchair Clemens occupied, while pointing the gun at him. She wanted to look him in the eyes while she pulled the trigger.

Axel Thompkins was the first to notice the weapon in her hand, but the Alpha immediately picked up on his wolf's change in attitude. Peter Clemens appeared more annoyed than afraid as she stood six feet from him, her weapon aimed at his chest. Large targets like the chest were harder to miss and Olivia could not afford to miss.

"What do we have here?" asked Clemens in a voice where Olivia thought she heard a hint of amusement. "Did my wife neglect to tip you last week?"

The other man was smiling, obviously enjoying the show. Neither one of them looked frightened or even nervous—unless they were particularly good actors.

"I am Olivia Harrington," said Olivia in a voice trembling with anger and fear. "You killed my parents and now you are going to pay for it."

Peter Clemens could not immediately place the name the woman had thrown at him, but as she drove three bullets through his lungs and heart, he remembered.

Chapter 96

Katia Olveda had been assigned the case of the assassination attempt against Michael. It wasn't the first time Detectives Lewis and Salazar had to work on a case with the Assistant DA, but that did not make the experience any less painful. For one thing, the two women's dislike for each other was so intense it was almost physically palpable. Samantha Lewis resented the way Katia walked around their office as if she owned the place almost as much as the fact the woman constantly looked like a model prepped for a photo shoot. Lewis had no respect for the type of women who spent this much time in front of a mirror every day. Katia, on her end, was quick to pick up on the other woman's antipathy and did everything she could to antagonize her in a subtly passive-aggressive fashion.

Ed Salazar was just an innocent bystander in the two women's cold war reenactment. Like most men, he was not insensible to Katia's charms, but he also felt loyalty towards Lewis, with whom he had worked day in and day out for the past eight years. As a result, when he and Lewis met with the assistant DA, he mostly kept silent, biding his time while the two women ran the show. Fortunately for him, this meeting was likely to be short.

"So you are telling me that you could not link any member of the failed assassination squad to organized crime?" asked Katia in a skillfully contemptuous voice.

"That's correct," answered Salazar before Lewis had a chance to voice a stinging reply. "We know a couple of them were associated with the Russian mob, but nothing we could prove in court."

"So I guess we don't have much of a case from that angle," said Katia. "What about a motive? Do we have any idea why the Russian mob would want Biörn dead?"

She already knew the answer to that question but she needed to find out how much the cops knew about this business.

"We think it has something to do with Harrington's murder, or the wolves' attacks in general," started Lewis. "But we don't know what exactly, and Biörn is not being very cooperative."

Katia rolled her eyes at the detective in a "How can one be so useless?" silent statement which sent Lewis' adrenaline pumping, while Salazar started wishing he were somewhere far away. Katia noticed the throbbing in the other woman's neck artery and silently savored her petty victory.

"Where can we find Biörn?" asked Katia casually. "Maybe we could interview him again together and try to find out what is really going on?"

Interviewing a suspect prior to indicting him was not the DA's office business and Salazar jumped in before Lewis could say so to Katia in a colorful fashion. "Michael Biörn has left town. He is back in Montana or Wyoming or wherever it is he lives."

Katia did not show any emotion at the information, but someone was going to be happy to know this.

"Well, I guess there really is not much for me to do in this matter," said Katia as she stood up from her chair and started walking towards the door. "Keep it up this way, Detectives, and I'll soon be out of a job."

"Now, that would be a pity!" Lewis managed to reply before the Assistant DA walked out of the office.

Chapter 97

As soon as the third bullet had left the gun's barrel, Olivia had turned her weapon away from Clemens and towards Axel Thompkins, only to find the man still comfortably sitting and staring at her with an annoyed look on his face. She had expected him to try and stop her, but he hadn't made a move to prevent her from shooting Clemens.

Olivia didn't have time to wonder about the man's reaction very long before something heavy slammed into her, throwing her to the floor. The gun flew out of her hand at the impact and landed on one of the coffee tables, shattering its glass top into a myriad of sharp pieces.

Olivia had hit the floor before realizing that what had just collided into her was an enormous wolf. The beast was now standing on her chest, effectively pinning her to the carpet while driving the air out of her lungs. She closed her eyes, knowing her time had come. The wolf went straight for her neck, a kill blow.

"Stop this, Bella! I need her alive."

The voice sounded to Olivia like Clemens', but it was impossible, the man was dead. She had killed him.

She could feel the beast's teeth sunk deep into her neck, but strangely enough the wolf did not seem in a hurry to finish her. Subconsciously, Olivia knew that with such a jaw the beast could easily crush her spine, but instead the wolf was just biting down on her throat without applying the pressure it doubtless could have.

Suddenly, Olivia started sweating heavily. Her temples were throbbing so intensely she thought her head was about to explode. An intense migraine the like of which she didn't know existed overtook her, but the pain did not stop at her head. Like a liquid flowing through her veins, the agony spread from her skull to her chest before reaching her stomach and finally her limbs. Not an inch of her body was spared from the excruciating pain.

"Look what you've done, Bella. We're not getting answers from her anytime soon," said Peter in a frustrated voice, while his wife, still in her wolf form, whimpered at his feet.

"We'll be lucky if she survives at all," said Thompkins, staring at Olivia's convulsing body. The woman had lost consciousness but her body remained continuously agitated by violent spasms.

"How did she find me?" asked Peter without expecting an answer. "What does she know about us?"

"Apparently not much if she thinks a few pop shots in the chest will bring you down," answered Axel Thompkins.

"Lock her up in the underground cache," ordered Clemens. "If she survives this, she'll know more about us than she ever wanted."

Chapter 98

Of the park's countless wonders, the Grand Canyon of the Yellowstone was Sheila's favorite destination thus far. They had only been in the park three days, but Michael had made a point of showing her a different one of Yellowstone's beauties each day. After a tour of the cabin's surroundings on the first afternoon, Sheila had discovered the upper geyser basin, starring Old Faithful, on the second day. She had never realized before that the park harbored over 75% of the planet's geysers, or that a geyser was only one of four possible thermal features one could find in the park, the others being fumaroles, mud pots, and hot springs.

And now, on an ice-cold but sunny Saturday, stuck between a multicolored mountain wall and a partially iced over river somewhere at the bottom of the canyon, she found herself wondering if she could spend her life in a place like this.

She had been a city girl all her life and had never felt the urge to venture into the wilderness. With Michael as a guide, however, she simply could not ignore the charms of nature's untainted beauty.

"When you come around a blind corner like this one," started Michael in the educational voice he adopted every time he told her something about the park, "you need to take it as wide and slowly as possible, just in case something is standing on the other side. Animals sometimes come here to drink and I have encountered mountain lions and grizzly bears more than once here in the canyon."

"Thank you for the advice, but I'm not planning on coming down here alone," replied Sheila with a smirk. Michael simply shrugged and kept walking.

"I like the way you look when you pout like this," said Sheila teasingly, but he ignored the bait.

"I bet that trick of yours comes in handy around here?" she said.

"What trick of mine?"

"You know... turning into a bear. You are probably the only living being in this park who doesn't have to worry about stumbling upon something meaner."

He shot her a sidelong glance but kept walking in silence. It took her a few seconds to realize her choice of words had maybe not been the most tactful.

"I didn't mean it in a negative way, I was thinking meaner in the sense more powerful... You know... intimidating."

Her embarrassment made him smile and she knew he wasn't upset at her. Over the past few days, she had grown increasingly fond of him, but besides holding hands now and then and a few kisses on the cheek, their relationship had not turned physical. The fact the man was essentially a bear had a way of tempering the excitement his muscles and stature would have ignited in her under normal circumstances, but this wasn't the only obstacle to overcome. Sheila wasn't getting the impression Michael wanted to take their relationship to the next level. He was pleasant enough around her, but he seemed more guarded than he should have been given the circumstances. Usually, shared adversity had a way of acting as a relationship catalyst and tended to bring people closer together in record time, but it didn't have this accelerating effect on Michael, and Sheila was starting to wonder why. She was confident he liked her—there were definite signs of this—so why was he holding back? Her sixth sense suggested that the wife he never talked about could be part of the explanation, but Sheila didn't want to bring her up. She had seen his reactions the few times the word "wife" had been mentioned, even in a subtly disguised manner, and she knew it tormented him deeply. What she didn't know was the reason for his torment.

"You've told me you were born a werebear, but can someone be turned into one?" she finally asked out of the blue.

"In theory… possibly. In practice, no! At least not anymore," he replied enigmatically.

"What do you mean by that? Why not anymore?"

"Because for someone human to be turned into a werebear—or any werebeing for that matter—they would need to be bitten by a werebear and survive the ordeal. You should think about the process as a microbial infection. The *microbes* are passed from the werebeing's saliva into the victim's bloodstream. After contamination, the victim's body turns into a battleground between the infectious entity and the victim's antibodies—"

"Does it hurt?" interrupted Sheila.

"The process is extremely painful, and the outcome uncertain. Sometimes the infection wins and the victim turns into a werebeing. But more often the antibodies win and kill the individual in the process."

"But why did you say it can no longer happen? Why can't people be turned into werebeings nowadays?" she asked inquisitively.

"I never said people couldn't be turned into werebeings anymore. Only werebears…"

"Why is that?"

"Because as far as I know I am the only one left alive, and when I have good enough reasons to bite someone, I make sure they don't survive the experience."

Chapter 99

For the second time in less than a week, Clemens had summoned the pack to his house. The first few had already started trickling in and were gathering in the assembly room on the second floor, but several of the wolves weren't scheduled to arrive until late afternoon.

The information Katia had delivered to Clemens was at the origin of the pack summoning, and the two of them had been behind closed doors in the Alpha's office for over an hour. Lately, Clemens had been feeling like a spectator in a show he was supposed to be running. Too many unforeseen events had occurred in the past month, and someone in his position could not afford to be caught by surprise. Michael Biörn was, of course, on top of his list of headaches, but unfortunately he was not his only concern. The journalist Sheila Wang, Ivanov, and now the cop's daughter were all issues that required to be dealt with, one way or another. In order to regain control of the situation, Clemens needed as much information as possible, and he counted on Katia to help fill in the gaps.

"You're sure the information is reliable?" asked Clemens for the third time, and for the third time the assistant DA assured him it was.

"Why didn't your boyfriend inform you of this?" he asked with a hint of suspicion.

"He didn't get the opportunity. I heard the information through Detective Salazar before I had a chance to talk to David. But David confirmed Salazar's info. Biörn and the journalist left Houston on Wednesday and are now staying at Biörn's cabin in the heart of Yellowstone National Park."

Clemens got up from behind his desk and walked to a cork board where a detailed topographic map of Yellowstone's Grand Canyon area was pinned up. A red thumbtack marked the location of Michael's cabin.

"And no one knows who tipped Biörn off about our arrival on Tuesday?" asked Clemens dubiously. "It can't be this difficult to find out! How many friends does the bastard have in Houston, for god's sake?"

Katia didn't have the answer to the riddle, and she decided to treat the query as rhetorical. Nothing she could say would have satisfied Clemens anyway.

"What do you know about Olivia Harrington?" asked the Alpha, temporarily changing the subject.

"I know she's the daughter of the late Lieutenant Steve Harrington, who was killed along with his wife at their domicile about a month ago by what seemed to be a wolf…"

"Could you please tell me something I *don't* know?" replied Clemens, irritated. "Like: what was the girl doing in my house two days ago and why did she try to kill me?"

The revelation brought a shocked expression on Katia's face.

"She did what?"

Clemens recounted how Olivia had shot him in the chest in an ill-advised attempt to kill him and apparently avenge her parents' death.

"What happened to her?"

"That's none of your business!" Clemens spoke in a voice that

precluded further enquiry. Surprisingly, Olivia had survived Isabella's
bite and would soon be a full-fledged werewolf in her own right, but this
was not something the assistant DA needed to know. The turning process was so traumatizing that it would take anywhere from a week to a
month before the woman would be able to answer any questions. In the
meantime, she would spend her days in a pain-induced daze, unable to
control the erratic morphing process. In her wolf form, she would go
through episodes of uncontrollable rage, but the underground cache in
which she had been locked up had been built to withstand anything the
rampaging beast could throw at it.

"What I want to know is how she obtained my name and address,"
said Clemens. "And since the reason people like you work for me is to
prevent this sort of thing from happening, I expect you'll be able to provide answers to these questions."

Chapter 100

Sheila was sitting on a surprisingly comfortable wooden chair on Michael's front porch. Wrapped up in a blanket, she was observing Michael busying himself with replenishing their firewood supply. He split
wood with lumberjack dexterity, his axe never missing the center of the
log, his cadence rivaling the best metronomes. He had only been working
around fifteen minutes and had already amassed what Sheila estimated
as a month's worth of firewood. Of course the fact he had been a lumberjack at the turn of the past millennium didn't hurt his performance,
but the journalist wasn't aware of this detail.

Michael was dabbing sweat off his forehead with the back of his
hand, when his attention was caught by a bird landing on the porch
guardrail. He immediately knew something was amiss. This bird did not
belong in Yellowstone; it did not even belong on the American continent
as a matter of fact.

The bird was almost a foot in length, with a black hood and black
wings, a gray bill, and a deep red body. The animal displayed all the at-
tributes of a Maroon Oriole, a species Michael had only encountered in
Asia.

Michael's pulse started racing when the bird flew from the guardrail
to the empty chair beside Sheila's. He sprinted towards the porch, but
before he could place himself between the young woman and the out-
landish animal, the bird changed into a frail-looking old man.

Sheila screamed in surprise as Michael started breathing again. Very
pleased with the result of his theatrical entrance, Ezekiel sat grinning on
his chair, his sharp eyes going back and forth between Michael and
Sheila.

The wizard's ageless gray cloak appeared a bit more wrinkly than usual and his pointy hat was standing on a slant on his head. He also seemed tired and was breathing hard.

"You're getting slow in your old age," said the wizard, looking at Michael with a mocking smile.

"Forgive me for saying so, but you don't exactly look to be in your prime either..." replied Michael, slightly concerned by the appearance of his friend.

"Nonsense! How do you think you'd look if you'd been chased by some idiotic bald eagle for fourteen miles? The moron finally gave up a mile or two from here, but it took some serious efforts to discourage him."

Sheila, who had quickly recovered from her fright, started laughing.

"That will teach you to turn yourself into hapless creatures," replied Michael. "Next time try a bear. I don't recollect ever having been chased by an eagle over the past millennium..."

Before the wizard could think of a witty comeback Sheila intervened. "It's nice of you to come and visit us, Ez. Aside from being mistaken for a raptor's snack, how was your trip?"

Ez did not miss the twinkle in the journalist's eyes.

"My trip was excellent, thank you," he replied in an overly serious tone before adding, "and I'm glad to see your sense of humor is wittier than his. He can be such a bore sometimes."

The wizard's answer widened the smile on Sheila's face but obtained no reaction from Michael.

"Will you stay for dinner or are you just flying by?" asked Sheila in the most serious voice she could muster, and this time even Michael smiled.

"I won't be staying, unfortunately," replied the wizard even more seriously. "I bear bad news, I am sorry to say."

The wizard's last words had caught the attention of his audience; nobody was smiling any longer.

"We're listening," said Michael.

"Clemens has already found out where you're hiding. He has sent the whole pack after you; they're on their way as we speak."

Sheila's face suddenly became very pale. She remembered vividly the battle between Michael and the pack delegation. If the whole pack came at him at once this time, he would have no chance whatsoever. She looked at Michael, but the expression on his face was as phlegmatic as ever.

Despite his apparent stoicism, Michael had reached the same conclusion as Sheila. He could not beat the Houston pack singlehandedly. This was how his species had been exterminated in the first place. Isolated werebears had been systematically hunted down by wolves' packs whose numbers had won over the bears' superior power.

"When will they be here?" asked Michael.

"They left Houston around midnight last night according to my spies, but they are driving. They should arrive early tomorrow morning."

"You have spies in Clemens' pack?" asked Sheila, bewildered.

Ez was amused by Sheila's ignorance and he answered her question with a kind smile. "Not all spies assume a human form, my child. Mine fly high in the sky and crawl underground, graze during the day and hunt during the night, breathe under water and flee the rain..."

"What Ez is trying to tell you in his own convoluted way is that he hired the animals of the woods surrounding Clemens' cabin as informers," interrupted Michael. Sheila felt thankful for the clarification.

Michael had known Clemens would eventually find out he had gone back to Yellowstone, but he had figured it out a lot faster than anticipated. Who had informed him? David Starks was the only person Michael had told about his plans and it was doubtful the detective had leaked the information to the Houston pack Alpha... So how did he know? There were always ways to learn about things, Michael supposed. Ez had had no problem finding him and Michael had not told the wizard where he was going either. Of course Ez was a wizard of the second circle and therefore in a totally different league than Peter Clemens, but still...

"I have business to attend in Alaska," said Ezekiel, "but I can stay here a bit if you need my assistance. Alaska can wait a day or two."

Michael thought about it for a minute before answering, "I thank you for your offer, Ez, but you know I cannot accept your help. You have already done plenty by warning us, you cannot get involved in my quarrel with the wolves. This is praeternatural business."

"Why?!" interjected Sheila. "Why do you reject his help? They will kill you Michael..." As she spoke she realized. "And then... they'll kill me."

Michael contemplated her last remark for an instant, thinking about ways to protect her without involving the wizard.

"I will find a way to protect you Sheila. Trust me," he said, but his voice lacked conviction.

"Why can't Ez help us?"

"Because there are unwritten rules we must follow. If a wizard gets involved in our business, it opens the door to others of his kind to join the conflict. And when supernatural beings battle each other, the consequences are always disastrous. Ask Ez what happened the last time he got into a fight with one of his buddies..."

"What happened?" Sheila asked the wizard.

Ez shot a dark look at Michael before answering, "Do you remember Mount St. Helens?"

Chapter 101

A low-intensity light bulb hung from the ceiling twenty feet in the air, giving the room a feeling of perpetual twilight. Locked up in this godforsaken place, Olivia had completely lost the notion of time. She was unable to tell whether she had been here a couple of weeks or a couple of months. She didn't think she had been locked up much longer, but she couldn't tell for certain. The only certainty she had was regarding her health: she was ill, very ill. The pain was not constant, but when it came it overtook her sanity, drowning her body and soul in an ocean of agony.

During these painful episodes, Olivia was losing consciousness, her mind drifting into a nightmarish reality haunted by a single monster. The creature—an impossible crossbreed between a man and a wolf—appeared to her in a state of perpetual rage. When the beast was not throwing itself against the walls of its cell—which happened to look exactly like Olivia's—it tried to claw its way through the concrete floor.

On at least five different occasions, Olivia had emerged from her disturbingly vivid dreams with torn fingernails and bruised limbs and shoulders. As if she had been acting out her dream… But every time, the bruises had healed and her nails had grown back, which seemed to indicate she had spent many weeks locked up in this place. Bruises tended to last a while on her pasty complexion.

From time to time, a trapdoor opened in the ceiling, and some food was lowered in a basket along with some water, but Olivia had no idea who was lowering the basket. She could not recall anything about how she might have found her way to this hellhole. As a matter of fact, she could not remember anything about anything, but she had not yet come to that realization. She had a vague awareness of the stench encompassing the room, but her brain hadn't realized the smell was coming from her own excrement, which she had been scattering across the cell ever since her arrival, three days earlier. The fact she was completely naked had been registered, mainly because she was cold from time to time, but she had not yet tried to understand why her torn-up clothes were littering the cell's concrete floor.

Chapter 102

Bill Thomason lived in a small one-story house at Mammoth, by the park's north entrance, close to a one-hour drive from Michael's cabin. Bill was wearing a pair of shorts and a T-shirt and looked like he was more than ready for bed when Michael and Sheila knocked on his door around 10.30 p.m.

"Michael?" Bill didn't try to hide his surprise. "What's going on?"

"Can we come in?"

Bill stepped aside to let his visitors in and closed the door behind them. The outside temperature was around twenty and Sheila was glad to be out of the cold.

Ezekiel's warning would have given them plenty of time to flee if they had chosen to, but Michael was sick of this cat and mouse game. He was no mouse! He simply refused to spend the rest of his life looking over his shoulder and worrying about when Clemens' wolves would finally catch up with him.

In leaving Houston, Michael had hoped for an instant the pack would lose interest. Now that they were tracking him down all the way to Wyoming, however, it had become clear Peter Clemens had taken a personal interest in him.

"Have a seat," said Bill Thomason, pointing towards a beat-up couch in front of a vintage TV set that looked older than Sheila. His house, although small, was significantly larger than Michael's, which had no proper living or dining room.

"Would you like something to drink? Tea maybe? I have caffeine-free varieties…"

"No, thank you," answered Michael. "I can't stay long. I came because I need a favor."

Bill looked at Michael attentively. He could tell by his friend's attitude that something serious was going on. "I'm listening."

"There's an urgent matter I need to attend to, and I would like Sheila to stay here while I am away. If that's OK with you."

"Of course she can stay here," replied Bill automatically. "How long will you be gone?"

"I don't believe I'll be gone much longer than a day," answered Michael vaguely. If he weren't back in a day, chances were he'd never come back. One way or another, the battle he was about to fight against the Houston pack was likely to be the last one.

"And why can't Sheila stay at your cabin then?" Bill's curiosity had been aroused.

"I would feel safer here," replied the journalist unconvincingly.

Bill Thomason looked at each of them in turn with a suspicious look on his face. "Can you at least tell me where you're going?" he asked finally.

Michael looked at his friend in silence for an instant before answering, "I'd rather you didn't ask, Bill."

Thomason nodded in understanding. "All right, no more questions. Sheila can stay here as long as she pleases."

Chapter 103

Michael knew his cabin would be the first place the pack would visit upon arrival. His address was public record, and Clemens had undoubtedly already obtained it. From there, they would pick up Michael's scent and track him down to wherever he would go.

That was why Michael had needed to return to his cabin and start from there if he didn't want the pack to follow the freshest trail he had left behind. The one leading to Bill Thomason's house... and Sheila.

The snow had started to fall, which could be viewed as both a good and a bad thing. A good thing because it would help erase the olfactory trail he had left going to Bill's house; a bad one because it would also make it difficult for the pack to follow the fresh trail, and Michael had no desire to spend a week waiting for the pack to find him.

He considered waiting for them at his cabin for an instant before discarding the idea. Although he lived in a pretty isolated part of the park, his cabin was still too close to Canyon Village to offer the absolute privacy the battle would require. In addition, the house would get annihilated in the battle and he had grown fond of the old shack.

There was another reason Michael had elected to wage his war far away from any trace of civilization. A trump he had not used in so many years he wasn't even sure he remembered how to use it.

Chapter 104

The snow was now steadily falling upon the evergreen-covered slopes Bill Thomason was currently climbing. Hiking in the snow at two in the morning was not exactly Bill's idea of fun, but Michael hadn't left him with a choice.

The snow-swollen clouds absorbed almost all the light from the stars and the moon, and cast a pitch-black veil over the treacherous trail Bill was following. Unlike Michael's, Bill's night vision was not any better than the average person's, but he had other resources Michael had never suspected. Bill's eyes did not need to see for him to know where he was going. His mind could feel the obstacles his sight didn't perceive.

About five hundred feet ahead of Bill, Michael, unsuspecting, was progressing at a steady pace, making his own trail in the midst of the vegetation, as he had done many times before. He was heading for his chosen battleground, a large clearing about seven miles northwest of his cabin. The clearing was just outside the caldera boundary north of a relatively small pond ironically named Wolf Lake.

Michael had visited this clearing numerous times over the years and knew its topography as well as the back of his hand. The near perfect flatness of the place had been a decisive point in his selection. Bears' front legs being shorter than their hind limbs, they had difficulties running downhill, a disadvantage over the wolves Michael wanted to eliminate.

Bill was progressing upwind from Michael. Under normal circumstances Michael would have smelled him coming from five miles away, but Bill Thomason had more than one trick in his bag, and being able to completely mask his scent was one of them—a handy one in the current situation.

When Michael finally arrived at his chosen destination, he stripped out of his clothes and placed them in the small backpack he had brought along. Leaving his bundle by a tree, he walked naked to the center of the clearing, apparently unaffected by the snow and wind accompanying the twenty-degree weather. He stood there for an instant, smelling the air before finally morphing, silently. Knowing he was in no rush, he took his time to transform. It was therefore almost an entire minute before an 800-pound bear stood in his place in the center of the snow-covered clearing.

Chapter 105

The convoy had arrived at Michael's cabin a couple hours before sunrise. A flat tire and the snow, which had been following them all the way since Denver, had significantly lengthened the pack's journey. Peter Clemens was not happy with the delay; he was eager to finish up Biörn and get back to Houston's more civilized climate. The fact they had found the cabin deserted had not helped improve Clemens' disposition either.

The pack had picked up on the Alpha's temper and was in an altogether foul mood. Clemens had been forced to intervene twice already to prevent his wolves from fighting each other.

They had picked up Michael's faint smell at the cabin and had followed the trail up in the mountains, morphing into their more efficient wolf forms as soon as they had been under the cover of the forest canopy. They had quickly noticed a second scent on the trail, a more recent one, as if Michael had been followed. Followed by... a woman! Axel Thompkins had finally identified the odor as belonging to Sheila Wang. He had been in close proximity with the journalist when he and his fallen comrades had fought Biörn at his hotel, and the woman's odor had been etched in his olfactory memory.

Why the journalist was following Biörn at a distance—a large distance based on the intensity of their respective odors—Clemens couldn't fathom. Nonetheless, one thing was clear: the two had been warned about the imminent arrival of the pack! They knew the wolves were coming for them! This was the only satisfactory explanation for their hike in the snow in the middle of the night. This once again raised the question of who was providing Michael with his intel? Who was the pain in Clemens' side? Katia Olveda, via David Starks, was an obvious possibility, but Clemens didn't think the assistant DA was stupid enough to betray him. She knew too well the consequences of such betrayal. Who else then?

Isabella, one of the pack's best trackers, was running with a couple of other wolves a couple hundred yards ahead of the pack when she noticed the woman's scent becoming significantly stronger—they were catching up with one of their prey.

Chapter 106

The sun was rising when Michael caught the first whiff of his hereditary enemies. The snow had stopped falling a short while before, leaving on the frozen ground a good foot of scintillating white powder. The clouds were starting to clear out, and Michael had lived in the park long enough to know with certainty that it would be a sunny morning. The air temperature, however, had dropped to zero, and the battle would therefore take place on a snow-carpeted ground.

The idea of the Houston pack having to fight in the snow did not displease Michael. Clemens' wolves were unlikely to be used to this type of conditions and would be at a disadvantage. Even praeternatural creatures suffered from the cold and the Houston wolves were unlikely to have coats thick enough to withstand Yellowstone's biting cold. Of course, once the battle was waged, adrenaline would keep them warm, but they would arrive at the clearing already weakened.

The pack scent was getting stronger by the minute, and Michael could start distinguishing individual scents out of the generic pack odor. He caught Isabella's scent first, followed by that of her husband. He then identified the scent of the wolf who had survived the battle at the hotel and escaped. There was a multitude of other odors Michael could now pick up: too many… As he realized Clemens had brought well over thirty wolves with him, Michael's hyper-sensitive nose detected a very familiar odor… Sheila's! He could not tell whether she was accompanying the wolves or if her odor was simply coming from their general direction, but one thing was certain—the pack was a lot closer to her than he was.

The woman had no reason to be anywhere near this part of the park. He had left her with Bill Thomason, so what was she doing here, a few miles away from his position, judging by the intensity of her scent?

Michael knew full well that, assuming they hadn't already done so, the wolves would catch up with Sheila long before he could. Going after them now meant losing all the advantages he had planned for; it meant certain death for both of them. He suspected Clemens would bring Sheila along unharmed, if for no other reason than to kill her in front of him. The best thing to do was to stay in place and wait patiently. They would be here soon enough. He just hoped he wasn't wrong about Clemens keeping Sheila alive. His wife Isibel, his childhood sweetheart, the woman he had loved the most in his entire life, had already perished because of him. If the same thing were to happen to Sheila…

Standing on his back legs, Michael put all his frustration, anger, and fear into a formidable roar, which echoed back against the surrounding mountains' walls to be heard in a five-mile radius.

Chapter 107

Shortly after Michael had dropped her at his boss's house, Sheila had noticed Bill Thomason's increasing nervousness. Wondering what this was about, she had pretended to be tired and Bill had shown her to her room. The journalist had only been in bed five minutes when she heard a car starting outside the house. In a flash, she was out of bed and heading for the front door. Anticipating Bill's departure, she had not undressed before lying down and was ready to take off at an instant's notice. She was deeply worried for Michael. Whatever Bill Thomason had in mind, he hadn't said a word of it to his employee, and she had a bad feeling about the whole thing.

Bill's personal truck was gone, but his official police vehicle was still parked in front of the house. She jumped behind the wheel, ready to hotwire the truck—a useful skill taught to her by one of her informants—but the keys were in the ignition. She started the truck and headed straight for Michael's cabin, speeding in the snow and almost losing control of the vehicle on several occasions. She was finally compelled to slow down after yet another close call involving a guardrail.

She eventually made it to the cabin to find Bill's truck parked next to Michael's. Using a flashlight, she discovered the trail left by the two men and started following it. The snow was quickly covering their tracks, however, and the trail became difficult to follow. Shortly after losing the trail for good, Sheila's flashlight died, leaving her officially lost in the middle of Yellowstone's wilderness. She walked in the snow aimlessly for hours before finally deciding she was too cold, too tired and too scared to care about who would find her first… as long as someone found her. It was only after seeing the first wolves closing in on her at the strike of dawn that she realized she had been wrong about this.

Isabella was still leading the scouts when they finally caught up with Sheila. The journalist had wandered off her boyfriend's trail, but she had been easy enough to find. The wolves, irritated by the thin mountain air, the steep climb, and the foot of snow on the ground needed to vent their frustration on someone and Sheila would do perfectly.

The scouts started circling Sheila who, paralyzed by terror, stood motionless with her back against the trunk of a large pine tree. The wolves were snarling like rabid dogs, showcasing canines that would have made most tigers envious.

Isabella quickly grew tired of playing the *scaring the defenseless journalist* game and started slowly closing the gap between her and the unfortunate woman. She was about to sink her teeth into Sheila's flesh when her husband pounced between them. The Alpha's command was unmistakable, and Isabella backed down. Sheila Wang was not to be harmed just yet.

Chapter 108

Although he had come prepared for the cold, Bill Thomason was still suffering from the drop in temperature that had occurred overnight. He had to remain almost entirely immobile to avoid attracting Michael's attention, and this forced immobility was not helping warm him up in any way.

Bill had reached the edge of the clearing just in time to witness Michael's transformation. Although the clearing benefited from a better light quality than the surrounding woods, Michael was standing a hundred yards away and Bill could make out little more than the outline of his silhouette. It had therefore taken some time for the ranger to finally realize he was staring at a colossal bear. The revelation wasn't exactly shocking, as Bill had suspected Michael's praeternatural nature for many years now, but it was definitely surprising since supposedly werebears had been extinct for centuries.

After Michael had stood in his bear form in the center of the clearing for several minutes without showing any desire to move on, Bill understood that he was waiting for something. It hadn't taken the ranger very long to guess a fight was coming, and since he was still standing on the trail made by Michael, there was a good chance that whatever was coming after the werebear would follow the same trail…

In order to avoid being sandwiched between the werebear and his incoming enemy, Bill had decided to go stand on the opposite side of the clearing. Very slowly and as silently as he could manage, he gave up his eastern position and circled the defoliated area from the north to land at the most western point of the Wolf Lake clearing.

He had been standing there for over six hours now and at times wondered if his feet were not frozen solid inside his boots. At least the sun had risen and he now had absolute confirmation that Michael was, in fact, a monstrous werebear. This sight was worth the trip in itself…

Suddenly, Michael, who had been lying motionless in the snow for the better part of the night, got up on his four legs and, neck extended towards the east, started frantically smelling the air.

Chapter 109

When the pack's scouts emerged from the same trail he and Michael had used to reach the clearing, Bill Thomason congratulated himself for moving to his current position on the opposite side of what would soon become the battlefield.

The wolves immediately started howling, warning the remaining members of the pack that the enemy had been found. Five minutes later, the clearing was teeming with werewolves.

Bill counted thirty-seven wolves, and by the size of the beasts he knew immediately these weren't your National Park variety wolves. They quickly formed a circle around the bear, effectively preventing any potential retreat, but Michael did not attempt to evade the maneuver. He hadn't come here to avoid the confrontation. Standing on his hind legs in the center of the clearing, the bear looked agitated but displayed no fear as far as Bill could tell. Each exhaled breath projected a thick cloud of vapor out of the bear's mouth, further increasing the surreal atmosphere of the scene. The ranger wasn't sure whether bears and werebears shared the same display of emotions but if they did, Michael seemed both angry and worried… or maybe annoyed?

At a call from the Alpha, the wolves started slowly converging towards Michael, gradually closing the circle they had formed around the bear. Peter Clemens had learned from his mistake and knew Michael was not to be underestimated. The attack needed to be coordinated to guarantee victory. This was now a personal feud for the pack. The bear needed to pay for what he had done to their brothers.

Although the wolves were closing in, the werebear's attitude did not alter. He was still looking annoyed, mostly staring in one direction, almost ignoring the now quickly approaching threat. It all changed when a naked man walked out of the woods dragging behind him a disheveled, bruised up and half frozen Sheila.

Axel Thompkins was not particularly happy with his babysitting assignment. He not only wouldn't get to participate in the fight, he was also freezing. His werewolf metabolism prevented him from turning into an icicle, but the near zero degree weather was still way too cold for not wearing any clothes. When he noticed the way the werebear was looking at him, a rush of adrenaline flowed through his body, raising his core temperature by a degree or two.

The bear was now rocking from side to side on his hind limbs, uttering loud and intimidating growls and roars while the wolves kept closing in on him. When the pack had tightened their ring to the point where they only stood thirty feet from Michael, the bear dropped back on his four legs and started charging towards the Alpha, easily recognizable by his all-black fur coat. The wolves on each side of Clemens instinctively rushed on an interception course towards the rapidly incoming werebear to protect their leader and were the first ones to reach Michael, but they could do little against the enormous momentum of the sprinting 800-pound beast. Michael rammed into the first one, sending him flying fifteen feet in the air before sinking his teeth in the throat of the other without even slowing down. The wolf's spine splintered under the pressure, but Michael kept the beast's lifeless body locked in his powerful jaws, using it as an improvised shield against the incoming tidal wave of the pack.

Before he could reach Peter Clemens, half a dozen wolves were on Michael, who was now using his victim's corpse in the manner of a medieval flay, slamming it left and right against his enemies. The abused carcass did not hold together very long. Soon its severed head flew in one direction and the body in another.

The battle was now raging, the sheer power and wrath of the werebear against the speed and viciousness of the wolves. Michael made quick work of the first two or three wolves who had made the mistake of going for his throat, but the rest had gotten smarter. Under the Alpha's guidance, they were now executing a well-organized harassment strategy aimed at wearing out their prey.

After twenty minutes of constant persecution, Michael started showing the first signs of exhaustion. He was slower to react when one of his opponents sank his teeth into his back or thigh and, most importantly, he was bleeding a lot more than any of them.

Although he had not yet bitten Michael, Clemens could already taste the blood of his enemy in his mouth. The werebear was obviously exhausted and would not stand a chance against their combined number. The Alpha gave the signal and the whole pack rushed toward Michael.

Chapter 110

The warehouse was located in a scary part of town, an area the cops didn't patrol and where they generally refused to set foot after dark. The chemist was standing, although barely, between two of Ivanov's henchmen, looking scared out of his mind. He had been dragged from his home early that morning and brought to the warehouse without a word of explanation. There he had found Ivanov waiting for him in person along with his lieutenant, Igor Petrovich, and two other gorillas. Victor had been almost relieved to find out his kidnappers worked for Dimitri Ivanov. The mobster was the opposite of a nice guy, but the

Chemist was less scared of him than he was of his mysterious customer. His relief had been short-lived, however. He had been strapped to a chair upon arrival, and the Russian boss had been directing the questioning ever since. Questioning that had taken its toll on Victor's physical condition.

"I will rip your tongue out of your mouth with red hot pliers if you don't start telling me what I want to know!" bellowed Ivanov, squeezing the chemist's throat in his right hand. "Do you doubt my word, Victor?"

The Chemist shook his head vigorously since Ivanov's chokehold prevented him from uttering the slightest sound.

"So start telling the truth," said Ivanov, finally letting go of the man's throat. Victor's face was quickly losing its oxygen-deprived purple color and returning to a more ghostly shade of gray. He was sweating profusely, and held-back tears could be seen in the corners of his eyes.

"I swear I am not making drugs for anyone, Dimitri. I extract a specific molecule from some plant and that's it. All the orders are placed over the phone, and I have never seen the man. I swear to you, it's the truth," he answered imploringly.

"What's the plant's name and what's that molecule you're isolating if it's not narcotic?" asked Ivanov in a slightly less threatening voice.

"The plant is called wolfsbane. I tried to look up the extract's effect and all I can tell is that if used as such, it would be a deadly poison. The man must have someone else modifying the substance after he gets it from me, but I don't know what for. It doesn't look anything like any drug I've ever made, and I've made a lot in my days..."

"How do you deliver, if your customer doesn't pick up the merchandise?"

"Some black guy, the mean-looking type... He drops off the plants and comes back to pick up the finished goods," replied Victor in a slightly more assured voice.

"What's the delivery boy's name?"

"He's never told me, and for the longest time I didn't know," started Victor, relieved he finally knew the answer to one of Ivanov's questions. "But one day he answered his phone in my lab and said: 'Thompkins'. I also heard the guy over the phone calling him Axel. So I know he's called Axel Thompkins... Do you recognize the name?"

Ivanov didn't recognize the name, but his second did.

"It's one of Clemens' men, boss," offered Igor Petrovich.

The revelation confirmed the boss's suspicions. Clemens was setting up shop in town and this was going directly against the agreement he had with Ivanov's organization. Something had to be done about it.

"We're through here." Ivanov picked up the jacket he had laid on the back of an empty chair.

"What do you want to do with this one?" asked Petrovich, a thumb pointed in the direction of the unfortunate Victor Grey.

"Surprise me…" answered Ivanov as he walked towards the exit.

Chapter 111

The werebear was panting and exhausted. Michael knew the battle was lost, but he would go down swinging, taking as many of his enemies with him to the grave as was superhumanly possible. It wouldn't be long now, Clemens had given the signal and in a second they would all be on him.

He could see them closing in, only fifteen feet away now, ten feet, five feet, three… As the wolves were now pouncing on him in a perfectly choreographed macabre ballet, Michael felt a surge of magical energy growing all around him. *Had the pack brought a witch with them on top of it all?* wondered Michael for a split second before the wolves collided into an invisible but very real barrier, which seemed to surround him. But the beasts looked as surprised as he was by the unexpected obstacle. After trying to force their way through the invisible force field a short while longer, without success, the wolves started probing for weaknesses in the energy field. They tried jumping over the barrier and coming down on Michael straight from the top, but they kept bouncing back.

Michael was thankful for the much-needed break, but he couldn't help wondering who was responsible for this clearly magical salvation. He had asked Ez to stay out of the fight, but maybe the old wizard had only pretended to agree to his request… This was going to open a whole new world of issues in itself if the wizard was involved, but for now he was simply grateful for the help.

He could see Sheila standing motionless at the edge of the clearing, a wolf in his human form guarding her. She suddenly started wobbling before finally collapsing to the ground, unconscious. Michael's heart sank. He wanted to run to her, save her from these monsters, but he was exhausted and the pack was still standing between them. Giving up was not in his nature, however. No matter how tired he felt, no matter how old he was—and he was very old—he simply wasn't ready to die yet. Not now that Sheila needed him the most.

This thought unlocked in him a source of energy he had not yet tapped into. A forgotten but powerful source that had lain sleeping in his core for untold decades. With this new power unleashed, his strength came rushing back to him, engulfing him like a tsunami. He was now ready for the battle of his life.

Chapter 112

Seeing his wolves bouncing back off thin air unable to reach their help-less prey, Clemens immediately knew a magician of some sort was protecting Biörn. He just didn't know who or where the pest was. The location of the spoilsport depended greatly on his power. A witch would have to be close, but a wizard or warlock could have been casting his spell from twenty miles away… Hoping Michael's unwelcome helper was not a wizard, Clemens sent a dozen of his wolves on a recon mission around the clearing's perimeter.

Bill Thomason had made sure his scent would be imperceptible by the wolves as well as by Michael, but invisibility spells were unfortunately above his pay grade, so if one of Michael's enemy were to catch sight of him, the situation would switch from bad to worse in a hurry. As he focused all his strength and concentration on maintaining the energy bar-rier between Michael and the wolves, he did not even realize that simply climbing a tree would have significantly improved his chances of remain-ing undetected.

When the witch heard the loud snarls behind him, it was already too late. The wolves killed Thomason before he had a chance to turn around.

Chapter 113

Calling Brenda Pennington's apartment clean and tidy would have been an understatement. Magazines lay in a perfect pile on the living room's coffee table, each niche of the large decorative shelf lining the wall hosted a single bibelot placed at its exact center, and it would have required a magnifying glass to find a single speck of dust on any given piece of furniture.

Detective Lewis had already placed the woman in the OCD category. Not a bad category for the purpose of their visit. People with OCD were so detail-oriented that they were usually reliable sources of information.

The two detectives were sitting next to each other on the sofa, while Brenda Pennington, sitting straight as an arrow on the edge of her arm-chair on the other side of the coffee table, looked nervous despite the fact her visitors had clearly stated the objective of their visit. Her pale complexion was flushed with pink and her blue eyes kept flying from Salazar to Lewis as if trying to assess which one of them was the most worrisome. She wore small, frameless spectacles which made her already plain features look even more devoid of personality. Her dark hair, pulled into a tight braid, only emphasized the boniness of her neck.

Salazar had found the woman's address in Jack Moore's apartment, along with a picture of her in the company of the now deceased assassin.

The two had been romantically involved at some point, but according to the woman, they had broken up over two years ago.

"Why do you think Jack still kept a picture of you in his apartment after two years?" asked Salazar in his friendliest voice.

"I don't know," answered the woman. "Jack had a hard time letting things go, I guess..."

"Did you break up with him?" asked Lewis.

"Yes."

"Was there a particular reason?"

The question made the woman uneasy. She kept silent for an instant before finally answering in a hesitant voice, "He changed..."

"Could you elaborate?" asked Salazar gently.

Brenda Pennington looked at him with distress in her eyes. She had learned about Jack's death from the news days before the detectives had knocked on her door, but talking about him still seemed to make her sad. Salazar suspected the woman was not over her ex-lover and it made the question of her breaking up with him all the more interesting.

"It's difficult to explain..." She swallowed hard. "You see... when we first started dating, Jack was the kindest man I had ever met. He was always surprising me with gifts and attentions, always placing my desires above his..."

Now tears were slowly trickling down the woman's cheeks, and she got up to go fetch a box of tissues from the bathroom.

"Sorry about that," she said, settling back down into her seat.

"No problem at all," answered the two cops simultaneously while flashing her their most sympathetic smiles.

"You were saying Jack used to be very sweet to you..." encouraged Lewis.

"Yes," answered the woman. "We had been dating for over a year when things started changing. He started becoming more distant. Initially, I thought I had done something wrong, but that wasn't it. I tried to talk to him, but he would always deny anything was wrong. I suggested we'd go to counseling and that's when he started becoming angry. I had never seen him lose his temper before, and it scared me to the core."

"Did he hit you?" asked Salazar.

"No, at least not that day, but from that moment our relationship dramatically changed. I was afraid of him. He started growing increasingly violent as time went by. He would punch holes in the walls, kick the furniture around, and if I was in the way, he'd hit me. That's when I moved out and broke up with him."

"How did he take it?" asked Lewis.

"Very badly initially, but after a week or so of almost constant harassment, he simply gave up," replied Brenda pensively.

"Do you have any idea why?"

"Not really..."

"But you have suspicions?" queried Salazar.

The woman looked at him intently as she was sorting her thoughts in her head.

"I think maybe someone told him to stop…"

"Do you know who that someone was?"

"No. At least not really… Before he started changing, Jack had met some guy at his job. They hung out a few times and Jack really seemed to like the guy. When he started becoming violent, he stopped talking about his new friend, but I was always convinced they were still seeing each other. I think that friend was responsible for the change in Jack's behavior. I brought it up once, but Jack almost destroyed the apartment in response, and I never dared mentioning it again."

Chapter 114

The wolves had given up trying to penetrate the protective bubble enclosing their enemy and were now pacing relentlessly outside the inaccessible hemisphere, testing its resistance from time to time.

The magical energy Michael had been sensing for the last few minutes vanished, and he knew immediately the shield had disappeared. The wolves were significantly younger than Michael and although praeternatural in nature, they were not as finely tuned to the magical world as he was. As a result, they did not immediately realize the force field had disappeared.

Taking advantage of the wolves' inexperience, Michael crashed into the biggest one he could find in his immediate vicinity before any of them had a chance to react. The wolf emitted a startled bark as Michael pierced his heart with the razor-sharp claws of his right paw, before snapping the spine of another opponent in his powerful jaws.

Their surprise passed and the wolves quickly reorganized their offense, but Michael had fully recovered by now and was offering a solid and often lethal defense. Under their Alpha's guidance, the pack returned to the harassment strategy that had successfully worn the bear out a few minutes earlier, and Michael realized that unless he did something different this time, the same outcome would result.

The wolves were becoming increasingly bolder in their attacks, and Clemens was now taking full part in the assault. Michael had felt the Alpha's teeth penetrating his flesh on two occasions, and he knew the man was both experienced and vicious, a true Alpha. After fifteen minutes of relentless pestering, Michael started feeling tired again, but this time he had several werewolves' bloodied bodies to show for his effort. Unfortunately, the number of wolves' bodies littering the clearing was nothing in comparison to that of those still standing, and Michael was starting to lose hope when he finally sensed their energizing presence. A jolt of adrenaline sent his heart racing with anticipation and excitement at what was to come. Reinforcements had arrived.

Chapter 115

Lucy Harrington had gone back to college shortly after her parents' funeral. Now, a month later, she was back in Houston, looking for her sister. She had been unable to reach Olivia by phone, email, or on her Facebook page for the past four days. Since the two sisters typically called each other on a daily basis, Olivia's silence was starting to seriously worry Lucy.

The cab dropped her at her parents' house where she knew her sister was staying, but she found the place deserted. A putrid smell assaulted her nostrils as soon as she passed the door, and her mind directly jumped to the worst possible scenario. After investigation however, she identified the smell as coming from the kitchen's trashcan whose bag had clearly not been changed in some time.

Lucy replaced the bag, and opened the windows to get rid of the nauseating atmosphere before going up the stairs and reluctantly checking every room on the second floor, keeping her parents' bedroom for last. The room had not yet been repainted or the carpet replaced, and Lucy started crying hysterically at the sight of the blood-stained walls and carpet.

After thirty minutes in the house, Lucy was fairly convinced her sister had not been there in a few days, but she still had no lead on where Olivia might be. She felt sick to her stomach at the prospect of losing the last member of her family and left the house, deliberately inhaling and exhaling several times before walking towards the neighbors' house. Someone had to know where Olivia was.

Chapter 116

One by one, they started slowly trickling out of the forest—Michael's reinforcements. They had taken their time, but they were here now, answering the call for help Michael had sent after first sensing Sheila's presence in the woods.

The wolves were too focused on the werebear to immediately notice the newcomers, but when a 600-pound grizzly bear charged towards one of them, they were forced to.

Around two dozen bears had answered Michael's calling. They were grizzlies for the most part, the breed with which Michael had the most affinity, but a few black bears had shown up as well. Michael immediately felt bad for the black bears, as they would be no match for werewolves, but he had no way to send them back. Caught in the magical spell of their praeternatural brother, the bears would fight to the death to protect him.

The arrival of the bears' army completely rebalanced the conflict and totally caught the wolves by surprise. In spite of his many years of existence, Peter Clemens had had no idea a praeternatural being could call upon regular animals. Surrounded by an unexpected wave of enemies, the werewolves could only pay limited attention to Michael, who now only had to fight a few of them at a time. As Michael had predicted, the black bears were being quickly dispatched by the wolves, and the slain bodies of three of them were already painting the clearings' immaculate snow-carpet a crimson red. The grizzlies, on the other hand, were much more fearsome enemies for the wolves. They were, on average, bigger than the werewolves, and just as mean. What the grizzlies lacked in viciousness they made up in power, and in a one on one battle they were more than a match for Clemens' wolves. Of course the werewolves were praeternatural creatures, and short of beheading them, they were a hell of a lot harder to kill than purely natural bears, but the bears were infused with Michael's instincts, and they knew how to exploit the wolves' weaknesses. They didn't necessarily need to kill the werewolves to knock them down and out of the fight. Of course, the wolves would eventually recover from any serious injuries, but it would take them some time.

Peter Clemens and his wife Isabella were among the dozen wolves still harassing Michael, but in spite of their number, they were unable to get the better of their enemy. At one point, they had all pounced on Michael simultaneously, trying to smother him under their numbers, but the bears had immediately abandoned their respective opponents to rush to Michael's rescue, and it had only taken a few seconds for the situation to get back to the original standoff.

After almost an hour of fighting, the bears' stamina started paying off. The animals, just like Michael, were acclimated to the park's thin air, to the cold, and to the snow. The foot of snow on the ground was still a nuisance to the bears, but their longer limbs were a definite advantage over those of the wolves who were significantly more hindered by the white powdery substance.

Sensing the battle was turning in his enemies' favor, Clemens and the five wolves still dealing with Michael were growing more desperate and therefore more aggressive by the minute. Michael's vigilance was unfaltering, however, and all their attempts resulted in further injuries to them.

The black bears had all been dead for some time, but there were now more slain and dying werewolves on the ground than dead grizzlies. Peter Clemens assessed the situation with a quick scan of the battlefield, realizing to his horror that his wolves were now outnumbered by the bears.

Reluctantly, the Alpha conceded his defeat and howled the retreat signal. An instant later, the wolves had fled the battlefield.

Chapter 117

Michael was gently holding an unconscious half frozen Sheila between his gigantic paws. After stripping the clothes off the catatonic journalist, he had changed back into his bear form in order to bury her naked body inside his thick fur coat. Clothing posed a barrier to heat transfer and, in cases of severe hypothermia, a naked body warmed up significantly faster than a clothed one.

Long minutes went by before the young woman started becoming responsive, and almost an hour had passed when she finally regained consciousness. Startled at first to find herself waking up wrapped in some warm and furry cocoon, she quickly came to her senses after recognizing Ezekiel as the funny-looking old man gazing down on her. If the wizard was here, the breathing blanket wrapped around her could only be Michael.

Ezekiel had walked out of the woods as soon as the pack had fled and had watched Michael finish off the wounded werewolves. If his bear form had been able to shed tears, Michael would have wept over the carcasses of the thirteen bears that had fallen defending his life... but he couldn't. Ezekiel had quickly started erasing all traces of the battle from the clearing, and by the time he was done, the place had recovered its virginal beauty.

A few minutes after waking up, Sheila had recovered enough to slip back into the clothes Ezekiel had warmed up for her. Michael morphed back into his human form and put his own clothes back on before turning towards his friend. "Why did you get involved, Ez? You know what—"

"I did not get involved," interrupted the wizard.

"What do you call the force field you placed around me when I was at the wolves' mercy?"

"I had nothing to do with that," answered Ez, and Michael knew his friend was telling the truth. "After you rejected my assistance, I decided to stay as a simple spectator. I just wanted to see how the battle would turn out. At no point did I interfere in any way during the fight."

"Who did it then? Who placed that shield around me?" asked Michael, turning a suspicious eye towards Sheila.

"It wasn't Sheila either," answered Ezekiel calmly. "You will find the man responsible for saving your life under those trees." He pointed towards the edge of the clearing where Bill Thomason's body lay slain.

The bulk of Michael's body had been swallowed by the trees on the opposite side of the clearing and Sheila was left in Ezekiel's company. She still felt exhausted, but she was now warm again and she had recovered enough from her ordeal to break the awkward silence and ask the obvious question. "Who is hiding under these trees? Who saved Michael's life?"

"Bill Thomason." The wizard's eyes were still fixed on the edge of the forest where Michael had disappeared. "But he is no longer hiding. He is dead."

"You didn't kill him, did you?" asked Sheila, suddenly worried.

"Of course I didn't kill him! The wolves did! Why would I do such a thing?!"

The journalist did not answer Ezekiel's rhetorical question. She wanted to ask him why Bill had been killed, how he had saved Michael, how the bears had known to come to Michael's help, and a myriad of other things, but she wasn't sure how long Michael would be gone and there was one thing she wanted to know above all.

"Did you know Michael's wife?" she asked after an instant.

The wizard's eyes dived into her own, an intense gaze, uncomfortably piercing, and she felt as if he could read her soul.

"No. Isibel died a long time before I met Michael," he answered finally.

"How did she die?"

"She killed herself... attached a stone to her feet and threw herself into the river. Not the way I'd choose to do it, personally, but I suppose if you reach that point, the way you go doesn't matter much anymore."

Sheila stood silently for a moment. This wasn't the answer she had expected, but it explained why Michael seemed gloomy every time he thought of her.

"Why did she kill herself?" she asked.

"This is something you should ask Michael," answered the wizard enigmatically. "And I would suggest you pick the right time to ask your question," he added very seriously.

"What do you mean? Why should there be a right time?"

"Because he won't like your question... and you won't like his answer."

Chapter 118

It was the time of the month where Detective Edward Salazar caved under the pressure of his partner's disgusted expression and finally cleaned up his desk. The files scattered across the entire surface of the large metallic desktop were coated with a thin layer of a mixture of dust and powdered sugar. The powdered sugar's decorative touch, easily traced back to Salazar's weakness for fried dough delicacies, nicely complemented the detective's coffee-ring collection proudly displayed on the cover of most manila folders.

"You're a pig, Sal! I have no idea how your wife puts up with you," said Lewis, observing her partner expertly blowing the grime away one file at a time, before placing the folders on a quickly growing pile on the floor.

"My wife loves me as I am. She doesn't mind my mess, she just cleans up after me," replied Salazar, not the least offended.

"I knew love was blind, but apparently it has no sense of smell either…" said Lewis ironically.

"The word is anosmic." Salazar wiped the empty desk surface with a wet paper towel.

"What?"

"Anosmic! Someone deprived of the sense of smell… If you spent less time criticizing people, you'd have more time to educate yourself," answered Salazar with a triumphant grin, which Lewis pretended to not notice.

"I'd forgotten about that one," said Salazar, holding a folder labeled *The Serb,* before Lewis had a chance to retort.

"What is it?" enquired Lewis.

"The Serb… Were we in charge of that case?"

"I guess…" Lewis thought it over for a minute. "But this whole wolf story took priority over everything else. And to be honest, the disappearance of a scumbag bookie does not affect my sleep much…"

"You sleeping like a baby is beside the point, Lewis. The guy was working for Ivanov, wasn't he?"

"I believe so… yes," replied Lewis contemplatively.

"The Russian mob seems to be somehow tied to our wolf case, so maybe the disappearance of Danko has something to do with it as well…"

Lewis stared at her partner in silence for an instant. He was a slob, but a slob who could use his brain when needed.

"You may have a point," she conceded finally. "We should probably take another look at his file. Maybe we'll find something interesting."

Chapter 119

Isabella had a really upset look on her face when she opened the door, and discovering Detective David Starks on her front step did not improve her mood.

David knew that showing up at the Houston pack den alone and uninvited was not the smartest thing he could do, but he didn't think Clemens would chance hurting a cop on official business knocking at his door. The Alpha was smarter than that.

"What do you want now?" asked Isabella, not trying to hide her irritation.

"I would like to ask your husband a few questions." David stepped forward to try and get a better peek at the inside of the house. The angle wasn't great but he could still see a good part of the living room, and he counted a half dozen individuals there. They all looked upset and the detective knew full well the reason for their distress. He smiled internally, but his face showed no sign of emotion.

"My husband already answered all your questions. So unless you have a warrant, get the hell off our property. You're trespassing!" Isabella slammed the door in David's face.

"That went well..." thought David, getting back into his car. The Clemenses had ten cars in their driveway, but David didn't think there had been many more than ten wolves present in the house. The detective knew about the unfortunate turn of fate the pack had suffered in Yellowstone, and he had knocked on Clemens' door as much to assess the damages withstood by the pack as to enquire about the disappearance of the Ferguson brothers.

He drove off the Clemenses' property without noticing Andrei still perched in his tree on his spying mission. Although he did not fully understand its necessity, the low-level mobster kept religiously applying the scent neutralizer Ivanov had given him.

David stopped his car a couple miles down the dirt road and parked it between trees a few feet away from the road. He got out of his car and started heading for the location from where the Fergusons had dialed 911.

After almost an hour of painstaking searching, David found a small clump of human hair trapped in the bark of a tree. He placed his find in an evidence bag and shoved it in his pocket before resuming his search.

Chapter 120

Michael and Sheila had just gotten back from Bill Thomason's funeral and were sitting at Michael's kitchen table, the only table in the small cabin.

The ceremony had taken place on the shores of Yellowstone Lake, in the heart of the park. Bill had never married, and only a dozen friends and remote family members had attended the service. Following the deceased's desires, his ashes had been scattered over the lake.

Although Michael had not directly involved Bill in the events that had led to his death, he could not help feeling guilty. He was the only reason the pack had come to Yellowstone in the first place, and Bill had died trying to protect him...

At first Michael had scolded Ezekiel for involving Bill in this mess, but Ez had vehemently denied any connection between him and the ranger. Bill had acted on his own, not following anyone's influence. When Michael asked Ez if he had known about Bill's magical powers, the wizard had simply replied that it wasn't his job to keep track of every solitary witch on the planet, and that he had never actually met Bill in person before his death.

Later, Michael had remembered the day a few years back where he had suspected his boss and friend of being a sorcerer after discovering crow remains in his trashcan. His suspicions hadn't been far off...

Sheila, for her part, couldn't help feeling relieved after the scalding defeat Michael and the bears had inflicted upon the Houston pack. Some wolves had survived the battle, but they were few, and she didn't think they would come back after them anytime soon. Clemens had learned his lesson.

She felt sympathetic towards Michael who hadn't been himself since Bill's death, however. He had been speaking even less than he usually did and had only been eating twice as much as her, a definite sign something was off.

Although the epic battle against the Houston pack had finally boosted their relationship to the next level—a level where they no longer had to choose who slept in the bed and who was left with the couch— Michael still had a hard time opening up to Sheila and mostly kept his feelings for himself. For her part, Sheila wanted nothing more than to ask Michael about Isibel, but Ezekiel's warning still echoed in her head and she was afraid of what the question would do to their burgeoning relationship.

"Why don't we take a look at this list of yours to see if something jolts our deductive powers?" she said, hoping the exercise would distract Michael from his melancholic state. He looked up at her as if not understanding the words for an instant before finally getting up. He walked to the bedroom and rummaged through the pockets of several pairs of pants that lay scattered on the floor before finding the folded sheet of paper in the back pocket of some jeans. He came back to the kitchen, list in hand, and set it on the table in front of Sheila who started reading the list aloud to force Michael to focus on the task at hand:

1) Deputy Chief Sullivan and his two Rottweilers were killed at home by Wolf-A, who escaped through a window. Window broken from the inside indicates escape point and not entry way.

2) Two guns were found on the floor in Sullivan's living room, but only one set of paw prints.

3) Steve and Marge Harrington were killed in their home by Wolf-B, who too escaped through the window. Same observation as above for the window.

4) David Starks attacked at home by Wolf-C, who was shot repeatedly by the detective but managed to escape...

5) There is an active Wolf pack in Houston whose association with the mob is likely.

6) I was attacked by the mob shortly after visiting Peter Clemens, the Alpha, at his house in the forest. Possibly the pack headquarters.

7) At least one wolf has infiltrated the local police, possibly more.

8) Sheila was attacked by Ivanov's henchmen after writing an article hinting at a connection between the mob and the wolf attacks.

9) Clemens keeps a file with my name on it in his desk.

10) Clemens sent his Wolves to try and kill me.

11) Wolf-A was killed by me while trying to kill Sheila. He had previously assassinated a known associate of Ivanov, presumably sent to kill Sheila as well. Strangely, Wolf-A morphed back into his human form after his death and the wolf scent had completely disappeared from the body.

"Do we have any new points to add to this list?" she asked after completing her reading.

Michael contemplated the question for a minute before saying, "I still wonder how Clemens found us at your house. I hadn't told anyone about my intent to visit you."

"That's strange indeed," concluded Sheila. "It's probably worth writing it down, even though it may be completely unrelated to the wolves' murders in Houston. It's also strange how quickly they found us here in the middle of Yellowstone…"

"They're definitely well informed. I just wish we knew who's giving them their intel."

Sheila added point number twelve at the bottom of the list:

12) The pack has an uncanny way of finding out about our every move even when no one is entrusted with our plans.

"Anything else to add to the list?" she asked, still holding the pen an inch above the sheet of paper.

They thought about it silently for a few minutes, but neither of them came up with anything else worth committing to paper.

Chapter 121

The phone rang, and the Alpha picked it up.

"He's dead! The Chemist is dead!" said Axel Thompkins' voice on the other end of the line.

"How do you know? What happened?" asked the Alpha, mentally analyzing the implications of this unexpected piece of news.

"I had been looking for him ever since we got back from Montana. I still needed to drop the last load of plants. I've been carrying them around in my car for a week now…"

The Alpha did not point out the danger of being caught by their enemies with a trunk full of unprocessed plants, but his silence was remonstrance enough, and Axel knew it.

"Anyway, since I could never catch the Chemist at home, and since he never gets out, I started worrying about it. I called Fanning and Maxwell to see if the cops knew anything about it and they didn't. But Maxwell called me back ten minutes ago. Houston PD found our friend

Victor Grey floating face down in the bayou late last night. He looked pretty beaten up... According to the coroner's office, the Chemist had been in the water between twenty-four and thirty-six hours by the time the cops fished him out. They also think he'd been dead no longer than eight hours prior to being dumped in the bayou."

"This is not good for our plans," stated the Alpha in a controlled voice.

"I know. What will you have us do?"

"We will have to move to the next phase a bit earlier than we had anticipated. We cannot afford to run out of the drug while the threat has not yet been neutralized."

Chapter 122

Steam was rising from the mugs of freshly brewed tea and Sheila had her hands wrapped around her cup. What Michael referred to as the *toasty 62 degrees* inside the cabin was not nearly toasty enough for the native Houstonian who, wrapped up in two sweaters, kept moving her chair closer to the hearth where small flames were working lazily on a mostly consumed log. Michael, apparently unimpressed by the raging blizzard outside the cabin, had not bothered throwing a jacket over his thin, taupe-colored ranger shirt before walking out to the firewood shed located at the back of the house. He had come back a couple minutes later covered in snow, carrying a dozen logs. After laying the logs in a neat pile beside the fireplace, he had gone back to his seat at the kitchen table, and Sheila had reluctantly given up her spot by the fireplace to join him.

They were now once again staring at Michael's list in the hope of finally finding a pattern or at least a connection between the apparently unrelated facts Michael had scribbled down on the page.

"OK Michael, let's go over our current theory one more time," said Sheila in a matter-of-fact voice. "Your friend Steve was killed because he was working on the wolf-assassin case, and his wife was unfortunate collateral damage."

Michael nodded and Sheila continued. "The same reason also explains why David Starks was attacked. He, too, was working on the case. The fact that the pack has not gone after him since the case was reassigned to Detectives Lewis and Salazar seems to confirm our hypothesis."

"But if working this case was the sole reason to go after Steve and David, why haven't Lewis and Salazar been targeted so far?"

"Maybe Steve and David were onto something without knowing it. Maybe they were getting close and Clemens couldn't allow them to dig any deeper..." answered Sheila after a second of reflection.

"Maybe..." Michael sounded unconvinced. "Assuming Clemens is truly behind all this."

"Who else could it be? Who else could readily send werewolves on killing sprees on Clemens' turf?"

Michael didn't answer. He had no other name to suggest.

"In addition, Clemens most likely came after you because you started working this case."

Michael pulled a face clearly expressing his skepticism. "Clemens came after me as soon as he learned of my existence. I am pretty sure he would have done the same if I had been in Houston on a trip to visit the space center. The wolves and my kind are hereditary enemies; we don't need reasons to tear each other apart. The feud has been branded in our genes over millennia of violent clashes between our two species."

He could still remember his first confrontation with werewolves in a frozen forest of Markland. He had met very few wolves in his early life—given its historical werebear population, Norway had not been a place for werewolves—and it wasn't until the early 1300s that he had faced off his first hostile pack. He had been living in Markland for two hundred years by the time the Thules had arrived from western Alaska. The indigenous Dorsets had been stronger than the Thules but poorly armed. In the end, the invaders' superior weapons, their dogs, and their werewolves had prevailed over the skrælings who had become extinct two centuries later.

Michael had not waited that long to leave Markland and migrate south to the werewolf-free Great Lakes region, where he had finally settled in the state now known as Michigan in 1323.

"OK, fine," replied Sheila, effectively drawing him back to present time, "but that doesn't invalidate our hypothesis in anyway."

Michael grunted in agreement.

"What we need to find out is a motive. If we understand why the first wolf killing took place, we'll have solved the puzzle," resumed Sheila.

Michael still wasn't convinced, but he did not voice his doubts. "Steve and David were working on a series of cop assassinations, and they thought Chief Deputy Sullivan's murder was probably related to those."

"I know, I wrote a piece about this implicating the mob. And since Ivanov's goons sent me to the hospital shortly thereafter, there might have been some truth in it..." commented Sheila, mechanically rubbing her recently mended ribs.

"We need to find out everything we can about these other murders, and maybe then we'll be able to find a motive," said Michael thoughtfully.

"I think your buddy David Starks would be a great asset in this matter..."

Chapter 123

The small army had made it to the rallying point an hour before sunrise and had waited there in silence. None of the men were expert navigators, but with the advent of GPS navigation, anyone with half a brain could get to a designated point nowadays.

With the exception of the lieutenants, easily identifiable in their black commando suits, the men wore camouflage army fatigues. Their faces were painted in black and green and only their weapons gave away their nonmilitary affiliation. A few of them had heavy duty M-16A1 assault rifles equipped with 40-millimeter grenade launchers, but the bulk of the group was armed with Russian AK-47s, the cheap, versatile, and reliable assault rifle favored around the world by rebels, regular armies, and terrorist groups alike.

In agreement with Ivanov's orders, every shell in every clip was equipped with silver-head bullets, an expensive and mostly useless precaution. The mobster was under the misconception that silver bullets could kill werewolves more surely than regular bullets… an urban legend! Granted, silver being harder and therefore less malleable than lead, silver bullet fired at short range might have a more damaging impact than their lead counterparts, but the armor-piercing steel or tungsten versions would still have been a better and much cheaper option.

Ivanov had given clear instructions to wait for daylight before launching the assault, for he knew the wolves had better night vision than humans. He also knew the wolves would be more likely to detect the incoming strike force if his men were to wait for sunrise too close to the Houston pack HQ. Therefore, following their boss's orders, the fifty-odd men had waited for the break of dawn to start walking the final mile to their target.

The forest was still doused in the early morning light when Ivanov's men took their positions at the edge of the clearing, completely surrounding Clemens' cabin.

Chapter 124

Lucy Harrington arrived at the precinct six police station shortly after 8 a.m. and walked straight into David Starks' office, only to find it empty. She sank into one of the only two chairs not covered with files and started crying silently, alone in the austere room. After three days spent looking for her sister in every possible place and interviewing everyone who had even a remote chance of knowing Olivia's whereabouts, Lucy had finally come to accept the fact her sister had disappeared and that she wouldn't be able to find her on her own.

She was still crying a few minutes later when David walked in, holding a steaming cup of coffee. The detective hadn't seen Lucy since the funeral, and he didn't recognize her right away without the huge sunglasses the young woman had sported then.

Recognizing her dad's old partner standing in the doorway, she said in a sob, "Olivia has disappeared."

The name jolted David's memory. "Lucy? I didn't know you were still in town. I had heard you'd gone back to college."

"I had… I just got back into town three days ago. I couldn't reach Olivia and I started worrying. I came back to look for her, but I still can't find her anywhere and I am afraid something happ—" replied Lucy, breaking into an uncontrollable sob in mid-sentence.

The detective extended a box of tissues towards the crying woman and waited patiently for her to regain enough composure to continue her story.

"Olivia never mentioned she was planning to take a trip," resumed Lucy, making a visible effort to keep her sniveling under control. "She's all I have left. If something happened to her—"

Not knowing what else to do, David placed a comforting hand on the weeping woman's shoulder and waited for her tears to run out.

Unable to bear the idea of sleeping in the house where her parents had been murdered, Lucy had decided to stay with a friend while in Houston. Sitting on the floor in the middle of the living room, she dialed Michael's cell phone number for the fourth time in less than an hour and, for the fourth time, the call went straight to voicemail. Growing increasingly frustrated with her lack of progress, Lucy hung up and angrily threw her phone on the couch. It bounced back and barely missed the coffee table before landing on the living room rug in one piece.

After filling out the paperwork to initiate a police investigation of Olivia's disappearance, David had given Michael's phone number to Lucy. The young woman had been trying to get in touch with the ranger ever since, and at every failed attempt she was shedding a few more tears. She had been crying on and off all day, and her puffed-up eyes were black with smeared mascara.

Suddenly, she remembered the detective mentioning Michael's return to Yellowstone and went to pick up her smartphone from the carpet. After a couple minutes of online searching, she dialed Yellowstone National Park's information and asked for Michael's landline number. Unfortunately, the lady on the phone apologetically explained this was not the type of information she could give out to the public.

"Could you at least pass on a message? It is very important…" said Lucy, sounding just desperate enough for the woman to agree.

She had expected to wait several hours for Michael to call her back, but five minutes later her phone was already ringing.

"Hello?"

"Lucy? Hi, this is Michael Biörn speaking. I believe you were trying to get a hold of me?"

"Yes, yes I was," said Lucy eagerly. "Is my sister with you?"

"No…" answered Michael, not at all liking the direction the conversation was taking. "Why would she be with me?"

He heard Lucy explode in sobs on the other end of the line and waited for her to calm down.

"She's gone missing," Lucy managed to say after a minute. "I've had no news from her in a week and we usually talk every day…"

Chapter 125

No light was visible inside the house, and Igor Petrovich hoped their enemies were still sound asleep. Ivanov had asked him to lead the attack against Clemens' organization, and since Igor was not an idiot, the boss had been forced to explain to his lieutenant why silver bullets were necessary for the job. Although Petrovich had long suspected Clemens' involvement in the wolf attacks, his logical brain refused to accept the absurd werewolf stories that had escaped from Ivanov's mouth. Maybe Clemens' men truly believed they were wolves and fought as such, or maybe they used trained wolves as weapons… The killings in Houston had been all over the news lately, and although the journalists had wrongly accused the mob of being behind the series of assassination, they could have had the rest of the story right…

Every member of the large execution squad was equipped with a radio headset to facilitate communications. When Petrovich gave the signal, the men located on the south side of the house dropped to the ground, while the men on the north side stood and started opening fire. Bullets poured out of their automatic weapons for a full minute, turning the cabin's north siding into Swiss cheese. Still following their lieutenant's orders, the men on the north side ceased fire and lay flat on the ground while their southern counterparts stood up and in turn opened fire. This strategy was aimed at targeting every possible angle of the house without suffering casualties from friendly crossfire.

Soon the south siding was equally well ventilated as the north one and Petrovich ordered a ceasefire. He had not expected werewolves to storm out of the house to tear his men to pieces, but after observing that absolutely no one—and nothing— had made a run for it, he felt slightly disappointed.

Given the look of the bullet-riddled building, it was doubtful anything could have survived the assault, but he still sent a dozen men inside the house to go investigate and confirm the success of the mission. The recon team had not been inside the cabin thirty seconds when terror screams erupted over the com system. The shrilling was short-lived and soon silence returned. Petrovich, convinced his scouting team was dead, ordered his men to resume fire and this time the use of the M16-A1 grenade launchers was strongly encouraged.

Pieces of hardiplank and sheet rock flew everywhere as the structural integrity of the building started to fail. Before the house had a chance to collapse, a group of gigantic blood-covered wolves exploded out of it and rushed towards Igor's men who did not wait for his authorization to open fire on the beasts. The monsters were impossibly fast and agile, however, and it was simply impossible to keep an aim on them. They dodged most bullets and the ones that actually reached them didn't seem to slow them down in the slightest. They were on Petrovich's group in an instant, ripping throats and stomachs open as if they were made of paper. Before long, the beasts were the only ones left standing on the bloody battleground.

After making sure there wasn't a single enemy left alive, the great black wolf who had led the onslaught let out a long howl and took off running towards the woods. The trees soon swallowed his silhouette, but none of his wolves made a move to follow him—they knew better. They, too, had seen the mangled body of the Alpha's mate lying amidst the rubble of their house. Isabella had been on the receiving end of a grenade and hadn't survived the detonation.

Chapter 126

"I had lunch with Salinger today," announced Salazar conversationally.

"Eastside Salinger?" enquired Lewis. Her partner nodded.

"How are things going over there?" she asked, maneuvering her way between lanes of traffic. There was never a good time for traffic on the 610 loop, but 5.30 p.m. was definitely one of the worst.

"Same shit, different place…" replied Salazar cynically. "He's working the murder of a smalltime crook nicknamed The Chemist, who was found floating in the Port of Houston a few days ago."

"Was the guy's real name Victor Grey?" asked Lewis, suddenly interested.

Ed Salazar thought about it for a second before answering, "Mmh, I think so. Why? Did you know the guy?"

The rain, which up to now had only been a drizzle, started pouring heavily on the already saturated freeway.

Most of these morons already can't drive on dry roads, this is definitely going to help clear up traffic, thought Samantha Lewis. She answered, "Yeah, I knew the guy. He was a small fish himself, but he worked for pretty big ones. I busted him once when I worked in narcotics, but he ratted his way out of the slammer."

She slammed on her brakes as the file of cars in front of her came to a complete stop.

"Looks like we're going to be here a while," she said, exasperated.

"Who did he rat out?" asked Salazar.

"Some bigtime dealer, but it's been twelve years and I doubt anyone would remember the guy. It was before the Russians' era, when the Italians were still running the show."

Salazar meditated his partner's answer while looking at the rain bouncing off the hood of the car beside them. "Do you think The Chemist's death could have something to do with Ivanov or our case?"

"Victor had supposedly retired from the drug-processing business, but you know how these guys are..." answered Lewis thoughtfully. "I suppose he could very well have been back in business, and since Ivanov controls the drug trafficking across the city... there is a chance, although slight, that Victor's death could be related to our headache."

Chapter 127

The ground surrounding the house was littered with the dismembered bodies of Ivanov's defeated army. The mercenaries' blood had seeped through the clearing's ground to form a macabre patchwork with the fallen tree leaves. Here and there, small patchy clouds of fog hung in the air like ethereal ghosts, further increasing the surreal atmosphere.

Karl Wilson, a woman, and six other men David Starks did not recognize were standing in silence in front of the house. The group looked utterly disheveled and wore ragged clothes, torn to pieces by what David assumed had been unplanned morphing.

The detective had surveyed the mobsters' bodies for teeth or claw marks, but he hadn't found anything truly definitive. Numerous bodies were riddled with bullet wounds to the point of being torn to shreds. David suspected the wolves had shot the bodies postmortem to erase all traces of their true fate. If it were the case, they had been very thorough in their work.

Since the lab team had already finished taking pictures and sampling whatever they felt needed to be checked out, David notified the team from the coroner's office that they could start taking away the bodies. He then walked towards what was left of the Houston pack to try and figure out what exactly had happened, and, more importantly, where the hell Peter Clemens was.

Chapter 128

The flight had been bumpy and Sheila had felt sick for a good half of the trip. Once she started feeling better, she had been in a chatty mood, but Michael wasn't, and despite all her attempts she had been unable to obtain more than monosyllables out of her boyfriend who appeared once again lost in thoughts. *Boyfriend...* she wondered. Was this how Michael saw their relationship? They had been intimate a few times and he seemed to appreciate her company as much as she enjoyed his, but did he consider her his girlfriend? She would have paid a lot of money to know what was going on in that brain of his, and to know how much room Isibel was still occupying.

The plane landed in Houston with only a five-minute delay, and Michael and Sheila drove straight to the friend's apartment where Lucy was staying to meet with the young woman. Lucy was glad to see Michael, but she didn't seem to have much more to tell him than what she had already disclosed over the phone.

Michael asked about the last few discussions Lucy had with her sister in the hope Olivia would have mentioned something which, although seemingly irrelevant at the time, could now shed some light on her disappearance. Unfortunately, nothing Lucy recalled appeared remotely useful, and Michael quickly realized he knew more about the situation than Lucy did. He refrained, however, from mentioning this to the young woman.

During his last discussion with Olivia, she had confessed to taking a maid job in order to get access to Clemens' house. Michael had warned her of the risks she was taking and demanded she never returned to Clemens', but the discussion had turned into an argument and it had been the last time he had talked with Olivia.

He now strongly suspected Clemens was involved in the woman's disappearance, but he did not know what to do about it. Although the pack had suffered major losses during their last confrontation in Yellowstone, there were still enough of them left to be a problem. Michael could not count on any help from his furry relatives this time, so he decided it was time to touch base with David Starks and see if the detective could help.

Chapter 129

Forty-five minutes of questioning hadn't enlightened David Starks very much regarding the exact circumstances of the bloodbath. Karl Wilson had been the only one answering his questions while the others had simply agreed to every statement made by the pack's second in command.

According to Wilson, Peter Clemens had not been around when the small army had given the assault, and no one knew where he was. Nobody seemed to know who the men were who had attacked them or why they had tried to kill them.

When David had asked how such a small group had been able to defeat such an overwhelming force, Wilson had simply invoked luck and God's protection of the innocents.

Because the evidence was so heavily indicating that the pack had acted in self-defense when they had decimated the fifty heavily armed men, David could not arrest any of them. Of course they had lied to him over and over again, but you could not arrest someone for suspecting them of lying. In addition, he already knew the answers to the most important questions: Peter Clemens was still alive, Isabella was dead, and there was no doubt in the detective's mind that the strike force had been sent by Ivanov.

Chapter 130

Ed Salazar was standing in Katia Olveda's living room trying not to stare too much at the assistant DA's particularly low-cut silk blouse.

"Where is your partner?" asked Katia casually.

"She had some other business to attend, so I told her I'd come alone to not waste any time," lied Salazar. Lewis was actually waiting for him in a coffee house a block away. She had simply refused to come and ask a favor from the woman she typically referred to as The Slut.

"I see," replied Katia, clearly unconvinced. "So, what is the emergency?"

"We need a warrant to search Peter Clemens' property."

"Why do you need to search his property? From what I hear, there isn't much left of his house anyway. It would seem someone decided to use it for target practice."

Salazar brushed some imaginary dust off his sleeve before answering. "Detective Starks informed us an hour ago that a clump of hair he had found nearby Clemens' cabin and had analyzed by the lab actually belonged to a Danko Jovanovich. A bookie for the Russian mob who went missing six weeks ago. The hair sample also had traces of Danko's blood. We were suspecting Ivanov's involvement in the wolf attacks, but we had no tangible evidence to go by—"

"What does Ivanov have to do with this now? Don't tell me you need a warrant to search his house as well?! And how do you link the bookie to the wolf attacks?" interrupted Katia, apparently irritated by Salazar's irrational reasoning. In reality, she was more concerned by the Alpha's reaction to her involvement in obtaining a search warrant.

Salazar took a breath to give himself time to formulate his reply.

"Clemens is a suspected associate of Ivanov," he said finally. "He lives in the middle of a forest, a much more appropriate location to keep wolves than Ivanov's residence in River Oaks—"

"This doesn't even get close to circumstantial evidence, Detective," interjected the assistant DA. "What you have, at best, is a theory, and no judge in their right mind would ever grant a warrant on such flimsy conjectures. And I would never embarrass myself asking for such a warrant either..."

"This is where Danko comes into play, Ma'am. He may not be linked to the wolf assassinations in any way, but he has known association with the Russian mob, and we are therefore justified in suspecting Clemens could have something to do with the bookie's disappearance."

Katia rolled her eyes in a *I can't believe I'm listening to this shit* kind of look, but Salazar carried on, oblivious. "Danko has probably never seen a wolf in his life, but it's irrelevant. He's just our way into Clemens' house. One—the bookie has been missing for six weeks. Two—we can establish a link between Clemens and Danko through Ivanov. Three— we now have physical evidence placing a bleeding Danko near Clemens' property. I don't believe it's unreasonable to assume Clemens may have something to do with Danko's disappearance and request a warrant to search his house."

"I see," replied Katia thoughtfully. She had dropped the attitude and seemed to be genuinely thinking about Salazar's request. "You do realize that finding a judge willing to grant a search warrant on a Saturday isn't going to be a walk in the park, right?"

"We know that, Ma'am, but we need it. With everything that went down yesterday, we think Clemens has become a flight risk, and we need to try and arrest him as soon as possible."

Katia pondered his remark for an instant before saying, "Let me see what I can do. I'll be in touch as soon as I have news for you."

Salazar thanked the assistant DA and took his leave. He was about to close the front door on his way out when he heard Katia say, "And please, say hello to Detective Lewis for me."

Chapter 131

Peter Clemens hadn't uttered a single complete sentence since Isabella's death twenty-four hours earlier. After spending the whole day and night in the woods, the Alpha had returned to what was left of his pack shortly after eight the next morning. The cops were long gone and his wolves had started cleaning out the mayhem inside what a few hours earlier had still been the pack's command center.

Although he should have been expecting it, Clemens had entered into a destructive fury upon realizing the coroners had taken away

Isabella's body. The survivors of his pack, knowing better than to try to calm their Alpha down, had watched from a distance while Clemens had methodically started destroying the few things still standing in the torn-down building. Once satisfied there was nothing left to destroy, the Alpha had pointed a finger at Karl Wilson. "You come with me." Then he'd turned towards the others. "Make sure there is nothing incriminating left in this house. Once this is done, go back to your homes. I'll contact you later."

"Where are you guys going?" asked Axel Thompkins as Clemens and his second were getting into Wilson's corvette, but Clemens did not reply.

It was mid-morning by the time they parked the car along the wall on the east side of Ivanov's estate. The street was deserted, and the two wolves wasted no time looking for a door. In an instant, they had jumped the wall and were among the Texas oak trees, walking at a quick pace towards the mansion's front door.

No guard could be seen on the grounds surrounding the manor, but as the duo was closing on the house, two Dobermans and three German Shepherds came rushing from various corners of the property. When the dogs were about twenty feet from the two men, they stopped dead in their tracks, turned around and started running for their lives. Unlike bewitched bears, dogs knew when they were outmatched, and their noses had told them all they needed to know about the two trespassers.

Clemens did not bother with the bell and instead gave a powerful kick to the center of the French doors, which went flying off their hinges and landed fifteen feet away on the vestibule's freshly polished hardwood floor.

The Alpha crossed the vestibule in four strides while Wilson, more cautious, kept an eye open for incoming trouble. No one came to meet them in the vestibule, however, nor in the living room, kitchen, or library. Although the house looked deserted, the two wolves could sense people within its walls, and one of them was Ivanov.

After rummaging through another couple empty rooms, Clemens and Wilson found themselves in the mansion's west wing standing in front of yet another set of closed French doors. The smell emanating from behind the doors immediately told them they had found what they were looking for. Before they had a chance to push the doors open, an avalanche of bullets erupted from inside the room, reducing the wooden doors to rubble and sending the wolves running for cover.

Most of Ivanov's forces had perished in their assault against the wolves, but the mobster had surrounded himself with the few he had left to make his last stand. Judging by the look of what a few seconds earlier had been two-inch thick solid wood doors, the mobster's bodyguards were packing serious fire power.

"You didn't think killing me would be that easy, did you?" asked the Russian accent-laden voice of the boss, but Clemens did not bother replying. From the direction the voice had come from, he had a pretty good idea of Ivanov's position inside the room.

He turned towards his second who had pulled his 357 Magnum out of its back holster and was crouching behind a rosewood secretaire.

"I'll morph, you shoot," he said in a low voice, before adding, "But Ivanov is mine... no matter what!"

Clemens stripped out of his clothes and quickly morphed into his 300-pound wolf form. A second later, he was storming through the office door, Wilson a few feet behind him.

As soon as the wolf entered the room, the deluge of silver bullets resumed, and several of them reached their impossibly fast moving target, but that did not slow Clemens down as he took a sharp right turn to pounce onto Stanislas Erzgova who was shooting a fifty caliber. The gun—the same model as the one mounted on Apache helicopters—looked gigantic even in the giant's grip, and when one of its bullets hit Clemens' chest in midair, it sent the wolf crashing against the opposite wall.

But the shooters, too focused on the nightmarish beast, had overlooked Wilson and when he entered the room, gun in hand, a second behind his Alpha, no weapon was trained towards him. Quickly assessing the situation, he placed a bullet in the heads of the three bodyguards, starting with the one holding the biggest gun, Stanislas, before shooting Ivanov in the right shoulder. Under the impact, Ivanov's gun dropped to the floor.

As he stood in a corner of the room holding his bleeding shoulder, the corpse of Stanislas Erzgova lying at his feet and his other bodyguards scattered lifeless across the room, Ivanov wondered if letting Clemens have a share of his business wouldn't have been a better idea after all.

The Alpha lay unconscious on the carpet in a pool of his own blood, a gaping crater in his chest. The hole had already stopped bleeding, though, and Wilson knew the Alpha would be all right... eventually. His gun still trained on Ivanov, the pack's second in command patiently waited for Clemens to recover while ignoring the mobster's alternating queries, pleas, and invectives.

It took a full thirty minutes for Clemens to be in good enough shape to get back on his paws, and Wilson had spent the whole time wondering whether the cops, alerted by the shooting, were going to show up, but in the end Ivanov's house was far enough from the street and surrounded by enough trees to absorb the sounds of the battle.

Under Ivanov's bewildered eyes, Clemens finally morphed back into his human form, a nasty scar in the center of his chest. The Alpha then walked towards the mob boss and, grabbing him by the throat, lifted Ivanov two feet in the air before throwing him against the opposite wall like a rag doll.

The impact drove the oxygen out of the mobster's lungs and he was still gasping for air when Clemens picked him up from the floor and sent him crashing this time through the room's bay window. Ivanov had barely landed onto the terrace when Clemens was already upon him.

"You shouldn't have killed my wife," were the only words the Alpha pronounced before crushing his enemy's skull against the stone floor.

Chapter 132

The clearing harboring the Clemenses' devastated cabin was teeming with police officers and search dogs. It had taken Katia Olveda the better part of her Saturday to find a judge willing to sign off on the search warrant Salazar had requested, and the cops had been forced to wait until Sunday to execute the search. The officers had shown up at the break of dawn on Sunday only to find the house deserted.

Out of courtesy, Lewis and Salazar had extended an invitation to David Starks, who had been the one to find Danko's DNA in the vicinity of the property, and the three detectives were now busy rummaging through the rubble in search of anything incriminating against Clemens and his gang. They had been at work for over three hours, searching through drawers, filing cabinets, and other less likely hiding spots, but to no avail. All they had to show for it so far were two bullet-riddled computers, whose hard drives were conveniently missing, and a collection of suspiciously empty drawers. The only artifact of interest had been a set of titanium shackles found by an officer inside a metal trunk in the garage, but with the exception of David Starks, nobody had grasped its significance.

Outside, special canine units were searching the grounds in ever expanding circles around the house, but the dogs' behavior was curiously erratic. The hounds were running from one spot to the next, seemingly unable to follow a trail to its end. The handlers, who had never seen their dogs behaving that way, were at a loss for an explanation. To David, however, it was obvious: olfactory overstimulation. The entire perimeter smelled of wolf—and not a lone wolf either. The area was impregnated with the smell of several dozen wolves and the poor dogs simply didn't know which trail to follow in this olfactory labyrinth. The wolf smell was so pungent and overwhelming that it effectively covered every other scent. In comparison, the faint odors left behind by Danko and Olivia were as noticeable as a cat hair on a Persian rug. In consequence, the officers searching the grounds walked over the underground cache in which Olivia was kept prisoner three times, and three times they failed to notice anything unusual about the clearing's leaf-covered ground in this particular location.

Chapter 133

Buried twenty feet under the surface, Olivia hadn't suspected a thing about the swarm of officers who, less than a day earlier, had spent hours searching the grounds directly above her head. Her prison had been designed to be perfectly soundproof, and the proofing worked both ways.

The young woman was slowly starving to death. Between Michael Biörn and the Russian mob, the pack had been too busy to remember feeding its prisoner, who hadn't had a thing to eat or drink in over a week. Had she still been human, Olivia would have been dead by now, but she was no longer a mere human and her werewolf metabolism was working overtime to keep her alive a bit longer.

Too weak to move, she spent her days lying naked on the bare ground amidst her own feces. She was too frail to morph even involuntarily, and that part brought her peace. Olivia had figured out by now that, against conventional wisdom, werewolves could be found outside overactive imaginations and movie theaters. She was the living proof of it.

For days, she had wished she had followed Michael's advice and returned to school instead of playing the amateur avenger in a league so far from her own that just thinking about it made her head spin. Those days were gone, however. The only thing she desired now was for death to come and set her free.

The light in the cell suddenly changed quality. It started shining with more intensity and looked somehow cleaner, but she was so disoriented that she did not realize the beams of light were pouring from the opened trapdoor above her head. She only started realizing what was going on when Axel Thompkins landed two feet away from her head and leaned towards her.

"She's alive," she heard him say to someone she couldn't see and who was probably still on the surface, "but it's a fucking mess in here!"

"I can smell it from here," replied a voice somewhere above them.

Axel placed her on his shoulders and effortlessly started climbing out of the hole using a rope hanging from the opened trapdoor.

Olivia was in no shape to fight off the muscular man carrying her, but even if she had been, she probably wouldn't have. What she desired above all was to get out of this stinking cave that had been her home since the fateful day when she'd had the horrible idea of confronting Peter Clemens.

After they reached the surface, the man who had been waiting outside the hole pulled the rope back out, closed the trapdoor, and started covering it in dirt and leaves to make it once again invisible to passersby. In the meantime, Thompkins started carrying the barely moving Olivia to their car parked on a dirt road, two hundred yards from the underground cache.

Once at the car, Olivia was tied up, gagged and unceremoniously tossed inside the vehicle's trunk.

"And now, let's go see the boss," said Thompkins, shutting the trunk on her.

Chapter 134

The doorbell rang and David Starks got up to answer it. He came back to the living room a minute later carrying four extra-large pizza boxes and placed them on the coffee table in front of Michael, who was holding out forty dollars as his contribution to the pizza fund.

"Keep your money," said David. "It's my treat tonight."

Michael thanked him for his generosity and pocketed the two twenties.

Monday night football was playing on the television in the background, but David had muted the sound so they could have a real conversation. Michael had been staying with Sheila since their return to Houston, and if he had driven an hour from her place to David's beach house in Kemah, it was not to watch football.

"Are you planning to move back into the city at some point?" asked Michael, thinking about the detective's daily two-hour commute.

"Eventually… but I like living here. I find the proximity of the sea very calming, though the commute is definitely getting to me." David got up and headed for the kitchen. He came back an instant later with two plates and a roll of paper towels, which he put down next to the pizza boxes.

"Whoever attacked you in Houston has had plenty of time to figure out where you relocated by now," said Michael, ignoring the plates David had just brought from the kitchen and settling down on the floor in front of an open pizza box. "If they have left you alone this long, it's probably safe to move back."

"Whoever attacked me? You don't think it was one of Clemens' wolves?" asked David, surprised at Michael's choice of words.

"There is a very good chance it was, based on what we know so far," agreed Michael, "but he's innocent until proven guilty… you know that better than I do."

"Right!" David sounded unconvinced as he sank his teeth into a slice of all-meat pizza. "So, what's new on your side?"

Michael swallowed down a piece large enough to choke a horse before answering, "Well, I believe you know most of it. For one, the Houston pack has been seriously downsized in the past week."

"You told me. And I got firsthand confirmation."

"Meaning?"

"I was at Clemens' three times in the past few days and there were never more than eight or nine wolves around. Given the recent events, the pack should definitely be operating in crisis mode, and therefore the members should stick together most of the time. That means the wolves I saw are probably all that's left of the Houston pack…"

"That sounds about right," answered Michael, remembering the handful of survivors who had fled the battlefield after their confrontation in Yellowstone. "But why did you go to Clemens three times these past few days?"

"Don't tell me you haven't heard?!" replied David skeptically.

"Heard what?"

"Heard what??! You're joking, right?" But David could see from Michael's face he wasn't joking. "I thought, with a girlfriend journalist and all, you'd keep yourself better informed."

Displeased by the girlfriend comment as much as by the fact David still hadn't mentioned what the big news actually was, Michael remained silent and focused an unsettling stare at David.

David finally obliged and related in detail the recent events to Michael. Starting with the attack on Clemens house that had claimed Isabella's life, the detective then followed with his interview of the survivors before recounting the execution of the search warrant, which unfortunately hadn't turned up anything incriminating against Clemens. "How did you manage to not hear about this?" he asked finally.

"I have no idea. I guess we've been pretty focused on looking for Olivia ever since we got back. And it's only been a couple days too… Talking about Olivia, have you heard anything? Any lead? The last time I talked to her, she was heading for Clemens…"

"What?!"

In a few words, Michael told David how Olivia had somehow found out about Clemens, and how she had decided to get a job with a maid service agency in order to be sent to the man's house and get a chance to snoop around.

"I agree with you," said David once Michael had finished his story. "It would be a miracle if Clemens wasn't involved one way or another in her disappearance, but we searched the grounds with dogs and they didn't find her. Of course, that could also be a good sign. That could mean she's still alive somewhere."

"The dogs would have been thrown off by the wolf stench anyway," answered Michael, before adding pensively, "I'll have to go take a look for myself." "Do you have something to drink?" he added as an afterthought.

"I have beer, water and that's about it," replied David apologetically. "Water will do."

David got up to go fetch Michael his drink as the other pulled out a small notepad and a pencil from his pocket. "Could you give me the names of all the officers assassinated execution-style?"

"I should be able to find those for you. I used to have them committed to memory but it's been two years for some of them… I remember there was an Elaine Blent from Houston PD, and now Mark Sullivan and, of course, Steve."

Michael jotted down the names on his notepad before showing it to David for spellchecking.

"I'll have to get the other names from Lewis and Salazar. They have the files now," added David.

An hour and three pizzas later, the two men had shared every potentially relevant piece of information in their possession and David was getting ready to unmute the game on TV when Michael's cell phone rang. He checked the caller ID and, seeing Sheila's name on the screen, decided to answer.

"I know, David just told me," replied Michael to whatever revelation Sheila had just made before adding, "Ivanov? Are you sure?"

He listened intently for another couple minutes before turning to David. "Ivanov is dead. He was killed in his River Oaks mansion along with three of his bodyguards. They just found the bodies, but it looks like they've been dead for at least a couple days."

Chapter 135

Michael rolled to a stop on a dirt road a mile from Clemens' cabin shortly after midnight.

It was three days past the full moon, and in the forest's cloudless sky the light dispensed by the lunar body was so bright that one could see almost as well as in broad daylight. Michael was not pleased with the eerie quality of the forest's lighting; the cover of darkness would have suited his current enterprise far better.

Leaving his car parked under the trees a few yards from the road, Michael started heading across the woods straight for the cabin. Ten minutes later, the house was in sight and, keeping a respectable distance, he circled the impact-riddled building twice while constantly smelling the air. Satisfied no one was hiding inside or outside the house, he started removing his clothes, piling them into a disorganized stack at the foot of a tree. Once thoroughly naked, he gave a last circular look at his surroundings before morphing into his bear counterpart.

In his animal form, his nose was as sensitive as a grizzly's, and therefore seven times more powerful than a bloodhound's, the best canine tracker on the planet. And, unlike the police dogs that had searched the grounds a day earlier, Michael knew exactly what he was looking for. Olivia's scent was as fresh in his olfactory memory as if the young woman had been standing right beside him. Now all he had to do was to ignore the hundreds of trails left by the pack and focus on Olivia's unique aroma. Of course this was easier said than done as the wolves' odors were so powerful they were nearly impossible to disregard.

Michael decided to start his search inside the house since it was the one location he knew for a fact Olivia had been. As soon as he passed the threshold, he picked up the woman's scent. It was very faint and barely noticeable under the overwhelming stench of Clemens and his wife, but it was there nonetheless.

He started following her trail across the house, but as he reached the stairwell he realized the seriously damaged stairs would most likely not support his 800-pound body. In all likelihood, the cops would have probably found Olivia had she been detained somewhere on the second floor, so he decided not to bother.

Back outside, snout against the ground, Michael started tracking Olivia's movements across the parking lot. Disappointingly, just like the immediate vicinity of the building and the garage, the parking lot did not appear to have any hidden trapdoor under which Olivia could have been kept. He was about to give up on the parking lot when suddenly he picked up a fresh trail, one that couldn't have been older than a day or two. Olivia had been here and alive in the past forty-eight hours.

This discovery boosted Michael's moral and motivation, and he resumed his search with renewed energy. The fresh trail did not seem to lead to the road, unless of course Olivia had been placed in a car, which would make a lot of sense if they were going to move her away from the original prison in which they had kept her... and that Michael had yet to find.

Starting from the parking lot, Michael slowly tracked Olivia's fresh trail back to the woods. The olfactory path ended abruptly two hundred yards from the cabin, in a place that had nothing to distinguish it from the surrounding woods. Michael knew trails did not simply disappear into thin air. The trail ending in the parking lot made sense if Olivia had gotten into a car; the trail ending in the middle of the woods in a location no enclosed vehicle could have reached could only have one explanation: this was the location where Olivia had been held captive.

Michael started rummaging through the dead leaves covering the grounds, sending massive amounts of dust and grit flying through the air in the process. It only took him a minute to uncover the hidden trapdoor kept locked by a deadbolt, and not much longer to pry it open and confirm what he already suspected. This hole in the ground had indeed been Olivia's holding cell, but it was now empty. It also smelled of werewolf.

Chapter 136

As a good investigative reporter, Sheila Wang had sources in most areas of society. The Houston PD was no exception. Working her magic with one of her informants, she had been able to obtain a copy of Jack Moore's file. She did not need any excuse to justify her appropriation of the information contained in the document, but assuming she did, the fact the man had broken into her house to murder her in her sleep was justification enough.

Sheila had begun retracing the steps of Detectives Salazar and Lewis, starting with a visit to Brenda Pennington, Jack's ex-girlfriend, but had learned nothing more than what had been in the file.

She was going through the police reports when she noticed that, strangely enough, the cops had not yet gone to the car shop where the would-be killer had been working as a mechanic. *A rather large oversight*, she thought, marveling not for the first time at the fact the police ever succeeded in apprehending criminals. An instant later, she was in her car on her way to the shop.

Judging by its size, the place looked like a small family-owned business. Sheila was mentally rehearsing her made-up story about the Mini's erratic behavior above fifty miles per hour as she pushed open the door of the front office. She started describing her car's invented issues to the middle-aged woman wearing a baggy floral blouse sitting behind the counter, but she didn't get a chance to finish her tale before the woman interrupted her. "Do I know you from somewhere, doll? You see, I never forget a face… and you look reaaal familiar. You've come here before?" The woman's southern drawl was as thick as it got.

Under the woman's intent gaze, Sheila started denying having ever set foot in the premises in the past, but the woman looked utterly unconvinced. Before Sheila could pronounce another word the woman recognized her. "You're that journalist, the one he tried to kill!" she said excitedly.

Taken aback, Sheila stood there uneasily as the woman started frantically searching for something apparently misplaced under piles of invoices. The broken car story was clearly not going to hold the water…

The woman eventually pulled out an abused press clipping from under a pile and handed it to the journalist with a triumphant, "That's you, ain't it?"

The clipping, an article written by one of Sheila's colleagues while she was still in the hospital, featured pictures of Jack Moore, Vadim and Sheila herself.

Overcome by the undeniable piece of evidence, Sheila confessed to her prosecutor, "Yes, Ma'am, it's me."

The triumphant grin that illuminated the woman's face was hard to ignore.

"I knew it! As soon as you walked through the door I said to myself: 'I know this face!'"

Sheila shot an uncomfortable smile back at the woman. She needed to figure out a way to turn the situation to her advantage now that her original plan had taken on water.

"How can I help you, doll? Are you really having car troubles?" asked the woman suspiciously.

"To tell you the truth... I was wondering if you would be so kind as to answer a few questions for me about Jack."

The woman contemplated the request for a moment before answering, "Well, after what he did to you, I suppose that's the least I can do."

"Thank you so much." Sheila flashed her most appreciative smile. "You see, I'm trying to make my peace with what happened, and I believe this will help me a lot."

The woman's face adopted a benevolent, if slightly boastful expression. "What would you like to know?"

"First of all, what sort of a man was he?" asked Sheila to test the water.

It took the woman twenty minutes to confirm what Sheila had already heard from Brenda Pennington's mouth. Jack had been a kindhearted man, but things had taken a turn for the worse and no one really knew why. He had become an ass, apparently out of the blue. An ass with a short fuse and a really bad temper...

"Did Jack have any friends among the mechanics?" enquired Sheila.

"We're a small business, you know. We typically run with two or three mechanics including the owner. And at the time Jack worked for us, the owner was the only other mechanic in the shop."

"And do you think the owner would agree to answer a few questions?" asked Sheila in a hopeful voice.

"He's off today and he's usually real busy..." answered the woman. Sheila could tell by her face as well as by her tone that she was reluctant to share her moment of glory.

"Well, I suppose you can answer any questions as well as he would," Sheila added quickly, in an attempt to appease her.

The woman took the bait. "I'll do my best, dear."

"Was Jack friendly with the customers?"

After a minute of reflection the woman answered, "No... not particularly. But he wasn't rude either."

"I thought maybe he could have befriended the wrong guy, and if Jack was the impressionable type, maybe the guy's bad influence could have rubbed off on him," explained Sheila.

"Now that I think of it," started the woman, "he *did* befriend one of our customers."

"Do you remember the man's name?" asked Sheila expectantly.

"I don't," answered the lady, looking distraught. "Never been good with names. Not like faces... His face I remember, that's for sure. Came to the shop several times for car troubles, but I can't remember what his car looked like for the life of me either. But I don't think this guy was a bad influence on Jack. He looked like a nice enough guy... He was even a cop if I remember correct."

Chapter 137

"It looks like they're talking about David's girlfriend again," said Sheila from the treadmill where she was running at a quick pace. Ever since her assault at Memorial Park, the journalist had traded her outdoor jogging routine for indoor exercising.

Michael, who was sitting on the floor with his back against the wall, turned his gaze towards the muted TV screen mounted in a corner of the bedroom they had converted into Sheila's new exercise room.

"Nothing they haven't said a thousand times before, I'm sure," he commented.

Katia Olveda's face had been all over the news ever since John Macfly had been gunned down in the middle of the street in broad daylight. With Macfly gone, Katia was the most logical choice to replace the soon to retire district attorney who had announced he wouldn't be seeking reelection.

"You know us journalists... Once we have a story, we milk it for all it's worth, or at least until something juicier comes along," replied Sheila with a smirk, as she wiped beads of sweat off her forehead.

The black skintight body suit she was wearing wouldn't have left Michael indifferent under other circumstances, but he was currently too busy beating himself up to notice Sheila's revealing outfit. If only he had been smarter, if only he had searched the grounds around Clemens' house earlier... He had missed Olivia by a mere forty-eight hours, but now she was gone and he had no leads to follow.

Michael had learned from David that with the pack's lair all but destroyed, Clemens had temporarily moved in with Karl Wilson. Wilson lived in suburbia, however, and it was very doubtful they would have taken the chance of hiding Olivia in his backyard.

"We are getting close, I can feel it," said Sheila more cheerfully than she really felt. "The Russian mob is out of the equation—"

"We don't even know if they were ever *in* the equation," interrupted Michael.

"True... But now they're definitely out. That can't be a bad thing, can it? We need a positive attitude here, Michael."

The treadmill timer's chimed, indicating Sheila had been running for forty-five minutes. She grabbed the towel and mopped her face and then her neck. She went to sit by Michael on the carpet and took his paddle of a hand in hers.

"You're sure the lady at the mechanics' yesterday didn't say anything else?" he asked, knowing perfectly well that Sheila was smart enough to recognize useful information.

"Nothing I haven't already told you. Jack's mysterious friend was apparently a cop, but we aren't even sure it is the same friend that his ex-girlfriend mentioned. Assuming it *is* the same guy, the garage lady seemed to think he was a nice guy, but I would rather put my money on the girlfriend as far as being a good judge of character."

"Did she tell you what kind of a cop he was?"

"She didn't know. He could have been FBI for all she knew, but I find it doubtful. If someone's a fed, that's usually what they say, they don't typically introduce themselves as cops…"

Michael contemplated Sheila's last statement for an instant before answering, "That still leaves plenty of agencies to fish from. He could be Houston PD, belong to the Sheriff's department of one of the twelve thousand counties around the city, or be a state trooper…"

"Yes, he could be all that. But that still narrows it down!" she retorted.

"At any rate, solving this case is no longer a priority. We need to find out where the pack is keeping Olivia before we do anything else."

Chapter 138

From her drug-induced coma, Olivia heard what appeared to be something heavy sliding on a rail, quickly followed by the more easily identifiable sound of a car engine. A car door was opened and shut, but Olivia had fallen back into a deep sleep before she could register the familiar noise.

Peter Clemens did not bother locking up his car—nobody was going to steal it inside the building—and walked straight to the staircase leading to the part of the warehouse which had been converted into a 2000-square-foot loft.

The warehouse, located in an industrial zone on the west side of town, had been purchased by Karl Wilson under an assumed name years earlier. It was to provide an emergency shelter for the pack in case of need; until very recently, it had seen little use.

The loft's furnishing resembled the second-floor meeting room of Clemens' destroyed cabin. Now, however, with only a handful of wolves left alive, the large open floor looked gloomily empty.

On the warehouse's ground level, a few feet from the pack's improvised parking garage, lay an unconscious Olivia. Face resting on the concrete floor, she was handcuffed to a four-inch-wide metal beam, which rose all the way to the building's high ceiling. She was so sedated that the cuffs were probably superfluous, but one could never be too cautious. The pack had enough problems as it were without adding a berserk pup to their headaches. A newly turned wolf needed to be handled very carefully the first few weeks, and none of them had found the time to try taming Olivia. Under different circumstances, Clemens would probably have executed the woman already rather than burdening himself with an additional liability. Now that three-quarters of his pack had been annihilated, however, he couldn't afford to kill a potential recruit. Turning a human into a werewolf was a lot harder than Hollywood made it look. Of course, there was still the minor issue of Olivia having shot him repeatedly, in all likelihood to kill him... but she could maybe come around to him. After all, he had done nothing to her.

Without a word to his wolves, Clemens crossed half the room to go sit, eyes shut, in a reclining sofa in the center of the loft. He looked weary and in a foul mood, but he had been looking that way ever since Isabella's death. He opened his eyes five minutes later, and the others took this as their cue to gather around the Alpha.

"This isn't our finest day," he said after they all took their seats, "but we'll survive this. If we stay united, no one will be able to take us down."

"What about Biörn?" interrupted Rachel, who was now the pack's only female. "I hear he's back in town."

Clemens looked at her straight in the eyes, and she had to look away, unable to resist the Alpha's stare.

"So he is," he replied unperturbed. "And he's looking for that one," he said, pointing a finger in Olivia's general direction.

"Isn't it dangerous to keep her with us then?" asked Axel Thompkins. "If he finds out where we are, he'll come for her, and he won't be happy."

"He won't be happy but he won't risk harming her either. In the worst case scenario, she is our best bargaining chip, and in the best, she can help us take him down once she is one of us."

"I still think we should get rid of her," replied Thompkins. "She's just too big a liability."

Clemens got out of his seat and walked straight to Axel Thompkins who stood to meet the Alpha.

"If you think you can take me, Axel... go for it! And then you can lead the pack. But until that day, we will do as I say," said Clemens, an inch away from Thompkins' face.

Thompkins sat back into his chair in silence looking sheepish.

"So what's the plan?" asked Rachel.

"We wait."

Chapter 139

After making sure no one was in sight, Michael quickly slipped into the backyard of the house and skillfully punched a hole through the back door's window. Unlatching the deadbolt took him only a second, and then he was inside.

It had only been a week since the Chemist had been found floating in the Port of Houston, but one wouldn't have guessed it by looking at his living room. In addition to the usual disarray of takeout cartons and crumbs littering the floor and every single piece of furniture, a fetid odor assaulted the nostrils of anyone brave enough to pass the home's threshold.

Michael quickly identified the smell of decomposition that simply came from the less than fresh garbage bag in the kitchen and tried to block it out in order to focus on more subtle aromas.

He had come to this house more out of despair than conviction, or even hope. He had run out of places to look for Olivia and was now fishing for leads from the file Sheila had obtained from a source at Houston PD—an exact copy of Lewis' and Salazar's dossier.

The only reason the Chemist was part of the dossier in the first place had been his past affiliation with organized crime. Organized crime in Houston nowadays was synonymous with Ivanov—at least until very recently—and his organization had been the prime suspect for the cops' assassinations. All in all, the chances that following the Chemist's trail would lead Michael to Olivia were more than thin, but it wasn't as if he had many better things to try.

Attempting to tail Clemens in order to find out where the pack was hiding these days would have been more logical, but this wasn't a job Michael could tackle on his own. Any wolf would have smelled him coming from a mile away, and this was too likely to jeopardize Olivia's life, assuming the young woman were still alive. Michael did not want Sheila to do the tailing either. The journalist was less likely to be detected by the wolves, but they knew her scent all too well, and Clemens would no doubt love to work out some of his pain and frustration on poor Sheila if she ever fell under his claws.

Fortunately, David Starks had agreed to take on the job and was to report to Michael any useful piece of information he could gather. Beside the fact Clemens had officially moved into Wilson's suburban home, however, nothing useful had yet percolated to Michael's ears.

Michael walked through the house, carefully avoiding the empty pizza boxes and soda cans, but identified no hint of Olivia's scent anywhere in the building. As he reached the laundry room, however, a curious smell tickled his nostrils: a smell he couldn't quite place, which in itself was highly suspicious given his near perfect olfactory memory, and the colossal library of odors he had accumulated in a millennium of existence.

The smell appeared to come from the garage, whose access door was in the back of the laundry room. Michael opened the door and stepped into something he had definitely not been expecting: a spotless laboratory. The two-car garage had been expertly converted into a lab. The ground was covered with a white epoxy resin and the garage doors were invisible behind white walls. Rows of benches, covered in scientific glassware, lined every wall. In one corner an exhaust hood designed to absorb toxic chemical fumes had been installed. Its exhaust, apparently rigged into the house's air handling system, was venting to the roof.

Michael was still trying to identify the unusual odor, but something was off about it, as if it had been altered somehow. It was a fragrance that should not have existed by itself, as if someone had isolated it from a more complex broth. He was getting closer now, he knew it. What was the broth this particular fragrance came from? From which complex mixture had this odor been extracted? And then it came to him: wolfsbane! This could not be good. Wolfsbane was one of the very few things that could actually harm a praeternatural creature. As a plant, wolfsbane was highly irritating to praeternaturals' skin; if ingested in a large enough quantity it led to death after a long and excruciating agony. What in heaven's name was the Chemist doing with wolfsbane in the first place? And what was the molecule he had been isolating from it? Even more importantly, who had been commissioning his work?

As his brain was working through the potential implications of his discovery, Michael caught a whiff of another familiar scent, a wolf scent. Not just any wolf either... this one definitely belonged to Clemens' pack. Michael did not know Axel Thompkins by name, but he knew he had been the wolf in charge of keeping an eye on Sheila during the battle in Yellowstone. Against all expectations, coming here had been a good idea after all.

Chapter 140

Michael had just squeezed back into his car when his cell phone rang. Though he still despised the concept of people being able to bother him anywhere he went, he had started to grow accustomed to the object over the past month. Overall, the few people who had his number did not abuse the privilege and simply called him when there was something important to say. Even Sheila did not use his cell number for girlfriend-boyfriend frivolities. She knew Michael better than that.

"Hello?"

"I have the names you asked for the other day," answered David's voice.

"Wait a second, I need to find something to write on." Michael started looking for a scrap of paper somewhere in the car, but found none. He tried searching his pockets, but stuck as he was in the under-sized habitat of the vehicle, his range of motion was seriously limited.

"What's going on there? Where are you?" enquired David, who could hear the rummaging over the phone.

"I'm in my stupid rental and I can't find anything to write on," re-plied Michael in a frustrated tone that did not go unnoticed by the de-tective.

"How about I text you the information?" asked David, trying to help.

"You do what?"

"I *text* the names to you, Michael. You *have* heard of texting, right?"

"Of course I've heard of it. What do you take me for?" retorted Mi-chael. "I've just never done it before."

"I just sent them to you," said David, adding in a falsely embarrassed voice, "And I'm sorry I was the one to take your texting virginity."

Michael did not bother gratifying the detective with an answer.

♋

"I got the names," said Sheila, pen in hand and phone still stuck to her ear. After a few seconds of frustration, Michael had given up on try-ing to forward David's text to her and had just verbally given her the list.

"Matt Wilkinson, Brad Shatwell, and Elaine Blent," she read back to him. "And now I suppose we can add Mark Sullivan and Steve Harring-ton to the list."

"Probably, but it remains to be seen," replied Michael. "Could you please try and find out everything you can about these people?"

"I'll do my best."

Chapter 141

Sitting in a wooden rocking chair, the witch was looking up at the Al-pha through the tangles of her stringy tousled hair, her calculating eyes trying to assess how much cash she could pull out of him.

"What you are asking me to do is very different from our usual busi-ness transactions," she articulated in a low husky voice.

The Alpha did not take the bait and simply kept staring at her from the corner of the room where he was standing five feet away.

"It requires more skill... yes! Quite a few more skill... And it is dan-gerous, very dangerous. This Biörn is not someone to trifle with; his type is perilous," she continued in the same falsely reflective voice.

"Will you do it?" asked the Alpha, not trying to hide his growing irritation.

She slowly raised herself from her chair. "I would have to do it from a distance. And the further you are from the target when you cast the spell, the more taxing it is on your strength and energy. Especially with a death spell! It would leave me drained and vulnerable to my enemies for days…"

"How much?" interrupted the Alpha, weary of her rambling.

She had been gradually closing the gap between them and now she was only a foot away from him, standing directly under his nose. She lifted her head and her eyes locked into his as she answered in a raspy voice, "Five hundred!" At the exact same instant a fire blazed into existence in the hearth on the opposite side of the room.

One had to admit, the old hag had a gift for theatrics.

"Two hundred!" replied the Alpha, in a subtly threatening voice aimed at discouraging any counter-offer, but it failed to impress the witch who retorted, "Four hundred."

The Alpha seemed to meditate her reply for an instant before saying, "Three hundred, and it has to be done by noon tomorrow."

The witch's lips twitched into a humorless smile. "You have a deal. But I will need the three hundred thousand in cash before I get to work."

"You'll have the money this afternoon," answered the Alpha as he exited the room.

Chapter 142

"I have a bad feeling about this," said Peter Clemens in a worried tone as he paced the living room of Karl Wilson's four-thousand-square-foot cottage. Wilson was a corporate attorney, and although his pockets were not quite as deep as Clemens', he wasn't hurting in the finance department.

"I feel like we are missing something… like we're being played. Do you know what I mean?" continued Clemens.

"I'm not sure I do," said Karl thoughtfully. "I know everything went to hell for the pack ever since Biörn came into the picture, but I don't see how he's been playing us."

Clemens stopped pacing for an instant and went to stand in front of the bay windows facing the golf course. Only a handful of players were visible on the greens: pretty typical for a Wednesday afternoon.

"I am not even sure Biörn has anything to do with any of this," he replied finally.

"He decimated half of the pack!" answered Wilson, bewildered at the Alpha's comment.

"That's not what I meant," answered Clemens in a weary voice. "Of course he is the enemy and needs to die. It's a given point, not worth debating. I'm just saying we might have been overlooking other less obvious threats."

"Like Ivanov?" ventured Wilson.

"Yes... like Ivanov."

The thought of this insignificant human turd being responsible for the death of his beloved Isabella still made Peter want to retch. He had always known Ivanov was dangerous, but he had never considered him a real threat. Men like Ivanov were perilous to the human population, not to the likes of Peter... or so he had thought. How wrong he had been... and Isabella had paid for his oversight with her life.

"Ivanov will never be an issue again, Peter. We've made sure of that. I understand what you're going through, I really do. Your losses were my losses. Isabella was like a sister to me, you know that. But you cannot let pain cloud your judgment."

Clemens was tired, so very tired. He would never have let another wolf see him vulnerable, doubting himself, but Karl Wilson was not just any wolf. He was not simply the pack Beta, he was also Clemens' best friend and had been for twenty years. "I suppose you could be right. Maybe I'm imagining things that aren't really there." He stood silently staring at the deserted golf course for a good five minutes before going straight for the front door.

"I have an errand to run. I'll be back in a few hours," he said as he left the house.

Chapter 143

True to his word, the Alpha had brought the money—a suitcase full of hundred-dollar bills. The witch had first protested his staying to witness her work, on the pretext of needing absolute concentration which was impossible to achieve with spectators, but he had made it extremely clear he was not parting with the money unless he knew for a fact she had accomplished her part of the bargain. Faced with a three-hundred-thousand-dollar conundrum, the witch had conceded to his staying as long as he made himself invisible.

She had then drawn the thick curtains in front of the windows in the alcove she used as her laboratory, effectively plunging the room into total darkness, before lighting what seemed like a hundred different candles. The majority of the candles were placed around a small wooden altar in the center of the room.

She approached the altar and fished into her pocket for a small Ziploc bag. Inside were three human hairs, which she placed in a silver platter at the center of the altar.

"You are sure these belong to Biörn?" she asked in her croaky voice.

"I'm positive," answered the Alpha, who had picked up the hairs from a shirt he had found in Michael's bedroom.

Using the tip of a sharp dagger, the witch pricked her own arm, letting a few drops of blood fall onto the hairs. Her skin looked a lot younger than the Alpha would have expected, and he started wondering how old the woman truly was.

She then grabbed a flask containing a foul-smelling liquid and added two drops to the platter, pronouncing incantations in gibberish that the Alpha did not bother trying to understand. A few other ingredients, including a raven feather, were added individually to the nauseating brew, which the witch stirred with one of her two-inch-long fingernails before announcing, "And now, for the final touch…" She pulled a small vial containing wolfsbane extract from a pocket hidden in the folds of her robe. She poured the entire vial into the platter, chanting in a voice almost inaudible. The brew immediately started seething and, as a white smoke rose from it, her chanting became progressively louder and louder. Finally, it reached such a level that the Alpha was sure one could hear it from the street.

The witch kept chanting at the top of her lungs, rocking back and forth in front of the smoking mixture, her eyes shut in concentration. From where he was standing, the Alpha could only see her profile, but he was pretty sure there were tears escaping from her shut eyelids. Suddenly, as if it had a will of its own, the smoke emanating from the alchemic broth started shaping itself into something resembling a visage. Sensing something wasn't right, the witch opened her eyes to find Ezekiel's face staring her down.

No words were exchanged, but by the time the wizard's face had disappeared, the brew was no longer simmering and Michael's hair had vanished.

The witch looked exhausted and scared out of her wits. Slouching into a chair, she whispered, "Take your money back. I cannot help you with this."

"Why? What just happened here?" the Alpha replied angrily.

"He is under the protection of the second circle. I am no match against such wizards."

Chapter 144

There was a time where investigative reporters gleaned all their information on the ground by talking to informants, blackmailing corrupt government officials, and spending hours on stakeouts, but this time had passed. Nowadays, Sheila was finding a good half of her material comfortably sitting in front of her computer in the safety of her home—although the safety of her home had been somewhat lacking of late. If only details about Michael's past could be obtained this easily, but the internet was rather lacking when it came to events a millennium old…

And she still hadn't worked up the courage to ask Michael about his deceased wife.

She had spent most of her day working on Michael's request, trying to find out as much information as she could on the assassinated cops. All in all, the cops who had fallen under the bullets of what had clearly been professional assassins seemed to have had little in common with each other.

The first victim, Brad Shatwell, who had been gunned down in front of his house in February 2008, had been a family man. Two of his kids had been in college at the time of his death and the third one was a junior in high school. His wife, from what Sheila could gather, had quit her job at the birth of their first child and had been a housewife ever since. Shatwell had apparently enjoyed playing golf on weekends, was fond of cats and wasn't a big fan of religion. Sheila was basing this last piece on the fact the man's funeral service had taken place in a funeral home in the absence of a priest, imam, rabbi, or preacher of any denomination.

Elaine Blent had been the second victim. The woman had been found in January 2009, lying in a pool of her own blood on a sidewalk in her neighborhood. She had been jogging at the time the killer had caught up with her and, just like the others, had been shot twice in the head. Elaine Blent had been a workaholic, and had never found time to marry or start a family. She had been an evangelist, and was very active in her church where she served as a deacon. She was also pro-animal rights and anti-gay marriage.

Matt Wilkinson, the third victim, had been shot nine months later in the middle of traffic on his way back home from the main police station in downtown Houston. A motorcycle had stopped next to his car at a red light. The instant the light had turned green, the motorcycle driver had shot him twice in the head before disappearing in traffic. Wilkinson had been divorced and a known womanizer. He was estranged from his two teenage kids, who didn't seem to approve of their father's numerous relationships with females. He had also been an avid hunter and a vocal member of the National Rifle Association. He was supposedly Baptist but did not appear to go to church very often if at all.

After hours of staring at her computer screen, Sheila's eyes were starting to hurt when she heard the front door opening and Michael's familiar gait on the hardwood floor. She turned around to find him behind her, looking dreary—the way he had been looking for days now.

Sheila was worried about him and was hoping they would soon find Olivia safe and sound, both for the young woman's sake and for Michael's.

"Any progress?" he asked.

"Some."

She started giving him a detailed summary of her findings as he slumped into a chair.

"It doesn't sound like these guys have much in common with each other or with Sullivan… and even less with Steve," commented Michael wearily as she finished her account.

"I agree, but there's one thing most of them had in common," she announced in a teasingly enigmatic voice.

"What?" asked Michael, not willing to play the game.

"Their rank… Sullivan was Chief Deputy for the Harris County Sheriff department, which means he was second in command of the largest Sheriff department in the state. Wilkinson was Executive Assistant Chief of Police for the Houston PD, which translates into: number two for the city's largest police department. Elaine Blent was a captain in the Texas Rangers force, which signifies she was only two spots behind the force's highest ranking officer…"

"Now that's interesting information," replied Michael thoughtfully. "It's a bit too much of a coincidence for it not to be relevant. What about Brad Shatwell?"

"Shatwell was a Captain in Houston PD, so it doesn't fit the pattern as well. A captain is more like middle management if you know what I mean."

Michael nodded. "Steve had just been promoted Lieutenant, so it doesn't work for him either… unless…"

"Unless what?" asked Sheila, interested.

"Unless…" But Michael did not voice his idea. He sat lost in thought an instant longer before adding, "I wonder if Shatwell was up for promotion."

Chapter 145

The wolves were never to separate from their cell phones, their main communication device, and Axel placed his on the bathroom countertop closest to the shower stall before stepping under the spray. He had just finished washing his hair and was about to get started on the rest when his phone rang. He quickly stepped out of the stall, grabbed a towel to mop off most of the moisture from his hair and face, and answered the phone somewhere between the third and fourth ring.

"Thompkins."

"It will happen today," said the voice of the Alpha on the other end of the line. "Call the pack around noon and have them assembled at the warehouse by 2 p.m. Once everyone has arrived, give me the signal."

"What about the wolfsbane extract?" enquired Thompkins.

"It's being taken care of. Fanning and Maxwell are handling it. Just remember, everyone needs to be at the warehouse by two."

Chapter 146

Michael was lying motionless next to Sheila, but unlike her, he was wide awake and had been for some time. He had never been able to sleep past six o'clock for as long as he could remember, and sleeping in a strange bed only made things worse. His head turned towards the sleeping journalist, and he admired the impeccable complexion of her olive skin, the soft curve of her neck, the impenetrable blackness of her hair.

His relationship with Sheila had taken an unexpected turn in Yellowstone, and he was still struggling with the realization. There had not been many women in his life since the passing of his wife Isibel, and although a few of them had tried, none had ever taken much space in his heart. It wasn't their fault, some of them had been very decent human beings... they had simply never stood a chance. Michael's heart had been locked inside an impenetrable fortress for a thousand years. A fortress he had built not only to protect others from the beast within him, but also for safekeeping of his terrible secret: a secret that had plagued his conscience with unbearable guilt for the past millennium. Now, against all expectations, the fortress had fallen to the gentle assaults of a cute journalist, and Michael simply didn't know what to make of it.

He slipped out of bed and silently got dressed before tiptoeing his way out of the bedroom. It was time for his daily morning walk around Sheila's subdivision.

The air felt nice and crisp, a rarity for the region, and Michael was enjoying it while he could. Walking around the small lake from which the subdivision took its name, he was thinking things over. Sheila had been a tremendous help so far and he felt grateful he could count on her to help him with the case. Her research skills far exceeded his, and, unlike him, she knew exactly where to look for information. After weeks of spinning their wheels on the case, he felt as if they were finally starting to get somewhere. The majority of the murdered cops had been high-ranking officers in various branches of law enforcement, and that definitely looked like a pattern. What they needed to find out now was who benefited from their deaths. Were these officers sitting on some sort of committee that could potentially impact on Ivanov's business... or someone else's? Michael was less and less convinced that the mob had anything to do with the assassinations. There were still many unanswered questions, but with Sheila's help they were now definitely heading in the right direction. Olivia's whereabouts was another matter. David Starks was actively working on locating Steve's daughter, but so far his search had not turned up any new information. Of course he had been on the assignment less than two days, and Michael knew it would take the detective some time to find out Olivia's location. Regardless, every minute she was still missing could be her last and this knowledge gnawed at

Michael's conscience like a dog at a bone. It was not in his nature to sit idle.

Suddenly, Michael felt a presence behind him. Already on the defensive, he started spinning around to swing at his opponent when his brain registered that the presence was familiar and unthreatening. He was back to his usual calm self by the time he completed his one eighty to face Ezekiel standing five feet behind him.

"You'll get hurt sneaking up on people like that," said Michael in a warning voice.

"Nonsense!" replied the wizard. "We both know you wouldn't hurt an old man, you big teddy bear."

"You can keep your fragile elder act for someone else, Ez," announced Michael with a scorn. "Someone who might actually buy it."

They started walking side by side around the lake, teasing each other about their respective age and fragility.

"What are you doing here, Ez?" asked Michael finally.

"What a question! I'm visiting an old friend, of course," replied the wizard, falsely offended.

"And the old friend appreciates your visit. But let's face it, we hadn't seen each other in over ten years and now I see you almost once a week. Which would be nice if not for the fact you only appear to foretell new calamities coming my way."

"You'd rather I didn't warn you?" asked Ez, but he knew the answer, so Michael didn't bother responding.

"I'll have you know, Michael, that you once again misjudged me," started the wizard in a lofty tone. "No calamity coming your way this time, at least none that I know about."

Michael looked at his friend for an instant, trying to assess the veracity of his statement, before answering, "I stand corrected. I guess you are giving me a courtesy visit after all."

"That's better, and since I am a magnanimous wizard, I forgive you," announced Ezekiel, still using his most condescending voice. "There *was* the small matter of a witch trying to do away with you from the comfort of her home. However—"

"Here we go," interrupted Michael, raising his eyes skyward.

"But since the threat has been dispatched, compliments of yours truly, it really doesn't qualify as a foretold calamity. If you stop and think about it for a second, it's technically a post-told calamity," continued the wizard, almost managing to keep a grin off his lips.

"Is she dead?" asked Michael.

"No, she's alive and well. But I strongly doubt she'll try anything against you anytime soon. She knows you are under my protection and won't dare cross me."

Michael thought about that for an instant before asking, "How did you find out about this?"

"A simple sortilege really... If anyone attempts to cast a spell against you in a hundred-mile radius around Houston, I know about it," replied the wizard looking very happy with himself.

"And what if they cast it outside your hundred-mile radius?"

"Then you're on your own. But don't let that eventuality concern you too much. There are only five or six wizards who could cast a lethal spell from such a distance, and odds are none of them are after you."

"You wouldn't happen to know who paid the witch for her service?"

"I'm a wizard, not an oracle," replied Ez dramatically, "but I suspect she wasn't working for herself. I have her address though... if you'd like to go and ask her."

Chapter 147

"**B**ring him in," said Thomas Maxwell without preamble as he entered the room. Lewis and Salazar looked at each other enquiringly. It was the first time the Houston PD second in command visited them in their office, and they weren't too sure what had brought him. They hadn't heard from the executive assistant chief of police in over two weeks. The wolf-attack media frenzy had died down, and Maxwell had apparently started relaxing about the case.

"Bring who in?" asked Salazar after an instant.

"Clemens! Who else?!" Maxwell looked at Salazar as if he were simple-minded.

"And on what charges?" enquired Samantha Lewis skeptically.

Maxwell turned his attention towards her and replied sarcastically, "Yes, on what charges... tough to decide. How about the disappearance of Danko Jovanovich whose DNA was found near Clemens' estate? Or what about the two hunters who, oddly enough, also disappeared near his house? Of course one could decide to bring him in for the fifty odd people he and his friends slaughtered not a week ago..."

Maxwell had so far always been professional, if somewhat pushy, towards the two detectives, but he had clearly gotten up on the wrong side of the bed today.

"We have no proof for the disappearances, and the search of his house uncovered no evidence that the slaughter of Ivanov's men was anything other than self-defense," retorted Salazar in a matter-of-fact voice.

"And you're going to tell me that Ivanov's being murdered in his mansion was another act of self-defense, maybe?"

"Once again, no evidence whatsoever, Sir," answered Lewis.

Thomas Maxwell, still standing in the middle of the office, shut his eyes as he started slowly rubbing his temples.

"Detectives," he started, "I am not telling you to arrest the man. I am simply asking you to bring him in for questioning. Maybe that way we can actually learn something useful for our case against him."

Chapter 148

The house was located in the Heights, a neighborhood where old run-down houses from the twenties and brand new constructions intermingled amidst a patchwork of cute residential streets and industrialized sections. Whatever Michael had imagined, the witch's house was not it. He hadn't really expected to find a gingerbread house with giant candy canes serving as columns in front of a nougatine front door, but the clearly new three-story Victorian construction he was looking at was still a bit of a shock. Although Michael was no real estate expert, he knew the neighborhood's reputation and a house like this had to run close to five hundred thousand dollars. Apparently, the witch was operating a profitable business.

Michael had dealt with witches in the past, mainly in association with the Native American tribes. The Dorset witches he had encountered in Labrador had been fairly powerful, much more so than those of the Potawatomi he had met later on in Michigan. The Lakota and Cheyenne tribes alongside which he had fought at the Battle of the Little Bighorn had used witches as well, although only as medicine men and women. So far, his encounters with witches had been mostly peaceful, but this trend seemed about to rapidly change for the worst.

Given the circumstances, Michael did not believe that etiquette dictated he rang the front bell. No need to warn his wannabe assassin off... assuming she was stupid or arrogant enough to stick around in the first place. He turned the handle on the front door and found it locked. No surprise there. He gave a slow but firm push on the door and, with a barely noticeable cracking sound, the frame gave in around the deadbolt insert.

As he entered the house Michael caught a glimpse of the bottom of a black robe as it disappeared around a corner. It would appear the witch hadn't fled after all... He rushed in the direction she had taken but stopped when he reached the kitchen. The sliding door to the backyard had been left ajar, and Michael wondered if this was a trick or if she had truly escaped through the door.

He cautiously stepped out onto the patio and immediately caught a whiff of the familiar aroma: magic. A spell had just been cast. The deck was a mere two feet above ground level and a quick survey of the back yard revealed no trace of her. The odds she had disappeared into thin air were slim. This type of spell was typically above a witch's pay grade, but so were killing spells, after all. More likely, she had made herself undetectable to his senses and peacefully made her way to the street.

Back inside the house, Michael conducted a thorough search of the rooms, one by one. Satisfied the witch was gone, he returned to her laboratory. He had discovered it on the third floor during his exploration, and was hoping the room contained some clue about the identity of her employer.

A few fading scents still lingered in the room. None of them were familiar to Michael, which in itself was odd. He had expected the place to be stinking of wolf, but could detect no trace of their stench. He supposed the witch could have erased their odor, but why would she? The most persistent scent in the room was also found everywhere in the house, and Michael concluded it belonged to the witch herself. There was also an aroma he could not place, which seemed vaguely familiar.

The laboratory looked disorganized at first glance, but it was just an illusion to throw off visitors. Although the room appeared messy, everything had its place. The potions were scattered on a shelf, but kept together. What Michael would have called, for want of a more technical term, the *dry ingredients* were spread out on the fireplace mantelpiece. The *cooking utensils* were strewn around a small wooden altar in the center of the room. The floor was coated with dust, feathers, hair, and a variety of crumbs of all sizes, but the mess looked more staged than the result of poor housekeeping.

Michael had been hoping for a scent he'd recognize to put him on a trail, but having been unlucky in this department, he resorted to old-fashioned snooping around. It didn't take him very long to go through the entire lab and decide there was nothing useful there. He was about to leave the lab when the vaguely familiar odor that had been tickling his nostrils since he entered the room finally found a match in his subconscious. Not an exact match, however. The smell was definitely reminiscent of wolfsbane, although not quite the real thing. It was *wolfsbane with a twist*. Michael would probably not even have linked the two together had he not smelled wolfsbane the day before in the Chemist's laboratory.

In an instant he realized the implications of this discovery: he had just found a link back to the wolves, back to Clemens. The scent of one of Clemens' wolves had been all over the chemist's lab, and it was therefore hard to imagine the two labs weren't somehow related. It would have implied two distinct factions in Houston were plotting to use wolfsbane as a weapon at the same time—since there really wasn't any other use for it. What were the odds?!

Chapter 149

Of late, Karl Wilson had been working from his home office, where he spent more time helping Clemens plan the future of the pack than he did on the work for which he was actually getting paid. He still had to go to his downtown office from time to time for meetings and other tasks he simply couldn't accomplish from home, but he tried to make these trips as short as possible. Peter simply hadn't been himself since Isabella's death and Karl worried about both his friend and the pack. The pack needed a strong leader, and he wasn't sure Peter was still up to the task.

Returning from a meeting he had to attend that morning, Karl found the house empty. Peter had not mentioned he was planning on leaving the house, so he started looking for a note Peter might have left him… to no avail. This was somewhat out of character since Peter typically kept him informed.

He had reached the conclusion the Alpha had simply gone to grab something to eat when his cell phone rang.

"Karl?" asked Axel Thompkins' voice.

"Yes. What's going on, Axel?"

"Peter called me a few minutes ago; he wants the whole pack to be assembled at the warehouse by two o'clock this afternoon."

"And he called you? Why didn't he call me?" asked Karl, surprised.

"I don't know, he didn't say. Maybe he tried to call you and couldn't get through?"

Karl thought about this eventuality for an instant. He had been in a meeting all morning, but his phone had been on vibrate in his pocket, and he hadn't missed any calls. Still, he supposed it was possible. Weirder things had happened with cell phones in the past.

"Maybe," he replied finally. "Did he tell you why he wanted us to gather?"

"No. I thought you would know," answered Thompkins in a surprised voice.

"I don't."

Chapter 150

By quarter to two, every wolf had made it to the warehouse with the exception of Clemens who was still conspicuously absent. He wasn't going to show up, but this only one of them knew.

The pack leader had been picked up at Wilson's house earlier in the morning by Detectives Lewis and Salazar, who had brought him in for questioning. Despite the lack of evidence against Peter Clemens, Thomas Maxwell had insisted he was brought to the station. In the end, the two detectives simply couldn't say no to Houston PD's number two.

"Are you positive Peter meant today?" Karl Wilson asked Axel Thompkins inquisitively.

"Of course I'm sure," replied Thompkins, discreetly searching for his phone inside his pants front pocket.

It was two o'clock now, and there was still no sign of Clemens. Karl Wilson was getting nervous and the other wolves could sense it. In the absence of Clemens, Wilson was in charge and they were all looking at him for guidance. Under normal circumstances, a few minutes delay wouldn't have worried anyone. They would have simply waited it out chatting around. The pack had recently suffered severe losses, however. It had been reduced to a quarter of its size, and these weren't normal circumstances.

Thompkins pressed the Send key on his phone, and his hand was immediately gratified with a vibration acknowledging the command had been executed. He only had a few seconds to wait now.

"I don't like this," said Wilson suddenly. "We're out of here. Now!" he added to get the pack's attention. He turned to Thompkins who an instant earlier had been standing by the ladder leading from the loft part of the warehouse to the ground level, but Axel was gone. Before he had a chance to go after him, canisters began to land on the hard wood floor of the loft. They seemed to come from all directions and emitted a bluish acrid smoke into the air as they landed. The atmosphere of the warehouse quickly turned toxic.

Sensing immediate danger, the majority of the pack began morphing into their wolf form, but morphing required taking large breaths and breathing meant sucking in the noxious fumes. As the vaporized wolfsbane went to work, their breathing slowed down and eventually stopped. Most of them were in cardiac arrest before they had fully morphed into their wolf form. A few of them managed to fully change, but the fumes were as toxic to their wolf selves as they were to their human counterparts and the beasts collapsed to the ground before they even got a glimpse of their assailants.

Only three wolves, including Wilson, had had the sense to hold their breath and jump to the ground level in search of fresher air, or at least someone to sink their teeth into. They were werewolves, but they did not have to be in their wolf form to be lethal.

The smoke canisters having landed mostly on the loft level, the visibility on the ground level was slightly better. Wilson, still holding his breath, could distinguish at least five aggressors, all wearing military grade gas masks. Some of them looked as if they had some sort of guns in their hands, but some weren't holding any weapons. *Fools*, he thought, rushing towards one of them, ready to drive his bare fist through the man's chest.

The man anticipated his charge and caught Wilson under the jaw with a punch that sent the Beta to the ground.

The impact drove his breath from his body and Wilson finally had to inhale the smoke-laced air. His lungs immediately began to burn as if someone had filled them with vitriol. The Beta did not consider himself beaten just yet, though. In an instant, he was back on his feet, swinging at the other man who clearly wasn't a mere human. After a few minutes of struggle, Wilson managed to knock his opponent out. He then took a circular look at the battleground and quickly realized this was a lost cause. Aside from himself, Rachel was the only pack member still standing, and she was surrounded by three men who were giving her the beating of a lifetime… which meant they weren't human either. Two other thugs had just finished off a wolf named Chris and were now turning their attention towards Wilson. They were still a good twenty yards away, however, and Wilson was only a few feet from his Corvette. In an instant, he was behind the wheel starting the engine. He briefly considered using the car as a weapon to try and rescue Rachel, but he wasn't sure he could survive another breath of the lethal atmosphere. Finally, he decided to do the only sensible thing and he drove full speed through the warehouse garage door.

He floored the gas pedal as he entered the freeway a minute later, windows wide open to take in the fresh air. His lungs were still on fire, but thankfully he wasn't dying. At least, he didn't think so. He needed to warn Clemens and give him the news that the remainder of the pack had been eliminated. They were the only survivors. He reached for his phone, but found his jacket pocket empty. He had lost his cell phone in the battle.

Chapter 151

"What the fuck was this?" asked a furious Clemens. On the other end of the line, Katia Olveda attempted to sound calm.

"I didn't get a chance to warn you, Peter. I assure you. When I learned about it, they were already on their way to pick you up," she replied in an uneasy voice.

Clemens had been shocked to find Katia waiting for him at the police station when Lewis and Salazar had brought him in for questioning. In her capacity as assistant DA, she had been present for the entire interrogation, sometimes asking her own questions. The interview had gone nowhere and after a couple of hours he had finally been released.

"If you had called me as soon as you had heard about it, I would have had a chance to leave the house!" he retorted, practically screaming.

"I was never alone, I simply didn't get—"

"Shut up!" he interrupted. "I need to see you now. I suggest you make it to Wilson's within the next thirty minutes or you are as good as dead," he said, before hanging up on her.

Chapter 152

"You were right!" announced Sheila triumphantly, putting her phone down on the coffee table in front of her.

"Right about what?" asked Michael.

"Right about Shatwell. It hadn't been made official yet but Captain Brad Shatwell was about to be promoted to the rank of assistant chief of police when he was murdered," explained Sheila enthusiastically. "Which means, except for Steve Harrington, all gunned-down officers held high-ranking positions."

This was what Michael had been suspecting for some time now, but he still couldn't see a motive for killing his friend... let alone his wife. It was likely Marge had simply been in the wrong place at the wrong time.

"I can see how Steve and David suspected the mob of being involved in the assassinations," started Michael thoughtfully. "Cut the head of the beast and the legs don't know where to go... Murdering high-ranking police officers would disrupt the functioning of the targeted law-enforcement agencies. And disruption in those organizations could potentially benefit organized crime."

Michael did not really believe in this explanation, however. It seemed too simplistic, too much of a long shot. The officers would quickly be replaced, and things would be back to normal before long. The risks seemed to exceed the benefits. A bad business decision, and organized crime was all about business.

"But if Steve was murdered because he was getting too close to the answer," mused Sheila, "that would also explain why David was attacked. They were working the case together, weren't they?"

Michael nodded but did not reply, still absorbed by his own train of thoughts.

"What happened to the assistant chief of police Shatwell was supposed to replace?" he asked after a while.

"He retired. Why?"

"Do you know who replaced him?"

Sheila glanced at the notepad she'd written on while on the phone with her source. "Thomas Maxwell. What do you have in mind?"

Once again Michael didn't reply. Sheila could see he was lost in thought and was not likely to give an answer in the near future. Her curiosity had been piqued. She grabbed her laptop and settled back down onto the couch to dig up more information on Thomas Maxwell.

The first article she opened immediately raised her curiosity. The article didn't refer to the man as Assistant Chief but as Executive Assistant Chief. After another ten minutes of fierce browsing, she found an answer to Michael's unformulated question.

"Now that's interesting," she said in a mysterious voice aimed at drawing a reaction from Michael. She was satisfied to see him raising an eyebrow.

"What is?" he asked.

"This thing I just found about Thomas Maxwell," she answered casually, without actually telling him what it was.

Michael waited for her to go on for a few seconds before saying, "Fine, you have my undivided attention. You can tell me now!"

She gave him a playful smirk. "Thomas Maxwell is no longer Assistant Chief. He was promoted to Executive Assistant Chief of police in less than two years. He was named to his new position two weeks after Matt Wilkinson's assassination…"

"Are you telling me that Maxwell benefited from the death of both Shatwell and Wilkinson?" asked Michael, visibly excited by her revelation.

"It sure looks like it!"

Chapter 153

It had taken Katia thirty-four minutes to make it to Karl Wilson's house. Exactly four minutes longer than she had been given, but Clemens had not mentioned anything about it.

Pacing the room back and forth like a caged animal, Clemens looked exceptionally nervous. Katia wished she were somewhere else, or at least not alone with the man. She knew exactly how dangerous he could be, and the fact he held her responsible for his morning spent at the police station did nothing to ease her anxiety. She did not have a choice, however. The Alpha wanted her here and she was not about to cross him, not now, not so close to the goal.

"I can't reach any of my wolves, not even Karl," stated Clemens, but Katia wasn't sure whether he was talking to himself or to her.

"Do you know anything about it? Did you have them arrested as well?" he asked in a threatening voice. His eyes, intently trained on hers, were watching for any sign of guilt.

"Of course not, Peter," she replied, quivering and trying her best not to make eye contact. "Do you think I'd be standing in front of you if I had? I have no death wish, I can assure you."

He stopped his pacing and came to stand directly in front of her. His face was so close to hers she could feel his warm breath on her forehead. He grabbed her by the shoulders and effortlessly lifted her from the ground so that her eyes were at his level.

"You wouldn't lie to me, would you?" he asked in a soft voice, which somehow sounded even more threatening than his angry tone.

"No! Of course I wouldn't," whimpered Katia, vehemently shaking her head.

"Liar!" he replied, flinging her across the room like a used towel. She landed on her feet, but not before colliding with one of the living room's walls.

She was scared, truly scared as Clemens started walking towards her. She shot a quick glance at her purse where she had left it on the couch and decided she could not reach it before he got to her. As Clemens was closing the distance, the front door opened and a disheveled Karl Wilson entered the room.

Momentarily forgetting about Katia, Clemens asked Wilson, "Where were you? I've been calling you for thirty minutes." Eventually registering the untidy look of his second he added, "What in heaven happened to you?"

"It was a trap, and I fell for it," answered Wilson as he started relating what had happened at the warehouse.

"I never asked Thompkins to gather the pack," said Clemens angrily once Wilson concluded his recount of the events.

"I figured as much… but a little too late." Wilson remained sheepishly in the entryway. Although he could never forgive himself for what had happened to the pack under his watch, the knowledge he had let his Alpha down was even harder to bear.

"What about the girl?" asked Clemens.

"What girl?"

"The cop's daughter. She was at the warehouse, wasn't she?"

Wilson tried to remember seeing Olivia, but could not. In the mayhem he had completely forgotten about her. She had been kept sedated and tied up to a pillar on the warehouse ground level, but he had not noticed her while fighting his way out of the poisonous atmosphere of the warehouse.

"I don't know," he replied finally. "I didn't get a chance to check on her. I suppose she's still attached to her pillar… dead by now."

He seemed to notice Katia for the first time. The woman was now standing behind the couch, her purse within hand's reach.

Chapter 154

Sheila was once again surfing the internet in search of more clues to support Michael's theory. Sitting close to her, Michael had pulled out his now thoroughly beaten-up list of facts and was intently peering at the piece of paper as if he could will the answers to jump out of the sheet directly into his brain.

There were still many unanswered questions, but he had a feeling they were now on the right track. Someone was infiltrating the various law-enforcement agencies operating in Houston. Strategically placing agents in high-level positions, and murdering if necessary to get their puppets in powerful seats. The million-dollar question was: who was pulling the strings behind the curtain? Who was the puppet master?

The fact that Ivanov's organization had been essentially eradicated while waging an all-out war against the Houston pack seemed to testify against its involvement. If the mobster had had the decision makers of three different state and local law enforcement agencies on his payroll, he could probably have found a more discreet way to deal with Clemens than sending an army to his cabin.

Clemens was also an unlikely suspect. If the Alpha had the cops in his pocket, Michael would never have been called in to help with the case in the first place. Even if Clemens had not been able to prevent Michael's involvement, the cops he had in his pocket could have easily made the ranger's life so miserable that leaving the city would have been his only option.

"Does the name Paul Garber mean anything to you?" asked Sheila, turning her computer screen towards Michael to show him the picture of a middle-aged man with grayish hair and round spectacles.

Michael glanced at it an instant before saying, "No, never seen the man, and the name isn't familiar either. Why? Who is he?"

"Sullivan's replacement. If your theory is correct, he should be one of the bad guys."

Michael nodded in agreement.

"Interestingly," continued Sheila, "Garber wasn't the favorite for the position. The papers quoted several police officials expressing their surprise at his nomination. Apparently a certain James Fanning had been foreseen as the logical replacement for Sullivan. Maybe our puppeteer pulled a few strings to have Garber named in place of Fanning..."

"Or maybe he hadn't seen it coming and Garber's nomination threw a wrench in his plan. In which case, James Fanning would actually be one of the bad guys, not Garber," replied Michael pensively.

Seeing Michael once again absorbed by his list, Sheila returned to her research. An instant later, she startled him with her scream. "Oh-My-Gooosh! Look at this."

On her screen was the picture of an African American, the very same man who had been in charge of watching her while the rest of the pack battled Michael in the heart of Yellowstone.

"Where did you find this?" asked Michael, showing more enthusiasm than Sheila had ever seen him display before.

"On the Texas Rangers website. His name is Axel Thompkins, and guess what his rank is."

"Captain?" answered Michael who had caught her drift.

"Bingo! He is Elaine Blent's replacement! Promoted one week after her assassination."

She gave Michael a minute to grasp the implication of the news. Not only did they have serious proof supporting their theory, they also had established the wolves' involvement.

"I guess Clemens *is* behind the whole thing after all..." said Sheila.

"I suppose you're right." Michael sounded almost regretful.

"What's the problem?" asked Sheila.

"Nothing. It's just that somehow I never truly believed he was behind it."

"The man's a psychopath, Michael. He tried to kill us both repeatedly. He kidnapped Olivia. What more do you need to be convinced of his culpability?"

The thought of Olivia threatened to drag him back to his self-deprecatory state of mind, but he forced himself to snap out of it.

"Clemens is a dangerous killer, but he is not a psychopath," he replied finally. Somewhere in the back of Michael's mind, something was nagging at him. There was an element he was missing and its importance, he was convinced, was essential in seeing the full picture, in breaking the case open and finally seeing it for what it was. Instead, he felt they were peering inside a box through different pinholes, each only showing a unique distorted view of what the box really contained.

Sheila was looking at him trying to comprehend his reluctance at finding the Alpha guilty. She failed to come up with a sensible explanation and decided to get back to work on her computer.

It had been an hour since Sheila had discovered Axel Thompkins' identity and the excitement had now receded. She was searching for more connections linking Clemens to the murders when she landed on a page about John Macfly. Macfly was the assistant DA who had been gunned down on his way to work a couple weeks earlier. He had been slated to replace the soon to retire district attorney. With him out of the picture, Katia Olveda was likely to land the highly coveted position.

When Sheila suddenly realized Macfly had also been executed by an assassin on a motorcycle, she started connecting the dots. She jumped on the notes she had taken about Wilkinson and began reviewing them frantically. The two murders were a perfect match.

"I believe we can add David's girlfriend to our list of suspects," she told Michael enigmatically.

"Meaning?"

She explained how both Macfly and Wilkinson had been executed using the exact same *modus operandi*, and how Katia was the one benefiting the most from Macfly's death.

Michael listened carefully before finally agreeing with Sheila's convincing arguments.

"I guess David should choose his girlfriends more carefully, or at least keep better tabs on them," she added jokingly.

"What did you just say?" interjected Michael.

Sheila repeated herself, but Michael was no longer listening. He had grabbed his precious list from the table and was avidly reading it line by line.

After checking every single point on the list against his new theory he announced, "I believe I know who is behind the curtain. It explains everything, including Steve's death and David's attack."

"Please do tell, don't make me beg," replied Sheila.

"I'll do better than that. I'll show you."

He grabbed her computer and typed a name in the search bar. After a few minutes he found what he was looking for. He showed the picture to Sheila.

"You're joking, right?" she exclaimed.

"Not even a little. Could you please print this picture for me? I'd like you to go and show it to someone." As an afterthought he added, "It looks like Ez was wrong after all."

Chapter 155

"What are you doing?" asked Clemens, looking at Katia with murderous eyes. She did not answer but quickly reached into her purse and pulled out what looked like a gun. The weapon's chamber, however, had room for a single slug and was currently loaded with a small vial containing a colorless liquid. It took Clemens a second to identify the weapon as a dart gun.

"Are you trying to put me to sleep, Katia? Like some type of wild animal? Have you forgotten who I am? Have you forgotten who *you* are?" he asked, laughing sardonically while walking deliberately slowly towards her.

She had the gun aimed straight at his chest, the largest target, the hardest one to miss.

"You have no idea who I am, my dear Peter," she answered. All fear had disappeared from her voice. She knew he had arrived. She could feel his presence in her skin. "You never had."

"Enlighten me… please," he replied sarcastically, still moving towards her while Karl was slowly approaching from a different direction.

"I am one of the traitors, Peter, always have been, just like Axel… Do you really believe I would have bedded lover boy over there for any other reason than getting to you?" she asked amusedly. "But don't judge me too harshly, Peter. I only followed orders; they just happen to have never been your orders," she added provocatively.

"You're dead, bitch." Clemens lunged at her, but he was still ten feet away, and his anger and arrogance made him oblivious to the gun she was pointing at him. She pulled the trigger and the dart punctured his skin right under the heart. He immediately snatched the dart away, but the contents of the pressurized vial had already entered his bloodstream.

The poison hit him before he could get to her, but it wasn't enough to deter his desire to strangle her. As he reached for her throat, she quickly stepped back and kicked him straight in the chest with the bottom of her foot, her stiletto heel puncturing his abdomen below the ribcage. He stared at her in shock, a look of utter surprise on his face—he hadn't seen that one coming.

Clemens lay prone on the floor stunned by the turn of events. He was still wondering whether Katia was particularly strong or whether the dart had made him particularly weak—a more likely explanation—when Karl collided into Katia, sending her rolling to the floor.

Karl easily pinned Katia to the ground despite his diminished strength from the wolfsbane gas he had inhaled at the warehouse. Back on his feet, Clemens started walking towards them holding his bleeding abdomen with one hand. He smiled maliciously as he advanced with the intent of crushing the woman's head under his heel.

"I grew fond of Katia, and I don't think I will let you hurt her," said a booming voice that startled both Clemens and Wilson. Clemens quickly turned around to find two men standing a few feet away from the trio. Diminished by the wolfsbane, the two wolves had not even sensed their presence. One of them was Axel Thompkins, the traitor, but the other one… Clemens simply could not believe what he was seeing.

"What are *you* doing here?" asked Clemens, bewildered, while Karl's jaw dropped in astonishment. Katia took advantage of the situation to free her hands from under Karl's knees and hit him simultaneously on both sides of the head with open palms, before pushing him away from her. An instant later she was standing by Thompkins and the other man.

"A fair question," answered the man in an approving voice. "I guess one could say I am here for a succession of power… You see, Peter, you have been the top dog in town for a long time. One might even say too long. It is time for a change of leadership."

"You may not have noticed, but there is no pack left to lead," answered Clemens, still bleeding on the carpet. The wound should have completely healed by now, but it didn't look like it was healing at all.

"Wrong again, my dear Peter, there is a pack—my pack. We have lived in your shadows for some time now, carefully preparing for the day we would snatch the control of the city from your incompetent hands. And that day has come… I am glad to say. But don't worry, it is for the better good of the species. Under my leadership, wolves will be more powerful than they ever were under yours. My shadow pack has already infiltrated government organizations at the highest level, both in the city and in the state. But we won't stop here, the sky is the limit. One day we might even have a wolf as President of the United States."

"You are insane, completely insane. You aren't even a wolf yourself. How do you expect to lead a pack?"

"Wrong again!" answered the shadow pack Alpha as he turned into a black wolf of about 250 pounds.

Astonished, Clemens tried to morph, but the wolfsbane flowing through his veins made the process extremely slow and painful. Wilson was able to morph faster but he still wasn't at the top of his game, not by any stretch of imagination.

Wilson had just finished morphing when the shadow Alpha leapt on him. The two wolves tumbled on the floor in a deluge of fangs and claws, quickly joined by Clemens in his wolf form. Clemens' wolf was significantly more experienced than the two others, but he was in such a diminished state that it didn't matter.

The three wolves battled across the living room under the watchful eyes of Katia and Axel, destroying virtually every piece of furniture in the process. After only a few minutes, Karl Wilson was lying motionless on the ground, blood gushing from the severed artery in his torn open throat.

The two Alphas circled each other for an instant before clashing once more. In the end, Clemens was simply too weak to triumph, and the shadow Alpha dispatched him the same way he had finished his Beta.

Morphing back into his human form, the shadow Alpha looked at the mess in the room and said to Axel and Katia, "Discard the bodies and get a witch to clean up this mess. I need to find some fresh clothes."

Shirtless, he walked towards the staircase. His pants were ripped and hung from his waist. He was the only Alpha left in Houston. Things were finally the way they were supposed to be. He only had one more problem to address: an 800-pound problem.

Chapter 156

The warehouse looked like any other warehouse Michael had ever seen, and nothing from the outside hinted that the building was used for anything other than storage. The place had a pedestrian entrance on its side in addition to roll-up industrial doors large enough to allow eighteen-wheelers in and out of the building.

Michael slowly turned the doorknob and was surprised to find it unlocked. This was suspicious if anything ever was, and he decided the odds for this to be a set-up were high.

Sheila had been able to dig out the address after an entire afternoon spent almost equally on the phone and on her computer. The journalist was well connected and one of her connections happened to specialize in financial investigations through means whose legality could sometimes be questionable. An in-depth search of Clemens' finances hadn't turned up anything interesting, but when Sheila and her connection had started looking into Karl Wilson's assets, they had noticed a large withdrawal made from an account in the Cayman Islands. Following the money trails, they discovered the wire had been used to purchase a warehouse some years ago. The warehouse had been bought under an assumed name, which explained why they had been unable to find it earlier, but Sheila seemed pretty confident it belonged to Wilson.

Michael carefully slipped through the open door and was immediately convinced Sheila had been right. He was equally convinced something had gone very wrong in the warehouse. He recognized immediately the acrid smell as it started burning his nostrils and irritated his throat. The odor was the one he had smelled in the Chemist's laboratory: concentrated wolfsbane extract. Apparently, someone had managed to disperse it as an aerosol into the room.

He cautiously started circling the ground level, making as little noise as possible. It wasn't long before he discovered the first body... and then another one. Immediately, his heart started pounding; preparing for the worst, his mind unconsciously got ready to discover Olivia's lifeless body. When he tripped over a pair of shackles wrapped around a pillar in a dark corner, however, he wasn't sure whether to feel worried or relieved. The shackles indicated that the pack had recently held someone captive, and Olivia was a likely candidate for the position. It also meant she was probably lying dead somewhere in the room... On the other hand, she might have escaped or been dragged out of the warehouse before the attack, for Michael was now convinced there had been an attack. The Houston pack had fallen victim to a chemical weapon that had laced the air with volatilized wolfsbane. Since the traces left in the air were potent enough to seriously irritate Michael's throat, no doubt the concentrated version would have been lethal.

After convincing himself Olivia was not lying dead anywhere on the ground floor, Michael carefully walked up to the loft level where he discovered four more bodies. Thankfully, none of them belonged to Olivia. The loft level was a lot easier to search and it only took Michael a couple of minutes to make sure there weren't any additional bodies hidden out of sight.

Wilson and Clemens were not among the victims, which meant they had almost certainly been absent during the attack and were probably still alive. The mastermind was getting close to his goal, however. The Houston pack was on the brink of extinction.

When he got back to his car, Michael noticed he had a voicemail on his new cell phone, the one Sheila had purchased for him earlier that morning. He had left it in his car to make sure it did not ring at an inconvenient moment while he was searching the premises. In retrospect, it was unlikely the ringtone would have alerted the corpses inhabiting the warehouse, but he hadn't known that before walking in.

The message was from Sheila, which was to be expected since she was the only one who knew his new number. It simply said: *You were right... again. I showed the picture to my "friend", and she positively ID'd him. See you at home. Kisses.*

Chapter 157

Michael had driven straight back to Sheila's from the warehouse, only to find the place empty upon arrival. He'd spent the whole drive back thinking about what his next move would be. If Olivia were still alive—and he was starting to believe she probably was—he needed to find a way to rescue her as soon as possible. The rescue mission needed to be well planned. It had to be both swift and conducted in a way that would minimize potential harm to Olivia. After careful consideration, he'd finally come up with an idea which had a reasonable chance of success. It was far from perfect, but time wasn't on his side.

Waiting for Sheila to return, he walked to the kitchen and picked up his old cell phone from one of the countertops. He dialed David's number. The detective answered on the second ring. "Michael! What's going on?"

"I have news," replied Michael. "I have found the warehouse where Clemens used to hold Olivia."

"Used to?" answered David inquiringly.

Michael told him about the bodies he had found in the warehouse, the scent of wolfsbane extract in the air, and the empty pair of shackles lying on the ground.

"What the hell is going on? Who went after the pack?" asked David, bewildered.

"I believe we've been looking at it the wrong way from the beginning. Clemens was never responsible for the wolves' attacks or the cops' assassinations. He was framed. The whole Houston pack was framed."

"Who by?" David sounded clearly unconvinced.

"That's what took me some time to figure out," answered Michael, "but I believe I finally know the answer to that question. Everything fits."

"Who?" asked David impatiently.

As if to build suspense, Michael remained silent an instant before slowly articulating, "Detective Ed Salazar."

"You're joking, right?"

"I'm afraid I'm not. This morning I sent Sheila with a picture of him to the garage where Jack Moore used to work. The lady at the desk recognized him right away. Salazar was the cop who befriended Moore."

Michael spent another five minutes explaining to David how he had found out Salazar was behind it all. By the end of his explanation, the detective sounded at least partially convinced.

Sheila walked through the door at the same moment Michael was hanging up. He quickly told her what he had found at the warehouse and let her in on his plan.

"You are a sneaky one, my big Teddy Bear," she said, smiling. "But it just might work."

He did not particularly like it when she called him a teddy bear, but he hadn't particularly liked any of the other pet names she had tried on him either.

The wheels had been set in motion. He had just one more phone call to make before rescuing Olivia. He picked up the receiver and dialed Detective Samantha Lewis' number.

Chapter 158

Katia was staring at her visitor from across a large cherrywood desk, which had been stained a dark crimson. The temperature in the room had plummeted ten degrees the second Samantha Lewis had entered the assistant DA's office.

"To what do I owe this honor?" asked Katia, barely hiding the sarcasm in her voice. Lewis did not take the bait and simply answered in a weary tone, "I need both an arrest and a search warrant and I thought you might be able to help."

Lewis had received a phone call from Michael Biörn an hour earlier. She had been very surprised to hear from the man in the first place, but after she had heard what Biörn had to say, there was simply no word to describe accurately Samantha's blatant astonishment. It had taken some serious convincing for her to even admit the possibility he might be right—as opposed to simply out of his mind—but in the end she had agreed to do as he asked.

"Possibly," answered Katia in a more professional voice. "Who are we arresting, and what evidence do you have?

A part of Samantha was praying for Biörn to be wrong; this was simply hitting too close to home. However, if he were wrong, Salazar would never forgive her for listening to him in the first place. She did not even want to start considering what would happen to her career in the case Biörn actually was full of shit. As if implicating a fellow officer of her pay grade was not bad enough, she was also involving Executive Assistant Chief Maxwell as a suspect in this affair. This of course was equal to career suicide and she knew it, but it was simply too late to change her mind.

Lewis presented Katia with all the pieces of the puzzle Biörn had given her and demonstrated to the best of her ability how well they all fitted together, all converging to point towards a same and unique individual: the mastermind of the whole scheme.

Katia Olveda switched from laughter to chuckles to impatient sighing before finally falling completely silent as Lewis got further and further into her surprisingly convincing demonstration.

"You do realize what this will do to your career if you are wrong?" asked Katia once Lewis concluded her demonstration. The concern in her voice sounded as fake as it was.

"I do," replied Lewis, who was vividly aware of the consequences she was facing, and facing alone. Following Michael's request, she had presented the evidence as if she had been the one to unearth them.

"At any rate, this is all circumstantial evidence Detective. You will never find a judge willing to deliver a warrant based on this heap of spec- ulations," said Katia in the voice of the one who knows. "I am sorry, but I can't do anything for you."

Chapter 159

After Lewis left the room, Katia waited three excruciatingly long minutes before jumping on the phone and dialing the Alpha's num- ber. She kept a prepaid cell phone in her purse for just this type of emer- gencies: one whose number could not be traced back to her.

"Hello?"

"She knows. Lewis knows. I don't know how, but she figured it out!" erupted Katia over the phone.

"Calm down and tell me exactly what you mean."

"I mean she knows everything. She knows about Maxwell, she knows about Fanning, she knows how you befriended Moore, and she knows you're running the show," answered Katia in a worried voice.

There was silence on the other end of the line while the Alpha tried to understand what had gone wrong. His plan had been perfectly exe- cuted; everything had fallen nicely into place. Jack's mishap on the Sulli- van assignment had been troublesome, but they had managed to use it to their advantage by turning Biörn and Clemens against each other. A great idea if ever there was one, since Biörn had wiped out three-quarters of the Houston pack by himself, effectively clearing the road for the shadow pack by making the task of finishing off the remnants of Clem- ens' wolves a mere formality.

"How did you find out?" asked the Alpha after a while.

"Lewis just walked out of my office. She wanted a warrant for your arrest," answered Katia nervously. "I told her the case was too weak. That I couldn't do anything for her, but it will only buy you a little time. She'll try to go over my head and convince a judge."

"I wonder how she found out," said the Alpha pensively.

"Never mind how she found out. You need to get out of town, and get rid of the girl. If they catch you with her tied up on your bed, they'll add kidnapping to the charges against you and their case will be airtight. Trust me on that one."

The Alpha knew Katia was right, but he still couldn't comprehend how quickly things had gone so wrong. How had Lewis figured it out when she had been so oblivious until now? It simply made no sense.

"If Lewis knows about Maxwell and Fanning, I wonder why she isn't suspecting you," were the Alpha's last words before he hung up the phone.

Chapter 160

Katia was pondering the Alpha's last statement when her office door was slammed open and Lewis marched in, followed closely by two officers in uniform. The detective walked straight to Katia's desk and removed the small microphone she had hidden under it a few minutes earlier.

It only took a second for Katia to realize the bitch had played her like a fiddle.

"Katia Olveda, you are under arrest for obstruction of justice, complicity in the assassinations of five police officers, and complicity to kidnapping," announced Lewis in a loud, neutral voice that contrasted sharply with the immense relief she felt inside. Executing Biörn's idea had been a huge gambit, and she felt as if an elephant had stepped off her chest now that some of his assertions had been proven right. She knew deep inside that her visceral dislike of the assistant DA had played a significant part in her willingness to play the gambit suggested by Biörn, but no one else had to know that.

"Officer, would you please read the prisoner her rights?" she added, looking at one of the officers while the other officer handcuffed a fuming assistant DA.

If Katia's eyes had been daggers, Samantha Lewis would have been pinned to the office back wall, dangling two feet from the ground. As it was, the detective was simply trying hard to suppress the uncontrollable smile she could feel growing by the second.

Lewis walked to Katia's desk and, with a slightly theatrical gesture, reached for the prepaid cell phone.

"No!" exploded the assistant DA as Lewis was closing her fingers on the phone. "You can't touch that, you need a warrant!"

"We'll let the judge decide about that," replied Lewis defiantly. "In the meantime, I think I'll take it for safekeeping."

The detective placed the cell phone into an evidence bag and, gesturing to the officers, added, "You can take her away now."

Chapter 161

After hanging up with Katia, the Alpha walked straight to his laptop. The screen showed a street map of Houston displaying several individually colored dots. *Good! At least Biörn didn't get the memo*, he thought, looking at a blue dot blinking sixty miles from his location.

Still trying to figure out how things had gone so wrong so quickly when everything had seemed to be going so well, the Alpha hurried up to the second floor. He probably had a little bit of time before the cops showed up, but it was safer to assume he didn't.

In addition to the master bedroom, the second story harbored three guestrooms, two bathrooms, and a large open-floor family room. The Alpha walked straight to the alarm system keypad located by the door inside the master bedroom, but he didn't enter the four-digit code used to activate the alarm. Instead, he dialed a ten-digit combination that was followed by a low popping sound. A four-foot-wide wardrobe was now standing four inches away from the bedroom wall against which it had stood an instant earlier. The left side of the wardrobe was on hinges, which allowed the Alpha to effortlessly spin the piece of furniture away from the wall to reveal a metallic door equipped with another keypad. He entered another ten-digit combination, and the greased heavy dead-bolts started noiselessly sliding out of their notches to unlock the vault.

The secret chamber was the size of a small prison cell with stainless steel walls, floor and ceiling. In a corner, a toilet bowl made of the same metal constituted the only furnishing of the room. In the opposite corner, next to a plastic tray cleaned spotless of any trace of food, sat Olivia.

The Alpha's men had picked her up half-conscious during their final raid against the Houston pack. Following the Alpha's instructions they had brought her back to him. He had immediately noticed the woman was no longer human, her scent was unmistakable, but he had not judged it necessary to sedate her. She was just a pup... His first intent had been to tame her and eventually integrate her into his pack. That ship had sailed, however. With no time left, she was now strictly a liability. He had to get rid of her and then disappear... at least for a while.

Olivia was now fully awake and was staring at him with murderous eyes. The effects of her captivity and transformation were now mainly visible in her thin form and slightly puffy eyes

"It's time to get out of here, Olivia," he said in a commanding tone. Despite her hatred for the man, she got up to obey the Alpha's order. It was nearly impossible for her to do otherwise. She could feel the Alpha male's raw power pouring out of his mouth at every word he pronounced, and she simply could not resist the urge to submit to his will. She might have tried to resist a bit harder had she known he meant to kill her and let the alligators deal with her dismembered corpse in a bayou.

The Alpha grabbed her by the arm and pushed her out of the cell. As he did so, he caught a whiff of something that told him he had been deceived. The stench was unmistakable; he had been breathing it way too often lately not to recognize it right away.

"Good morning, Michael," said the Alpha, still holding onto Olivia as Biörn walked into the bedroom. "I see you abandoned the phone I so graciously gave you."

Michael gave David Starks an unreadable look. "It simply wasn't reliable. It just seemed to attract trouble on a too regular basis."

"It took you long enough to figure it out," replied David condescendingly.

Olivia was trying to break free from the Alpha's grip, but he was much too strong for her. "Let me go!" she snarled, but he simply ignored her.

"Let her go now, and I will try to not take too much pleasure in killing you," said Michael in a voice deprived of humor.

"You threw a wrench in my plan, Michael. I'll give you that. Seeing you here, I now have no doubt you were behind Lewis' sudden breakthrough. Without you, she would have never suspected me in a million years."

David was correct in that respect. Michael had been the architect of the plan, with Lewis and Sheila his mere assistants. Michael had suspected the Alpha was keeping Olivia locked up in his beach house—a secluded place, where screams would likely get drowned by the sound of crashing waves. In order to get to her safely, Michael had needed to make sure David did not feel immediately threatened by him. He had therefore called David to let him know he was suspecting Salazar to be behind it all. Salazar was such an unlikely suspect that the perspective was almost comical, but the Alpha had taken the bait. Knowing the phone David had given him was bugged with a tracking device, Michael had entrusted Sheila with it and sent her north of town, while he had started heading south towards David's beach house.

Figuring out what to do with Katia Olveda had been a challenge. The evidence against the assistant DA had been circumstantial at best. Not nearly enough to indict her. Unless of course she were to get caught red-handed… That was when Michael had come up with the idea to enroll the help of Samantha Lewis. The plan had not been without risk. Michael knew Olivia's life would be forfeited the minute Katia let David know the cops were onto him. Timing had to be perfect, and he had made sure of it. Michael had found the Alpha's car parked in the driveway upon arriving at the beach house. Even from a distance the fresh scent of Olivia had been easy to detect. Once satisfied that the Alpha and his hostage were on the premises, he had given Samantha the green light to walk into the assistant DA's office and request a warrant against David. Taking the bait, Katia had immediately called the Alpha to warn him. In the meantime Lewis, following Michael's instructions, was letting him know his plan had succeeded. This had been his cue to enter the house.

Michael took a step towards David and his hostage, but the Alpha drew a 44-Magnum from his back and placed the barrel under Olivia's jaw. Michael froze.

"Since you are going to kill me anyway, what stops me from killing her first?" asked David with a humorless smile.

"You count on killing her with that gun?" replied Michael skeptically. "Unless my nose is deceiving me, I don't believe your gun would do her much permanent harm."

Michael had smelled the wolf on Olivia, and knew the young woman had been turned into one of his hereditary foes.

"You should not underestimate your enemy, Michael," threatened David. "Do not make the same mistake Katia did with Lewis... I suspect my sweetheart is on her way to jail as we speak. Am I correct?"

Michael did not answer the Alpha's question. Tears were visible in Olivia's eyes, but he couldn't tell whether they were caused by fear, anger, or a mixture of both. David cocked the gun's hammer but Michael rushed him before he had a chance to pull the trigger. This was the reaction the Alpha had been expecting and turning his gun towards his enemy, he shot Michael in the chest four times before he could react. Anyone shot at close range with a 44-magnum would have been projected and nailed against the wall behind them, but Michael wasn't just anyone and the impacts barely slowed him down.

As soon as the bullets entered his body Michael knew they weren't ordinary ammunition. Now he understood what David had meant about underestimating the enemy. Reacting on instinct he began morphing as the poison started spreading from his punctured organs into his bloodstream.

David jumped to the side to get out of the way of the incoming hybrid monster, which was already halfway between man and bear, and simultaneously started to morph as well. An instant later, a bewildered Olivia was staring with unbelieving eyes at what looked like a clash between Titans. The sheer size of the beasts, accentuated by the comparatively small proportions of the bedroom, was already a good indication these weren't mere animals. The way the two monsters fought each other would have convinced any remaining skeptic. The viciousness displayed by the monstrous bear and equally horrific wolf could only have originated in the beasts' human brains.

Michael's transformation into a bear surprised Olivia but did not shock her nearly as much as it would have a month earlier. Her threshold for awe and bewilderment had been drastically raised since she had come to grips with her new identity as a werewolf. Michael would have quickly dispatched the much weaker Alpha under normal circumstances. With the wolfsbane extract flowing in his veins, the battle was much more balanced. Olivia wished she could change into her wolf form to help Michael in his struggle, but she simply did not know how to morph voluntarily.

Suddenly, the Alpha's jaws clenched onto the bear's throat and for an instant it looked as if Michael wouldn't be able to shake himself free of the wolf's powerful bite. When he finally succeeded, the Alpha was sent flying across the room. Unfazed, the Alpha landed on his paws and was back harassing him in an instant.

Olivia could see Michael growing weaker by the minute. She was starting to fear not only for his life but also for her own. For she was certain this bear was the only thing able to prevent the Alpha from killing her the same way he had murdered her parents. Seeing the wolf slowly gaining control of the battle, Olivia decided to make a run for it and darted out of the room.

Michael's movements appeared sluggish now. His attempts at swatting his enemy were becoming feeble and largely unsuccessful. After a while, he simply stood motionless, nose down in the middle of the room. The wolf warily circled around him at a safe distance while assessing the situation. Sensing his instant of triumph had arrived, the Alpha closed in for the kill. He was too arrogant in his approach, however, and got too close to Michael's deadly paws. The bear suddenly lashed out at the wolf with a resurgence of vitality, tearing his throat open with razor-sharp claws. The Alpha leaped backwards, blood flowing from the deep gouge across his throat.

The Alpha knew that, given enough time, the wound would heal, but he needed to end the fight quickly if he wanted to live to see it. Michael had used the last of his strength in the surprise attack and was now ready to collapse to the ground. When the wolf jumped on his back and sank his fangs on the side of his neck, he did collapse.

The wolf was now hacking at his neck and throat with desperate efficiency, tearing off mouthfuls of muscles and broken vertebrae. David was significantly weakened by his injury and unable to carry out the task with the celerity he would have otherwise displayed, but he felt confident Michael could no longer fight back. Already celebrating his victory in his mind, the Alpha felt a mixture of surprise, disbelief and anger when the teeth of Olivia's wolf form locked down on his throat to finish the job Michael's claws had started.

Chapter 162

Michael had recovered his human form but was still lying motionless on the ground by the time Sheila arrived at the beach house. A beheaded David Starks, also in his human form, was lying in a pool of blood not three feet from Michael.

Michael had morphed back into his human form only to pronounce two words before passing out: "Call Sheila." Olivia needed to be in her human form to do that, however, and it had taken her an additional fifteen minutes to successfully will her body into transforming. Her human body finally reintegrated, Olivia had found Michael's cell phone inside a pocket of his torn-up pants and had dialed Sheila's number.

The journalist was kneeling by Michael, her face a mask of anguish and concern. She was trying to stir him out of his unconsciousness but couldn't get any reaction out of him.

"Is he dead?" asked Olivia as Sheila was wiping a tear from the corner of her eye.

"No. I believe he's in a coma." Sheila's voice choked on the words. "I wish Ez were here," she added to herself.

"Who's Ez? A doctor?" asked Olivia, but Sheila simply didn't know what to reply.

"What can we do?" asked Olivia after a minute had passed without Sheila answering her previous question.

"We need to move him," said Sheila, trying to sound confident, but the doubt and the pain in her voice were obvious. "The cops will be here shortly and they can't find him here. He can't be brought to a hospital either, so we'll have to drive him to my house."

Olivia nodded as Sheila added, "I just don't know how we are going to get him to my car. He's no lightweight."

Before the journalist could think of a solution to the problem, Olivia threw Michael over her shoulders and headed for the door.

"Let's go," she told Sheila who was staring at her, bemused.

Sheila was delighted when they bumped into Ezekiel on their way out, but her joy was short-lived.

"There is nothing I can do for him, my dear," he told Sheila right away. "No one can. He is a strong lad, though; he might beat the poison and pull through this."

The wizard's words did not bring any comfort to Sheila.

"Why are you here then?" she asked angrily.

"Because Michael asked me to come and clean up the mess before the authorities arrive."

Olivia was looking at the frail-looking old man in his Halloween costume with a look of utter skepticism. "Oh, really? And when did he ask you that, Merlin?" she asked, a bit too aggressively.

The wizard looked at her with a mixture of amusement and compassion. He knew what the young woman had been through and understood her cynicism. "Let's just say he wished it," he responded enigmatically.

Chapter 163

The faces of the shadow pack's now infamous members were once more occupying the entire TV screen. "How many of them do you think there were in total?" asked Sheila. "I mean Starks' wolves? How many?"

"Hard to say," answered Michael reflectively.

It had been almost three weeks since the police had found the body of David Starks in his beach house along with a suicide note. Ezekiel had done such a thorough job at cleaning up the mess that the detective's suicide was never once put into question.

After four days spent in a coma, Michael had woken up on the fifth morning to find Sheila bent over him. It had taken another two weeks for him to fully recover from his ordeal, but now he was as good as new. The caliber of David's gun had been Michael's salvation. The 44-Magnum was so powerful that two of the bullets had simply exited through Michael's back, leaving only two of them to spread the poison inside his body. A smaller caliber would have probably left all four inside his body and most likely killed him. The fact the Alpha had used bullets instead of poisoned darts had also played in Michael's favor. A dart could be quickly ripped out but it also held twice as much poison as a bullet.

"Do you think they are all werewolves?" asked Sheila, still staring at the television.

The pack had been all over the news for weeks now, except no one ever called it the shadow pack. To the media, it was the *conspiracy affair*. As far as the general public was concerned, David Starks had been leading a secret criminal organization in the process of slowly infiltrating governmental institutions at the highest levels. Wide disagreements were expressed in the media regarding why wolves had been used to execute Chief Deputy Sullivan and the Harrington couple, but werewolves had not been mentioned a single time as a possible explanation. To everyone, including the police, the shadow pack had simply been another criminal group, sophisticated, but not unnatural in any way.

"Either wolves or wolf-wannabes," replied Michael pensively. "It's hard to tell. At any rate, they should be taken very seriously just in case."

The police had found enough evidence in David's computer to arrest Maxwell and Fleming, but Thompkins had managed to disappear into thin air. An additional three lower profile arrests had been made in conjunction with the case. The inclusion of Katia Olveda to the lot made a total of six pack members behind bars.

"What about Katia? Do you think she is a wolf?"

"I don't know," answered Michael, slightly irritated. "The witch brew hides the wolf scent completely. That's why it took me so long to figure out David was a werewolf. I disliked him the first time I met him, but I simply couldn't explain why. After Steve's murder I just forgot about my gut feeling and started trusting the guy."

"How do you know the witch brew was responsible for it?"

"Ez told me. He found some vials at David's when he went there to clean things up. The Chemist was extracting the wolfsbane toxin from the plants, and the witch converted it into some form of serum. Unconverted, the extract was a powerful poison, which they used against the

Houston pack and myself, but once converted by the witch, its properties were different."

"It's the serum form that masked the wolf scent?" asked Sheila.

"Yes, but it did more than that; it had a variety of virtues. Being made from wolfsbane, it was also toxic to some degree to the wolves, and David used this property to his advantage while staging his own attack. Without the serum in his blood stream, he would have healed unnaturally fast and I would have been onto him right away. But the serum acted on his praeternatural functions and significantly slowed down his rate of recovery."

"He was a son of a bitch, but a smart one," commented Sheila. "How did he manage to maul himself in the first place, anyway?"

"I am sure he had one of his wolves do it. Self-inflicted wounds would have been too obvious. I am not sure which one of them was kind enough to oblige, but it wasn't Jack Moore. It wasn't his scent I picked up at David's after the attack."

"What about Steve and his wife? Do you know which one killed them?"

"Definitely! David did. I recognized the odor as soon as he morphed. I think it was partially what kept me fighting as long as I did. Realizing he had executed Steve and Marge himself increased my hatred for the man just enough to keep me going."

Michael fell silent as Olivia appeared at the top of the stairs. The death of her parents was not something the young woman needed to hear about.

Chapter 164

The showers were like everything else in the penitentiary, clean and austere. Two white walls facing each other harbored a total of twenty showerheads where the convicts could scrub amidst the total lack of intimacy that was the trademark of the place.

As a former assistant DA, Katia was a prime target for the animosity of her fellow inmates. The guards were relatively protective of her, however, and after two weeks spent in the penitentiary she could only complain of a few instances of verbal abuse.

It was nearing dinnertime and the showers were emptying quickly. Soon Katia found herself alone with a single other inmate: a small puny thing with scrawny arms, who was rinsing the soap off her body while carefully avoiding eye contact. Overall, the woman reminded Katia of an underfed scarecrow.

Four women walked into the shower room and immediately the scarecrow exited, making a visible effort to keep the greatest possible distance between herself and the newcomers. The four had no interest in her though, and completely ignored the sickly looking thing. Their attention was fully focused on Katia's luscious naked body.

Katia was acting as if she hadn't noticed their interest and was proceeding dutifully with her shower as the four women started approaching her. They all wore their hair cropped close to the scalp and were as feminine as a Picasso painting. The tight muscles, clearly visible on their naked bodies, testified to numerous hours spent lifting weights. They formed a half circle around Katia and stared at her in silence for an instant. The assistant DA's body was in sharp contrast with their own. All curves and grace, it was an open invitation to debauchery in a place like this. The lust in the women's eyes was unmistakable, but Katia pretended not to notice.

"She's mine," said one of them, in a voice used to being heard. She wasn't the biggest one of the four, but she looked to be the meanest. She stepped towards Katia and grabbed her under the throat with one hand, pinning her against the wall while the others watched with visible excitement. Her free hand started caressing Katia's breasts but as she moved it down towards her vulva, the ADA gave the woman a powerful shove that made her lose her balance. She landed on her butt as Katia stared at her with a provoking grin.

"You little bitch!" said the woman with a snarl, while getting back on her feet. "Now you gonna get it. You gonna get it good!"

"Hold that bitch," she added in a commanding tone to the others.

The three of them rushed the assistant DA eager to obey their leader and put their hands on Katia's body.

A second later, Katia was effortlessly lifting the gang leader into the air with one hand, her fingers wrapped around the woman's throat in a grip that was as strong as a vice. Terror was clearly visible in the rapist's eyes. The other three women all lay dead on the floor, their necks broken.

"It looks like you fucked with the wrong inmate, you pathetic little turd," said Katia in a cool threatening voice. "I was the Alpha's mate, and now I am the Alpha. Who the fuck do you think you are for even daring to look me in the eyes?" she asked the woman. To no avail... she had already choked her to death.

Chapter 165

The doorbell rang as Olivia was reaching the bottom of the stairs and she went to answer. She came back a few seconds later, closely followed by Detectives Lewis and Salazar.

"Good afternoon, Detectives," said Michael, standing in the middle of Sheila's living room.

"Mr Biörn, Ms Wang," answered Samantha Lewis while her partner simply gave a nod by way of a greeting.

"Please make yourselves at home," said Sheila in a cheerful voice. "Would you like something to drink? Coffee? Beer?"

They all agreed coffee would be nice with the exception of Michael who preferred tea. Olivia headed for the kitchen as Lewis was saying, "I believe we still need answers from you, Mr Biörn."

"Please call me Michael."

"All right, Michael it is. How about those answers, *Michael?*"

Lewis and Salazar were the only humans in whom Michael had confided, with the exception of Sheila. He had done so more out of necessity than choice. There were simply too many potential loose ends the police could stumble upon. Too many problematic questions could be raised: questions with the potential to jeopardize the necessary secrecy surrounding the existence of praeternatural beings. Having the detectives in charge of the case on his side had been Michael's only option. After all, if a journalist could keep quiet about the whole thing, two detectives should be able to do the same. Michael also took comfort in the fact they would likely be taken for lunatics by their colleagues if they started going around the station talking about werebears, werewolves, and witches…

"I guess I'd better start at the beginning," said Michael, comfortably settling back into his armchair. "Since you already know what Starks' goals were, and by which means he had planned on achieving them, I'll focus on how I figured things out."

"That would be much appreciated," commented Salazar, who liked people who got to the point without rambling on about useless details.

"When Steve called for my help and I arrived in Houston, I was working under the false assumption there was a single pack operating in the greater Houston area. And after Steve's murder, Starks skillfully manipulated me into thinking Clemens was behind the police officers' assassinations, even though it never felt right. The idea that Clemens was maybe not responsible for the attacks kept nagging at me, but for the longest time I purposefully suppressed it to focus on the most logical explanation, which of course turned out to be the wrong one. It was only much later that I realized Starks' hidden agenda. David recognized me as a threat the moment we were introduced. And by playing me against Clemens, he hoped to kill two birds with one stone. He didn't know whether the Houston pack or I would finish on top, but it was a moot point. No matter the outcome, it was a win-win situation for him."

"What about Ivanov?" asked Lewis as Olivia was coming back with a tray carrying five steaming mugs.

"Ivanov was just a cover Starks used when he was in charge of the assassination case. His plan was to use the mob as a scapegoat for the whole thing. He hadn't planned on one of his wolves losing control and leaving compromising evidence behind him at Sullivan's domicile, but even then he caught a lucky break. He knew of Clemens' and Ivanov's business relationship and used it to explain Clemens' involvement in the killings. It worked too… since I bought it. I don't believe Starks had planned for things to degenerate between Clemens and the mob, it just happened—"

"But how did you figure out that David was behind it all?" interrupted Salazar.

"We have Sheila to thank for that," replied Michael, turning towards the journalist who looked as surprised as the others by the revelation. "I was banging my head against the wall trying to make sense of all this when she said something that made me understand a point which had been puzzling me for weeks."

"What did I say?" asked Sheila, clearly taken aback.

"You said that David should have kept better tabs on his girlfriend."

"And that statement solved the case?" asked Lewis dubiously. By the looks on the others' faces, she wasn't the only one in need of convincing.

"It did," replied Michael, unmoved by his audience's skepticism. "You see, one of the things which had been bothering me for a while was how quickly Clemens was able to find out where I was, no matter where I went, and no matter who I told. Even when I didn't tell anybody about my intentions, Clemens was able to find out within hours where I had relocated. When Sheila made her comment, I had been upset with Starks for a couple days. He was supposed to help me locate Clemens, as I was certain the pack had Olivia in their custody. It shouldn't have been too difficult for David to obtain the information I needed but he never gave it to me. When Sheila started talking about him keeping tabs, my mind immediately jumped to the cell phone he had given me to keep in touch in case of emergency. I opened the phone and found the tracker he had placed in it. Once I figured out Starks was a bad guy, the question became whether he was working with Clemens or against him. No matter how I looked at it, I couldn't find a good explanation to Starks' actions if he had been working for Clemens. I therefore decided he was against him, and in this light, things started making a lot more sense."

Michael took a break to grab the cup of tea Olivia had placed in front of him. He took a few sips and quickly returned to his story.

"At this point, Sheila had just found Thompkins' picture online and had identified him as a Captain in the Texas Rangers. We knew for a fact Thompkins was part of the Houston pack, which left only two possible explanations. Either Clemens was behind the murders, but in this case what was Starks' agenda? Or Starks was behind them, and Thompkins was truly one of Starks' men. I found the second explanation by far the most satisfying as it also explained how Starks was leaking information to Clemens concerning my whereabouts. If Starks' agents had infiltrated the Houston pack, everything was starting to make sense… I was starting to have a pretty good idea of the way things had happened, but to make sure my logic wasn't flawed, I used Sheila as a sounding board."

They all turned towards Sheila who acknowledged the attention with an exaggerated shrug, while gesturing for Michael to resume his explanation.

"There were a number of points which needed to be elucidated and I went down the list one by one to make sure they could all be explained by my new theory. The first points were concerning the evidence found at Sullivan's. The window had been broken from the inside—a strange thing. Usually, an assassin or even a burglar would break a window to gain access to a house, not to leave it. The broken window indicated to me that whoever left the house had entered it a different way. I knew from the beginning that Sullivan's murderer was a werewolf, so the fact he had left through the broken window indicated he had been unable to regain his human form before leaving the house. This could only have happened with a relatively young individual who had morphed into his wolf form by accident in the first place. The accidental morphing could have been caused by the unanticipated presence of Sullivan's Rottweilers for instance. This explanation also accounted for the two guns found at the crime scene. Jack Moore had come with the intention of shooting Sullivan but had been unable to retrieve his gun once he had morphed into his wolf form."

"That also explains the shoes," intervened Salazar, suddenly very excited.

"You and your shoes…" retorted Lewis, emphatically rolling her eyes.

"We found a pair of size eleven shoes at Sullivan's. Except that Sullivan's shoe size was a nine," explained Salazar to the others. "But Moore *was* a size eleven…"

"That doesn't explain how the shoes landed on the shoe rack," objected Lewis.

"Actually the wolf could have easily placed them there himself. The rest of his clothing would have been most likely still sticking to his body, or at least easy to carry away with him in his retreat, but the shoes would have been problematic," intervened Michael supportively. "By placing them on Sullivan's shoe rack, they were more likely to be overlooked, I suppose."

Salazar gave his partner a condescending look, which Michael took as a cue to resume his account.

"But if the wolf attack at Sullivan's had been the result of an involuntary morphing, the evidence found at Steve and Marjory Harrington's simply did not make sense."

Sheila shot a discreet look at Olivia, but the young woman's face betrayed no emotion at the evocation of her parents' murder.

"The evidence didn't make sense… unless it were staged! The window had once again been broken from the inside, and a werewolf was clearly responsible for the attack—"

Suddenly Olivia excused herself, got up, and went straight to her room.

Her departure was followed by an awkward silence quickly broken by Sheila. "I'll go check on her in a minute."

Visibly relieved, Michael nodded and resumed. "Clemens would have had no interest in attracting attention to his wolves, but Starks would. By killing my friends and making sure I knew a wolf had done it, he was pointing me towards the Houston pack, effectively turning Jack Moore's botched assignment to his advantage."

"Did he have Steve killed simply to throw you off track?" Lewis was clearly bothered by the possibility.

"I had to think about that one for a while," replied Michael, "but I think I finally found out why he killed Steve. Of all the murdered cops, Steve was the only one who didn't fit the profile. All the others had high positions in their respective organizations, positions that would benefit Starks' agents if they were to be promoted into them. But no one would profit from Steve's murder. David had no reason to kill Steve. That is, unless Steve knew something about Starks he shouldn't have. If Starks saw him as a threat he would have killed him without a second thought, and I believe that's exactly what happened. The day I arrived in Houston, Steve took me to a restaurant to meet David. During dinner, there was a mix-up with their phones and Steve ended up checking David's text messages. I don't think Steve found anything compromising on Starks' phone or he would have mentioned it while driving me back to my hotel, but maybe he did and simply hadn't realized it yet. At any rate, Starks would have very likely been unwilling to take any chances and I believe he decided to kill Steve before he became a liability. Marge was just collateral damage..."

"Bastard!" interjected Samantha Lewis, and no one disagreed with her.

"Starks could sense I didn't like him, so he staged his own attack to throw me off his trail. A very clever move. But the fact he was the only one so far to have survived an attack, and more importantly the fact his enemies had not even tried to correct their failed attempt, started becoming suspicious after a while."

Sheila got up and walked upstairs to Olivia's room.

"What about the Chemist? What was his role in all this?" asked Salazar.

"The Chemist extracted and refined the toxic molecule contained in the wolfsbane plant, one of the few poisons which can harm a werewolf. Starks had two usages for the toxin. Part of the extract he used as weapons against the Houston pack and me, but another fraction of the toxin was converted by a witch into something entirely different. The shadow pack was using the witch brew as a drug they administered to themselves as intravenous injections. The drug had several virtues, but the most important one was to mask their scent to other praeternatural creatures.

Without the witch brew I would have picked up on Starks' scent the first time I met him, and so would have Clemens for that matter..."

"How did you even start suspecting Starks was a werewolf if you couldn't smell the wolf on him?" asked Lewis.

"I only found out about the function of the witch's brew recently," replied Michael, not giving details about the way he had found out; Ezekiel was off limits to the detectives. "But I had seen its effects without knowing the cause. Jack Moore had been in his wolf form when I killed him in Sheila's bedroom. A normal werewolf would have remained in its wolf form in death, but Jack reverted to his human form. Even more surprising was his odor; the wolf scent had completely vanished from him. Once I remembered this fact, I knew whoever was behind this could be a werewolf without smelling like one."

"Werewolves, witches, werebears... I sometimes wonder if I'm not dreaming," said Salazar, only half joking.

Sheila and Olivia walked back into the room. Olivia had obviously been crying, but she had a timid smile on her lips now.

"I believe you now know as much as I do," said Michael, and since the two detectives did not ask any other questions, he assumed they were satisfied with his account.

"Will you have dinner with us, Detectives?" asked Sheila. The two detectives accepted the offer, and after a brief debate they all settled on ordering pizzas.

Epilogue

Olivia picked up her MP3 player from the coffee table and, without a word, walked upstairs to the guestroom she occupied.

"Did you notice how pale she looked?" asked Sheila.

"No... but I wasn't really looking," answered Michael, who was absorbed in an Agatha Christie novel.

"I think I'll go talk to her for a minute. Just to make sure she's OK," said Sheila, heading for the stairs.

Michael uttered a sound which could have been interpreted as assent, but which more likely meant he wasn't listening.

Olivia and Michael had both been staying with Sheila over the past few weeks. The young woman had helped Sheila tend to Michael, and now that he was better, she remained in the house because Michael refused to let her out of his sight. It wasn't that he was overprotective of his friend's daughter; he simply didn't trust her. The woman had recently been turned into a werewolf, and he knew from experience that it would take her a long time to be fully in control of her furry alter ego.

Lucy Harrington had gone back to college two weeks earlier, unaware of her sisters' lycanthropy. Ignorance truly was bliss in certain cases.

The student would have been ill-equipped to act as a werewolf-sitter, even for her own sister, and Michael had taken upon himself to assume that particular duty. He was struggling with the fact the young woman was now a werewolf—a sworn enemy of his species—but he was feeling responsible for what had happened to Olivia under his watch.

After thinking things over, Michael had decided the best option would be for Olivia to go back with him to Yellowstone. He could not think of a better place for a pup to learn control. The park was virtually deserted in winter and she would have plenty of time and space to learn to resist her instincts. He estimated they had about six months to a year before Olivia's instinct kicked in and she saw him as the hereditary enemy. Then things would get interesting.

They were scheduled to depart the following week. Sheila was to remain in Houston for her job, but she would go and visit them on weekends as often as possible. At least that was the plan.

As he finished reading the last page of his novel, Michael suddenly became aware that Sheila still hadn't returned. He seemed to recollect she had said something about going to talk to Olivia, but she had been gone at least twenty minutes now… He supposed this was not very long for two women to discuss feelings, but since he was not a specialist on the subject, he decided to go check things out and make sure everything was all right. He realized things were everything but all right as soon as he entered Olivia's bedroom.

Sheila was standing livid and utterly still in a corner of the bedroom, while a 170-pound wolf named Olivia was growling at her, all fangs out. It took Michael less than a minute to control the beast, but he had the feeling it would take a lot longer for Sheila to recover from the shock.

"What happened here?" asked Michael, sitting on the floor and stroking Olivia's mane gently. The arm he had around the wolf's neck was meant to look more like an embrace than a hold, but Sheila was not fooled.

"The room was empty and the curtains were drawn as I entered. I went to pull them open and the next thing I know there is a wolf standing between me and the door," answered Sheila, her voice still vibrating with fear and barely contained anger. "Now *you* tell me what just happened!"

It didn't take a Ph.D. in psychology to see Sheila was very upset by the incident. It was one thing to be threatened by a pack made of dangerous criminals and quite another to be threatened by a guest in your own house.

"Olivia's not responsible for her behavior," pleaded Michael. "She has close to no control over the morphing at this point… and she spent the little control she had stopping her beast from attacking you."

"I suppose I should be grateful for that…" retorted Sheila, only half earnestly. Michael remained silent; there was nothing to reply.

"How long will it take before she has full control over her impulses and instincts?" enquired Sheila.

"It's hard to say. I'm not very intimate with the intricacies of self-control in werewolves. I know they learn faster than we do, but I don't know how much faster. It could be months, or even years I suppose."

"How long before *you* were able to control your beast? How long did it take *you*, Michael?" asked Sheila. She was shaken by what had just happened, but she didn't truly hold it against Olivia. She knew the poor woman was not responsible for her actions, but she could read Michael's face and saw how responsible and guilty he felt. There would never be a better time to get him to talk about his past.

"Over thirty years…" replied Michael who did not like the turn the discussion was taking. Before he had a chance to wonder where Sheila was going with this, she asked the question he dreaded the most.

"What happened to Isibel? Why did she kill herself?" Sheila was pretty sure she knew the answer to that question, but she needed to hear it from Michael's mouth. The guilt in his eyes was like a confession: he was responsible for his wife's death. In a fit of rage he had attacked her and she had been unable to cope with the psychological trauma.

Michael looked at Sheila for a long moment. His hand was now resting still on Olivia's fur. He did not even bother asking her how she had learned about Isibel. When he finally started talking, his voice sounded resigned and almost mechanical. "My wife killed herself because she could not accept the death of our son."

Sheila suddenly felt a wave of relief wash over her. Michael hadn't attacked his wife… she had only lost her son… But her relief was short-lived as Michael continued.

"A grizzly sow is only in heat when she has no cub to care for. This is why a grizzly boar will kill any cub that isn't his own. For his genes to spread, he needs the female to be in heat, and killing her offspring will trigger her cycle." Michael paused an instant to give Sheila time to understand what he was saying. She was looking at him intently, drinking in every word he pronounced. He saw in her eyes the instant she connected the dots. All he had to do now was confirm what she already suspected. "Unfortunately my son was born a human, and my bear form never recognized him as his own. My son was only three when I killed him… he was only three."

The End

A word from the author

I hope you enjoyed this Michael Biörn story, and I wanted to thank you for being one of my readers.

With over 300,000 books published in the US every year, new authors face an uphill battle when it comes to making their work visible to the public. So, if you enjoy my stories, I would greatly appreciate if you could help me get the word out.

If you believe Michael Biörn deserves to be discovered by a wider audience, please tell your friends about the books. This would make a real difference and help me publish more stories at a faster pace. Even a simple post on social media or liking my Michael Biörn Novels Facebook page would make a significant difference.

Of course, if you truly love these novels and decided to write a brief review for any of my books on Amazon, I'd be eternally grateful. Whatever you choose to do, thanks again for reading my stories; it means a lot to me.

Thanks,
Marc Daniel

http://bit.ly/ReviewShadowPack
http://bit.ly/MichaelBiornBackStory
https://www.facebook.com/MichaelBiornNovels
@MarcDanielBooks

Excerpt from

UNHOLY TRINITY

1

After a short discussion on who would remain sober to drive them back home safely, the two young women had elected to walk to the party. The pleasant early September weather made for a relaxing stroll through the pedestrian-friendly streets of the small college town. Fall leaves, ranging from dark red to bright yellow, crackled under their feet while a gentle breeze pushed the two women towards their destination.

They were both fairly new to Bozeman and still unfamiliar with its streets. Thankfully, they could hear the music from a block away, so they simply followed the loud thumping of the bass.

With its jettied second floor, pillared porch, and half-timbered façade, the house was a prime example of Tudor Revival architecture. It'd been many things over the past century, but today it was simply the largest frat house in town.

The party had spilled out onto the porch and the front lawn, with empty cups, beer bottles and drunken students disseminated throughout the mess. The cops, who would no doubt pay the party a visit later, were going to have a field day.

Cautiously avoiding an incoming freshman who had obviously consumed his fill of alcohol for the evening, the two women stepped into what could only be described as full-blown mayhem.

The music was so loud that one could only communicate through gestures or by screaming into each other's ears, which didn't seem to bother the students in the least. Clearly, they preferred body-language communication as illustrated by the grinding taking place on the numerous improvised dance floors.

"Brad told me he'd be here," said the younger woman.

"Do you see him?" replied the other, a brunette who could have been attractive if she'd tried, but clearly didn't intend to waste any time with makeup or with revamping her rather conservative wardrobe. Her ostensible lack of concern for her looks was in stark contrast with the studied beauty of her companion whose long, straight red hair and almond-shaped emerald eyes were already attracting a number of woozy male students.

"No, but he might be upstairs. I need to find him; he still has my driver's license from last night," replied the redhead, pointing towards the wide staircase on the other side of the room.

After skillfully dodging the numerous human obstacles hurled at them along the way, they finally made it to the second floor where they were nearly puked on by a 5-foot tall little thing clad in a dress that would have barely covered a Barbie doll.

Carefully tiptoeing around the nauseating puddle, they walked to the first room on their right to find a very intense video game contest of which they wanted no part at all. On a mission, they didn't notice the peculiar way one of the gamers was looking at them.

They didn't find Brad in either of the next two rooms; but, when they pushed on the door of room number four, it only partially opened before being slammed shut in their faces.

"I saw him. He was sitting on the floor and he looked sick," said the redhead.

The brunette forced the door open and stepped into the room to find a mountain of a man blocking the way. He started turning them away but quickly changed his mind, apparently having just noticed the hot redhead standing behind the brunette; the woman's fair complexion, highlighted by her bright red lipstick, seemed to his liking. Strangely, he didn't appear to notice the revealing cleavage of her curves-hugging summer dress right away: a lapse easily attributable to the nine beer bottles scattered at his feet.

There were five other guys in the room in addition to the doorman, and all but one looked as if they belonged on a football field's line of scrimmage. The exception, who also happened to be the object of the two women's search, was sitting motionless on the floor in a corner of the room.

The barely breathable atmosphere of the room was laced with smoke, and a distinctive smell floated in the air: an odor which couldn't be mistaken for pure tobacco.

When the redhead bent over to check on her boyfriend the males in the room took advantage of the opportunity to check her backside. The lustful looks they exchanged weren't lost on the brunette.

Kneeling next to the man, the redhead tried to wake him up, but even a good shake didn't bring him out of his self-induced coma.

"He's out. Had one too many." The doorman pointed towards the empty cans of beer littering the floor.

"But we're still up for it!" The last comment came from a guy with a crew cut and a pointy chin who easily weighed more than the two women combined. His beady eyes were undressing the redhead, who was now standing next to the brunette. Their lewd glimmer hinted towards an outcome the two women wouldn't enjoy.

"Let's go," said the redhead, suddenly conscious of the threat, but her sentence was punctuated by the sound of a deadbolt sliding into its groove. The men's attitude was noticeably threatening now; they were making howling sounds and slowly surrounding the women who had nowhere to go.

Realizing their screams would be drowned out by the deafening music playing throughout the house, the redhead started shivering.

"Have no fear, pretty thing, you gonna enjoy what we're about to do to you," said Crew Cut, while the others assented with guttural sounds which would have made a tribe of apes proud.

When one of the men placed his massive hand on the redhead's left cheek in a parody of a caress, the brunette, who'd been silently fighting an internal battle to maintain control, decided it was time to lose it. In a quick motion, she grabbed the offending digits and snapped the four fingers at their base. The man screamed in agony while his companions, shocked by the unexpected move, simply stood there, unable to react. But the brunette wasn't done with them. Grabbing the closest man behind the neck she hurled him at the wall, where his head made contact with enough momentum to leave a dent in the plaster.

Snapping into action, the four men still standing jumped on the woman. One of them grabbed her waist to bring her down, but to no avail. She'd planted herself in the middle of the room and was as unmovable as a rock. She did seize the opportunity, however, to grab two of them by the head, bringing the craniums on a violent collision course which ended with a loud thump and two collapsing bodies. The man around her waist was still putting all his weight into bringing her down. Had he been given another thirty minutes, he might have eventually succeeded, but freshly out of skulls to crush, the woman's attention landed on the hapless man. The determination with which she grabbed his throat quickly convinced him to release the hold he had on her. Still holding him by the throat, she smashed his head against the porcelain sink, breaking the basin in half.

Trying to escape, the man with the broken fingers was in the process of unlocking the door when the fury launched at him. Colliding brutally into the man, she brought him to the floor and started pummeling his chest and face with her small fists which, at this instant, were anything but harmless. The man's face was bleeding profusely and without even knowing it she went for the kill.

"Olivia, stop it! You'll kill him!" screamed the redhead, jerking her sister away from the man's throat into which her teeth had been about to sink.

Olivia, still in a trance, was struggling to regain the control she'd sur-rendered to the beast within her. She turned to face her sister and tried to smile, but Lucy was staring at her in awe. Before Olivia could say a word, Lucy started running for the door. She was halfway down the stairs before Olivia realized what had scared her sister away. Staring at her re-flection in the mirror above the broken sink, she could clearly see fangs where her canines had been a few minutes earlier. Closing her mouth to hide the fangs, she made a run for her sister.

As she exited the room, she bumped into one of the men who'd been playing video games but didn't recognize him. She was too intent on finding Lucy to pay attention to him.

The gamer immediately recognized the brunette as she collided into him without a word of apology. Wondering why she was leaving the party in such a hurry, he peeked inside the bedroom. He wasn't shocked to find the beaten-up football players scattered across the floor.

Quickly making up his mind, he decided to follow the woman who had so eloquently demonstrated that the weaker sex wasn't so weak after all. A second later, he was out the door. He spotted the brunette a hun-dred feet down the street and picked up his pace to close the distance. He didn't want to lose her.

2

It was the middle of the night but Michael Biörn wasn't asleep. Instead, he kept tossing and turning in his bed, unable to find peace in merciful slumber.

After centuries of seeking solace in austere isolation in various parts of the world, the last few decades had felt as if he'd finally succeeded. But the peace wasn't meant to last. The past year had been rich in excite-ment. Within just a few months, he'd lost two friends to a pack of were-wolves and assumed custody of Olivia—a newly-turned werewolf. He'd also fallen in love for the first time in over 950 years but had lost contact with the woman. Probably for good, since she hadn't found a minute to return his calls in the past nine months.

Michael finally gave up his quest for slumber and slipped into a light shirt and a pair of shorts. The shorts looked a bit awkward on a man his size, but that was the least of his concerns. At 6'4" and sporting over 300 pounds of solid muscle, Michael looked anything but average. He had a square face supported by a strong jaw line that gave him a determined look. His unruly cropped hair was the color of dark chocolate, while his hazel eyes testified to a wisdom much older than the forty years reflected by his body. He wasn't handsome in a typical way, but he had a magnetic charisma.

Putting on his shoes, he walked out of the cabin and into the fresh air of Yellowstone National Park. He took a deep breath. It was early September but in Yellowstone the nights were seldom warm, and the air felt crisp on his exposed skin. He walked to the back of the cabin and started heading towards the bordering woods.

Where was his peace and quiet now? A year ago, he'd been serenely minding his own business, working as a ranger for the park and living alone, just the way he liked it. Now, he had a werewolf pup to worry about plus an ex-girlfriend who didn't return his calls. Truth be told, Olivia's lycanthropy had been easier to handle than he'd expected. The young woman had only been a werewolf for ten months, but she already had remarkably good control over her inner beast. This was why Michael had finally agreed to let her go back to college, albeit at Montana State and not Texas A&M where she'd been studying before. Located a mere two-hour drive from his cabin, the Bozeman campus was the closest university he could find. Lucy had transferred to Montana State six months earlier to be closer to her sister while Olivia stayed with him: a fact that had considerably helped in convincing Olivia to attend that school.

Olivia's departure for college had provided the two of them with a much-needed break. As a werewolf, she now belonged to the species that had hunted Michael's kin to the brink of extinction. The two preternatural species they represented had been at each other's throats for millennia and as such Michael and Olivia were sworn enemies. But Olivia was the daughter of the late Steve Harrington, Michael's Army buddy, and that made matters a bit more complicated. Michael also felt responsible for what had happened to the young woman, which added another layer of complexity to the mess.

He'd been hiking upslope for a good fifteen minutes and was completely covered by the canopy and surrounding trees when he stripped out of his clothes and hid them inside a hollow tree as he had done countless times before. It was close to 3AM and unlikely anyone would be following him, but still he took a last circular look before changing into an 800-pound bear. An expert would have been able to tell that it was not quite a grizzly, but most people weren't experts. To the overwhelming majority of the world population, Michael was now a gigantic grizzly bear.

Michael was hoping that by letting his furry alter ego take over he'd be able to escape his human troubles, at least for a while, and forget about Olivia and Sheila for the remainder of the night. In his bear form, Michael didn't forget about his human persona. He could still reason like a human being, but the bear's instincts were taking over his thoughts, occupying the front and center position, while those of his human half were relegated to the back of his mind.

As he casually walked amongst the thick groves of lodgepole pines, his extra-sensitive nose relishing the rich evergreen aroma of the trees, he suddenly felt a pang of hunger in the pit of his stomach. He hadn't been eating much these past couple days—barely more than a couple healthy teenage boys combined—and he could use some exercise. A good hunt would provide the perfect opportunity to satisfy both needs. Trusting his nose to point him in the right direction, he quickly picked up a faint but definitive elk scent. He followed the olfactory trail for a hundred feet before realizing there were actually two distinct smells, a mother and her calf. He dropped the trail right away. Unlike his cousins in the wild, Michael could afford to be picky in his diet; as a matter of principal he never targeted the young ones or their mothers.

He had started seeking another prey when he stumbled upon a quite different fragrance: bear pheromones, a female in heat. It took Michael's bear a few minutes to realize there was something very odd with this picture. The female was a full five months behind schedule. Sows typically came into season in early spring and this was September. He didn't get a chance to push this train of thought any further as the sow came out of the brush a hundred feet ahead of him. She stopped, staring right at him. She was a grizzly of maybe 250 pounds, on the small side for sure, but still pretty typical in the park.

His bear's instinct was to make a move for it, but his human half wanted nothing to do with that. Even though Sheila was clearly no longer interested in him, he would have considered it as a betrayal of her trust. He was about to turn away and head in the opposite direction when the female started moving toward him. *What the hell?* This wasn't the typical behavior of a sow at all. A sow liked to be pursued, and the pair only mated after days of courting, but that one just kept getting closer and closer. *What does she think she's doing?*

Frozen in bewilderment, Michael simply stood there, watching the female close the distance between them. She was a mere ten feet away when he finally snapped out of it and started heading away from her. She followed him, however. He started running so she would get the message, his 800-pound body skillfully negotiating subtle changes of direction to avoid the evergreens' trunks, but she didn't get the message and kept pace with him. He accelerated but the groves' thickness made the operation difficult; no matter how hard he tried, he simply couldn't shake her.

Fifty feet directly ahead of them was a clearing Michael knew well. He decided to make a dash for it. Bears weren't distance runners; he could probably out-distance her in a sprint, but she would quickly catch up with him as his body forced him to slow down. Michael's patience was wearing thin. If she didn't get the message quickly, there would be confrontation. A male fighting off a female! What was the world coming to?

They reached the clearing an instant later. Clearly visible in the cloudless sky above them, the waxing moon projected its eerie twilight on the protagonists of this unlikely tale.

Suddenly Michael stopped running and spun around to face his unwanted suitor who was still twenty feet behind him. She slowed down as Michael stood on his hind legs in a threatening posture. She didn't stop, however, but kept creeping closer until she was only five feet away. His eyes met hers in a domination contest, but the effect obtained wasn't the one he had hoped for. The sow seemed to be batting her eyelashes at him! Before Michael had a chance to grasp the full absurdity of the situation, the sow turned into an old man wearing a long gray cloak and a pointy hat: Ezekiel! The wizard was laughing so hard, he was having trouble catching his breath.

Michael's back story

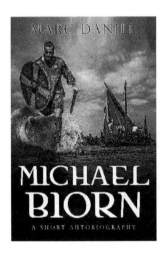

Download your free copy at:

http://bit.ly/MichaelBiornBackStory

Marc Daniel

After spending significant amounts of time in Ohio, France, and Montana, Marc is currently living in Houston with his wife and two toy Schnauzers.

When he's not writing, cooking dinner or playing with his dogs, Marc enjoys woodworking, going to the theater and escaping the city to reconnect with nature.

Contact information:
www.marcdaniel-books.com
https://www.facebook.com/MichaelBiornNovels
@MarcDanielBooks

Printed in Great Britain
by Amazon

40402891R00145